continued . . .

Milk in My Coffee

"Rich *Coffee* steams away clichés of interracial romance. . . . Dickey fills his novel with twists and turns that keep the reader guessing as he describes a true-to-life, complex story of relationships. Along the way he smashes one stereotype after another." —*USA Today*

"A fresh romance . . . heartwarming and hilarious."
—*The Cincinnati Enquirer*

"Frothy and fun. . . . Dickey scores with characters who come to feel like old friends . . . smart and believable. After the last page is turned you'll still have plenty to savor." —*Essence*

"His characters are people we have seen walking down the street, at church, or at the family picnic. . . . Plain old good reading." —*Mosaic*

"Dickey is just as adept at giving voice to female characters as he is to males." —*New York Daily News*

"Dickey demonstrates once again . . . his cheerful, wittily acerbic eye for the troubles that plague lovers."
—*Publishers Weekly*

"Controversial and sensitive." —*Today's Black Woman*

"Entertaining . . . humorous." —*Boston Herald*

"Juicy . . . a carefully woven tapestry of vibrant characters and turbulent situations that will have you hooked."
—*Advocate* (Orlando, FL)

"Engrossing, entertaining . . . the surprising twists and turns bring a good novel to a very satisfying conclusion."
—*Booklist*

Sister, Sister

"Dickey imagines [his characters] with affection and sympathy. . . . His novel achieves genuine emotional depth."
—*Boston Globe*

"Vibrant . . . marks the debut of a true talent."
—*The Atlanta Journal-Constitution*

"A hip, sexy, wisecracking tale."   —*New York Beacon*

"Bold and sassy . . . brims with humor, outrageousness, and the generosity of affection."   —*Publishers Weekly*

"Dickey is able both to create believable female characters and to explore the 'sister-sister' relationship with genuine insight."   —*Booklist*

"A good summer read you won't be able to put down. . . . Depicts a hard-edged reality in which women sometimes have their dreams shattered, yet never stop embracing tomorrow."   —*St. Louis Post-Dispatch*

"Will captivate your fancy . . . an engaging read."
—*Cincinnati Herald*

"One of the most intuitive and hilarious voices in African-American fiction."   —*St. Louis American*

"There's a little sumthin', sumthin' in this book we can all relate to. Buy the novel, read it. Relate. Relax. Release."
—*Crusader Urban News*

Other Books by Eric Jerome Dickey

Between Lovers

Cheaters

Milk in My Coffee

Friends and Lovers

Sister, Sister

Liar's
Game

ERIC
JEROME
DICKEY

 NEW AMERICAN LIBRARY

New American Library
Published by New American Library, a division of Penguin Group (USA) Inc., 375 Hudson Street,
New York, New York 10014, USA
Penguin Group (Canada), 90 Eglinton Avenue East, Suite 700, Toronto,
Ontario M4P 2Y3, Canada (a division of Pearson Penguin Canada Inc.)
Penguin Books Ltd., 80 Strand, London WC2R 0RL, England
Penguin Ireland, 25 St. Stephen's Green, Dublin 2, Ireland (a division of Penguin Books Ltd.)
Penguin Group (Australia), 250 Camberwell Road, Camberwell, Victoria 3124,
Australia (a division of Pearson Australia Group Pty. Ltd.)
Penguin Books India Pvt. Ltd., 11 Community Centre, Panchsheel Park, New Delhi - 110 017, India
Penguin Group (NZ), cnr Airborne and Rosedale Roads, Albany,
Auckland 1310, New Zealand (a division of Pearson New Zealand Ltd.)
Penguin Books (South Africa) (Pty.) Ltd., 24 Sturdee Avenue, Rosebank, Johannesburg 2196, South Africa

Penguin Books Ltd., Registered Offices: 80 Strand, London WC2R 0RL, England

Published by New American Library, a division of Penguin Group (USA) Inc.
Previously published in Dutton and Signet editions.

First New American Library Printing, May 2002
20 19 18 17 16 15

Copyright © Eric Jerome Dickey, 2000
Excerpt from *Between Lovers* copyright © Eric Jerome Dickey, 2001

[NAL] REGISTERED TRADEMARK—MARCA REGISTRADA

New American Library Trade Paperback ISBN: 0-451-20593-6

The Library of Congress has catalogued the hardcover editon of this title as follows:

Dickey, Eric Jerome.
Liar's game / Eric Jerome Dickey.
p. cm.
ISBN 0-525-94483-4
1. Afro-Americans—California—Los Angeles—Fiction.
2. Los Angeles (Calif.)—Fiction.   3. Divorced men—Fiction.   I. Title.
PS3554.I319 L57 2000
813'.dc21
99-087739

Printed in the United States of America

for erica nicole and dominique simone

1 Vince

I was making love to En Vogue.

Not the group, but one majestic woman in a royal blue negligee. She had Cindy's intelligent smile, Maxine's sexy disposition, Terri's womanly grace. Her negligee slipped off her shoulders, slid down across her breasts. Inside her moan, she sang my name. Inched me toward her warm soul.

Dana hummed with the feeling. "You love me, Vince?"

Okay, I was about to tell you my name, but I guess Dana beat me to the punch. Vincent Calvary Browne Jr. And the woman I was holding, the one who had my face flushed, toes curling while I sang her name, the angel who was squirming ever so slowly in pleasure, that was my woman. The one I wanted to have forever. The last one I ever wanted to make love to.

I'm almost thirty and don't have a lot of family. Not now anyway. Not since my divorce. Not since Moms and Pops died. Moms had colon cancer and it spread up. That was when I was nineteen. Pops had it in his throat and it spread down. That was right after I made sixteen. Moms didn't have me until she was almost forty; Pops was in his fifties. So I guess I came from an old egg and some old sperm. That's why people always tell me I have an old soul. People have always said that I acted and sounded ten years older than I was. A baritone voice makes anybody sound older. But I've always felt ten years younger. Mistakes make a man feel like that. Hard living and bad loving ages a man.

Divorce ranks right up there with death, so I've lost more in a few years than most men lose in a lifetime. The biggest loss was when my ex-wife had an affair, divorced me, then vanished with my little girl.

I met Dana a few months back, up at the Townhouse. That's a soul food restaurant that doubles as party central up in Ladera, a black middle-class part of Los Angeles not too far from LAX. That night Jaguars, Rolls-Royces, and Benzes were corralled at the east end of the strip mall, dark-haired Mexicans doing the valet parking. The club had a live band up front, playing sassy, Marlena Shaw–style jazz. An unknown all-girl hip-hop group, Dangerous Lyrics, was supposed to hit the small stage in the back room a little later.

In the meantime, a D.J. was keeping the flow going in the rear. A few sisters were under thirty, maybe under twenty-five, most showing as much flesh as legal. And a few were the victims of gravity and time: old babes in young dresses. This was where the generation gap collided over jazz and drinks. A few brothers had some age on them too; older-than-dirt players who were strutting around, Poli-Grip on their breath, acting like they knew they were still the shit. If this was a meat market, some of this beef needed an expiration date.

It was easy to make eye contact with the lonely and broken-hearted. I know because I was one of them. Hell, I was both of them. Right before Dana drifted into the room, I was kinda leery about trying to start a conversation, because I'd just gotten a rejection slip from one sister.

Earlier that night I'd met this long-legged creature with stilettos and a slinky dress. She'd come to me while I lingered at the bar in the back room. Said she worked at UPS, been there ten years. Her Bugs Bunny overbite said that she hadn't taken advantage of her dental plan, but the more I drank, the less that was a problem for me. She was perky and had personality. Stood out from the women who were clinging to dirty old men twice their daddy's ages. She made at least twenty duckets an hour, bragged about her 500-series BMW, even showed me a Polaroid of her new ride, but was crying broke because of the twelve-dollar cover charge.

We danced on the itty-bitty wooden floor, grooved to Blackstreet and Mary J. Blige, then hung out close to the fireplace and had a damn good time for the left side of thirty minutes. Bought her two glasses of wine while we laughed about this and that. Her eyes were all over my dark suit and off-white linen shirt, flirting strong, and my mack was on target, more persuasive than Johnny Cochran's closing argument.

Then she asked me, "So, brotherman, are you married?"

I told her, "Divorced. You?"

"Single." All of her youthful features started to sag, like air being let out of a balloon. "So, you have kids?"

I sipped my chardonnay. "A daughter. I have a daughter."

Midnight-colored clouds came from nowhere and darkened her brown eyes. Her shoulders slumped and she let out a sigh. Real quick, she gulped down the last of her wine, lost the pep in her voice, said, "Well, it was nice to meet you, Reggie."

I said, "Vince. My name is Vincent Browne."

"My head is hurting. I'm going home."

I asked, "Well, can I get your number?"

"Ahhhh . . . give me yours."

I did. My eyes were on the back of her head as she headed up the hallway, passed by the pictures of Billie Holiday and Malcolm X, kept moving by the exit sign, made a right, and vanished. Minutes later she was up front at the octagonal-shaped bar, on a new yellow brick road, jazzing it up, in another man's wallet, a brother older than Grady from *Sanford and Son*.

That wasn't the first time I'd gone through rejection. It wasn't always about the marriage thing; sometimes it was about income, even went on a date with a sister and she saw I wasn't rolling around in a new hoopty, the kind of ride she wanted to be seen cruising Pacific Coast Highway in. Nope, rejection ain't nothing new and doesn't discriminate geographically. It's happened at First Fridays. At the L.A. Social Club on First Saturdays. At the Los Angeles County Museum during a cultured happy hour. Happened at church on communion Sunday. On-line in AOL, sisters were either looking for an Adonis or a brother with a mega bankroll. Always looking for love in all the wrong faces.

So that's where my head was at: frustrated and pissed off.

I'd wasted an hour of my life, and because of the cover charge and the drinks my pockets were thirty dollars thinner. I was about to say three tears in a bucket and give it up; going to a club searching for a quality woman was like going to Target and hunting for Saks Fifth Avenue merchandise—ain't gonna happen.

Then I made eye contact with Dana. Rapturous midnight skin in a golden business suit. White pearls. Hair in thin, spaghetti-style braids, the kind that were loose on the ends and could be curled or put in pretty much any style. Classic, conservative, fashionable, and feminine. A womanly shape that should be engraved in stone from the heart of the motherland. A few brothers with their momma's breast milk still on their breath put down their cellular phones, craned their necks, and peeped. A number of the rusty players with Geritol dripping out of the corners of their mouths rubbed their receding hairlines and checked her out, head to toe.

She eased into the room, her tight eyes my way.

She smiled.

I smiled.

A smile is the shortest distance between two people. The musician Victor Borge said that. One-thousand-one, one-thousand-two—I counted how long she held my gaze. By one-thousand-five, Dana's superior gravitational pull had me bumping through the crowd, heading her way, adrenaline rushing.

By the time I made it to her zone, she stopped dancing in place. Her arms folded across her breasts. She shifted like she didn't want to be bothered. I would've let it go, but her eyes. Tight light brown eyes that hypnotized me. Her eyes, her build, the physical package was there. I couldn't walk away, not without a try.

I gave her another easygoing smile. Introduced myself. Dana Smith did the same. We shook hands. Her hands were soft, fingers thin, but she had a good grip. Very business, very questioning, that signal established a thick line. As far as I could tell, she'd come in alone.

Before I got cozy she said, "I'm meeting somebody up here."

East Coast. I recognized that metropolitan accent, flair, picked up on the bright lights, big city tone in her words. That with her straight back and straightforward posture, her urbane style, made her so different from the rest. Made her mysterious, exotic, and fascinating in my eyes.

She wasn't a born and raised L.A. woman. I didn't know if that was good or bad. Based on my track record with West Coast women, it had to be good.

I said, "Place is pretty crowded. You see 'im?"

"Not a he, a she. Geraldine"—she caught herself—"I mean Gerri Greene. We work in the same real estate office."

Nervousness ran through my blood, a fresh heat dried my throat. Her buddy's name sounded too damn familiar. I wondered if her friend knew my ex-wife, or me, for that matter.

I asked, "She married?"

"Divorced." Dana checked her watch. "She should've come by now. I should page her before she gets here and wastes twelve bucks."

"Uh-oh. What's wrong?"

Dana looked at the clientele, frowned. "No curb appeal."

"Curb appeal?"

"Don't look good from the outside. Real estate talk."

"Gotcha."

"Somebody call George Lucas, this looks like a Chewbacca convention."

I laughed.

She went on with her ranking: "And that sister over there needs to quit getting dressed in the dark. She has on more colors than a pack of Skittles. Quick, somebody give Grandma Cellulite a fun house mirror."

Comical. Intelligent, thick, bedroom voice that made a brother wonder what she sounded like when she whispered sweet things. Perfume dabbed behind her ears, in the crevice of her breasts. Long black braids pulled away from her face, clipped in place. Nails clear, not overdone with a million colors. One small diamond in each ear. Classic, classy, smooth.

And she had a job. She gets bonus points for being gainfully employed.

I wanted to know, "How did you end up in real estate?"

"I have an older cousin, Dawn, who was out here doing real estate. Did it for about ten years. Hubby dumped her for a singer. Dawn moved back to New York after she divorced, but always talked about how great the market was out here. Guess I wanted to pick up where she left off."

A waitress dressed in fake black leather, a purple wig, and a top that made her breasts look like pyramids stopped in our faces holding a tray of shots: "Would you like to try a Crown Royal tonight?"

I shook my head and asked Dana if she wanted a drink, my treat. She wanted a 7UP. I took out my wallet, invested four dollars in my future.

We moved over by the light blue rails and white walls, watched people who had denied their last ten birthdays struggle with a Lauryn Hill groove, and fell into the typical conversation people have when they're sizing each other up: the age, what do you do to make your ends meet, where you from thing. Told her I was twenty-eight, born July 17, in Pasadena. In between singing along, Dana said she was born at Mount Sinai, June 14, twenty-seven years ago, had packed up and come out here by herself.

I'm a moody Cancer and she's an unpredictable Gemini.

Fire and dynamite. A dangerous combination in any season.

Midsentence, she stopped and motioned. "There's Gerri."

Dana waved at an amazon of a woman who had on dark linen pants, white blouse. A small waist, everything the right size, in the right places. Cinnamon skin, round face, freckles, light brown hair in a bob. I saw all of that while Dana's buddy made her way through a crowd of ancient brothers who hovered over her like vultures on a prairie. Four men tried to stop her stroll; four men were ignored.

Dana and Gerri hugged, short and intense. I expected them to start talking in that silly, high tone that women use when they're trying to act like girls, but they didn't. Their voices stayed smooth, even. I stayed in the background, tapped my feet to the hip-hop, and played it cool.

Gerri frowned. "Dag. This place is usually popping."

Dana introduced us. Her buddy had a faint southern accent, added down-home sensuality to her strong presence. Gerri had a young face with a mature demeanor. That had to come from being a parent and raising kids. What stood out was the weariness underneath her eyes. To me it looked like she'd had a busy life. No dirt was underneath her fingernails, but hard workers recognize hard workers.

Dana asked, "What took so long? Had me waiting."

"Shit." Gerri took a deep breath. "Today has been hell on wheels. Had to drop my kids off at my ex-in-laws—that's where my ex is going to pick them up. His weekend with the crew, so I'm free from parental servitude for forty-eight hours. Anyway, my son didn't want to go. He met this girl."

"Oh boy."

"That's why I want him gone, gone, gone. I ain't trying to be nobody's grandmomma. Anyhow, to top that off, my daughter wasn't feeling good, so I had to stop and buy her some of that nighttime, sniffling, sneezing, coughing, aching, stuffy head, fever so I can rest medicine."

Dana laughed. "Could you just say NyQuil?"

"Then I ended up getting there the same time Melvin did, and we had a few financial things to talk about. We almost got into a shouting match, but you know I didn't want to show out in front of my kids."

"You tell him things have been a little rough?"

She nodded. "And I let him know that I'm tired of being patient and I'm talking to an attorney. A Jewish attorney at that. I don't want the white man all up in my biz, but like my momma used to say, when a nigga don't do right, call Mr. White."

"You're taking him back to court?"

"I don't want to. But a sister gotta do what a sister gotta do." Gerri tsked. "So, I'm going to have to keep working my other paper route twice a week. That extra cabbage is really making a difference."

Dana was single, no kids. Gerri was the one with two kids and an ex-husband, a profile that was damn close to mine. For a few seconds I wished that Gerri had sashayed in the room first. Empathy would live in her corner. Maybe. But then again, maybe her plate was already too full.

A tall brother peacocked his way across the room, tapped her on the shoulder, then leaned in and smiled like he was auditioning for a Colgate commercial.

He said, "Mind if I talk to you for a minute?"

"Do I know you?" was Gerri's stiff reply.

"Not yet."

He had a reddish complexion, built like a solid oak tree, goatee trimmed, hair short and texturized to make it look curly, dressed head to toe in Tommy Hilfiger jeans, shoes, probably had on matching Hilfiger drawers. The walking billboard had jumped right into the flow of our verbal intercourse, burglarized his way into our conversation.

His name was Jefferson. He was the proud manager of the rap group Dangerous Lyrics, which was about to hit the stage in the back. He bragged, told Gerri how the group had just got back from Atlanta. They'd won a talent show for HOT 97, had a big after party at someplace called Plush.

Chris Tucker. Holyfield. Chilli. Miki Howard. In the middle of his flattery and nonstop macking he dropped a lot of names.

Gerri asked him, "Ain't you kinda young to be playing me so close?"

"I ain't young. I'm twenty-six."

"Well, this chunk of Little Rock is thirty-six."

"Damn, you don't look no more than twenty-one."

"Thanks, but look. Let's not waste time. I'm divorced with two kids. My daughter is in middle school. My son is sixteen, almost your age. What you wanna do, come over and play Nintendo with him while you baby-sit?"

"Hey, age ain't nothing but a number."

"In some states it's ten-to-twenty singing jailhouse rock."

"Five minutes, that's all I ask. Let me buy you a drink and we can talk, and in the end if you wanna step off, cool."

He didn't back away. Stood in front of her like he had been appointed the spring to her summer. Six foot five, thick, and when he strutted, most of the sisters looked like they were ready to start throwing him their panties and keys to hotel rooms and charge cards.

Jefferson took Gerri's hand, pulled her away from us, got her a glass of wine, hemmed up in a private spot, and got his mack on.

When they left Dana smiled, looked the young buck up and down, let her eyes dance to a rhythm of envy and delight, then made a sexy, humming sound.

I asked, "What was that all about?"

"What?"

I mimicked her scandal-lust humming.

She laughed. "You weren't supposed to hear that."

While me and Dana tainted our souls with a strong and smooth French Connections, I played the role and hid from my memories, told Dana I was a black man working hard every day, as single as a dollar bill, no kids, no ex-wives, no problems. With every word I dug my hole deeper. Dana shifted closer, gave me serious eyes, said she had the same résumé.

Dangerous Lyrics took the stage. A group of five girls. Most of them barely looked legal. All dressed in tight-tight black pants made of that trendy, stretchy-tight material that let you know where a woman's panty lines are. Colorful halter tops—satin lying across their majestic breasts—made them look like rainbows above the waist. All of them with nicknames like Big Leggs, Goldie, Butter Pecan, Pooh Bear, Chocolate Starr.

Butter Pecan stepped up like she was the leader of the crew. From her looks, her nickname was based on her complexion. The D.J. kicked on a preprogrammed tape. People stepped back and the group found some space on the tiny wooden dance floor, danced with the same ferocious energy M.C. Hammer did when he had a job, sounded like TLC with a NWA edge and did an edgy song of possessiveness of a lover. They set the room on fire with a catchy melody that praised sex, retribution, violence, pretty much everything wrapped in one tune.

Gerri was on wearing out the carpet, hands up high, pumping it up and grooving. At thirty-six she danced better, had more choreography than most of the girls in the rap group.

Dana smiled, bebopped where she stood, shoulders bouncing to the beat.

I spoke up over the music, asked her, "Wanna dance?"

"About time. I was wondering when you were gonna ask me."

She took my hand, anxiously led me through the heat. We had to settle for the carpet; the floor was only big enough for about ten people. It was awkward because the carpet was worn, held stains that made the fabric sticky to my shoes.

That stylish native New Yorker had wicked rhythm. She adapted to the carpet, turned up the volume on her rhythm, moved so good that other men tried to sneak a peek and women tried to mock her style.

After Dangerous Lyrics finished two records, the room applauded loud enough for the girls to O.D. on their egos, then the group went to another room. Gerri and Jefferson were between the fireplace and the exit sign in the back, slow dancing, laughing, talking non-stop, her southern grin gazing up at that roan-colored statue with dreamy eyes. Dana turned down my offer to slow dance, didn't let me get that close. The music changed.

Then Gerri vanished with the spring to her summer.

Dana said, "Gotta go potty."

"I'll be right here."

I headed for the narrow hallway between the front of the club and the back, where the loud music from the front collided with the loud music in the back, canceling each other out. The girls from the group came out of the bathroom. Somebody sounded upset, like she was holding back tears with every pissed-off word: "I don't believe that fucker brought us down here, then was all over that old-ass bitch, dumped me like I ain't shit."

"Why you tripping, Butter? He ain't your man. He set your ass straight down in Atlanta. Stop playing up on him and quit tripping."

"I ain't trippin'. He the one trippin'."

"Well, you need to think about the group. Like he

told you, this is business. That other stuff you running off at the mouth about ain't—"

They felt me listening. Ten eyes snapped my way at the same time. Butter stepped out, gave me a cold what-the-fuck-you-looking-at expression before she stormed away. Her girls followed their leader.

As soon as Dana came out of the bathroom, she said she was ready to raise up out of here, so I escorted her out to her car. We talked and headed beyond the Brenda's Talk of the Town and the Chinese dry cleaners, strolled down on the far side of Ralph's grocery store. Dana stopped in front of a dark-colored Infiniti Q45. Her ride was ten years old.

She looked disturbed. "Full moon."

"Full moons means romantic."

She shook her head, her mood changing, becoming dark and distant. "Drama. A full moon is a flashlight so everybody can see your drama."

I opened her door, peeped inside before I let her get in. No child seat, no sign of those cheap throwaway toys that come inside a Happy Meal. No man's belongings. No leftover cologne scent.

Dana kept the door between us, that subtle yet straightforward move a woman does when she's letting a man know that she ain't in it for the kissing. Her lips, full and dark with color. All evening, every time they opened and closed, my mouth watered. She tossed her purse over to the passenger seat; it turned over and some of the woman stuff she had inside spilled across the seat.

Makeup. Pager. Checkbook. A coal black stun gun.

That caught my eye.

She followed my eyes to the stun gun and said, "I was mugged on the subway."

"Mugged?"

"Got jacked for my little old purse. Damn near fell in front of a freakin' subway train and got run over." She cleared her throat like she was trying to cough the

memory out of her system, then picked up her urban assault weapon, let it rest in her lap, in ready position. "I
was almost run over by a train, but this guy caught me
before I fell."

"Good thing he caught you."

Her tone turned flat. "Good thing, yeah. Bad thing
too."

She fired up the engine; it purred like a newborn
kitten.

She took my digits, gave me her red-white-blue business card. Her office was near the golf courses in white-
bred Westchester. The card had her smiling face on the
front, an office number, pager number, web site, e-mail
address, but she didn't give up the home number. That
made me question whether she really lived alone. Or
was single. I've been on a few dates with sisters, and
when we made it back to their crib, a boyfriend or a husband that they'd forgotten all about was waiting in the
parking lot. Not a good way to end a night.

It's all part of that dating game. You lie about this, I
lie about that, you don't tell me this, I don't tell you that,
we date a while, have sex, some lies come out, we mention the unmentioned, we realize how incompatible we
are after about six months of fun in the sun, then by-
gones.

I offered, "Wanna hit Roscoe's for some chicken,
maybe coffee?"

"My girlfriend in New York said Roscoe's stole the
idea from Well's Chicken and Waffles on Seventh Avenue in Harlem."

"Never heard that. Never heard of Well's, actually."

"Said Roscoe stole everything but the recipe."

"Is that fact or fiction?"

"Well, my fact is this: I support my people back in
Harlem."

She gave me a firm good-bye handshake, then drove
away.

Three tears in a bucket, motherfuck it.

I headed three parking spaces over to my old 300ZX. A ride that needed a set of new tires and new fuel injectors. With the layoffs, I'd been cutting corners. Aerospace had been as steady as a two-legged table during an earthquake.

When I came down a moment ago, I hadn't looked out across the lot, had been too focused on the woman from New York. Her friend, Gerri, was standing between an Eddie Bauer and a Range Rover, under the full moon, living in the broken shadows with Jefferson. His arms were wrapped around her like he was her protector. They were kissing and I heard their sound. Moans and groans that come from hardness and wetness. Her slim arms up around his shoulders, intense tongue dancing like high school kids.

I watched them until heat warmed my groin and envy burned in my lungs.

Yep, once again I'd wasted half the night and too much money on the wrong woman. I tossed Dana's ReMax business card facedown on the black pavement. I knew that I'll-call-ya routine.

During my three-mile drive, I passed by bus benches. Saw Gerri's photo plastered on a few. Felt relief. That was why her name and her face were familiar. It had nothing to do with my ex-wife, nothing to do with my past.

2 Vince

When I made it home I had a message. It was from my
ex-wife. I heard her soft, cultured voice of deception
and my blood changed to ice. Her first call in over a
year. That was about how often she rang my phone.
She'd talk for a hot minute, but she'd never let me talk
to my daughter. Never gave me a way to get in contact
with them. It was her way or no way.

No matter what happened between us, I'd still been
sending checks. Womack's daddy, Harmonica, told me
to keep up with that because it'd come back to haunt
me. So I'd been doing right on my end, hoping she
would grow up and come to her senses on hers.

"It's Malaika. We're still in Germany. I just wanted to
leave you a message and let you know that Kwanzaa is
fine. Getting tall. We're living on base. She's speaking a
little German." There was a pause, an emotional stammer. When my ex-wife spoke again, anxiety, maybe
guilt, was in her tone. "She's a smart girl. Too smart for
her age. Maybe when we get back to the States, after
I've talked to Drake and we've gotten settled . . ."

Then there was noise in the background. Maybe her
chicken shit husband walked in the room. I don't know,
and when you don't know you imagine.

What I do know is that Malaika hung up.

Disconnected once again.

Nonstop rain. Anger. Screams. Fighting.

On that night of thunder and lightning, when I stood
under a crying sky and let my temper take control, I did

shameful things that have marked me as a criminal in the eyes of my ex-wife's family. I wished I had done things differently. Wished I hadn't given my pain to two other people.

Dana called me early the next afternoon. I'd run in the a.m., put in eight miles flat, then came back and tried to decide what I was gonna do with the rest of my weekend. My friends, Womack and his family, lived right over the hill, and I was thinking about going over that way. He has a house full of kids, three little boys and a brand-new little girl, so we'd end up either shooting hoops in his backyard, playing Nintendo, or watching a Disney video that we'd seen a thousand times. That was my plan until Dana called me from a cell phone, a technological device that players use.

I cut to the chase. "I wanna see you today."

She maintained her business tone: "You don't waste no time."

"Nope. Tomorrow's never promised, have to go for what I know today."

"Before we go any further, do you have a girlfriend?"

"Nope."

"I'm not looking for drama. Been there, done that, wrote a postcard."

"Same here."

There was a pause. In the background I heard her car radio whistling soft jazz, the echo of traffic too. She said, "I'm leaving church."

"Want to meet me for lunch at either Aunt Kizzy's or Dulan's?"

"No can do. I have an open house today with Gerri."

"Open house can't last all night. Wanna catch a movie after that?"

"I'll call you when I get some free time."

"Well, can I get a number where I can reach you?"

"I'll call you."

Then she was gone again.

After my wife, I didn't have a lot of faith in women, not on a romantic level, so I didn't expect Dana to be a woman of her word.

Monday evening after work, Dana and I met up in Ladera at Magic Johnson's buzzing Starbucks, another overcrowded meat market for the twenty-something that's been disguised as an extravagant coffee house. We talked for about an hour, then she glanced at her watch and said she had to go. Her pager had been blowing up the whole time. I figured she must either be living with somebody or had somebody in her life. Tuesday, on my lunch break, I called her job, had a short phone conversation. Wednesday, didn't hear from her at all. Thursday, another brief conversation during lunch.

Finally, she gave me her home phone number. But that was because she was having problems with her PC, needed me to come by and look at it.

Wanted to get some free work out of me. Just like a woman.

A one-bedroom condo in Culver City, the side of town that used to be all movie studios but now was overpriced condos. Her place wasn't a castle, but it wasn't a dungeon either. IKEA-style furniture, gray carpet, white walls, vaulted ceilings, black-and-white pictures from Harlem, a lot of books. I mean, way over three hundred books, some new, most of them old, some stacked in a corner, some on a bookcase, a stack in the loft next to her white computer stand—and those were all she kept when she left Harlem.

When I got there, her phone rang. It was a dude. I could tell by the way her tone dropped, the way she sucked her jaw in, the way her body shifted away from me.

Dana wore black stretch jeans, dark blouse with three buttons open and sleeves rolled up to her elbow, silver bracelets on her right arm, scarf over her braids, glasses with small oval lenses, her look more genius than diva.

Her hand went over the receiver and she whispered uncomfortably: "Long-distance. I'll be back."

I pretended I was so into her computer that I hardly noticed.

She left me in the loft, reformatting her disc drive, reloading all of her software, making sure her modem and fax were connected. She took the phone downstairs, went into her bedroom, stayed gone for almost an hour.

When she came back, she had a confused lover's disposition.

I finished her PC. She thanked me with a handshake. I left.

Told myself, don't waste your time.

"Black Man Negro, where you at?"

I laughed along with my buddy, then told him, "I just got in from the gym, Womack. How's UPS treating you?"

"Same way they've been treating me for the last ten years. Working me like a Hebrew slave."

We talked for a while. His three boys all hopped on the phone at some point, all wanted to say hi to their uncle Vince before they got ready for bed. His little girl was asleep. I'm the godparent to his children. He's the godparent to mine.

Womack asked, "You see my wife up at the gym?"

"Nope. Didn't see Rosa Lee."

"She wasn't in Evelyn's class?"

"She always works out up front by Dwayne. Didn't see her."

"She came in a few minutes ago, huffing and puffing. Said she was bone tired because she had been up there working out. Ain't but one aerobics class at six-thirty, right?"

"Didn't see her."

"You drinking water?"

"Yeah. Sorry about that. Thirsty."

"Ain't got no kinda phone etiquette," he said, then asked, "Were you there the whole class?"

"Didn't miss a move."

"Where were you in class?"

"My same old spot, up front by Robert and Jodi. Everybody asked about you."

"Yeah. I need to get back to going to the gym."

"Maybe Rosa Lee was downstairs riding the bike or something."

"Said she was in class. Told me that five minutes ago."

"Where she at now?"

"Upstairs at Daddy's place. She ran up there to put clothes in the dryer. We're doing all of our laundry up there and down here at the same time."

He made a troubled sound, something so unlike him.

I asked, "What was that all about?"

"Nothing, nothing." Then my buddy changed the subject. He perked up. "How thangs working out with that girl you just met?"

"They ain't. She's a flake. I'm done with New York."

But two days later, I called Dana again. Irresistible impulse.

Four weeks of hit-and-miss conversations, another brief moment at the Starbucks in Ladera. Then for days, not a word or a returned phone call.

Friday evening, since our conversations had been going downhill, since it was an I'll-call-you-don't-call-me kinda thing, I had pretty much written Dana off as another flake. I didn't expect her to ring my phone as soon as I got in from work and ask, "So, what we doing tonight?"

We ended up at Magic Johnson's theater, ragging on people, wondering why black people in the neighborhood were so damn loud at the movies, chomping popcorn warm enough to melt the Raisinets we scattered on top.

Saturday night we drove out Pacific Coast Highway, ate dinner at Gladstones, then went out on Malibu Beach. Under a half-moon we rested on smooth rocks and talked. Wave after wave rolled in and dampened the dirty brown sand. She wore a short jean skirt that exposed her smooth legs, kissable thighs, a faded over-size Levi's jacket, a red and yellow tam on her head. She looked like a rebel artist. I had on jeans too, baggy Levi's I'd bought at Robinson's-May that day just to wear while I hung out with her.

The temp in L.A. dropped at least fifteen degrees at night, and the beach was even cooler, borderline cold, so the chill that came with the night made Dana snuggle next to me to keep warm, her shoulder against mine, close enough to know there was a taste of magic riding the ocean's salty breath.

She was relaxed, serene enough to talk about how she grew up. Went to four elementary schools in three years. A rough time for her and her mom. Her dad was in Florida, remarried his first wife and started a new family. Things were tight. In those early paycheck-to-pay-check years, her mom moved a lot, sometimes trying to stay one step ahead of the landlord, but things got better.

"So." Dana sighed. "I said what the hell. I needed to get away. Nothing was keeping me there. Nope, nothing at all."

Leftover love was in her voice.

Dana told me, "I used to put on events with this guy I was seeing. Bands in Harlem, did quite a few book signings with some writers—those were a headache. Rappers were hard to deal with, but some writers and their Talented Tenth egos . . ."

This wasn't the conversation I wanted to have, didn't want to hear her ramble on about her ex, not when I was sitting on the beach on a star-filled night. This was buddy plan kinda talk. She'd put me on the friendship train. I sneaked a peek at my watch, gave up on the romance, ignored the sounds of the ocean and the glow of the moon over our heads, and went with the flow. "So, what happened between you and your ex?"

"Picture this: middle of the night, we're in bed, this girl shows up."

"Sounds scary."

"It was. When I woke up, she was over me, screaming. I

hadn't figured out left from right, or up from down, before she attacked me."

"What happened?"

"I opened up a family-size can of whup ass on that big-titty heifer. Police came." Her words trailed off, faded the way a person does when they wish they hadn't told you the first part. "It was a mess. Wretched."

"That was when you broke up?"

"We got together a few times. Wasn't the same. Didn't want to keep doing a circle dance in a yo-yo relationship."

I should've told Dana then.

I opened and closed my fingers the same way I was opening and closing my mind, imagined my ex-wife's damp, curly hair, the strawberry scent it held after she washed her mane. Remembered the last time I touched her the way a man touches his wife. I'd loved her to a depth I never thought possible. She'd hurt me to a depth I never thought curable, betrayed me and I'd lost my motherfucking mind. Went insane. I'll never live it down.

Dana spoke on other things. With every word, she was more real to me. So far from being perfect. That was why I was so attracted to her.

I asked, "Where're your folks?"

"I buried my mother three years ago, the Saturday before Mother's Day."

"Sorry to hear that."

"Momma worked at a publishing company in the Village, busting her butt housekeeping, moved up to the cafeteria and got a job as a cashier, went to school in the evenings, eventually became an editorial assistant."

"Impressive."

"I was so proud of her."

"Your dad still in Florida?"

She tossed a rock out toward the ocean. "He died right before Momma did. Heart attack."

"Sorry to hear that too."

"Don't be," she said in a joking way, but still with the kind of finality that let me know a deep story lived there. "It's not like they remembered to put my name on the obituary."

I nodded. Had empathy for her old man.

"I loved 'im, just didn't like the way things turned out. I said some things that hurt him, but I apologized. It hurts a kid when their old man promises to call, or promises to write, and doesn't."

No words were spoken into the light winds for a moment.

She mumbled, "Yep, I come from a family of weak hearts."

Dana didn't have to say it, but for a woman to leave New York and jet to Los Angeles, a place where she had no friends or family, ran here before she had a job, things had to be pretty rough in her life at the time.

Me and a past I couldn't erase.

Her and a past she was trying to escape.

Between us, we had more issues than Stephen King had books.

So much baggage, so few baggage handlers in this world.

She asked, "You want some gum?"

I answered, "Sure."

She pulled out a stick of Big Red, licked the stick top to bottom, then eased it into my mouth. Did that without expressing any emotion.

Around three a.m., we pulled up in front of my peach stucco apartment complex at Stocker and Degnan. Stocker Avenue is a main east-west throughway, lined with two-level stucco apartment buildings that have been here since the 1940s. Single-family homes were on the side streets—the sections that had less traffic and pandemonium. This was a world of African Americans, Hispanics, and others, all living under the shade of palm trees in Mexican-style homes and apartments.

At the same time I turned my engine off, a golden CJ-7 Jeep parked right behind me. Two women got out before we did, passed by my car laughing and giggling. Naiomi, the dark one who had big legs and a short black dress, saw my face, perked up, and waved. Juanita, the mulatto one, looked back to see what her buddy was waving at, what had slowed her giggles, then briefly smiled.

In a skeptical tone, "Who're those women?"

"My landlords."

"Uh-oh. Sure that's not your woman?"

"Nah. Just my neighbors."

She paused. "Mind if I use your bathroom before I head home?"

"Just don't be critical. Martha Stewart didn't show up this month."

A soft, uneasy chuckle. "At least have two-ply tissue."

"I can handle that."

We crawled out of my car about the same time as Juanita and Naiomi disappeared into our shared stairwell. By the time we made it into the staircase, Juanita and Naiomi were up at the top, in front of their door. So close that I couldn't tell where one of them ended and the other one began. Juanita had on a red miniskirt, yellow blouse thin enough to show the outline of her dark bra, colors that looked good on her skin. Naiomi's black dress clung to her Jamaican-born backside. Not a big butt, just noticeable, shapely, and hard to deny.

They were breast to breast, sounding like they were about to explode with desire, sloppy kisses, voracious noises, hands rubbing on each other, tongues wildly snaking in and out of each other's mouth. Naiomi wore a lot of silver jewelry, and every piece sang when she raised her hands and eagerly cat-stroked the sides of Juanita's face.

Dana had frozen.

I blinked out of my voyeurism, cleared my throat. "Evening, ladies."

Naiomi caught her breath and backed away from Juanita, let her purse slide to her right shoulder, then ran her hands over her reddish brown braids. "Hey, Mr. Browne."

Naiomi was a couple of years older than me. I didn't know much about her, just knew that she was Jamaican, from Oklahoma, divorced with a kid. She works part-time at a health center, counseling people with STDs, does the meals on wheels things and takes lunches to people with AIDS, teaches aerobics on the side.

Juanita ran a hand over her blond hair, evaluated Dana in the blink of an eye, but didn't share any words. With her left hand, she pulled out her keys, twirled them, then unlocked their dead-bolt and two other locks.

Juanita's in her early thirties, from Compton, the well-maintained section that no one ever sees on the news, went to Berkeley, teaches at UCLA's extension program from time to time, but as far as I know, outside of keeping this building in tip-top shape, she never does much more than that. With her trust fund, she's on easy street. Her folks own several pieces of property between here and the 110 freeway, this building being one of the nicest.

I had stopped halfway up. Wasn't enough room for all of us on the landing, so I paused. The passageway didn't have a breeze, so the stagnant air was filled with two kinds of sweet perfume, three if you counted Dana's, and a hint of wine and romance. Both of them were glowing, had lustful eyes.

Dana was two steps back, eyes on the peach walls, more than likely uncomfortable, but I was six steps behind two of the most beautiful women in L.A. County. Well, they were in my opinion. I wasn't trying to stare at Naiomi's mound of almond joy, but it was right there. A buried treasure hidden in plain view.

Juanita's head jerked, her eyes shot my way, caught me staring at the round of her woman's backside. I yanked my head up and away; our eyes collided like two cars in a head-on collision. She frowned. Gave me a grimace louder than the sirens in the background. Her lips moved like she was about to embarrass me in front of Dana, but Juanita put her hand on Naiomi's perky backside, held that embankment like it was her private joy, glared down at me as her bosom buddy opened their door.

A simple territorial nod from Juanita as she vanished.

Their door closed, three locks clicked on.

I breathed again, opened my door, and let Dana inside my place.

She dropped her purse, covered her mouth with both hands, and chuckled. "Yikes. Guess that wasn't your woman."

"Is that why you came up, to see if I was lying?"

"And to potty. Weak bladder."

"Hope that didn't disturb you too much."

"Sweetie, I'm from the big city. I've passed by Dumpsters and seen homeless people having sex. That was nothing. It just caught me off guard. Made me feel, I dunno, silly and nervous."

After the bathroom, she dried her hands on a paper towel in the kitchen, then lingered around the living room, made her way down the hallway, and checked out the rows of pictures.

"Wow. These are nice."

Dana was talking about my black-and-white prints from the civil rights era: Rosa Parks on a bus; blacks fleeing a burning Greyhound bus somewhere in the South; brothers marching, wearing signs that let it be known that I AM A MAN.

She moved on to the photos of my parents, made a few nice comments, then eased her way down the hall to my James Patterson, Walter Mosley, Stephen King, and other novels on my nightstand.

Then she was in my den of sin, my bedroom. Next to my old, cold bed.

Her eyes roamed, then she sang out, "Alrighty, then. What's up with the video camera in your bedroom?"

I said, "Just in case."

She smirked. "Nice boys are always perverts."

My eyes went to the videotape that was on the pine dresser. The video held erotic moments of me and my ex-wife.

Dana kicked off her shoes, and my bitter thoughts left the room.

I moved into her space, put my hands around her waist, pulled her hips up to mine. Her breathing thickened. Her eyes had the soft and sensuous glow a woman possesses when she wants to share her tongue, let it dance in a man's mouth for a while. I put my face close to hers, felt her warm skin, inhaled the sweet breath she exhaled, touched noses, moved from Eskimo kisses to tongues grazing, then deep tongue-on-tongue business.

The room's temperature shot up a thousand degrees when my hands strayed to her breasts. She crooned, face blossomed with an illicit smile, quivered and let me know that was a dangerous spot. In no time flat I had her blouse open, her breasts out of that satin vault, tasting her softness, licking the midnight off her rising nipples. Dana made sweet babylike sounds, moaned and squirmed away from that good feeling, but I didn't let her go. The heat was overwhelming, so I tried to stop, but she pulled me back for more nurturing.

So many things about a woman I had missed for too long: the voice, the sugary aroma, the intimacy, the conversation that came in the midnight hour. Trembles rolled through me, turned me on. More kisses. More erotic agony. She pulled me closer, adjusted my erection on the bull's-eye, pushed her flesh into mine and matched my slow grind.

Her body was famished for what my body was craving, I could tell.

"I'm serious about who I give my body to." She said

that with an edge and looked me dead in the eye. "You seeing somebody? Let me know now."

"Nope. I told you that. Nobody."

"I'm not saying I expect a commitment, I ain't that stupid, but at the same time I ain't looking for a one-time, two-time fuck."

"That makes two of us."

"And I don't want somebody walking in here starting no shit."

"No problem."

All of that sounded like a forthright business transaction, but in the end, after I signed on the dotted with my word as my bond, her expression softened, became innocent, let me know that she was a kitten, that her sarcasm and attitude, even her laughter, were her defense mechanisms, what enabled her to survive out in the world's concrete jungle on her own.

She tilted her head, chewed a corner of her bottom lip, whispered in a rhetorical tone, "We can't do this. I can't do this. Not this quick. Getting naked too soon always leads to problems."

Another hot and humid kiss rekindled our fire. I ached to become familiar with that New York woman in ways I could only imagine.

She groaned, "Damn, sweetie. What are you trying to do to me?"

My unrelenting, unending seduction was inside the next kiss.

Throbbing, aching, about to go crazy with these illicit feelings. Then came the sound of a woman having an orgasm. The moan started low, like a cat meowing, then grew. She praised God in the sweetest voice, called Jesus. Yet the slow ride to heaven wasn't in my apartment. The wail of passion had crept through my wall from next door.

Listening to them rock and roll just inches away had excited me for months on end. I bet they were over there, tipsy, feeling so good that their eyes were rolling into the back of their brains, touching each other.

Turned me on so much I'd sit up at night with my penis standing tall, looking at me with one eye, like Mr. Happy was pondering the origin of the universe.

Seconds later Dana had me against the wall, came to me like what she'd heard had turned her on just as much. She rubbed me, ran her hand over my crotch like she was trying to see if it was enough for her to consider changing her mind. Rubbed and rubbed and rubbed. Made wishful moans. My hand was under her skirt, fingers dancing inside a wet spot.

"Damn, Vince, why you have to go and touch me there?"

Thong panties. Very little hair down there.

While we stood in the fire we had built, lived in that heated moment of lust and indecision, we were breath to breath, eye to eye, her face saying that she didn't know if she should trust me. And to be honest, that was a two-way street.

Dana murmured, "You have condoms?"

"We can run out and get some."

She made crinkles in her nose. "Not even one?"

"Not one."

Which was a lie. Magnums were on standby. I didn't want her to think this was an every night thing, didn't want to devalue what she was offering me.

Then she nibbled my lips and whispered, "I have a couple in my purse."

I thought I had chosen her, but Dana had chosen me. Women always choose. Men, we just live with the illusion that it was our idea.

She lay across my bed on her stomach, propped up on her elbows, loose braids shadowing her face, the venetian blinds slit enough for moonlight to brighten her mystical skin. Jean skirt with white stitching caressing the round of her backside. Silver bracelet on her left arm, anklet on right leg. Watching me with dark eyes, eyebrows arched to perfection, silent, an unreadable expression, analyzing me.

She said, "Take your clothes off."

I kicked out of my shoes, unbuttoned my shirt.

She whispered, "Slow. Take 'em off slow. Let me watch."

I did and she worshiped me with voyeuristic eyes. I stood before her butt naked. Not dangling but not erect. Either way, no shame in my game.

Her eyes went up and down my body, lingering in the middle the longest.

She swallowed, lips barely parted, tongue running across her lips.

I undressed her. Rubbed, kissed, and praised her flesh.

She asked, "Your sheets clean?"

"Yeah."

She crawled under the covers, pulled the sheets and dark comforter up to her neck, became modest, while I unwrapped the condom she'd pulled out of her purse, first struggled with opening the damn thing, then with rolling it on, feeling like if I took too much time she would get turned off.

Then it was on. Secure and withstanding. My body went to hers.

She was nervous. I was anxious.

She squealed.

I backed off. "Ooops."

"Aim that thing—wait, sweetie, hold on, let me do it."

She touched me, then licked her full lips, those eyes filled with hunger and amazement. And challenge. Her face softened, became vulnerable as the tip of me broke her skin, went beyond those moist folds.

I went into her world, listened to her hiss sweet sounds that invited me deeper inside. "Perfect, Vince, you feel so perfect."

Short nails slid back and forth across my butt as I dissolved into the beauty of the feeling. Her head jerked up, those tight eyes went wide. She gasped for air, made eager, greedy sounds, nibbled my neck, and she rolled so subtle, so intense, so right.

She slowed me down, her words hot and sexy. "Hold on, sweetie."

"What's wrong?"

"Be a pace car, not a race car."

"Okay."

"Make it last longer than a Puff Daddy remix."

We sweated like a spring rain, moaned nice words, groaned religious phrases, laughed because it was so damn good. Then the nervous laughter faded, was suffocated by cannibalistic cries, swallowed by the slow and easy rhythms that echoed from rocking and rolling on my squeaky bed.

"Dana, baby, slow down—"

"Soooo purrrrrr-fect."

She was there; her nonstop chanting begged me to go faster. Her light brown eyes rolling, hips thrusting, back arching, face flaming with pain and pleasure, those small hoop earrings bouncing with her dance.

Slow and easy went away when I grabbed her braids, pulled her open mouth on mine, swallowed her tongue, ate all of her sounds. Pace car became race car. Unrestrained, uninhibited, desperate enough to make my headboard slap the wall in pulses. Down below, she was hotter than the desert sun, as soothing as a fire on a cold day. I loved a woman who could come like that. Loved the way En Vogue sang out her sensuality.

We consumed each other like we'd found water after a six-month drought.

When she was done, when I was done, when our hurricane was downgraded to a tropical storm filled with cinnamon kisses, my lady love put her damp face on my chest like she was listening to my inner rhythm. She panted out her words, "Put your hand on my chest, feel my heart. Whew. I had back-to-back moan-gasms."

"Moan-gasm?"

"Yeah. A moaning orgasm."

Then there was silence between me and the stranger in my bed.

It was like both of our minds were outside this room. The romantic fantasies and energy of lust had taken flight, our spirits in two different places. A beautiful New York woman was in my arms but my mind was on my old life, my ex-wife, my child I missed so much it blistered my heart.

I disturbed the quiet and asked Dana, "You have to work today?"

She jumped, came back to this room. "Yeah. Open house in Inglewood."

"Can you stay awhile, or do you have to raise up?"

"Sure."

More silence. Naked, vulnerable, not knowing what to say.

I told her, "Your legs are so toned. You a runner?"

"Nah. I've lived in walk-ups damn near all my life."

"Walk-ups?"

"Apartments that don't have elevators. You walk up five floors eight or nine times a day while you're carrying books and laundry and groceries, your legs'll have muscles too."

We spooned. She was different from L.A. women. Exotic in my eyes. I wanted her to talk all night long, but the sandman cometh. That was how the sun came up on us. In the blink of an eye, morning was there. Every day a million miracles begin at sunrise, and I'd woken with one in my bed, holding me close, keeping me warm.

She showered, did her female hygiene thing, then wore my black shirt over her black panties while she cooked pancakes and seafood omelettes. She never stopped talking, wore a smile that refused to go away.

When the fun was done, she said she had to go.

Minutes after I walked her to her car, I called my ex-mother-in-law's out in San Bernadino. Got the answering machine—she always screens her calls—but didn't leave a message. Didn't really know what to say.

The black tape I owned, the VHS with erotic memories of me and my ex-wife, loving on the same bed, the same worn mattress I was with Dana on last night, I took that six-year-old tape out and played it once again. Anger, love, confusion, all lived inside me as I watched. Pictures of my daughter were on that shelf too. I gazed at my child's image, saw traces of me in her round brown eyes, traces of my old man's narrow face on her chin, her full lips like my mother's. Seemed as if none of that life was real. I was dead to them. I tossed those memories from my failed life back on the top shelf of my closet, pretended that space was the back of my mind.

In the evening, I took Dana down to Long Beach, and we shot pool at this blues club right off the promenade. Back at my crib, I made her a salad and heated up some blackened catfish for dinner. She was in a great mood. A naughty kind of mood. Talking while we fed each other, sex while we rubbed sweet fruit on each other's flesh. Teasing and touching.

We sat out on my back porch for a while, wrapped in a blanket, staring up at the crescent moon, talked until it was the beginning of a new day. We showered again, changed sheets, and crawled back under the covers, kissed a while, touched each other. She told me, "I'm too dry. And sore. We're gonna have to get some kind of lubricant, sweetie."

"I'll get some tomorrow."

She yawned. "Don't buy anything with spermicide nonoxynol. That irritates me like you wouldn't believe. Make sure it's hypoallergenic."

An adrenaline rush came back, this time a wave of heated fear. Lines had been crossed. Too much talk about tomorrow, too many promises.

She chuckled. "You know the funny thing about sex? The more you do it, the more you wanna do it. Whatever brain cells are in charge of my sex drive, they're on fire. Make sure you have some Crisco tomorrow."

Laughter and yawns.

Dana closed her eyes and whispered in a sensitive tone, "Thanks."

"For what?"

Her words were fading. "God, I've been so stressed. Didn't realize how much bad stress good sex takes away. Haven't been this relaxed in months."

As I held Dana, I didn't ask her what she was troubled about. One way or another, we all had problems. My mind was on mine, but not so heavy.

Out of nowhere she said, "I'm getting my phone number changed to a private number on Monday. I'll leave it on your machine."

"Why you getting it changed?"

"To prevent problems."

"What kind of problems?"

She stalled, didn't answer, just laughed an uncomfortable laugh that told me she didn't really want to say, and switched the subject. "Gerri said I was smiling and glowing today."

"Guess she knows our little secret."

"She's been smiling and glowing for about a month now."

"Jefferson?"

"You better believe it. Her hubby has the kids, so Jefferson took her to Catalina Island this weekend. Stella getting her groove back big-time."

I made a sound and replied, "I'm not surprised."

"Why not?"

He was young, but he drove an expensive ride, wore designer threads, carried himself like he had power and position, things that attract certain mentalities, probably got him a special breed of poontang by the pound.

Me, I'm just an average, hardworking Bubba, one of the real men that make the world go round. My smile was rueful as I responded to Dana's question. "No reason."

She moved a bit, made her eyes stay open. *Sex and the City* was on HBO, volume down low. Every time they showed something outside, Dana told me exactly where in New York that was, what avenue and street.

She was struggling with her eyelids, her voice fading. "This is a trip. I'd given up feeling this good for working long hours and months of celibacy. Geesh. What the hell was I thinking?"

"You sound extreme."

"I am extreme, I guess." She jerked, made herself wake up. "I've lived hard. When I love, I love hard. Know how to hate hard too."

Then she was asleep. I changed the channel when her show went off, switched over to Fox and checked out the last half of *The X-Files*. While that fiction played, I kept her warm body close, touched all the soft parts I'd missed touching for so long.

That's the way it always starts out.

We were moving so fast. And it wasn't just me. It's never just the man pushing the envelope. Yes, we have an agenda, and mine extends beyond the desires in my loins. But women help propel a relationship where they want it to go as well, they strip away their clothes, put down their defenses, slap on blinders, and race toward their own Fantasy Islands at warp speed. No, we don't live in the times of my folks, where dating was a slow-burning candle. Now we move faster than technology.

3 Dana

I was in Manhattan at the Moonstruck Diner. Dishes clattering, cash register cha-ching-ing, heels clicking across the gray tile floors. At a table by myself. A little uneasy, but I didn't know why.

A sweaty Italian waiter dressed in a white shirt and black pants, thick arms, and a big belly yelled, "Gimme a mash to go."

Pancakes, sausages, eggs, hash browns, all of that was sizzling on the grill. I saw it, but I couldn't smell a damn thing. I inhaled to see if I was catching a summer cold, but my sinuses were clear as the sky outside.

I stared at the Italian man. I was about to get pissed off because of the way he winked and leered at me, but then I looked down and saw that all I had on were dark panties and a satin bra.

"Dana?" My name came from everywhere at the same time. "What are you looking at? Don't stare at people."

I blinked and turned around: "Momma?"

Momma and Daddy were on the other side of the table, laughing and touching. Momma had on a satin housecoat; Daddy was dressed in khakis and a bright polo shirt, chewing on a bagel the size of a loaf of bread, like the ones I used to get from Joe's Bagels on Fourteenth Street and Tenth Avenue.

Daddy said, "Dana, you know what the secret to the bagels are?"

I was confused. "What do you mean, the sec—"

"The water. The New York water is what makes the bagels so damn good."

Momma was eating Homegirls Potato Chips. I know because of the four spunky sisters dressed in four different colorful styles on the bright pink package. Momma was crunching. My mouth watered, my stomach growled, and I wanted to taste what I was missing.

Humidity and smiles were all over my parents' faces. Everybody who came in had sweat on their faces, dank under their arms, across their dark suits. Momma and Daddy kissed, touched each other like nobody in the room could see them. My mouth wouldn't open. I want to yell out, You two aren't together anymore. Daddy has another wife, Momma. Another life.

Momma grimaced at me, read my mind—I could tell by the way her brows raised up. She didn't like the pissed-off expression on my flesh. She opened her mouth to snap at me, and her voice rang like a telephone.

My eyes went to a yellow clock, it started melting.

Momma's lips moved, the sound of a phone ringing again.

All around, clocks started melting, the numbers falling to the floor in silence. The room started to get blurry, was going away.

My good old telephone was ringing me right out of New York.

I jerked awake, pulled my head out of my pillow, tried to get my head right and answer like I was wide awake: "Good morning."

"Dana!"

"Who's call—" I tried to focus my eyes and make out the number on my caller ID box. It was a 212 area code. In bold letters, her name was shouting at me from the digital display. One of the last people on this earth I wanted to talk to. I said, "Renee, that you?"

"This is a trip! I actually found your butt!"

Renee lived in the city I had left behind. Hearing her squeaky voice surprised the hell out of me.

"Your brother's not there, I hope."

"Claudio is out traveling. You know he's blowing up."

She's my ex-heartbreak's half-sister. When my relationship with Claudio went into a death spiral, I made some hard choices and divorced myself from that whole bunch. That was the hard thing about breaking up with somebody that you'd been with for five years. Not only did you have to break up with him, but you had to kick his momma, daddy, the dog, had to kick the whole family to the curb.

I asked her, "How did you get my number?"

"Grrl, I went out on AOL, was playing around doing this search thing, just having fun and acting like Eye Spy. I put your name in a search engine and whoop, there your number was. Damn, that was easy."

"Just like that?"

"Just like that. You live on Summertime Lane in Culver City, right?"

That chilled me. "All that info on me is out there?"

I peeped out my bedroom window, gazed down at Jefferson Boulevard. A few people were jogging, traffic was getting crazy.

"Yep. Dana, I don't know nothing about computers, and I found you in five minutes. Hmm. Maybe I can find KFC's secret recipe out here too. I could sell that to the Russians and make a grip."

Shit. That meant anybody with a funky Internet account could find me. Bill collectors I left behind. Ex-boyfriends I left behind. Relatives I don't want to talk to until the day after never.

She sort of snapped, "Why haven't you called?"

"I haven't called anybody."

Renee is my age, twelve years younger than Claudio.

She said, "If that's the case, Claudio was spreading rumors. He said that a few months back, you were talking about getting back together, had him packing and borrowing money to get his plane ticket. Then you just vanished and changed your number on him."

Right before I met Vince, I'd called Claudio just to see how he was doing. Shame on me for trying to be mature about the breakup, for still caring. We talked. He wanted to see me. So many I-love-yous came from his mouth. The next thing I knew, I was debating whether I should let him swoop out to L.A., thought maybe starting over in a new spot would do us some good. Besides, I'm not the type of girl who wants to meet every dick in town. But the reality of the situation was that, well, even before the police came knocking, things had been up and down with us, I mean for a long while. Then I asked him, hypothetically, what kind of relationship we were gonna have when he got here. Wanted to know if his intentions went beyond that weekend. He slowed his verbal stroll, put the seriousness aside, said we'd talk when he got here, face-to-face.

So, I told him I'd get back to him when I'd made up my mind. My heart and mind had an all-out brawl over what I should do.

That was the same night I met Vince down at the good old Townhouse. I'd been crying on Gerri's shoulder all day long, and she wanted to hang out as therapy. I walked in and saw Vince. Most L.A. brothers talked too damn much about nothing, like they have all of these extra words they have to get out of their mouths before their faces exploded. Vince's baritone voice was cool and smooth, like Eric Benet and Maxwell combined.

And, of course, Claudio started calling every day. He had rung my phone the night Vince came over to fix the hard drive on my computer. Called and wouldn't let me get off the phone when I told him I had company.

I cared about Vince, he was cool, but after that night when I was so rude, and he didn't get an attitude, stayed so mature about the whole deal, I started seeing him in a different light. Smart enough, tall enough, cute enough, so damn nice, always there for me, always lifting me up when I was feeling down.

And, of course, I felt him pulling away from my wish-washy ways.

Renee went on, "Momma asks about you. Claudio's momma asks about you, still calls you her daughter. She cares more about you than she does her own son. You just don't know how upset she was when she heard you had to file bankruptcy because of all those bills."

My bankruptcy was the last thing I wanted to talk about. I never talked about it. Humiliation ain't nothing but a word.

Even after all that, when I was out here, I was so lonely that I'd wake up crying. Wanting him, wanting to go back home, and crying like a baby in day care. I didn't want to be with anybody else, wanted to be healed and whole. I'd close my eyes, bring Claudio's face to my mind, and touch myself and squirm and feel good and be mad while tears rolled from my face to my pillow.

That first time that I spent the night with Vince, when he slipped inside my body wearing condoms left over from that New York relationship, Claudio whispered his way into my mind. His name was on the tip of my tongue while I held Vince and moan-gasmed. Thank God I was saying "Oooh baby" instead of calling out a name.

Something that Vince will never, ever know.

Thinking about that, remembering that moment, made me ache.

That was then, six months ago.

Now palm trees and an ocean breeze lived outside my window. I didn't feel like having a conversation that would cause me another good morning heartache, and I didn't want to just up and diss my old friend, so I did a switch-eroo with the subject. "You still slaving at Random House?"

"Yep. But I'm about to bounce to a bigger pot of cabbage."

"Where you going?"

"To Penguin. I'm bumping my head against a low glass ceiling. You know how the corporate game goes. You leave to get respect, show them how capable you are, then they bend over and beg you to come back."

"Just like in relationships."

"There you go."

"Tell me I'm lying. Niggas don't respect you until you step off."

My paranoia went down a notch. A little a.m. conversation wasn't gonna kill me, and we drifted into chitchat mode. I'd been working hard getting educated in this real estate game, and she'd been playing like there was no tomorrow. She let me know that Freaknic was weak this year, then told me she'd gone to the Essence Fest.

Ten minutes of gossip, my eyes moving on the clock.

Then came the real reason she had hunted me down. This was a search and recovery mission. Every time I've broken up with Claudio, somebody in his family has called and tried to put some glue on that shattered vase.

She said, "Claudio is missing you like crazy."

I was in front of my mirror, taking off my short cotton Tweety Bird pj's, getting ready to hit the shower. Diet and exercise, living where I could work out year-round has been too good to be true.

I told Renee, "Don't waste your ten cents a minute."

"I was just saying. He misses you, that's all I was saying."

"No, you were recruiting. I'm seeing somebody."

Naked in front of a mirror that was getting pretty steamed up, I peeped at my backside and thought of how Vince always called me En Vogue. That made me smile on the inside and let out a soft laugh. Somehow I doubt if Terry, Cindy, or Maxine have pimples on their butts.

"So, how long you been with this new boo?"

"Long enough."

She stalled, then bounced back with "I'm so happy for you."

"Stop lying."

"What makes you think I'm lying."

"You hesitated and didn't squeal."

She went right back to talking about Claudio, told me that he was promoting comics and was out in Dallas and St. Louis, then was heading to Atlanta to meet up with Chris Tucker and a few other comics.

She told me, "He'll be in L.A. soon. Supposed to be out there for a while."

No reply from me, not a single breath was taken.

She sounded hurt. "Dana, he's doing good. I'm telling you, you should call 'im, get back in the groove, because he's gonna blow up."

"Remind him about how much money he owes me when he does."

"Dana, give him a call. His number is 674—"

"Didn't you hear me say I've met somebody and I'm happy?"

"You didn't say nothing about being happy."

Jealousy mixed with my curiosity, and I asked, "What happened to Tia?"

"Hell if I know. After you got out of jail—"

"Wrong way up a one-way street. I don't want to hear all of that."

"Sorry, didn't mean to upset you," Renee responded softly. Then she perked up. "So, this guy you seeing, is he cute?"

"Yep. And not afraid of commitment."

"You sure he's heterosexual?"

We laughed, my chuckle faker than Diana Ross's hair. My light brown eyes were on the red glow from the digital clock.

She said, "You're moving too fast."

"Yep. This wound has been cauterized. My life is fantastic."

I didn't tell her anything I didn't want her brother to know.

I'd been on the phone long enough for me to end this

parley without being rude. I turned the shower on so she could hear it running, told her I had to get ready for work.

She said, "You're gonna keep in touch?"

"Yep. I'm glad to hear from you."

That was a lie. The day I called, every nationality in the five boroughs of New York would be on the Brooklyn Bridge, holding hands and singing "Kumbaya" while Giuliani tap-danced with Hillary Clinton.

I let her go back to her world. I went back to mine.

Part of a dream about New York came and went, bagels and potato chips. I had a sudden craving for both of those, but those desires faded and dissolved into the place wherever old dreams go to get their rest.

As I got ready for work, my eyes went to the mirror over my sink. The bathroom had misted up, and the writing that Vince had left in my mirror a few days ago came to life.

DAS

I ♥ U   I ♥ U   I ♥ U

VCB

That came from a Saturday morning two weeks back. After I showered at Vince's, I'd left a message in the glass.

VCB

I ♥ U   I ♥ U   I ♥ U

DAS

The night before, we had been cuddled, relaxed, sipping wine, laughing and pillow fighting and watching movies I had brought over, fantasy stuff like *Notting Hill* and *Runaway Bride*, did the cuddle and talk until the break of dawn thing. Somehow we drifted into a conversation about marriage. I don't know how, or which one of us brought that issue up, probably neither one of us, maybe both of us, hell maybe it was Julia Roberts in those damn movies, but he told me how I was the best thing to happen to him in years, how he wished he had met me about five years ago, how he hoped he could be with me in a forever kinda way.

Then he asked me the ultimate question, told me we should think about it.

I stopped blinking: "You serious about us getting married?"

"You know I am."

I was stunned. "Don't think you have to say that because—I mean, there ain't no pressure to—"

"We can make this unofficially official. I just want you to know what I want from you. When I get a little money, we can get you a ring and you can wave it at everybody."

"Wow." I didn't know what to say. Then out of my mouth tumbled, "Engagement ring, wedding ring, then suffering."

"What's that?"

"That's what—" I blinked out of my trance, cleared my throat, erasing that bad memory. "Nothing. Just thinking about something I heard some idiot say back in New York."

I had a hellified day. Had to pick up checks from a buyer in Mid City, then drive to a Crestwood escrow in Inglewood. I was zooming the streets, eyebrow pencil on standby, shades on, bottle of Evian at my side, looking Cali-fied. Most of the morn, my cell phone was glued to my ear, setting up appointments for a physical inspection on a property in Windsor Hills, making sure buyers were looking at property elsewhere, then to Edgehill for another physical inspection at one o'clock, biz that lasted two hours, so I sat there the whole time, going over the report.

Edgehill is in Leimert Park, not too far from Vince's ponderosa, and when I was done with the inspection, I had to go potty.

Two minutes later, I had parked across the street from Vince's, barely found a spot because Audubon Middle School was letting out. All the African American, Hispanic, and Asian parents were in their own separate-but-equal racial cliques, waiting for their noisy rug rats in their blue and white school uniforms, clogging up the sidewalk, school police driving back and forth, making sure the kids didn't get into any after-school fights.

Vince's mailbox was at the base of the stairs, and I saw that he had put out some letters for the mailman to pick up. Since they looked like they were about to slip out and fall, I tried to tuck them back into the narrow gap between the mailbox and the wall. Phone bill. Electric bill. Car insurance.

One was a plain white envelope. Written in his small handwriting, addressed to Joanne Jackson in San Bernardino.

I sniffed the letter. No cologne on the outside. It was sealed too tight to open and put back without tearing the damn thing. I held it up to the sunlight. The shape of a rectangular piece of paper showed.

"Can you believe they curse so much in public? They saw me and kept on using the b-word, f-this and f-that. No respect for adults at all."

I jumped. Juanita was walking up behind me, shaking her head, talking to either me or herself. She had on a black pantsuit, similar to the olive one I had on. I tried to stuff the mail back in, but I nearly dropped half of the letters. Such a fool for spying. Finally I got them wedged in.

I stooped to get the mail. "Hello, Juanita."

"Did you hear them cursing? The girls are worse than the boys. And I wished they would stop dropping paper in front of our property."

Pro-black sisters with blonde hair, for some reason

they look like oxymorons. But we came in all shapes, sizes, and shades of Miss Clairol.

She stopped to check her mailbox, which was empty, and out of nowhere, she asked, "Didn't I see you at FAME last Sunday?"

"Probably. Didn't know you went there."

"Naiomi and I usually attend Agape. Did you enjoy the message?"

I was ashamed to admit that I couldn't remember what the sermon was about, hell, who does, but I said, "It was cool."

"I had a hard time with a portion of the sermon. Naiomi and I didn't see eye to eye on the matter. Maybe I could get your opinion."

"Oh." I'd been sucked in. "Like what?"

"Following men wherever they lead, regardless if they are capable of leading. Propaganda like that is passed off as righteousness. It's aimed at keeping men in charge and women in a role of subservience. We should be getting empowered, not devalued. We get fed bigoted indoctrination with a smile, and forget all about the push ahead for equality. That biblical attitude that propagates a one-sided slave mentality is truly outdated."

"Did we hear the same sermon? Maybe we were at different churches."

She went on, "The white man used the Bible to justify slavery, held us down for centuries with the spirit of his God. Now our own men are still using the Word to keep a woman in a submissive place."

"Whoa. Submissive?"

"Yes, submissive. There is a lot of sexism in organized religion."

I sidestepped just in case lightning was about to strike. I played the whole thing off with a smile, glanced at my watch as we headed up the stairs.

She smiled a strange smile as she took out her keys. "Maybe you would like to meet and discuss some issues that we as women should address in order to move forward and claim our rightful place in society. We have the numbers, statistics show that, but true power is in unity and knowledge."

I blinked. Her voice had changed, softened up the way mine does when I'm talking to Vince. Couldn't make up my mind if she was hitting on me, schooling me, or just keeping me from going to the bathroom.

I pretended I didn't hear her last sentence. "I saw you out last weekend."

"Saw me out . . ." Her smile went away. "Really? And where was this?"

"Yeah, last Friday night, me and a girlfriend dropped in at Duets. I was upstairs, leaning over the rail, and I looked down and saw you."

She shifted.

"When 'Back Dat Ass Up' came on, you started backing that ass up."

"That was not me."

"I watched you dance with that girl for a good thirty minutes."

"You're mistaken."

We stared. She was trying to do a Jedi mind trick and make me forget that I'd seen her wild side when she was clubbing on the DL. Hell, we all have wild sides, and Duets was the place everybody let theirs run free.

She went inside, left without saying adios senorita.

I rushed inside Vince's apartment, danced out of my Enzos, wiggled to the rest room, did my biz. After that, I went to his nightstand, took out his box of condoms, counted them. Outside of the ones we'd used, none were missing. None were ever missing. Every other man I've dated has flunked the condom count at some point.

I took chicken and frozen veggies out, left that on the counter so it could thaw. Thought about Juanita. Yep, everybody has their wild side. I'm the leader of that pack.

The letter. I had forgot.

I grabbed my purse, my keys, hurried to the front door and got ready to satisfy my curiosity.

The mailman was at the foot of the stairwell, grabbing all the letters. That note to Joanne was getting stuffed in his mailbag.

That was the end of that.

When my errands were done, I rolled down Manchester into the bourgeois city of Westchester. So many palm trees and so much green grass, the scenery was redundant. All the way to my gig, my windows were down, music blasting until I pulled up into the parking lot at ReMax. My day wasn't done. Transfer-disclosure statements, affidavits, had to do all of that and complete an agency relationship letter, plus fill out an earthquake and hazard booklet.

My mind kept telling me something wasn't right.

I stepped in the door, spoke to a few of my co-strugglers. A couple were on their phones cold-calling and trying to drum up business. When I went to the receptionist area and pulled my mail, a familiar sealed envelope that came monthly was waiting for me.

A co-struggler walked up. She's tall with long legs, tanned and blonde. "Your desk fees have come in."

I made a displeased face. "How're you doing on yours?"

"Almost two thousand behind. I'd hoped I'd have a little money when my commission check came in, but they took half of that up front for my fees."

"Well, if it makes you feel any better, you're doing much better than me. I don't think I'm ever gonna get out of this hole."

I moved on, went to check with a superior on setting up a payment plan for what I owed ReMax. "I closed on a property in Inglewood, so I could be down some on my arrears."

The supervisor pushed a button on her computer, said, "Let's see. Your balance is right at three thousand, a little less."

Some stress crept into my mood. Right now there wasn't much of a difference between three thousand

and three million. "Tell me something I don't know, like the numbers to this week's lottery."

Laughter.

Small talk for a hot minute, then she lowered her voice and asked, "Dana, why has Gerri been looking so run down?"

"What do you mean?"

She put her hand on mine, sounded so sincere. "That worries me. I came in one morning, and she had her head on her desk. Snoring loud. I heard that things have been rough and she's working two jobs."

I chuckled, used that to stall while I thought up a way to skirt the subject. "Well, you know she's got two kids running her crazy. Plus, you met her young buck when he came down here to take her to lunch."

She playfully fanned herself. "That lucky girl."

"A young man will keep an old woman up all night."

We laughed that naughty laugh.

I went to my office, feeling more pressure because I'd been covering for Gerri for a while. I put the paperwork to the side, fired up the PC on my desk, and went into AOL.

BIG HOT TITS CLICK HERE
XXX SEX PICTURES OF PAMELA ANDERSON
BILL, HILLARY, AND MONICA BUTT NEEKED WITH A GOAT

That was the kind of crap people were forwarding all day every day. I deleted all of that junk, saw I had nothing important out there, then clicked on the People icon. Two mouse clicks later, I'd found AOL's search feature that Renee was bragging about this morning.

I filled in the blanks: put in Joanne Jackson's name. Put in San Bernardino. Clicked Find, folded my arms, and took a breath.

Only one popped up, just like that. The same address out in the boondocks that I'd seen on Vince's letter, plus a phone number, everything on her popped up.

Cyberspace is amazing and scary at the same time.

My throat dried up as I dialed, but I called.

A sister answered. Soft voice. My age, maybe older, but not much.

I had to swallow a swig of my bottled water and figure out how to handle this. The direct, no-bullshit route was always the best. The last thing I wanted was to get into a "do you know Vincent and what is he to you" conversation. But a woman had to do what a woman had to do.

I said, "Yes, may I speak with Joanne Jackson?"

"I'm sorry, but Miss Jackson is deceased. She recently passed."

My heart stopped. This déjà vu moment came, reminded me of when Momma died all of a sudden and people were still calling, and I had to say pretty much the exact same thing.

So much empathy was in my voice: "I'm so sorry to hear that."

"May I ask who's calling?"

"I'm just—may I ask who I'm speaking with?"

"One of her daughters. I came back from overseas to take care of things. Are you a personal friend or . . ."

"No, no. I'm a realtor. I was . . . I'm sorry to disturb you."

"No, it's okay. Momma wasn't organized, and we're trying to go through all of her stuff, find out what bills were paid, if any, and—"

Somebody picked up an extension.

"Mommy," the little girl said, her voice articulate, "is that Daddy?"

"No, Kwanzaa. Mommy's talking on the phone."

"I'm hungry."

"Put your shoes on and we'll go to McDonald's."

I blinked out of my trance, gave her my kindhearted condolences, then hung up as quick as I could, feeling foolish. Maybe that was a sympathy card that Vince had sent to the family. That was all it was.

4 Dana

I asked Vince, "Where's the bathroom?"

He shuffled next to me. "Downstairs in the basement."

"I gotta go potty."

"You always have to go potty."

It was seconds after the benediction of a jam-packed second service at FAME—First African Methodist Episcopal, just east of downtown L.A. Vince and I spoke to a few people leaving the mega church, shook a few hands, then mixed with the stampede leaving the upstairs section. It was hard to act cool and stay cute because my bladder had started speaking in tongues ten minutes before the ushers took up my tithe.

I asked Vince, "You see Ruby Dee and Ossie Davis?"

"Where?"

"Downstairs."

The lobby was crowded like Times Square. Ushers were directing traffic. Some peeps were trying to leave, others were trying to get inside and claim a seat for the next service.

Vince told me, "I'll be outside the door."

"Okay. Take my Bible. Won't be long."

The line for the ladies' room was longer than the line at Magic Mountain. Waiting gave me a moment to people watch. A few of my peeps looked like they had staggered in from Club Century. A sister in blue leather pants, a couple wearing short dresses, another was a cleavage factory. One was all up in an usher's face, giving up righteous words and devilish eyes.

No matter where, men are men, and women are looking for men.

I did my biz, put on a little more lipstick, and came out, climbed back upstairs, slowly. Pumps with narrow heels are not made for mountain climbing.

Vince was outside near the street, talking to a petite, bowlegged, bronze-colored sister with wavy dark brown hair. From where I was, her narrow face reminded me of Queen Nefertiti.

When she kissed Vince on the lips, my world halted. My heart became a brick. Can't leave your man alone for a minute.

Vince saw me and adjusted his coat. Looked so uneasy. Her eyes followed his and she looked uneasy too. I moved toward their anxious expressions like I was being sucked into a black hole.

Vince moved my Bible from his right hand to his left, then pulled me near his side. "Dana," he said, and motioned at her, "this is Rosa Lee."

"Nice to finally meet you."

I'd heard about Rosa Lee and her family, but we'd never met.

I said, "You're the schoolteacher, right?"

"Teacher, counselor, drill sergeant. And that's just at home."

We laughed.

"Rosa Lee," Vince continued, but sounded a little nervous, "this is my fiancée, Dana."

Her eyes did a quick peek-a-boo at my empty ring finger before her soft smile met my face. I scanned her ring hand, saw the huge rock on her finger.

We were interrupted by another woman. This one was a little darker than me, over six feet tall, in a dark knee-length multi-colored dress, holding an NIV Bible and her pink umbrella. She was excited to see Rosa Lee and Vince. So excited that she was rude enough to cut me off.

"Lord, I haven't seen either one of you in years. I see you're still keeping in touch with this knucklehead."

Vince said a few things, but he didn't introduce her to me.

She asked Vince, "Where's Malaika? I called out to her momma's house last week, but nobody answered."

Rosa Lee made an "oh boy" face, then glanced at her watch.

My beau moved closer to me. The woman blinked a few times when he held my hand. Her new look said she got the message.

Vince was very uncomfortable. "We broke up years ago."

"I didn't know. The air force had me stationed in Japan forever, so I've been out of touch with the real world."

Once again, Vince introduced me as his fiancée. And like they all do, her curious eyes ran across my empty ring finger.

My skin heated up. Anxiety all over my face.

She asked, "When's the wedding?"

I said, "We're looking at next summer."

"That far away?"

"No rush. We have to shop for rings. I have to figure out who's gonna be in it. If we're going to get married here in L.A. or back at my old church in New York, which might not be practical. Where the reception will be . . . photographer . . . music . . ."

Rosa Lee saved me from going on and on. "Getting married is more than a notion."

After that, Rosa Lee had to hurry and get a seat before the last show of the morning sold out. Vince waved adios to the tall one, then kissed Rosa Lee again, right on the lips.

My soul was in this weird place. A very unspiritual place. Where a woman has to be cautious and confrontational about things.

I said, "Sweetie?"

"Uh-huh."

"What kind of relationship did you have with Malaika?"

"Love at first sight, competition, conquest, contempt."

"Sounds like a very unhappy ending. When did you go out with her?"

"Years ago."

"She go here?"

"Nah. She doesn't go to church here."

"Where's she now?"

"Married. Last I heard, she was living overseas."

That made my sun brighter. But not bright enough.

He paused, turned, and stared at the huge brick church. He wanted to say something but didn't.

I should've let it ride away on the soft cool breeze. But my soul still wasn't satisfied.

In the car I asked, "Did you used to date Rosa Lee?"

"Nope."

"You kissed her on her mouth."

"Oh, is this your jealous side?"

"Not jealous, just, as the pastor would say, heedful. If you saw me go lip-to-lip with a man you didn't know, a good-looking brother that you hadn't been introduced to, then looked guilty when I saw you—"

"I didn't look guilty."

"Of course you didn't. If you saw me locking lips with a brother, I don't think you'd run out in the streets and start tap-dancing."

"Dana, all of us have been ace boon coon since high school. Me and her husband, Womack, have been hanging tight since elementary school."

He drove up Adams to Crenshaw, the Mostly Mexican part of town, made a left and went to Rodeo and made a right, the black side of L.A., headed back toward Culver City, where white people ruled the yard. The scenery changed, but my thoughts remained the same. A nerve had been struck. Reminded me of how I felt left out of my daddy's prosperous life.

As he passed the guard shack and headed toward the man-made lake on the edge of my complex, I said, "Sweetie?"

"Uh-huh."

"Don't you think it's time I met all of your friends? These peeps will be getting invitations to our wedding, right?"

He nodded but didn't say anything as he pulled over in front of the door to my three-story building. Building 9000. Separated from Overland Boulevard by a wall that a midget could jump over.

I asked, "Why don't you set something up? Nothing big. We could meet for coffee, or I could cook and we could kick back and play dominoes."

Again, he nodded.

I wished I hadn't spoken my mind, especially when I realized my mind was dipping in a well of memories, taking me to a place I was trying to leave.

After we kissed a few times, I asked, "You coming over later?"

"I can."

"I'll throw a lil' sumthin'-sumthin' together for dinner."

"Okay. Yeah. I'll be back after I do my laundry."

"You okay?"

"I'm fine. Why?"

"Your mood is kinda funky. You're so quiet."

"I'm cool. See ya in a little bit."

We kissed again, short and sweet, then Vince left.

I went upstairs, undressed, checked my messages.

I had a verbal note from my landlord: she had put her condo on the market. A slap in my face. She knew I was an agent. White people stick together like . . . hell, like Asians do.

The next message was from Gerri. She was supposed to have met us at church this morning. That was the third time in two months she'd pulled a no-call, no-show on me. I wasn't mad at her, though. She'd probably worked late last night. Child support was delinquent and she was impatient, working two jobs to keep it all together. And she had to go to that late-night paper route again tonight. A risky gig that not too many people knew about.

Being a single parent ain't no joke.

I thought about zooming over to Lula Washington's and hop in a dance class, but since it was gloomy and I was lethargic, I took advantage of the mood. I lit candles, turned on the music, turned on the shower, closed the door so the hot water could steam up the room, made it my own private sauna. The moment I stepped in, the phone rang.

Vince or Gerri, had to be one of them.

I held my breasts, hurried, dove across my bed and grabbed the cordless phone before the call rolled over to my service.

Happiness reeked in my voice. "Good afternoon."

"You left me hanging, Dee Dee."

"Claudio?"

My lungs filled with tears. That husky Brooklyn voice filled my apartment, thickened the air.

"Yeah, it's Claudio."

His voice was crisp. I could see him, every detail of his face, even the little scar behind his right ear. I was butt naked and he was in the room, all around me. I pulled the comforter down over my body and said, "How did you . . ."

"Get your number?"

"Yeah."

He chuckled.

I said, "Renee?"

"You know it."

My eyes went to my black lacquer dresser, IKEA-style decoration that came with this condo. A picture that me and Vince had taken down at Del Amo mall was set high on top. That new love gave me strength.

"What do you want, Claudio?"

"I'm gonna be in L.A. soon."

"L.A.? Los Angeles or Lower Alabama?"

"From what people tell me, most of the nigs out there are from lower Alabama. I hear clubs close before two in the morning out there."

"Look, Claudio, I'm busy and—"

"Your area code is 310 and I'm gonna be kicking it in the 310, so I guess that's not too far from you, right?"

"What difference would it make if it was?"

He paused long enough for me to hear HOT 97 on his radio.

"You left me hanging, Dee Dee. Thought we were gonna try again."

"Changed my heart."

"Well, can I change it back?"

I wanted to sound mean, but my voice was soft. "Don't do this, Claudio."

"You had me getting my funds right, bags were at the door, had the tickets on Tower Air in my pocket, then you changed your number. That was cold-blooded."

"I'm hanging up, Claudio."

"You really hate me, don't you?"

"I don't do hate. Can't heal when you hate."

"Dee Dee, I'm gonna be honest. This ain't easy for me. Being without you night and day has been rough. Look, I thought that after a while you'd call me up. I didn't sweat you because you know the old saying, if you love something set it free. Let's hook up when I land in L.A."

He started telling me about his company, TNT.

I asked, "Why you name it TNT?"

" 'Cause I'm blowing up."

"Corny."

Everything he told me, all of those were our ideas, our plans when promoting was my hustle. Working temp jobs in the day, doing everything from bill collecting to phone solicitation, then hustling at night.

"I saw Steve Harvey last week," he said, talking in a soft tone. "Brother is completely off the hook. We vibed; I hit 'em with a larger plan for hitting up sponsors and doing a major comedy tour starting on the West Coast, and his boys gave me the hookup out your way."

I said, "Thanks for the reach out and touch, but I gotta go."

"Wait, wait."

"Don't hold me host—"

"Hold on, just give me a sec. I was at Nell's last night. Saw our old crew. Everybody asked about you. Made me miss you more than I can stand. What I'm saying is, I'm doing all of this, I'm motivated and on the right track because of you. Everything is jumping off, I have my own Web page—"

"Ten-year-olds have Web pages. Hell, I have a Web page."

"Hold up, gimme a minute."

I listened and paced, chewed my thumbnail. I stopped moving and leaned against the wall, halted in front of my black-and-whites of Harlem: Eddie Rochester at the Theresa Hotel, a snow-covered Central Park at night-time, a World War II food-ration line outside of GE Votings Employment Agency.

I went back to pacing and said, "Sounds like you're back on your feet. You still living on Park Ave, or did you lose that place too and have to move back in with your mother again?"

"I'm hanging in Harlem. Eighth Avenue and 151st Street."

"Eighth and 151st isn't the best area to live in."

"That's where you grew up."

"That's why I know."

"It's huge. Only four C notes a month."

"Good for you. A thirty-nine-year-old man should have his own place." I nodded. "You have the money you owe me?"

"Look, let's not get into that right now."

"I take that as a no. So we can hang up ri—"

"I wanted to prove to you that I was about something. It's blowing up and I want you here with me. That was our plan."

"How's Tia?"

"See, that's why I didn't know if I should call."

"Always follow your first mind."

"Couldn't stop thinking about you when I was coming home on the subway. I'm sitting up now looking over the pictures we took in Puerto Rico. Well, the ones you didn't burn. Want me to hold it up to the phone so you can see it? This one you have on the thong."

"Good-bye, Claudio. Hang up the phone."

"Is this how you treat the man who saved your life?"

"Next time, let me fall. I've died a thousand deaths since then."

That shut him down for a few seconds.

I said, "I'm trying not to get angry, trying not to be rude by hanging up in your face, so find it in your heart to respect me. Say good-bye and get on with your life."

"Well, until you tell me not to call—"

"I'm getting married, Claudio."

Silence. The kind that comes after a bomb has dropped. I thought he had hung up, but he panted back to life, sounding dazed and confused. "Married?"

"Yep."

"Getting or got?"

"Getting."

"That was quick."

"Nope, you were slow. You had your chance."

"Damn."

"What, did you expect me to cross my legs, become a nun, and chant hymns to the moon? It don't work like that."

"You said that you'd love me forever, no matter what."

I rubbed my eyes. Inside my mouth every taste bud was swollen, infected by a soured love's bitter juice.

He said, "Until you get married, you ain't married, so I'm gonna try."

"Claudio, don't do this. You had your chance."

"I love you. We're soul ma—"

I hung up. I didn't whack the phone in the receiver. I pushed down on the button and let Mr. Dial Tone do the rest.

I waited for it to ring again. It didn't. A long second

later I slumped back to life. After that conversation, I'd tensed up and held my breath so long I had to be dark blue. His Brooklyn voice lingered like a bad cold. He had stirred up old feelings, ancient memories that felt like they happened yesterday.

He didn't lie. He had saved my life.

The phone rang again. It was Vince. He was done with his laundry, had rented a couple of movies from Blockbuster.

I wiped the frustration from my eyes and put some happy in my voice. "Sounds like a plan. What you get?"

"A flick called *Cappuccino*."

"Lots of sex?"

"Yeah. Lots of plot twists, drama, and sex."

"Juicy, juicy. Bring it on."

We hung up. In the background, my shower was still running, the humidity seeping from underneath the door, drifting into the hallway. So much steam that when I opened the door, the walls were crying.

I didn't shower. My mood had been stolen from me. I turned the water off and went into the kitchen. I put on a pot of vegetables, started broiling salmon made with a shrimp stuffing. That's what Vince likes, so that's what I make. I've adapted to his world, changed my eating habits, started becoming part of him. He's made changes too, become part of me.

Claudio was coming to L.A.

I had become Bess, wanting Vince to save me from being handled by my old lover's hot hands.

Dinner and a movie went by in no time flat. It was a hot, steamy movie with enough twists to keep my mind occupied. Vince showered while I cleaned up the kitchen. Then I hopped in and scrubbed while he ironed his shirt for work tomorrow. A few of my things were lying around, slacks and a cotton blouse that had a wrinkle or two, and he pressed those for me. He always did that without my having to ask.

A good thirty minutes went by with me standing underneath that shower. The water ran cold and I took the hint. Thoughts. So many of them at the same time. I rubbed my skin down with baby oil, stepped out wet from braids to toenails. I thought that Vince was waiting for me in the bed, maybe already dozing off, but he came to me in red silk boxers.

I joked, "You know you're wearing gang colors?"

No laughter from him. That insatiable look was in his eye.

Jazz was breathing through my shower radio, KTWV playing Cassandra Wilson and Luther Vandross's duet, telling the world that they were only human, bound to make mistakes. Eucalyptus-scented candles were already lit; that was the dimly lit, erotic environment I loved to hide myself inside when I was bathing.

One long kiss later, I had melted into the bathroom floor, legs open wide, his tongue dancing down where the honey was always sweet, massaging deep inside my Queen jelly. Plain and simple, Vince was tearing it up. Call me 7-Eleven because I was ready to stay open all night.

I couldn't wait; needed this so badly. Needed the escape.

Good loving was supposed to help a woman forget bad times.

Vince was almost on top of me. His hard penis touched my inner thigh, bumped my pubic hair, got too close to my vagina.

I tried not to sound scared when I scooted away a little, pushed my lips up into a smile, then whispered, "Get a condom."

He opened his hand, showed me the Magnum he was palming.

I gave up a real smile then. I shifted so no renegade baby juice would slip inside and go on an Easter egg hunt. I kissed on his neck and chest, waited for him to get ready.

My phone rang. Broke the spell I was under. I made a motion like I was going to go get it. Vince shook his head, and I relaxed.

In the moment it took him to roll on the latex, my mind rolled back east. To Claudio. To the night I experienced my first moan-gasm. I thought I'd been having orgasms, but when my eyelashes fluttered like a hummingbird in flight, and I moaned so long and strong, I had landed in a new world. After that big O, I was dazed for an hour, amazed for even longer. It was easy for a young and naive woman to confuse that sensation with love.

When Vince was wrapped up like a mummy, I wondered if he tasted like candy. I'd never done that with him. I pulled him up on me, reached between his legs, loved the powerful way he felt in my hand, loved how my nerves opened up when I slid him inside. His expression tells me how much he craves me, and that turns me on.

I murmured, "Perfect. Sweetie, you feel so perfect."

"Damn, slow down, Dana. Pace car, baby."

"Okay, okay."

I was in midair, floating to a wonderful place.

Every thought of Claudio went away.

Slow pushes, pulls, kisses. Things got heated up, my breathing faster and deeper, felt my blood flowing through my body, my skin so soft under his weight. Our groans filled the room from floor to ceiling, wall to wall. Vince was sucking on me like I was a scrumptious mango. I bit him, laughed; he bit me back, right between my breast and shoulder. So much fun. I was with him, saying things I'd never say in church.

His love should be able to cure the common cold.

I asked him, "Tell me."

And he did, in that baritone voice, he told me over and over. His words made me melt into the warmth of an orgasm, held on to that cloud as long as I could.

*   *   *

Morning rolled in like a soft fog in Bakersfield.

Six a.m. My digital clock was humming like a storm warning. I slapped the snooze button as hard as I could.

Vince said my name, kissed my face. His breath, Colgate fresh.

I groaned. "How long you been up?"

"Your phone rang and woke me up a while ago."

"This early? I didn't hear it."

"It rang quite a few times."

I yawned and played it off. "You okay? You were tossing and turning and mumbling half the night."

His face changed for a second. Lines grew in his forehead and he looked older. "What did I say?"

"Hell if I know. I was too busy talking in my sleep."

We laughed, soft and easy.

Vincent had on khakis and a short-sleeve shirt, one that had one of those designer triangles on the front. A blue windbreaker was under his arm. I envied how he could always dress Cali casual for his job.

He said, "Gotta go beat traffic."

"I'm hurrying, sweetie."

I moved too fast, wasn't awake. Bumped into the six-foot-high bookcase. Shelves were so full, some three deep, a couple of books fell off. I owned everyone from Shakespeare to the Harlem Renaissance up to the juicy-juicy novels by the *Waiting to Exhale* lady.

Hand in hand, I hurried him to the door.

He said, "Make sure both locks are clicked on."

"Okay, sweetie."

Another long good-bye kiss. Then he was jogging down the hallway with a slight bulge in his crotch.

I scratched my butt and stepped over the books.

Five messages. All from Claudio. The first call had rolled in about the time I was waiting for Vince to roll his condom on. The next, in the middle of a moan-gasm. I deleted every message as soon as I heard his voice. Deleted them and wished feelings could be purged so easily.

I'd pleased Vince last night. Had done it so many nights.

Once I had wanted to know why my sex, my love, my whatever wasn't good enough for Claudio. Was it her breasts? Because I'd put on a little weight? Yep. One jerk can make a woman insecure about all men.

I'd given myself permission to leave those foolish thoughts behind.

That night had been beautiful. Snow covered Central Park. Cold as hell, but I was wrapped around Claudio. In his bed, my head to his chest, his breath on my skin, all snuggled and warm. Tipsy because we had been out partying at Nell's, had a night filled with sweet wine and friends, then made love as a nightcap.

Screams came into my dreams.

I woke up, woozy and slobbering, with Tia hovering over me, in her blue flight attendant uniform, crying and wailing like Busta Rhymes.

To this day, I don't understand why the skank went off on me. I tried to stay cool and tell her that we'd been sharing a man, that this was a love triangle and nobody knew about it but him.

She doubled up and came at me talking shit, shoved me so hard I fell and almost cracked my face on the heater.

When I got up, I tilted my head, looked at her like she'd lost her mind. It wasn't about Claudio anymore. Nobody pushes me around. If she couldn't respect me, then fear would be a good substitute.

Her insults screeched to a halt when I picked up a knife, chased her big titties, had her bouncing from wall to wall.

Claudio grabbed me, wrestled me until I was tired, my braids were every which-a-way, had me looking like snake-headed Medusa. He pinned me and tossed the knife to the side. While I tried to wiggle myself free, Tia's bitch ass ran to the phone yelling bloody murder. The neighbors woke up screaming for one of us to go ahead and kill the other so they could get some sleep.

NYPD came, brought a new level of humiliation. Took me for a little ride. Crackheads were on every corner, people selling bootleg videos and pirated CDs out of every bodega, but they locked me up.

Two days later I met with Claudio, listened to him explain what couldn't be justified. He told me Tia didn't mean a damn thing to him.

And of course he reminded me of the on-ness and off-ness of our relationship, of how my phone rang from time to time with the jingle of an old lover. Nope, over that five-year stretch Claudio wasn't the only man I'd been with. He pleaded insane on the grounds of insecurity. I ended up in his bed that night.

We'd had twenty seasons of history. He'd been there for me when Momma died, and I couldn't handle the love being over just like that.

Yep. Reason had jumped out the window, and when the damage was done, I had stooped to that girl's level and met ignorance with anger. Resentment, when you don't control it, only leads to misery. Claudio made a fool out of me, then I turned around and made a bigger fool of myself. That's what I hated the most. Not the people, not what my daddy did, not what my momma allowed, not Claudio, not Tia, just the feelings they left behind.

I left New York. Called myself leaving all of that behind.

That was then, this is now.

Outside was cloudy, still overcast with a marine layer that made the morning cool, right at seventy degrees. I'd been blessed. I was seeing the perfect man in a perfect land.

I headed for the shower.

Vince's silk boxers were on the bathroom floor, bundled next to the black satin pajamas I never had the chance to slip on last night. A hurricane of pleasure had come through there.

That was only a few hours ago.

And this morning another man was clogging up my mind.

I had been tracked down like I was a runaway slave.

I stood under the hot water, no candle, no music, soaped my sleep-deprived body down, wanted Vince to come back and save me from these uninvited feelings. Needed him to crawl inside me, fill me with sweet pain, and steal my mind away from New York once again.

5 Vince

I was heading south on the 405 freeway, zooming underneath the DC-10s, 747s, and FedEx planes coming into
three runways at LAX, passing the HerbaLife building,
and the strip of mega-hotels, car dealerships, and fast-
food joints on Century Boulevard.

I'd left Dana's ten minutes ago, was doing at least
seventy-five, but most of the cars, SUVs, and minivans
were passing me like I was driving a Pinto with three
tires.

Whenever I was troubled, Womack was the man I
called. So, that's what I did. Took out my c-phone and
dialed his number.

He said, "Fool, why ain't you been by here? Thought
you were gonna help me sell all these doggone T-shirts
I had made up?"

"Been working overtime in case the layoffs come
down again."

"Ain't that much overtime in the world."

"Been spending time with Dana too."

"Aw, so it's like that now, huh? Negro Black Man, you
got family over here and you dumping us for a New
York woman?"

"Drop 'em off at the crib. I'll take a few to Boeing."

He reminded me, "First of the month is coming up.
You need to hit the strip. You know how peeps on your
side of Crenshaw become shopaholics when they get
those county checks."

We laughed. My tone was light-hearted, but I didn't

feel that way. This morning I was a man standing in water up to his chin, waiting for his fears to rise two more feet and drown him.

Womack has been my best friend since I was my daddy's sperm searching for my momma's egg. His dad, Harmonica, and my dad used to work at the Long Beach Naval Shipyard together, then hang out on Central Avenue, the West Coast version of Harlem, living in the gin and blues until way after midnight. Our mothers both sang in the same choir, both did hair, Momma out of our kitchen, Womack's mom out of theirs. Everybody worked hard. Too hard.

In the background, Womack's baby girl, Ramona, was crying. His three little boys—Louie, Mark, and Jordan—were rumbling. Their television was on an early morning kiddie show.

Rosa Lee picked up an extension, heard my voice. "I told everybody you almost got busted when big-mouth and ignorant what's-her-face showed up asking about Malaika."

The tall sister that we'd run into at church yesterday, she was at my wedding. Was at my ex-wife's baby shower too.

She said sternly, "Don't put me in the middle of your mess."

"See, I should've married you, Rosa Lee."

"Hey, hey," Womack cut in. "Don't flirt with my wife."

She retorted, "Vince, if you don't mind a woman with a few miles on her and a ready-made family, we'll move into your apartment with you by the time the sun goes down."

"Hey, hey," Womack snapped. "Don't flirt with my best friend."

Rosa Lee had to get ready for work. She was running behind. She told Womack to change the baby's diaper because she had deposited a stinky load of Colonel Mustard in her Huggie.

He snapped back at her, "Why can't you do it?"

"Can't you see I'm trying to get out of here?"

A few more spicy things were said.

Womack was my best friend. I'd lie for him. Go to jail for him. Die for him. If he died before me, I'd spend the rest of my days taking care of his children. I'd do that for him, and I know he'd take care of my little girl if anything happened to me.

But when him and Rosa Lee had words, I backed away.

Rosa Lee hung up.

I told Womack, "It's no biggie. I'll hit you back."

"Nah," he said. "I can handle it. Just have to give her a hard time so she won't forget who's in charge over here."

He was heading toward the baby. I knew because the crying was getting louder. Hearing his daughter cry reminded me why I had called.

I told him, "I had a dream last night."

"Martin Luther King Jr. had one first."

"Why you always got to be such a smart-ass?"

"Because you're a dumb donkey."

Since he didn't curse me back, that meant his boys were in earshot. Either that or he thought they might hear him through the monitors. When you have kids, monitors are in every room. I know that for a fact.

"Hold on for a quick sec," he said.

I was passing the Carson Mall, leaving the 405 and merging with the 110 north, riding with about a million cars. Riding and thinking about a lot of things. About how after we spent two years at El Camino Community College, Womack got Rosa Lee pregnant, found a gig at UPS, jumped the broom, and tossed his community college books to the side. I went on to Cal State Long Beach, did a year, couldn't afford the tuition, had to lay off a year. At least that had been my plan. I met Malaika. She was hot to trot, ready to party, and pregnant six months later. We married a month after the rabbit died, divorced two years after that.

Falling for a fine woman had changed my master plan.

An anxious dick, misplaced romance, and some misguided sperm have changed many a man's plans. Made him wake up every day wishing he could turn back the hands of time. Which proved that there's no such thing as free sex, only delayed payments.

As I was driving, surrounded by a million cars and still feeling all alone, I thought about the things that I don't think I'll ever be able to tell Dana. If I told her part, she'd want the whole story.

I'd found out Malaika was seeing her high school sweetheart. While I was slaving from six p.m. to two a.m., making that third-shift differential at Boeing, she was making booty calls in the desert.

Only she didn't know I had her followed.

Malaika had left my little girl in San Bernardino at her mom's crib. Lied and said she was going to party at Pinky's with her sister, Regina, but had gone on a rendezvous out in Moreno Valley. On that rainy night I went right up to that door. Banged like thunder. Called her name like I was sounding Gabriel's horn. She came out. Trembling. Shocked. Tried to talk. But I couldn't hear a word she said because I was so busy cursing her down for leaving our child while she ran the streets. Besides, it was hard for her to get the words out with my hands clamped around her throat tighter than an Indian necklace.

He jumped in. Big mistake. It was between me, my wife, and God, but he jumped in like he was the hero in an action movie.

I kicked his ass like it was the opening day of ass-kicking season. And when the smoke cleared, I unrolled my fists, went and got my child, took her over to Womack's crib. Went there because I was scared the police might come knocking. Not one of my proudest moments. My roughest hour. In my heart, that's my black beast. That personal violation felt like a slow death. My grief was so overwhelming it was oppressive. Almost got swallowed up by a wave of loneliness. Couldn't reach out to nobody. Nobody but Womack.

He came back on the line: "Man, didn't mean to leave you hanging, but that girl kept squirting mustard while I was changing her. I went through three doggone diapers."

He got settled and I told him about the dream that lasted all night. Seemed too real. It had done a real number on me.

In my dream, I was flying. Feeling good.

He said, "Power. Flying means you have power. Then what?"

I went on. Told him I had glided through a cloud shaped like a smile, then over a snowcapped mountain. Then somebody was pulling my pants, tapping on my leg. Felt like small hands, soft fingers. I looked back and Kwanzaa was flying right behind me.

My child had returned.

Her hair was in two ponytails. She was wearing a blue Kente dress, white tights, and patent-leather shoes. I took her tiny hand and pulled her softness up to me. Her face smelled like sweet breast milk. She kissed my cheek, smiled under her eager eyes. Then we flew side by side and laughed a million times.

A lot happened, words, we sang songs.

The sun started to set, went down too fast. With the darkness came coldness, and Kwanzaa started to fall. She fell and I forgot how to fly. My child screamed that I had said I would always protect her.

A huge shadow circled me. Malaika's husband. He didn't have a face, but I knew it was Drake. He flew by and caught my child. He slowed and held my baby steady while I continued to plunge.

This morning I woke up, heart beating too fast, shivering, sweating. I had expected Dana to be awake, lurking in the shadows, watching me and knowing, her cold eyes piercing at me through the darkness. But she wasn't.

Her phone rang. She didn't move at all. Sound asleep. Warm. Looking innocent. I watched her for a while.

I had wanted to whisper good-bye to that pretty sleepyhead, make sure she was tucked in tight, tell her I loved her and to take care of herself, sell those houses and become a big-time real estate agent, tell her all of that while she slept, then pack up my lie and leave forever. Hope that by the new spring she would forget about me. And maybe by the time old man winter rolled around again, I'd've gotten over her.

Womack said, "Don't let that worm dig too deep."

We said a few more things, made plans to get together over the weekend for a few minutes, if he had minutes to spare. He's married with four kids, so if he found a few minutes that would be a miracle.

He told me that he'd ride over to my side of Crenshaw and leave a box of T-shirts on my front porch sometime today.

Womack said, "Lauryn Hill or Jada Pinkett?"

I said, "Lauryn Hill till the cows come home."

"You a fool."

"Takes one to know one."

"Idiot, how could you pass up Jada Pinkett?"

"How could you pass up Lauryn Hill?"

He had me where I needed to be, living inside of friendship and laughter. When we hung up, my laughter faded, but the memories were still here.

I wished I was younger. Wished it was back when KDAY was on the air playing the hell out of NWA. Back when we cruised Crenshaw on Sundays. And Carolina West was the place to be, party from sundown on Saturday until nine on a Sunday morning.

That was way back then. Before Malaika. Back when Womack had planned on being an attorney and I was going to be an engineer and come up with something to knock IBM out of the market and help my buddy rule the free world. And his wife, before the unplanned pregnancy, she was heading down the road of medicine; that brilliant woman was going to be a doctor.

The choices we made diverted us all to another life.

Not bad. Just different. Unexpected.

I made it into Boeing, parked in the football field–size parking lot that faced the 91 freeway, grabbed my sacked lunch, and raced across the blacktop through the security gate. Smiled and laughed and ran with the rest of the fellows who were rushing to the nearest time clock so we could punch in before our corporate curfew, hurrying to work another day at the plantation.

I clocked in, stopped by the ARA machine long enough to grab a cup of flavorless coffee, then hoofed it into Building 270 with the rest of the crew. The white-collar people were in their groups. The real workers were in theirs.

I passed a pay phone near the bathrooms, paused, decided to try and set things right at both ends of my life.

The first call went to Dana. Told her I loved her, hoped she had a great day, that I wanted to get together with her and talk.

Then I called my child's grandmother's house. Hadn't dialed San Bernardino in about six months. Since the breakup, conversations with her had been brief, some a little tart to the taste, and no matter how much I asked, she never offered any help in contacting my child. Her voice always held hostility when I called. Ever since that night, every one in that family has held the same disdain.

Three tears in a bucket. I needed to get a direct international number to Malaika. No matter what they thought, I had to put my foot down, let them know I'd had enough of the bullshit.

I steeled myself, became firm, determined, and called.

The phone had been temporarily disconnected.

That Saturday was the first of the month. Everybody had started hawking the avenue named after George H. Crenshaw with the rising of the sun. In ninety-degree heat I was peddling designer T-shirts, stayed dog-eat-dog with Asians hawking video and cassette tapes, Mexican ladies offering cotton socks, and ashy-elbowed Iranians auctioning off quadruple-X-rated African American porno tapes.

I hit the crowded Crenshaw Car Wash, sold a few, went by three Nix Check Cashing places, Phillip's BBQ, the Arco next to the 98 Cents store, dropped in Magic Shears and sold a couple while a brother named Silk trimmed my hair and shaped up my beard for me. Everybody liked FUBU T-shirts. I did the best when I hit the barber and beauty and braid and weave and manicure shops. There are more vanity shops on one block of this strip than there are craters in the moon.

I went home, showered, changed into my 501s and a dark blue T-shirt, and drove over to Womack's duplex. His nest was in Old Ladera, three miles from my rambunctious part of town. Land that used to be all Armenian and white around twenty years ago, but now it was mostly African American with plenty of white people in the mix. Single- and two-story duplexes, Spanish-style homes, eucalyptus trees, and Neighborhood Watch signs on every pole.

Most people judge how safe an area was by the number of wrought-iron bars on the window. Womack didn't have any on his champagne-colored building, and neither did his neighbors.

A *Wave* newspaper was on his front lawn, covering a sprinkler. I picked the paper up, glancing at the front page. A woman police officer who lived in the neighborhood had gone ballistic, pulled out a .22, and shot her also-a-cop boyfriend four times in the upper torso.

The fight that me and Malaika had was bad, but not that tragic. It still haunts me. If I had've had a .22 on my hip back then, blood would've been flowing like the Miss'ssippi River. That just goes to show, because I would've taken Malaika back. Wanted her to come back. Would've gone to counseling because I wanted my child to have both of us in the house, a mother and father. Didn't care if me and Malaika never made love again. My child was all that mattered. My daughter sitting in my lap would make me feel wealthier than Trump and Perot combined.

Womack was in the back, near his three-car garage, washing his '64 Impala. His toy. Every man should have something that lets him hold on to the boy inside. His everyday car was out front, a plain-wrapped Honda Civic that he hardly ever washed. He'd had the Impala since the days we used to cruise Crenshaw on Sunday afternoons.

He still had on his brown UPS uniform. A manager at the hub over at LAX. He'd no doubt worked last night, then come in and hit the ground running, doing family stuff. My ace saw me coming down the concrete driveway, heading toward the backyard with the cardboard box, his newspaper in my other hand, and said, "You done already?"

"Yep. Sold about half of what you left on my door."

Womack said, "When I dropped that off, I saw Naiomi. Good-googity-moo. She was walking 'round in a sports bra and spandex, looking bootyful."

I chuckled. "Man, you need to quit."

He made a face. "You should find out when she gonna be home alone and tip across that hall and borrow a cup of sugar."

I shook my head. "Dana is enough to fill my cup."

Outside of a few premature gray hairs, Womack looks the same way he did when we went to Morningside High and El Camino College—skinny, six foot two, thick eyebrows on his honey-colored skin. He was scarecrow thin; a good Santa Ana breeze could slap him over on his homemade Jheri-Kurl.

I told him, "Somebody should've put an expiration date on that flammable hairstyle ten years ago."

"Don't hate me 'cause I ain't a conformist."

He inhaled his cigarette, a Djarum that made the air smell like cloves, dipped the end in a spot of water on the ground, flipped it into an open trash can, then leaned back on one boney leg and asked me, "Vanessa Williams or Chanté Moore?"

"Vanessa Williams, from dusk to dawn."

"You a fool."

"Takes one to know one. Besides, Chanté got a man." Womack said, then asked, "How much we make?"

I echoed, "We?"

"You heard me. We."

I answered, "Four hundred. We split it fifty-fifty."

"Shyster. I'm supposed to get more than you."

"How you figure? I'm in the sun sweating my butt off."

His face was stiffened. "I'm the boss. You the employee. Those my damn T-shirts, Black Man Negro. I invested the money. I gotta offset my damn costs. You shouldn't get no more than a hundred. Matter of fact, I got four kids and a wife, plus my daddy living over my head. Therefore, all you should get is fifty dollars. And you owe me twenty-five of that."

I shook my head. "Punk."

He frowned and said, "Gimme my money and the rest of my T-shirts, then get off my property, Black Man Negro."

I gave him two hundred fifty dollars; I kept one-fifty.

He smiled at that, then pushed the other fifty in my pocket.

Friends. Always friends.

We hopped in his tootmobile and rode two blocks up to Slauson and stopped in at LA Hot Wings. I'd been craving spicy chicken because I'd passed by all the BBQ chicken places on the strip.

Back at Womack's duplex, we went upstairs to his daddy's place. He had been living there for the last six years, rent free. Womack complains night and day, but he takes care of his own.

John Lee Hooker blues was playing strong when we made it through the back door. Harmonica—that's what everybody called Womack's daddy—had his silver harp to his lips and was bumping along with the gritty voice on that bluesman groove.

He smiled at me from the oak dining room table. "Well, if it ain't Vince. Ain't seen you since the last blue moon."

Harmonica's voice had a southern drawl and was bulldog mean, but he was one of the nicest men I'd ever met. He always wore fifties-style slacks, white T-shirts, and a colorful sweater, even if it was a hundred degrees in the shade. A receding hairline was on his dome, a crop of razor bumps lived under his neck.

I smiled because I'd missed him too. "What's up, old man?"

"Keep on livin', youngster, you'll find out."

I laughed.

He said, "I hear you done got yourself another one of those women that's trouble on two legs."

We laughed.

Harmonica winked at me, licked his chops, and said, "Brang her by so we can get acquainted."

I winked back at my mentor. "If you promise not to take her away from me and leave me heartbroken, I might do that."

"Oh, now you know I can't promise you that. I got what all the girls like, and I can't help myself sometimes."

Again, we shared locker room–style laughter.

A book rested on his table: *The Words That You Should Know*. That was my present to him the last time he got out of Cedar Sinai, right before I met Dana at the Townhouse.

I asked Harmonica, "Dionne Warwick or Nancy Wilson?"

He grinned so hard his teeth slipped. "Nancy Wilson. Now, that's a fine-looking young woman. Dionne all into that Psychic Friends voodoo mess. Can't deal with no mojo women like that."

Harmonica is old, about the same age my daddy

would be. His bronchitis has gotten worse; he has a medicine cabinet filled with more pills than a Rite Aid drugstore. A few times he'd been to the hospital; the last time he left in an ambulance and we didn't think he would come out breathing. I've already seen my folks get weak, hooked up to machines, then fade like sunshine at the closing of the day. I didn't want Harmonica to ever die on me.

He put his c-band harmonica up to his mouth and jammed with the blues like he was part of that southern-fried philharmonic.

The building shook, jerked like it had been hit by a small truck. Walls creaked, noise from the foundation. The CD player skipped, then stopped. Ceiling fans moved back and forth.

The room swayed.

Harmonica said, "Earthquake."

I yawned.

Womack said, "Poppa, how many pieces of chicken you want?"

"Put 'bout ten on the plate, son."

That made me miss my daddy. Made me miss my momma. I'd never be able to argue with them or make them a plate again.

Harmonica said that he'd seen where aerospace was still cutting back, then asked me how Boeing was holding up. I told him everything could be better, but it could be worse. For now, I'd hang on to the good.

He asked, "You keeping up with sending your girl money?"

"Yes, sir."

"Keeping records like I told you to?"

"Yes, sir."

"Good, good. Send her something to let her know that no matter who her momma laying up with, you her daddy down to the bone." His heavy face motioned at Womack. "I done took care of all nine of my children, and this one here the only one that even offered me a glass of water."

That was his pain, his way of telling me to do right, but not to expect anything in return.

Womack stopped eating his chicken long enough to tell his daddy, "Don't get too comfortable. Next week you're gonna start paying me some rent money. This ain't no free hotel."

"Boy, you crazy as a cat chasing a pit bull's tail."

Womack rambled about how this place—just like the one downstairs—had hardwood floors, a fireplace, den, bay windows.

Harmonica growled, "Vince, see how he comes in my house acting all bumptious and impertinent?"

I laughed, then overarticulated the same words he'd taught himself, "Bumptious and impertinent?"

The old man tapped the book on the table. He'd been studying. Again, me and Harmonica shared a chuckle and a wink.

Womack sucked his teeth and blew off a little steam. "I could get twelve hundred a month if I had a real tenant."

Harmonica said, "Let's see if you can get yourself a tenant who gonna baby-sit every day and cut the grass every Monday."

Womack shut up.

The CD player had come back on, but I hadn't noticed it until now. John Lee Hooker was singing about covering the waterfront. Harmonica played along with the mellow tune. Made me wish I had Dana in my arms.

I pulled out the dominoes, grabbed paper and a pencil. Harmonica had pictures of him when he was young, down South, playing in a five-piece blues band, The Night Blues, up all over the place. He was as slim as Womack, hair conked, a bona fide playboy. He had about a thousand photos of his eighteen grandchildren and his ten great-grandchildren. Outside of those memories, he had African figures in almost every room of his two-bedroom castle. Nkondi figures dating back to the 1700s, double-headed snakes, brass hips masks from

Nigeria, bronze heads from Benin. In his retirement he'd become a collector of culture. And new words.

Womack poured soda for everybody. He made his with Coca-Cola, root beer, Sprite, mixed it up like a kid.

We held hands. Womack blessed the food.

Then we ate, played bones, talked shit, and laughed.

Thirty minutes into our bonding, the garage door rattled open. A Ford Explorer came down the driveway. Classical music floated up from below. Doors slammed, kids laughed, and a set of petite feet came up the wooden stairs. A slim, bowlegged copper-colored sister with fascinating eyes, wearing a denim vest and long floral skirt. Every stitch of clothing on her said Rodeo Drive, but I knew better. Middle-school teachers slaving for L.A. Unified didn't make that much.

I said, "You're looking sweet sixteen, Rosa Lee. Still got that homecoming queen figure."

She sort of blushed, then bounced her gurgling baby on her hip and said, "Teach your buddy to be so sweet with his words, Vince. This marriage will be a lot better for the both of us."

The three boys were outside running around the yard. Basketball bouncing, hitting the rim, bouncing, yells, challenges.

"Momma, tell Louie to stop making faces at me."

"Nobody looking at you. Ask Jordan, Momma. I'm being good."

"Mark won't give me the ball."

Rosa yelled, "Knock it off before I come take that ball."

Dribbling, bouncing, no more arguing.

Womack said, "I left y'all some hot wings in the fridge."

Rosa Lee handed Womack their youngest, said, "Your turn."

Womack asked, "Where you going?"

Rosa Lee answered with an exhausted breath, "Beauty shop. Cynthia said she can squeeze me in if I get to La Brea and Olympic in thirty minutes. Maybe she'll make me pretty enough for my husband to notice what's left of my homecoming figure."

She kissed my lips, did the same with her father-in-law, then went downstairs to feed her three little men.

Me and Harmonica shared a look, then looked at Womack. I was going to ask him if life was okay downstairs, but he was busy smiling at his baby girl, asking her which bone to play next.

Harmonica said, "Son?"

"Yeah, Poppa."

"Son, look at me for a minute."

Womack's eyes went to his daddy's.

Harmonica asked, "Why didn't you get up and kiss yo' wife?"

"I'm tired. I did the grocery shopping, cleaned up when they left. She know how to kiss me when she wanna be kissed."

Harmonica said, "She been with the chirren all day. She's tired, son. A woman gets tired just like you do."

Womack shifted like he was a six-year-old child.

I stayed out of their family business.

Harmonica sighed, rubbed the razor bumps under his flabby chin, and put some daddy-tone in his voice. "Why don't you go downstairs, send my grandchirren up here with enough clothes to last them until the sun comes up, and spend some quality time with your wife? Give her some kind words, tell her how much you appreciate her while you rub her feet."

Womack looked at his daddy, then at me. I nodded.

Harmonica said, "Son, when a woman gets tired, and has the mind to stray, the man in her own home is the last one to know."

Womack handed Harmonica his grandchild.

When the door closed behind Womack, Harmonica turned to me. "Wisdom ain't seeing what's in your face, but recognizing what's about to come."

Two minutes later the three boys—Louie, Mark, and

Jordan—were in Harmonica's living room, watching television.

After they came up, I never heard Womack's door open downstairs. Never heard Rosa Lee leaving for a late-evening hair appointment. We heard love and laughter coming from downstairs.

I changed Ramona's diaper; Harmonica made her a fresh bottle.

Harmonica told me, "Straighten out your business with your woman. If she 'cepts it, y'all can move on. If she don't, y'all can move on."

"Should I tell about, you know, that night?"

That was all we ever called it, "That night."

"Nah," Harmonica said after he'd thought a few seconds. "That don't need to be discussed. A man's past is his own business."

"Wonder how she'll react."

"Man never knows how a woman will take thangs."

6 Vince

Dana lowered her candy apple and snapped, "You're married?"

"Divorced."

"And you have a kid."

"Yeah. A little girl."

Her candy apple slipped from her hand, rolled across the concrete into the thick of the crowd. She swayed, and I thought she was about to pass out, fall over the wooden rail and plunge fifty feet down into the murky sea. I put my fingers on her shoulder, but she moved my hand away. Held herself. Made a gasping sound.

We were on the boardwalk in Santa Monica, underneath the shadows of the Ferris wheel and all the other kiddie rides. Below us, the Pacific was rolling wave after wave into the fine sands on the beach. Air filled with laughter and the scent of cotton candy. A brother who passed by with his little girl high on his shoulders was what helped me stutter and stammer my way to my moment of truth.

A minute ago, Dana was snuggled with the butt of her wide-leg Levi's tight against the buttons on my 501s, and I was kissing flesh that was smoother than a Billie Holiday tune. Now her face looked like she'd never smiled a day in her life. Or would never smile again.

"Hold on, let me make sure I heard what I just heard. You're telling me you're married? And you have a child?"

"Divorced. Yeah."

"Why did you wait this long to tell me?"

"I'm facing the truth. Everything that is faced can be changed, and nothing can be changed until it's faced. James Baldwin—"

"Just what I need," she said, cutting me off with who-gives-a-shit sarcasm. "Another quote. You can save that bullshit."

I rubbed my beard as if admitting that was stupid.

She winced, then spoke in a soft and numbed voice. "Give me the details. Tell me the real deal."

I gave her the Cliff Notes to that portion of my life.

The sun was dropping from the skies, changing the smog-gray skyline into a magnificent hue of peach and strawberry.

Dana blew air so warm it fogged; her insides were on fire. "Womack and Rosa Lee and their daddy and her kids know about this marriage?"

"This is my mistake. They told me to tell you when we met."

"Duh, hello. Why didn't you?"

"Fear, I guess. I couldn't handle you not liking me."

"What, is this supposed to make me like you now?"

Harsh looks. Regretful expressions. Anger. Shame.

Dana continued, "What's her name?"

"Kwanzaa."

"Your wife is named Kwanzaa?"

"That's my baby's name."

"Your ex-wife's name is . . . ."

"Malaika."

She looked at me, remembering that name. Remembered it from a week ago at church. Dana showed me how precise her memory was, said, "Love at first sight, competition, conquest, contempt."

I added, "A very unhappy ending."

Dana fingered her hair. "So, now I know. How old?"

"Twenty-eight."

"I meant your baby."

"Five."

I told her that Malaika had remarried and left the country; I hadn't told her that part yet. I was giving information in doses, seeing how she digested each spoonful before I gave her the next. She looked like she was being force-fed castor oil.

Dana strolled away, dabbed sweat away from the tip of her nose, moved in short steps like she had shackles on her feet.

I followed, moved a little slower, gave her room.

She asked, "You're paying C.S. and alimony?"

"No alimony."

Crackling was in my ears, the sound from a wooden bridge that was burning under my feet.

Abruptly, Dana laughed a hard, very not right, belly laugh.

"What's funny?"

"I misunderstood you. I thought you brought me down here"—she took a breath—"because you were about to ask me to marry you."

"I want to marry you. I asked you to."

She waved her empty ring finger. "Not officially."

Time went by. Wasn't much. Just a corner of forever.

She forced a smile. "I'm glad you're an obligated brother. Most of ours don't take care of their own."

"White man does the same thing. Black people don't own sin."

We were moving toward people fishing on the backside of the pier, facing Palos Verdes and miles of open ocean. She hardball pitched a pebble over the railing into the ocean. Lowered her head, then raised it again.

She said, "I told you my daddy went back to his first wife."

"Yep."

I threw a pebble out into the waters, south toward Venice Beach. I wished that everybody's past could be tossed away so easily.

She mumbled, "Families always break up because of

some bitch. Brothers walk when they get tired of the pussy, or a woman becomes inconvenient."

"Sisters walk too. Switch up in a heartbeat."

She ran her tongue over her bottom lip. Her black-berry lipstick was almost gone. "When we met, I asked if you had kids. You said no."

"I wanted to tell you. I didn't know how."

"What do you mean, you didn't know how? There were one thousand ways you could've told me. You could've left a Post-it on my front door, left a message at my job, sent an E-mail, faxed, called on my car phone, did a beep-beep-beep on my pager, could've wrote a letter, sent a postcard, or even better, you could've been a man and told me."

"Did you tell me all about you in the first fifteen minutes?"

"I didn't share every little detail, but I told you enough."

I said, "Well, I wanted to be sure you were the one."

"So, all this time you were using me to get off."

I didn't say anything. She was the one who had showed up at my place, undressing and with the con-doms, but I carried the blame.

"Look, I'm going to be honest. My last relationship with Claudio"—she stalled when she said his name, frowned as her tight eyes became opaque—"was a wasted five years. That was a big chunk of my life that I'll never be able to get back. It shouldn't take a man five years of laying up with somebody to figure out if a woman is right for him."

"I know. We're on the same page."

"I don't know we're on the same page."

"Why not?"

"Because it shouldn't take a man half a year to tell me he already has a family."

"They're in Germany."

"I don't care if they're on the third ring of Saturn. You still have a family."

"If you want to cut your ties, I understand."

"What, you think my emotions are a switch? When something goes wrong I can click that unwanted feeling off? It don't work like that. I love you. I can't unlove you in two seconds. I can't act like we never met."

I couldn't bob or weave out of the way of her words.

She wiped her nose, asked, "You have pictures of your little girl?"

"Yeah. A couple."

"Never seen 'em. You've been hiding 'em."

Then Dana complained about being cold, and we drifted back toward my worn-out 300ZX. We headed east up the 10, left all the yuppies and people with green and purple hair in Beach Town, USA, got off at Crenshaw, headed over the rough and uneven pavement toward my home.

"Your car stinks like gas."

I said, "Fuel injectors must be leaking."

"A lot of things are leaking. Starting to smell."

I parked on the south side of Stocker, away from my building and nearest Leimert Park. Dana was still practicing being a deaf mute. The area was packed, hardly anyplace to park because Raleigh Studios had about twenty eighteen-wheelers down in the mouth of the park, filming a movie.

We walked across the street, Dana in front, moving slowly. Neighbors sitting on stoops, a couple walking a pair of identical pit bulls, heading toward Audubon Middle School. They saw us coming. Read the tension. Backed off.

One of my landlords was standing in their bay window. Naiomi. I recognized the crescendo of her breasts, the curves in her silhouette, saw her good enough to make out the shape of her head, braids, and to tell that she had on tight jean shorts and a midriff top.

She checked out Dana's aggravated body language. I pretended I didn't feel Naiomi's energy, didn't acknowledge her shallow wave or her curiosity.

Before I met Dana, I used to wish I was Naiomi's type, wished that because she seemed so damn easy to get along with. Divorced with a kid, just like me. Lonely days made me want her so bad that I fantasized about her tipping over to see me in the middle of a warm summer night.

But that was back then. I'm wishing on things that would make my present so much more pleasant.

At the top of the stairs, my landlords' door opened. Juanita came out, golden hair hanging straight, no makeup on her face, dressed in jeans and a white T-shirt that had red letters that read PUT WOMEN IN THEIR PLACE—FIRST PLACE.

She looked across at Dana, then down at me.

I said, "What's up, Juanita?"

"Three garages were broken in tonight. Not ours or yours, the people across the way. Two cars were stolen. Last week a couple of cars were broken in out on the streets too. Dana, your car is nice, so be careful and try and park in front of this building. It's safer."

Dana replied, "Safety and love are both illusions."

Juanita's eyes went from Dana to me.

Dana chuckled. "After tonight, I won't be parking on Stocker."

"Why is that?"

An awkward moment.

Juanita tendered her tone and asked Dana, "You okay?"

I came up a step or two and said, "Everything's fine."

"I was talking to Dana, Vince."

"And I'm talking to you: everything's fine."

Another one of those moments happened between me and Juanita.

She went on, "If you need anything, Dana, let us know."

Dana said, "Vince, the door please? My bladder."

Inside the huge living room of my one-bedroom apartment, after Dana had gone to the bathroom and come back, and a lot of minutes with no words had gone by, I asked, "What're you thinking?"

"Melting clocks. I'm thinking about melting clocks."

I didn't know what that meant, but the way she said it was soft and agonizing at the same time. A second or two went by.

She asked, "How long have you had that bedroom furniture?"

I shrugged. "Five, maybe six years."

Dana made a negative sound; blue devils were dancing in her lungs, swimming in her blood. She said, "So, you've been screwing me on the same furniture you laid with your wife on. That seems blasphemous."

For a hot moment she wanted to go off, but she pulled herself inward and subdued her rage as fast as it came. I curled my bottom lip in, wondered how many men had left semen stains on her sheets, how many condoms had been flushed down her toilet.

I offered, "I can get something new, if that'll make you feel better."

"If that'll make me feel better," she mocked. "It's kinda late to worry about my feelings."

I felt so bad. Never felt so low.

"Let me ask you something," she said, then cleared her throat. "Did you ever videotape you and your wife when you had sex too?"

She asked me that out of the blue, caught me off guard. I almost admitted that I'd dabbled in some video fun with my ex-wife, but from the look on Dana's face, now wasn't the time to add any more coals to the fire.

"Nope. Never taped anybody but us."

"Where's the tape?"

My insides jumped, made me think she had read my mind. "What tape?"

"The one of us."

"In the closet."

"I want it destroyed. You might be one of those perverts who would send X-rated crap over the Net." She rocked, did nervous things. Then in a no-compromise tone she said, "Get the pictures of your child."

She watched me go into the back of my closet and pull out a legal-size golden envelope. A VHS tape crashed to the floor. I played it off, kicked it to the back of the closet, then closed the door.

I opened the envelope, showed her the photos of my child.

Her voice turned tender when she said, "Only four snapshots?"

"Malaika took everything else."

"Wedding pictures?"

"Everything."

The unraveling of me hurt. Nobody was gunned down with a .22, but a finger was on the trigger and the night was young.

Dana said, "She's pretty. Nice-looking child."

I didn't know if she meant that, or if that was what people were supposed to say when they looked at the pictures of a newborn baby.

She asked, "Is Malaika a twenty-five twenty?"

"A what?"

"Is she white?"

"Nope. She looks more Creole than black, though."

She went on, "What you've told me doesn't make sense."

"What doesn't make sense about it?"

"Help me connect the dots. You said she abandoned you and married somebody else before the ink dried on your divorce papers. She never calls, never writes. Doesn't all of that sound kind of suspicious?"

"What do you mean by that?"

Dana was checking out my child's walnut complexion, round face, and slanted eyes. No expression. Totally unreadable.

She asked, "You ever take a blood test?"

"No."

"So you're not sure it's your child?"

"What, you know something that I don't know?"

"You never took a blood test after you found out she

was messing around. You said you didn't know how long she'd been messing around."

I emphasized, "She looks like Malaika."

She studied the photo. "Your ex-wife must be pretty."

That rang out like a trick statement, so I didn't bite. She gazed at my child's image until her eyes watered, then eased the pictures down and stared at me. Didn't blink.

I said, "What's wrong?"

Her lips barely parted. "I'm thinking about the big picture. This would be one hellified, complicated relationship when they came back. When we went to bed last night, when we made love, when we woke up this morning and made love again, while we sat at Boulevard Cafe and ate breakfast, while we had all that fun, in my mind there were only two people in this relationship. Now . . ."

A moment passed. "What are you saying?"

"I'm saying this plate is looking mighty full. I thought it was only me and you, but you've opened a friggin' day-care center on me."

"One kid. I only have one kid."

"A kid, an ex-wife, in-laws that you claim treat you like an outlaw. All of a sudden this makes me feel claustrophobic."

"It's just my daughter."

"Get real. If the child is there, the wife never leaves."

"Malaika is long gone."

"Well, from what I've seen in my own life, between my momma and my daddy, you two have a bond through that child."

"Well, our divorce unbonded us."

"Don't fool yourself."

Silence filled the room like water flooding a bathtub.

While we drowned, I asked Dana what she was thinking.

She said, "About something I heard in church, that divorce is one of God's consequences for not following

Him and doing it His way. In God's eyes you're still married, and every time I've slept with you, in God's eyes, I've committed adultery."

I joked, "If we had a dime for every time we sinned, we could buy our way into heaven."

Her face hardened. "Don't say that."

"I was joking."

"Don't joke like that."

"What's the difference between you sleeping with a divorced brother and the plain old fornication you were doing with your ex for five years, all the sex you've had up until you met me?"

"That's not funny."

"I'm not laughing. What's the difference?"

"Deception. Misrepresentation. My ability to choose."

"So you pick and choose what sin works for you?"

"Doesn't everybody?" Dana stood, did neurotic things with her hair. "All the way back here from Santa Monica, I thought about kicking you to the curb. My insides are, I dunno, all mixed up with thoughts of forgiveness and revenge."

I asked, "Is it more forgiveness or more revenge?"

Neither of us moved.

I said, "I'm sorry."

"Sorry? What you did was punk. Do you know how many women would've fucked you up for this shit you pulled? You're a coward. There is no room in my life for a coward."

She stopped like someone had suddenly taken the batteries out.

She hand-combed her hair, smiled a little, spoke softly. "I don't know you. I have no idea who you are."

She didn't move.

"I can't handle this now. This is too much," she said as she nodded with her other thoughts. "I'll send Gerri or somebody to get my stuff for me."

I stood in the doorway, watching.

She took her stun gun out of her purse. At first I

thought she was about to come at me, but she held the urban assault weapon at her side as she passed me by, bouncing it against her leg at a quick rate, the tempo of her thoughts.

She stopped at the front door. I stepped toward her, said her name.

She motioned to keep away, that same motion telling me to not say her name, made that rugged gesture with the tense hand gripping the stun gun.

She said, "I'm serious. No room for cowards in my life."

"So, this is over?"

"This never was."

Dana put on her dark shades, summoned her cool, world-conquering attitude, sashayed out my front door into the night. Crying, but not in a dramatic way. She gave up her salty river the way a person who had shed a lot of grief wept. Her footsteps echoed in the hallway, moved down the corridor at a pace that told me her head was held high, chest forward, was taking her time about going down the concrete stairs.

Being called a coward had driven a stake into my heart.

Bed squeaks and light moans came through my wall. Heard Naiomi moan like she was arriving at that special place, traveling in the express lane.

I stood in the window, stared down at the empty parking space.

Dana was gone.

After a lie has been spoken, there is never a good time to tell the truth. Never. I should've started with the honesty and taken my chances. That way my dignity wouldn't have a watermelon-size exit wound.

7 Dana

Some half-drunk Asian man wearing Dockers yelled at Gerri, "Cinnamon Delight, work that thang! Be my wife tonight, baby!"

She laughed, jiggled her booty, and took his crumpled money.

My road dawg was topless, damn near bottomless. The way her skin blended with her G-string, under those lights that were hitting the square stage and the rectangular runway, she looked like a butt-naked slice of Nubian nudity. Dancing her ass off in black high heels. Every plastic chair around the pyramid-style stage was packed.

An hour had passed since my bubble was burst. One minute I was pissed off and driving aimlessly; the next I was in Hollywood. In a smoky room. Large televisions all over the joint. A VIP area. Pool tables. I was alone at a round table in the back. Inside a gentlemen's lounge on the Sunset Strip called Blondies. A very kick-back atmosphere with concrete floors and psychedelic neon lights advertising pretty much every brand of liquid crack ever made. Everywhere, movie posters of every blonde from Marilyn Monroe in *Some Like It Hot* to Kim Basinger in *LA Confidential*.

From the sidelines, a white man yelled at Gerri, "Cinnamon Deeeeee-light, I've been waiting for you all damn night!"

Gerri licked her lips, shook her ass, smiled, and let the man slide sweaty and wrinkled-up money in her paisley garter. Her act was hotter than Joan of Arc's last barbe-cue; the men were going crazy.

This was a world she controlled.

I bumped through the crowd, fanned clouds of smoke out of my face, and made my way to the ladies' room. Now I'd have to wash my braids so I didn't run around smelling all funky tomorrow.

Married. With a damn rug rat. Masquerading like he was SINC all this damn time. Asked me to marry him and he hadn't told me any of that shit. How fucked up could fucked up get?

By the time I finished cursing out the woman in the mirror for being so naive and came back out, The Com-mitments were singing "Mustang Sally" and an Asian waitress was on the main stage, grinning wider than a virgin UCLA cheerleader, swinging upside down from a golden trapeze bar like she was auditioning for Ringling Brothers. I shook my head. Yep, that was a talent she should stick on her résumé in big, bold letters.

Gerri came through the rainbow-colored beads on the floor level, a few feet left of the stage. A note was in her hand; the napkin I'd written my message on and had delivered to the back. She had thrown on a white button-down-collar shirt, but the shirt was unbut-toned.

Disbelief covered her face as she strutted my way, buttoning the two middle buttons on her shirt. She ig-nored men who smiled and grinned at her like she was Ishtar, came to me with a tight face and an anxious, em-barrassed stride.

Her over-the-top mascara hid her freckles. The kohl-black made her eyes look deep and mysterious. She pulled a few strands of the fake curly blonde hair that framed her brown face aside as she said, "Somebody die?"

"No."

"Well, this is one helluva surprise. How long you been here?"

Nervousness was in my voice. "Not long. Got a minute?"

She paused. "Well this is very, eh, weird."

"I know it's inappropriate."

"I hope you didn't come down here to try and make me quit."

I told her, "No sermons."

"I've got two minutes. What's so important?"

I vented. Boy, did I ever get out everything. I opened up and emotions poured out like water from a ruptured dam. Told her everything.

"Whoa, slow down, Dana. Slow down." Gerri let out a slow groan. "Keeping an ex-wife and a shorty on the down low. That's whacked, but you could've waited until morning to tell me that."

She sighed and glanced toward the owner.

I said, "I'm sorry. I know you need to go."

"Well, O ye queen of stressed out, tonight you're lucky. A lot of girls showed up and there's a lot of time in between rotations."

She smiled at me like I was her best friend. I smiled too.

"Dana," her voice rang out with sensitivity. "If you want the truth, the lie was wrong, but Vince having a kid ain't that bad. At least he ain't HIV, on drugs, or fresh out of prison."

"Shit, ain't no telling what he ain't told me."

"Well, the only perfect people are dead people. They're the only one who can't make mistakes."

"I never said Vince was perfect."

She asked, "Cut to the chase. You love 'im, right?"

First I nodded, then I shrugged. Her eyes told me she had to go, people were watching us, but she wasn't rushing, not right now.

A couple of girls were on the stage, both working different sides of the room. They switched sides a few times. Part of me had always wanted to see what she did down here. That curious, naughty girl side of me. The truth be told, those girls onstage, the ones men were feeding money, I could outdance both of them, had a better body too.

I changed the subject. "How much can you make doing that?"

"I pulled close to two hundred dollars on my last set."

"Wow. You made that much cabbage in a few minutes?"

"That's way above the norm. I'm talking way. I still have to tip the D.J., but even with that, tonight's a good night."

"I don't see how you do this."

"Two kids, a mortgage, a car note, an unemployed ex-husband, and I'm behind on my desk fees. That's only the beginning."

I watched the show and twisted my lips with my other thoughts.

I asked, "How does it feel when you're up there?"

She laughed a little. "What, you wanna get your fantasy on?"

"Right now I'm numb, so I'm pretty much open to anything."

"You could try it one night."

"Is it as powerful as it looks?"

"More. It can be a rush."

"Wonder how long it would take me to get enough cash to get rid of the few bills and the desk fees I have."

"Not long. I'm here maybe twice a week. Some girls are here almost every night and make ends meet better than I do with my nine-to-five."

My eyes went to the Asian girl onstage, controlling every man in the room. Not one was laying a finger on her. Getting paid to get eye-fucked.

I folded my arms, sucked in one side of my jaw. That angel side of me slapped the shit out of the devil side of me.

Gerri saw my expression, then sounded defensive. "It helps take care of me and my family. Since Melvin only has to pay fifty funky dollars a month, Jefferson is the best thing going."

"Well, couldn't you do like normal women and pussy-whip a sugar daddy?"

That got a nice laugh out of her.

She said, "Baby, I don't want nobody older than me. An old man can't do nothing for me."

"You really care about Jefferson, huh?"

"Caring don't pay the bill." She nodded ever so slightly. "But it's nice to be with somebody who cares about me for a change."

"Uh-oh. Falling in love?"

"Love don't pay my rent. Never has, never will. Jefferson is gonna kick down half the mortgage, pay the utility, which will help a lot. If all goes the right way, I can give this up in about three weeks, maybe a month, say eleven Hail Mary's and move on with my life."

"You gonna miss this paper route?"

"Like I miss a yeast infection." She chuckled, short and weary.

I asked, "How do you get into it like, you know, like that?"

"Easy. I pretend that every man in this room is Jefferson."

My lips were tight, lines in my forehead.

She asked, "What's up with that look on your face?"

My words came out fast, on the wings of my emotions. "I was wondering how much fucking child support Vince was paying, if he is really paying or just giving up another lie to keep himself from looking bad. Thinking that Cali is a community-property state. If we were married, the court would look at the household income. Imagining how fucked up this could've been if I didn't find out about it until after the wedding. His ex-wife's hands could've been deep in my handbag, and I would've been spending my money to finance somebody's else's rug rat."

Gerri's expression rigidified, her eyes left my face.

I said, "What?"

Attitude was in her eyes. She said, "I'm gone."

"How long you working tonight?"

"Not long."

"You be careful, Gerri."

She took a step, stopped, then faced me: "Dana, do me a favor, okay?"

Her shrewd glare chilled me. "Yeah?"

"Next time you need to talk, don't come down here."

"Guess I was delirious and let my emotions take over."

Gerri was gone before I finished my sentence, headed to a back corner and doing an erotic table dance for a white man in a business suit.

Disgusting, hypnotic, and powerful. Very powerful.

God, I hoped that I wouldn't end up like that, having two babies, divorced, stripping for repulsive men in a smoky Hollywood bar.

A good-looking Italian man glanced at me and raised his drink like he was offering to buy me a round of liquid illusion. I moved a loose braid from my eyes and shook my head at that Robert De Niro. Headed for the door with my hand on my purse. Hurried by homeless people who were using the pavement as their pillows.

My secondhand Q45 was in a side lot, right next to Gerri's Camry. I sped out into traffic and drove through the wickedness on Sunset Boulevard, left this area that had miles of foreign stores, all the names in cryptic alphabets I didn't recognize, down past Larry Flynt's sky-high smut factory on La Cienega, rushed toward my corner of the world.

Thirty minutes later, I was back in Culver City, cruising through the guard gate at Lakeside. A maze of three-story buildings. Ducks waddling in the lake. Nicest place I've ever lived. Quietest. Buildings were spread out, nobody living on top of each other like my life was back in Harlem.

Momma would be proud. Very proud.

I cruised into the underground parking, a concrete

coffin that reeked of dust and mold. Tonight I hated
L.A. I really did. Wished I had stopped in Memphis, or
Dallas, maybe even Phoenix and tried to start over.

Never should've left New York. My home was in my
blood. Missed my old buddies. Missed partying on
Wednesdays at Twirl. Or at Magnum. Fridays at Shine.
Being on the list and squeezing behind the velvet rope
at Cheetah on Mondays. Friends and fun down on West
Fourteenth Street at Nell's.

Claudio popped into my mind. My throat tightened.
So many old feelings that I couldn't escape. That had to
be the way my momma felt for my daddy all those years,
the love that wore down her gentle heart.

Vince's imprint was deep inside me. He was in me,
moving back and forth, his voice more romantic than a
Brian McKnight song. Pissing me off because I had let
him get this close to me.

On the first floor, I stopped the elevator and grabbed
my mail. Junk from Anna's Linens, Good Guys, coupons
from Ralph's and Lucky's. I had a letter from my landlord. And a very thick, heavy letter from the IRS.

Yes, like Momma told me, bad news did come in
threes.

I crashed on the peach sofa, slid my *Heart and Soul*
and *Black Enterprise* magazines to the side. The letter
from my shyster landlord was on legal paper, thanking
me for being a wonderful tenant and reminding me to
pack up and move on in thirty days, less if I could.

The thick letter from the IRS watched me. It was
smirking.

Fingertips sweating, I ripped the edges of the letter,
peeped inside like it might be a letter bomb. It was
worse than a bomb. It was a damn extortion notice.

The bastards said that now that I was out of bankruptcy, even though I'd listed them as a creditor two
years ago, my debt was too new and bankruptcy
couldn't dissolve that debt. Long story short, with the
penalties and interest that I wasn't interested in, my

debt had damn near doubled. Now I owed Uncle Sambo more than three thousand dollars. And they politely threatened to put a levy on my wages, salary, and other income. If they froze my checking account, I'd be up shit creek.

With my desk fees, I was over five thousand dollars in the red.

An explosion went off inside my head.

The Pentagon was paying two hundred dollars for two-dollar hammers, NASA paid six hundred for toilet seats, and Uncle Sambo was acting like a Billy Bad Ass and coming after me.

A picture of Vince was on the end table.

I turned that image facedown, made him dead to me, sat fidgeting, glowering at that IRS letter, rocking, scraping the Black Opal enamel off my short nails, giving up a this-ain't-funny laugh.

Then I picked up Vince's picture. Grunted and threw it at the wall so hard it exploded. I shrieked, covered my eyes, hid my face as hundreds of fragments bounced across the carpet. My heart was pounding inside my ears while I crunched over the glass, yanked his smiling face out of the mangled frame, tore it into pieces, made it another one of life's puzzles.

I turned the stove on high, dropped the pieces of the photo onto the burner, let them burst into flames and die by fire.

8 Vince

In his rugged voice, Harmonica told me, "You done the right thing."

"Sure don't feel that way."

"Everything will come to pass."

Harmonica was on my sofa. He grunted the way old men do when they get up off a sofa a foot too low. After he was on his feet, he straightened out his dark, baggy slacks, did the same to the white shirt he wore underneath his red sweater, then made his way down my narrow hallway and stopped in front of the pictures of my momma and daddy. He always did that when he came by my place. Went to look at his friends.

Harmonica rocked for a moment, then his voice softened up. "Lord knows I miss y'all. Miss all the cussin'. Miss the fun. All of us'll be together again. Lord willin' and the creek don't rise, we'll be together. Y'all kiss Edna for me. Kiss her a hundred times a day till I get there."

Edna was Womack's mother. There was always one who set the standard. Always a woman that a man would never be able to live without.

I nodded. "Rosa Lee coming?"

Womack shook his head.

He was in my bay window, looking down at the courtyard. Something was troubling him. His arms were folded and he wasn't moving. Womack usually ran his mouth more than an ADD kid on caffeine.

I asked Harmonica, "The walk won't be too hard on you?"

"Son," Harmonica said, waving me off, "I started working in the country when I was eight years old. If you could walk, you could work. When you stopped workin', you was on your deathbed."

They had come by my apartment, not because of my state of affairs with Dana, but because of the state of affairs of our world.

Harmonica had to go to the bathroom before we made that two-block walk into the heart of culture. He called back, "I'm gonna need more toilet paper than what you got on the roll."

"Under the cabinet."

I went to the bay window and stood next to my best friend.

I said, "Tracy Chapman or Whoopie Goldberg?"

He tightened his face like he was having a root canal with no anesthesia. "Black Man Negro, you done lost your mind."

I patted his shoulder. "Now that I have your attention, what's up?"

Womack told me the abridged version. While he vented, there was a knock on my door. Soft taps, like they came from a feminine hand.

It was Juanita. She had on a green and gold Kente outfit, her hair underneath a matching head wrap.

She asked, "Are you attending the rally?"

"We're coming down."

"If we don't stand for something, we'll fall for anything."

On that note, she headed down the stairs.

I went back to the window and stood next to Womack.

Juanita was going door to door, spreading the word. A second later, I heard footsteps going down the stairs. Naiomi came out of the building in jeans and a cutoff Bob Marley T-shirt, her golden braids tied below her neck. Silver rings were in her nose, belly button, and left eyebrow.

She and Juanita headed toward the mouth of the park.

I asked Womack, "You think Rosa Lee's messing around?"

"The signs are there."

"What signs?"

"She's bought a few new things."

"Well, like?"

"New sexy underwear."

"So?"

"New perfume. Changed her hairdo."

"That don't mean nothing."

"Twice this week she packed for the gym, and when she got back, she left her gym bag on the service porch."

I said, "Okay, and . . . ?"

"She sweats buckets, so I was gonna throw her gym clothes in the washer before they started to sour and stink up the place."

In his eyes a storm was coming on. I said, "Uh-huh."

"She didn't have any wet clothes."

"You sure?"

"Nothing was damp. Not a corner of a towel, not a damn thing." He sighed, then picked at his cuticles. His fingernails were dirty, hands callused from a life of work. "Her stuff was still neatly folded. I sniffed the crotch."

"Whatever turns you on."

"Shut up, fool. Her draws were still Downy fresh. I ran my hand through her hair. The roots were as dry as Arizona in July. Kissed her neck before she ran and showered. No salt."

I digested his words. Years back, I'd run to him with a similar conversation. I put it out there: "So what do you think?"

"Like Poppa said, I'd be the last to know."

First I shook my head, telling him, telling myself, that Rosa Lee wasn't that type of woman. Then I said, "Maybe she was in the sauna."

"Dry towels, remember?" He took a deep breath, let it out slowly. "It wouldn't've been so bad, but she came in acting like she was tired from doing aerobics. She took a shower, fed the baby, the whole nine."

Womack went back to the window, stared down on the street.

We left my apartment, walked shoulder to shoulder up Edgehill. Harmonica liked going up that street because all of the trees have purple leaves. We were heading for a protest. Lately it seemed like there was one pretty much every weekend. One week it was Tyisha Miller being gunned down by Riverside P.D., then a few days later, a homeless sister, Margaret Mitchell, was killed by LAPD. It used to be black men; now it was open season on sisters as well.

A couple of hundred people were in the area.

I saw Dana in the thick of the crowd, a few people over from Naiomi and Juanita, up front facing the stage listening to the speaker. She had on jeans and a rainbow-colored tam, standing next to her buddy, Gerri. Dana was nodding her head, clapping her hands whenever a key point was hit, very involved in every word.

A thousand righteous words and two lengthy applauses went by.

Harmonica said, "Thangs don't never change. Different faces, but thangs never change. It was Medgar Evers back in my day. I've seent so many Medgars in my time."

My eyes went to Womack. Still quiet. Listening to the speech while his mind was brewing in thoughts of anxiety.

When the speech was done, Dana saw me. There was an awkward moment, but I went over. Gerri was holding hands with her young trophy man. Jefferson had on Kani jeans, matching sweatshirt, accessorized down to the boots.

He offered a cool and quick handshake. "Long time no see."

He handed me a flier advertising his group. Dangerous Lyrics was performing at a club in Westwood, opening for a rap group. Considering why we were down here, all due to a tragedy, I thought his timing was tacky, opportunistic.

But I was trying to be opportunistic too.

I said, "I'll try and check it out."

Dana moved away from them. I stepped with her, stopped in front of the Chinese laundry near Vision Theater. Coldness covered her face when we were away from the crowd, away from her friends. In her eyes I saw the electrical discharge of danger and anger.

Her breath chilled me when she said, "I'll get my stuff next Friday."

She walked away before I could answer.

9 Dana

When I walked away, I didn't look back.

Gerri asked, "You okay?"

My lips went up into a smile. "I'm fine."

Jefferson was holding Gerri's hand, had her close. They were so touchy-feely, which, considering my state of mind, was inconsiderate.

I went down on Melrose Boulevard and ate at Georgia's restaurant with Gerri and her beau. All evening they talked about the rap group. No space for one-on-one girl talk with Gerri. All Jefferson's talk was about the group and the studio, stuff that was way over my head: digital recording studios, mackies, mixers, DBX compressors.

In the backseat of Jefferson's Ford Expedition, I was forced to listen to his group's song "Kick the Bytch in the Azz" at least six times straight. Not exactly my cup of tea, but Gerri was ecstatic. Talking about what type of video the group should do, who should do the lead on what songs.

Gerri said, "Butter is pretty good with the lyrics, can dance a bit, but Big Leggs should be the lead on this cut. Butter should fill in the rap part. Chocolate Star should lead the other song you're working on."

"Butter wrote most of the songs."

"There's a difference between a songwriter and a singer. Everybody has to recognize their limitations. You have to go with the winner. Butter ain't the one. If you're going to be in charge of the group, then be in charge of the group. Ain't that right, Dana?"

"Sho' you right."

Seeing her making those kinds of starry-eyed plans with her man, having the kind of hopes that led to a windfall, reminded me of who I used to be way back when. I've left that hustle behind.

I'd hoped this was a regular hang-out, eat thing, but Gerri put the issue out there: "Dana, I told Jefferson how you used to do stuff in entertainment, the promotions gig, and we were wondering if you would be interested in doing some promo stuff with the group."

I told them no. That was the kind of life that put pressure on relationships and very little money in your pocket. Gerri pressed the issue. Again, I told her no. I'd get a job selling Slurpees at 7-Eleven before I tossed my hat back in that arena.

Gerri was disappointed, but I stuck to my guns.

Jefferson had to meet with the girls in the group at the studio. New material, new song, yada, whatever. Gerri's kids were at her ex's in-law's house, so she was tipping off to her late-night paper route.

I drove home. All alone with nobody but me. Felt so heartbroken, disappointed in myself because I didn't see the signs of Vince's other life. But I don't think there were any. Guess I'd been a classic woman, you know, looking for signs of other women. The typical stuff. Phone numbers. Late night calls. Missing hours that he couldn't explain. There was none of that bullshit. Hunting for things in his present, not worried about his past.

Eleven years ago. Time flies, but the feelings remain.

I was about to turn sweet sixteen. Our phone rang and Daddy was on the other end. Damn near shocked us into Stroke City. I guess after being MIA for eight years, that good old guilty feeling got heavy enough to make him pick up the phone and call the family he had left behind.

He said he had to come up to New York in a week or so, was going to take care of some business in Brooklyn, then head to Long Island and visit some old friends by the Green Acres Mall.

He wanted to know if I wanted to visit him for my birthday, go to Disney World, and then fly back up to JFK together. He thought that it was time I finally met my half-brothers and half-sisters.

I didn't think much of the promise—my own defense mechanism—but when the airplane tickets showed up in our mailbox, I started smiling, telling all my friends I was going to see my daddy, and packing all of my good stuff: best drawers, jeans I bought across the street from the Apollo, my gazelle shades I got from a hustler on Times Square, hair done all up in finger waves. I don't know if I was more excited about going to see him or just thrilled to be going anywhere. Plus, I'd never been on a plane. So the whole trip my insides were rumbling with fear at being so high in the sky, and my skin was jumping with electricity, anticipating seeing Daddy.

It was strange stepping off the plane and standing face-to-face with a tall, brown, slim man I recognized but didn't know. I looked just like him, especially around the eyes. Just seeing my daddy looking older with gray hair in his beard, around his hairline, made me forget everything wrong, made me feel like a kid with a big bag of candy.

That rich voice of his came to me with a smile. "Hey, Dana."

"I don't know what I'm supposed to call you."

"Well, whatever makes you comfortable: Chuck, Charles, or Daddy."

"Nice to see you again, Daddy."

I didn't know if I was supposed to hug him or shake his hand, didn't know how to touch him, but he gave me hugs to go with his smiles, told me how much I looked like a woman and resembled his momma. My grin was so wide it hurt my face.

He carried my bag, opened my door for me, sat me in that clean Cadillac of his, then cruised me out into the sunshine. On the way to his Cococabana, the warm breeze was pleasure on my skin. We drove through Fort Lauderdale, passed by buildings that didn't block the skyline, a bazillion *Miami Vice*-looking palm trees, headed into Pembroke Pines, a section called Town Gate.

Older people were cutting grass, getting tans. Everybody had their own yard. Kids didn't have to scrape up their knees playing on asphalt.

As he pulled up, I stared at a breathtaking stucco house and its Spanish tile roofs, a bodacious crib on the edge of a lake, hidden inside a spanking brand-new community. I took a deep breath and asked him, "This is your house?"

"Yep."

"Wow. Where do you work?"

"Me and a friend own a couple of auto-repair shops. One in Fort Lauderdale, another one not too far from the house."

"You must be making a grip."

He gave up an unsure smile. I guess he thought a sister was about to start asking him for money. I wasn't. Not my style to beg. I sold cakes, pies, did whatever I could, so I had my own money. Besides, Momma had already told me not to stick my hands in his pockets. I was just wondering what it would take for me to get a life like the one he had.

That's what I wanted. That's part of what I want.

While he kept on being a gentleman and grabbed my suitcase from the trunk, I stared at his house with my mouth wide open. I was in a dream, imagining him asking me to live with him. Spending time making up for lost time. I really did.

His wife came down the stairs like she was Norma Desmond in *Sunset Boulevard*, smiling like she was ready for Mr. DeMille to shoot her close up. She was around the same age as my momma, early forties. A pretty woman with a Texan accent. The skank gave my jeans the once-over, did the same with my mix-matched luggage, gawked like I was a Cambodian refugee.

"So, you must be Dana."

"Nice to meet you, Ann."

The heifer wagged her finger at me. "Never call me Ann. I'm old enough to be your mother. You may call me Mrs. Smith."

"And you may get your finger out of my face."

She chuckled, folded her hands in front of herself.

I stayed eye to eye. That was over before it started.

His other kids came down the stairs like they were a negrofied Brady Bunch. They checked me out like I was Thelma on *Good Times*. They had quite a spread. A living room damn near larger than our apartment. Five bedrooms. Three-car garage. Three and a half bathrooms. Two family rooms. Getting carpooled to karate lessons, piano lessons, gymnastic classes, all kinds of toys.

But most of all, they had Daddy.

I looked at all he had done for them, at all he'd done for his wife, then thought about what he hadn't done for me, what he'd never do for my momma. When a man met a woman worthy of being his queen, he showered her with gifts. And he'd showered a hurricane of blessings on his family. That let me know not to ever depend on him. On any man. That was a hard lesson, probably the best lesson my daddy ever taught me.

So the world my daddy was living in was—that existence that had weird pictures by Salvador Dali all over the place, unnatural pictures of melting clocks . . . I dunno—was strange to me. Why would anybody spend all that money on a picture of a melting clock?

I didn't get upset with my dad then.

That didn't come until after we hopped on a red-eye flight and headed to Harlem. He was going to kick it with his friends in Brooklyn.

Momma met us at the door of our fifth-floor walk-up. I kissed her and went in. Our apartment seemed so small, compared to his southern plantation. His neighbors had been so quiet. All day every day, right outside my window were all kinds of noises: buses, people yelling, sirens.

I hate long good-byes, so I held back my feelings, gave him a hug, told him thanks for the birthday trip. Momma had this strange look in her eye, said that they had to talk for a minute. She had said a few things, told my daddy that she was working at Random House, but wasn't making a lot of money and was thinking about moving on. At that point I assumed their conversation was going to be about money.

I showered.

When I was done, Daddy's luggage was gone. The living room was dark. Momma was in bed, the glow from her nightstand light slipping underneath the door; that meant she was reading.

I yawned, tapped on her door as I passed by. "Nite, Momma."

"Nite, Dana."

I stared at that empty spot where Daddy had left his luggage. Didn't know when I'd see him again. Sadness went through my body in nonstop waves. But after I stole a little bit of Momma's wine out of the fridge, sleep took away the sadness and pulled me into a world with no dreams.

I woke up in the middle of the night when these ghostly noises, these moans and groans, crept into my room. Sounds that came from Momma's bedroom. Momma's catlike whines. She'd never let hard times with one man keep her from moving on to another. I thought that the man she'd been seeing had come over to spend the night.

My bladder was talking to me when I woke up, so I headed to the bathroom. When I passed her door, I heard her sing out my daddy's name.

I stood there shaking.

With the sunrise came the street noises outside my

window. The city was one loud-ass alarm clock. Momma was up early, sounded like she was tap-dancing and singing while she cooked breakfast—Momma *never* cooked breakfast. Heard her moving around, talking to my daddy. I stayed in my room. Wanted to stay sequestered until I was sure he was gone.

Momma called me to come eat breakfast. I didn't answer. Then she said my name in her no-nonsense, I-know-you-heard-me tone, the one that made me hop up, grab jeans and a T-shirt, and get moving.

I went out into the living room, our front room that was smaller than my old man's southern-fried foyer. Me and Momma looked at each other.

My lips were turned down, hers pursed.

She was defensive: "Now, you know if he had left here in the middle of the night, fools down there would have mugged your daddy before he got out the building."

"We have a sofa," I retorted. "How could you?"

Softly she said, "He's your father. Don't act up."

Daddy came out of the bathroom, freshly showered, looking embarrassed, all duded up in blue linen pants and a beige cotton shirt, ready to eat and run to take care of his business in Brooklyn. I sat in the middle chair.

With a difficult smile he said, "Morning, Dana."

"Daddy, what you did was wrong."

That jarred him, stunned Momma.

"Momma, how could you? He's married. You know you're gonna be upset when he walks out that door and goes back to his wife—"

Daddy said, "Respect your mother."

I tilted my head sideways like that RCA Victor dog, dropped my fork, and snapped, "Respect? I know you're not trying to come into my life and act like you have some real authority. Momma has done everything."

That wasn't exactly what I said, but that was whatever words jumped out of my mouth meant. My head was about to pop. I went off. I didn't throw my head to the sky and break into a Klingon death howl, just stayed firm and vented about how he had been living, all the stuff he'd done for his kids.

Momma was telling me to stop it, but I kept on reading him the riot act, told him how fucked up it was that he never responded to my letters, how many of my birthdays he'd missed, went over every lie I remembered.

I said, "You're a coward. A liar. And since you spent the night in my momma's room, I guess I can call you a thief too."

Nope, my teenage words didn't come out exactly like that, not that crisp and articulate, but I do know that liar, thief, and coward were in there holding hands like the cousins they are.

Before he could wipe his watery eyes, I left the kitchen table, threw on my clothes, and left. Didn't come back up those five flights of concrete stairs until it was almost a new day.

By the time I made it back, Momma was in bed. A tattered Bible was on her nightstand next to an empty glass of water. I stood in her doorway for a while, knowing that she was pretending to be asleep. We had five old, noisy locks on our metal door, so there was no way anybody could sneak in any time of the day or night.

I softly asked, "How could you do something like that?"

Momma moved her feet like she did when she was irritated. Her eyes were open; I saw the corner of her left eye when she blinked. She didn't turn and face me. Her response was soft, damaged, and given to the wall, "How could you not want your momma to be with your daddy?"

"He ain't my daddy."

"How can you say that?"

"Because you've been my momma and my daddy. That's why I give you Mother's Day and Father's Day cards. And get a grip, you know he's married, he ain't your husband no more, never will be again."

She made a wounded noise. I was ready for her to snap and put me in my place, but all she did was bounce her feet and make a series of hurting sounds, creaks and groans that mirrored what I felt inside.

I knew when to fight with her. Knew when I'd gone too far. Knew when she needed me like I needed her.

I sat on the edge of her bed. "You never got over him, huh?"

"Guess not." She sighed again. "Guess not. When you've been in a relationship that meant anything, I don't think anybody ever really gets over it. Not even in your grave."

I didn't understand that she was telling me that Daddy hadn't gotten over her either. It never occurred to me that those type of feelings ran up and down a two-way street. I rubbed the hair on the back of her neck, told her, "Scoot over."

"Hot-comb my hair for me tomorrow."

"Why don't you just get a perm?"

"No chemicals will ever touch this head."

I lay next to Momma in the bed. She reached back and patted my leg.

Momma spoke tenderly, "What his wife look like now?"

I described her better-than-thou attitude. Ragged on my half-bros and -sister. Let Momma know that PBS bunch was weak and spoiled. Described their castle, his car, everything down to the beige paint on the walls.

Then we didn't talk for a while.

I know it was wrong the way I had snapped on my daddy, had dogged out his rug rats. So much jealousy was in my eyes. I wanted my daddy to myself. Maybe that's why I want any man in my life to myself. Anything less is, well, less.

I asked, "He leave a number?"

"Yeah. You gonna call him and apologize?"

I was surprised she asked me that instead of demanding.

Softly, I answered her, "Okay. He leave any money?"

"A little."

"Little won't do a lot. Why didn't you ask him for more?"

"I ain't never begged a man for nothing. Never will."

"Shouldn't have to. Why don't he send money?"

"Never expect a man to do something his own daddy didn't do."

I didn't agree with that, not at all, but I keep my opinion inside.

A few tick ticks later she mumbled, "Can't blame a man for being human when human is all he'll ever be."

That was the end of that.

When all was said and done, I put my arms around the woman who birthed me and held her like she'd been holding me since the day I was born. She was a strong woman who had suffered a weak moment. Even the strongest woman falls from time to time. And Momma bounced back up every time.

Maybe if I'd put my head to her chest, maybe I would've noticed her heart was slowing down, that so much hard labor and complicated loving had taken its toll. Hypertension and what the doctor said was mitral valve prolapse, something that Momma thought were just her nerves acting up.

I asked, "Want me to read to you?"

"Not tonight. Tired."

"You're working those long hours, no wonder."

"You don't get to be an editor by resting while other people are working. Especially a black woman. Five times as hard for a black woman."

I put my arms around my favorite Harlem girl. Lay there in a room that was two inches bigger than a phone booth, my eyes to the ceiling most of the night. I'd been so mad at her for losing her mind when Daddy showed up, but the way I had packed up my best clothes and hopped on that plane the moment I heard his voice, I guess I hadn't gotten over him either. I loved him so much. He just didn't know.

When I closed my light brown eyes, instead of darkness I saw melting clocks. Remembered the name of that eerie picture: *Persistence of Memory*. My daddy's life, that trip would always be persistent in my mind.

So, that memory was part of what scared me. Vince could lose his mind when his ex came back. Whether it's ten days or ten years later, they always come back. If he had kicked her to the curb because it was over in his heart, it would be different. That would mean his heart had gone cold for her. Maybe, just maybe and not guaranteed, I'd feel different about the situation. But she had broken his heart. And she had his child.

10 Vince

Under an overcast sky, I was running from the devil on the route known as the Inglewood Ten, ten miles of concrete hills. Once I ran Presidio back to Stocker again, it would be almost over. Downhill all the way, less than a mile. Opened up my stride until I stopped at Degnan, breathing hard.

My Indiglo stopwatch read 1:11.56. Two minutes longer than my best. Legs ached; I was walking on raw muscle. Knees yelled for me to lighten up and stop punishing myself. My body was soggy from the top of my head down through my Thorlo socks.

The moment I made it to my building, a golden hardtop Jeep pulled up and parallel-parked right in front of me. A classic 1980-something CJ7 with wide tires. Naiomi was sporting cherry USC shorts over black spandex, and a dark, damp SHEILA'S AEROBICS midriff top. Her navel ring sparkled, so did the ring in her right eyebrow.

She put her Club on, hopped out, slung her orange gym bag over her shoulders. Lean arms. Small hips. Fist-hard Jamaican booty that was hard to ignore. Her braids were rust-colored, I think her hair had been dyed again. At least ten bracelets jingled a perky tune as she walked my way.

"Hey, Mr. Browne."

I wrung sweat out of my tank top, said, "What's up, Miss Naiomi?"

Under a tree, one with green leaves and pink things

blooming on the tips, was where I had stopped. Three of those trees were in front, framing the walkway to the building.

She smiled. "Nice legs. Never noticed all that before."

"Better watch that kinda talk."

Her smile changed into a mild laugh. "Especially since we're standing out here half-naked."

Her cherry USC shorts were damp, some on the back-side, mostly in the crotch area, probably from her work-out. Dried sweat was on her face, made her right jaw look ashen, but wasn't enough to damage her cuteness. Naiomi went natural most of the time. Hardly wore makeup.

"Neighbors have been talking since Miss Smith left here fuming."

"I bet they have."

"Ten-to-one odds that you're an old maid again."

"You putting in your application or just being nosy?"

She motioned toward her apartment. "I've got enough drama."

"Ain't you two getting married?"

"Don't know. We wanted to, but—" She stopped and hunched her shoulders with her thoughts. "Ever feel like you're just not good enough for somebody? She can be too extreme. It would be easier pleasing God."

"You two seem like the perfect match."

She sighed. "Heck, I don't know, might be me. I've got too much gypsy in my blood. This is the longest I've stayed in one spot for years. Heck, my first marriage didn't last this long."

Naiomi dropped her gym bag so she could tie her braids back.

I asked her, "How's your little boy doing?"

"Otis is fine. Maybe you'll get to meet him one day."

Naiomi pointed east. Dana was pulling up, parking a few cars back, closer to the other end of the block at Edgehill. She chuckled. "Who taught her how to parallel-park?"

My wall was going up. I didn't say anything.

Naiomi talked until Dana got out. They made brief eye contact, waved. Naiomi told me a halfhearted good-bye, adjusted her gym bag, jogged up the three steps in front of our building, her silver bracelets jangling.

I glanced upstairs. Juanita was in her bay window. I didn't know how long she'd been there. Didn't know if her windows were open. No one had air conditioners in this part of town, but it wasn't hot, so there was a chance. I waved. She did the same, then vanished from her window.

Dana had on khaki shorts and a red and yellow Winnie-the-Pooh sweatshirt. Dark baseball cap on her head. Wearing dark shades on a cloudy day. Like she was trying to change the season. She motioned at the darkening sky with a nod, made a face like she was pondering something.

"Can I get my belongings before it starts to storm?"

I wiped my salty face with a corner of my Speedo tank top and headed toward the stairs. She followed, stayed five or six steps away.

All of the panties, bras, her precious books, and other stuff had been neatly placed in a long white box, right along with her liquid soap, cotton balls, tampons, and candles.

I told her, "If you wait a minute, I'll carry it to your car for you."

She went to the tower of CDs that were next to my twenty-four-inch television. The Nas, DMX, Mase, TuPac, all of those kinda CDs were either hers or ones I didn't really care about. Bobby Blue Bland, Etta James, B.B. King, John Lee Hooker, those were mine. Chanté Moore, Regina Belle, Ginuwine, the newer R&B CDs that we'd bought since we've been together, we agreed that we'd have to decide who would get what.

"If it's okay with you," she said, "I'll make three stacks. Yours, mine, and a gray area. I'll do the same with the videotapes we bought."

This was a déjà vu. Same exact thing, damn near the same words that I'd shared with Malaika about a week after that night. Only then Kwanzaa was in the room, crying, restless, like she was picking up on the bad vibes that were in the room at the time.

It was the same, but it was different. There were no shared bills to be discussed, no visitation, no talk of courts and rights, no being mad because she'd been fucking around, no watching her pack up her life and hurry out of my place only to drive to another man's home.

It was too much to bear, so I headed for the shower. Cleaned myself, caught my breath, tried to center my soul before we started doing the petty things people did at the end of a romantic journey.

A tap on the door.

"Yeah," I said.

The door opened. She opened the shower curtain.

We stood there for a moment, staring at each other. She rubbed her hands up and down her arms, lower lip trembled, skin reddened. Tears rose to the surface. She showed me all of the damage I had done. That made me uneasy, rub the back of my neck, struggle to breathe.

She said, "I can't handle this."

Dana stepped in the shower, came in with all her clothes on.

She kissed me. Did it like she was trying to see if anything was left between us. I gave her all I felt. We kissed awhile, warm water soaking her clothes.

Her words had the intensity of a Maya Angelou poem when she said, "It's been so damn rough without you. Haven't been able to sleep."

"Same here."

"This is too abrupt."

More kisses.

"If I stay in your life," she told me, "I'm gonna make you suffer."

Right there she undressed. We left her soaked khaki

shorts and Winnie-the-Pooh sweatshirt, her drenched panties and bra on the bathroom floor, made it as far as the hallway before passion weakened our knees and dragged our wet bodies to the carpet. I spread her wings wide, wanted to make her fly, licked her deep, licked her shallow, made her melt like chocolate on a hot sidewalk. Did that while she scooted her wet bottom across the carpet, tried to escape my fervor and earned rug burns on her backside. The wall slowed her retreat, but I didn't stop my feasting on her natural juices. She held the top of my head, fingers raking through my short hair, cried out a song so soft and sweet, a melody that told me how much she cared about me.

After I put on a condom, Dana pinned me down on the carpet and loved me with so much intensity it scared me. In the middle of all that goodness, while my toes were curling, my mind exploding, for a quick second my thoughts drifted. Memories had been stirred up. While I made love like I was trying to cast a spell that would make her mine forever, I thought about Malaika. Thought I was about to say her name when my love gushed out and my little soldiers charged into the thin barrier between me and Dana's womb.

Years of repressed frustration seeped out, made me ride Dana like I wanted to brand her for the scars somebody else had left behind. And the more maniacal I became, the more her face winced in torture, and her moans and pleas for me not to stop became high and hysterical.

When we were finished, silence. Silence and the fear of the unknown.

Pain woke up my knees. I touched two spots of raw flesh. Rug burns.

I had wanted to escape inside her as far as I could. Yes, escape. I needed to escape all that was wrong, from everything I was afraid of, from what I couldn't run from, and find myself in a warm place, the womb of a woman.

Sniffles. Rugged breathing. Dana was still crying, but it was the end. She put her head on my chest, wiped her eyes, chuckled.

"You tried to kill me with your penis."

"Sorry."

"That's okay. Part of me wanted to die."

I downed about a gallon of water, put on my jean shorts, white socks, and sandals. Made myself look like a black Spartacus. Dana put on my sweatpants and T-shirt, some Nikes she'd left over, put all of her panties and candles and CDs back, then made us a huge cup of French Vanilla Kaffee.

We sat on my back porch, overlooking the rows of garbage cans in the T-shaped alleyway, sipping exotic Java, breathing fresh air, eating fruit. Dana massaged my legs, rubbed my back, put me in a divine trance.

She asked me about Malaika. Drilled me. Wanted to know where we got married. Vegas. Where we honeymooned. Maui. How long we honeymooned. A week. If I had wedding pictures. Malaika had snatched 'em all. And if I did have them, with the stiffness in Dana's voice, I didn't think it would be a good idea to share those kinds of memories.

She stated firmly, "I need to see your divorce decree."

"For what?"

"I have to be sure."

"No problem."

Her words were easy, but there was a look in her eyes that was new to me. Something crafty, sly, maybe cruel. Could've been all of those things, could've been none, just my own derangement come to life.

Then she wanted to know how tall Malaika was, how much education she had. Five foot five; a business degree from U.C. at Riverside that she never used. She had been working part-time at Mervyn's jewelry counter when I met her, and after we married, she made it my job to make all of the money.

Dana said, "I feel threatened."

"Ain't no need to be."

Dana sipped her coffee. "No need at the moment."

We were outside, glancing toward our future, but the past was rat-tat-tapping us on our shoulders.

My phone rang. I stepped in and grabbed the phone on the kitchen wall, clicked it on. Nobody was there.

Dana asked, "Who was that?"

I sat back down on the steps, told her it was a hang-up.

She went inside, picked up the phone on the wall in the kitchen. She said, "You really should get a cordless phone."

"I will, if that one breaks," I called out. "Checking your messages?"

"Doing a *69."

That was the first time she'd done that to me. There was a difference in her. In us. A hardness that comes when trust has thinned. Both of us had flipped, become the other side of a dented coin. Some sort of a smile was on her face, but traces of her history were in her eyes.

Things had changed. No way to go back and be who we were before.

She said, "A recording said the call came from outside this area."

Sounded like her skepticism wanted a stronger justification.

Dana held my hand. Gray skies darkened. Air was getting cooler.

She said, "Six times. I've moved fifteen times in my life. Six times in the last three years. Always packing and unpacking. Afraid to buy anything because I know I won't be anywhere too long. I want to get somewhere and be stable."

She told me that her landlord had sold the condo, and she'd been out all day trying to find another place to live.

"It's easier finding somebody else a house than it is for me to find my own apartment. The areas that fit my budget are dangerous."

"Move in with me."

"No can do. Don't think because we had sex that everything is settled. If we're going to move on, we have a lot of issues we have to talk about."

"Like?"

She sighed. "Since you're telling me things, there is something that I did that you should know. You'd find out sooner or later."

A steel hand clutched my heart, squeezed so tight. I waited to hear about her and another man, waited to hear her tale of infidelity.

In a counterfeit tone of reassurance I said, "I'm listening."

"Part of your income will be going into someone else's household. Money that would impact our quality of life. This wasn't exactly what I had planned. That's a whole new kinda life. I'm really into debt management, really want a quality life for myself, and that's not just talking about money. But a lot of it is. If I sound too extreme, it's because . . . well, okay, let me back up."

"Okay."

So much stress was in her body, its aroma rising from her pores. She confessed, "I'm having a hard time getting an apartment because everybody wants to do a credit check."

She said that like I was supposed to understand, maybe ask something. I waited a second. "And?"

She asked, "Want some gum?"

I answered, "Sure."

She opened a pack of Big Red, licked the stick top to bottom, then eased it into my mouth.

"I'm coming off a bankruptcy."

"What bankruptcy?"

In a nervous tone she told me about her jacked-up credit, how she had run up her cards into the five-digit arena doing her promotions thing, started borrowing from Visa to pay MasterCard, from Discover to pay American Express. In the end, she'd gotten almost as much in cash advances to start over, filed Chapter 7 right after that, spent quite a bit of her nest egg when she bought her car, paid cash because with her credit rating they wanted to charge her damn near credit card rate, took real estate classes, got her career started. Not all in that order, but that was the sum of what she confessed to me. Something that would definitely make a difference if we married, would be in our faces every time we went to make a major purchase for the next seven years.

I wanted to know, "How did you get your condo?"

"Gerri cosigned. I don't want to ask her to do that again. I want to get something on my own. People are a trip. Even when I offer them a few months' rent up front, and I show them I'm working and show them a stub, my business cards, they look at me like I'm trying to get over."

"Well, it's not a forgiving world."

"Not at all. Not at all. And these are black landlords."

"You know we don't trust each other."

"With all these black-owned signs up everywhere I look, I would think that they would have some empathy for a sister."

"Those signs are up so they won't get looted and burned when there's another riot. Ain't got nothing to do with solidarity."

Seven years with her monkey riding on my back. So, getting a loan for a house, or buying a new car with a decent interest rate, the weight of all that would be on me. I had hoped that with our combined income and credit, we'd be able to qualify for a larger house, in a nice, quiet area.

"When did you file?"

She told me again, let me know that it had been discharged.

She needed to see my divorce decree; I had to see her credit report. That and her bankruptcy-discharge papers.

Then she broke down and told me about her heavy bill from Uncle Sam.

And being delinquent on her desk fees.

There comes a point in every relationship when you realize that the person you're dealing with isn't as unblemished as you thought.

I still loved her. Like she said, love wasn't a switch that could be turned off. It was more like a battery, had to run until there was no more energy left.

I smiled, spoke in a soft and supportive way, "You have less than three weeks before you have to move. Might as well come over here."

She hemmed and hawed. "Living together and not being married ain't right. We start shacking, you'll be getting the milk for free and we'll never get married. And I don't want to spend five years cohopulating."

"Co-which-a-what?"

"Cohopulating. Cohabitating plus copulating equals cohopulating."

"Nice equation."

"Learned that in algebra." She chuckled, then went back to serious mode. "If we shack, and I'm not saying that I will move in here, we should get away from this apartment living and lease a house instead."

"You just said your credit needs a few stitches."

She fidgeted. "It would have to be leased in your name."

"What's wrong with kicking it here until we get our money right?"

"Well, parking on Stocker sucks. Would be nice to have a driveway. A backyard. Sixteen people live in this building with one washer and dryer. If we had a house, we could split the write-off. If I can't get Uncle Sambo's hands out of my purse, I can stop him from digging so deep."

That was when I told her that my job was cutting back. Ten thousand people were getting the short end of the stick. Another restructure move. Right in my face, six hardworking men that had been with Boeing for the last ten years had been laid off in the last two days. Last in, first out. I was three people from getting shoved out the door, so I needed to lay low. That was part of the stress that I had been trying to run off.

She asked, "What are your plans?"

"I e-mailed an app to Dan L. Steel."

"I'm showing houses to a guy who works there. Give me a résumé and I'll give it to him for you."

I kissed the side of her face, her ears. She wiggled closer.

Teamwork. This was gonna take a lot of teamwork.

We didn't say anything for a while. I was remembering the pain from when Dana had called me a coward. I'd never forget that look in her eyes when she cut my dignity down to the bone. It was ironic. Not being a coward on a cold, stormy night was what had gotten me where I was today.

"Vince?"

I said, "Yeah."

"Since we're laying it all on the table, I want to make sure I say this, and I want to say it the right way. I don't have anything against you sending your kid money, but I don't think you should mail money if they won't let you see her. If she is your daughter, they could at least call you and let you talk to her."

Her honesty burned like fire. I guess that's the way truth is, the uncomfortable way the truth always feels.

She went on, "We have to set our goals. Let's get everything ready for the wedding first, save for that."

"What kinda wedding you want?"

"Nothing in Vegas, I know that much. I want something blessed, not damned. I want what I deserve."

"What we can afford or what you deserve?"

"What I deserve."

I didn't say anything.

She said, "After we're situated, if she hasn't called, put that C.S. money aside, open up a special account and let it draw some interest. I think we should do that until you get that straightened out with Malaika."

I patted her leg. Didn't agree or disagree. Vocabulary was on lock-down. Defensiveness came alive, made me question if she was going to try and control that aspect of my life. Until she said that, I hadn't realized how personal that part of my life was for me. I had wanted to keep one separate from the other.

She went on with what sounded like my conditions of surrender. "You are gonna eighty-six that bed of yours, right?"

"I just told you my job was cutting back, so with an ax swinging at my head, it would be stupid of me to go out and buy new furniture right now."

I hoped my words didn't come off too harsh, echo too much of my frustration.

"Then what I said about making a plan and putting that C.S. money in the bank till you hear from them should really make sense, right?"

Again, I patted her leg.

She rocked awhile, but didn't say anything.

Her issues had arisen. I wondered what else she hadn't told me.

From my back porch, part of the HOLLYWOOD sign was visible in the rolls of the mountains that stood behind the Griffith Park observatory. A few drops of rain came down. Cool water that soothed my warm skin.

Dana sat between my legs, leaned back, moved her braids in a sweeping motion, held her face back and let heaven's water dampen her skin. Raindrops raced from her face down into the crevices of her breasts. She arched her back, made her bosom stand out. She had on one of my plain white V-cut T-shirts. A very thin T-shirt. No bra. Her dark nipples were alive, pushing their way out of that cotton. I rubbed my fingers over her skin, around her nipples, watched them grow, felt how erect they were.

Dana licked my hand, took in two fingers as they

passed her lips, sucked them deep. Rain steamed off my skin like a bowl of hot soup. My free hand traced around her neck, to her breasts, did that over and over.

She stopped long enough to say, "That really makes you hard."

"You noticed."

"You're about to poke a hole in my back."

Police sirens screamed like Richard Pryor on fire. Big motors revved; LAPD was chasing some fools through the neighborhood. Bouncing over dips, screeching, and swerving. When the noise level dropped, voices came from the other upstairs apartment. Soft-hearted talking changed into the sound of two beautiful women laughing.

Dana purred out a sound that sent a chill up my spine.

She took my middle finger again, slowly licked it from fingertip to my palm, sucked it over and over. "This morning I got in the shower and pretended the hot water was your hands touching me everywhere. And I made love to myself, but it was with you at the same time."

She pulled my back firm against her crotch. Rubbed against me. Made small circles. She licked my ear and whispered, "Feel my fire?"

"I feel the heat."

"Wanna?"

"Again?"

She whispered, "Yeah."

My tone tendered, "I wanna if you wanna."

"With you I always wanna. That's part of the problem."

Both of us heard the clatter at the same time. Somebody dropped a piece of silverware. The jangle came from the back door of the apartment behind us.

"Juanita's eavesdropping." That was me whispering.

"Let her listen. She might learn something."

"Stop it. She might hear you."

Their back door creaked opened. Naiomi bumped her way out, a blue plastic laundry basket filled with white clothes on her narrow hips. She'd put on tight Levi's and a baggy gray sweatshirt, one from the post office that had Malcolm X's picture on the front. She hurried down their side of the stairway, moved like she wanted to get to the laundry room before anyone else did. When she made it to the bottom, she paused her stride, looked up, and smirked. She saw my hard-on, I know she did.

Naiomi turned the corner facing the alleyway and the row of garages. Another noise came from their apartment. Juanita was in the kitchen window, cordless phone in hand, dialing. She nodded, closed the blinds. Her voice was still there, talking very low in Spanish, her voice soft and rushed. *"Mami—ella se fu a la lavandería . . . puedo hablar por un minuto . . . cuando te puedo ver?"*

Her voice faded, like she was walking away.

Dana rubbed between my legs, whispered, "I wanna strip for you."

"Strip?"

"Yeah. Like they do at the strip clubs."

I hummed out a good feeling.

She kissed me. "I wanna tie you up, put on a Janet Jackson CD, and do my sexy table dance for you. Think you might like something like that?"

While candles burned, Dana danced slow and easy, ethereal, defying gravity. Took off one piece at a time, did that for a long while. Sat me in a kitchen chair and did all kinds of flexible things with her body, moved with the smoothness of a contortionist, tied my wrists with satin scarfs, did all kinds of erotic things to me, put her mouth in places that had never met pleasure. She was smiling, but she was serious. Got into it like I never thought she could.

Another side of her I'd never seen.

I called Malaika's mother ten times. The number, disconnected. I mailed another check and put a note in asking them to call. The check didn't come back. It didn't get cashed either. No phone call.

Dana moved in before two weeks had gone by. Put most of her boxes in my garage. Then she was gone, off selling property to people with decent credit and higher incomes. Opportunity was there so I glanced through some of her stuff, the boxes that hadn't been taped down. Wanted to get to know who she really was, find out things she hadn't told me. Found photos of her and her dad at Disney World, hugging and smiling. Cards from Claudio, but no pictures. Notes that spoke of long nights with her in his arms.

I looked through her stuff because she never talked about going back, never offered to give me a tour of her old life, never wanted me to meet her old friends. I'd driven her all over L.A., showed her everything from elementary school to my old colleges, the house I grew up in on Chanera.

She was still a mystery, a mystery with no real history.

I let that go. She was in L.A. I let go of whatever she left behind.

The arrangement worked pretty well. She cooked. When it was too hot to turn the oven on, I grilled on the back porch. She was pretty neat but not anal. She didn't clean up after me. If I left a shirt in the living room, she'd say "Your shirt's in the living room." She'd say that in a soft tone, like I was looking for the shirt and couldn't find it. I woke to the soft beeps of her alarm clock. Sometimes she played that old Desiree song first thing in the morning, "Gotta be tough, gotta be stronger . . ." Either that or that 1980-something flaming disco tune some woman sang about being a "native New Yorker." Sings and dances and struts and showers to those messages while she made herself wake up.

She bought a few things at Target, pretty much redecorated the whole place. Beige curtains replaced my darker ones. Plants were in every room. Her pictures depicting New York were put up with mine. Her mother's pictures went up with my parents' photos. The apartment had a new kind of flavor. A family flavor. Fresh, colorful towels in the bathroom. Perfumes and incense. That made the john the nicest room in the house. Her library of books were added to mine.

Ain't nothing like a woman's touch.

But I still had that same bed. We made love in the shower, living room, hallway, in the kitchen, marked our territory from corner to corner, but rapture was never comfortable when we were on that old bed.

Every day Dana asked me a hundred questions about Malaika, something that left me feeling uneasy, then kept asking about putting Kwanzaa's pictures on display. I stopped by Robinson's-May and picked up a four-section golden frame for my child's pictures, fell into a sentimental mood and spent over thirty dollars, then put that image on the same worn dresser I had Dana's picture on. I arranged all of them so they were the last thing I saw before I went to sleep, the first thing I saw when I woke up.

Days after that, I went to the Jewelry Mart in downtown L.A. Spent all day shopping for rings. Found a nice rock for two thousand. That was a big piece of my savings, but it was a good investment.

First I took Dana to the Ahmanson Theater to see *Rent*, a musical about struggling artists in New York's Greenwich Village.

As soon as the curtain came down, I whizzed Dana south to Orange County's Laguna Beach for a weekend getaway in a suite at the Hilton. I dropped down on one knee, told her I didn't want her cohopulating, asked her if she would be my wife, even though she wanted a man with a different résumé, with lighter baggage and less of a past.

She accepted.

11 Dana

Intense voices came through the wall from next door.

Warm water ran down my back. I said, "They're cat-fighting."

Vince and I were soaping each other down, acting like Adam and Eve, the smell of a slow burning incense and perfumes making this humid room our Garden of Eden. My back was against Vince's chest, his arms around me. Heaven has gotta be like this. We'd been taking a long, lazy shower, standing under the water and lollygagging about nothing.

The phone rang.

I said, "I'll get it."

"It's either Gerri or Womack."

We were supposed to hook up with Womack and Rosa Lee in a little bit, then a late-late social-thang dinner with Gerri and Jefferson. We were being social butterflies all day today.

Water dripping off my body, soap sliding from my breasts. When I stepped on the gray carpet in the hallway, I stroked my bare feet with smooth catlike motions and dried off the water I'd picked up from the bathroom floor. Vince peeped out, checked out the show I was putting on. I purred, made a sound that let him know that I always landed on my feet.

"Hurry, Dana."

I held my soapy breasts to keep them from bouncing and hurting, did a tiptoe-run by all of my black-and-white pictures from Harlem, squeaking like a teenage girl all the way to the bedroom. The phone hummed for the third time.

The sun was MIA for the night, so it was dark outside. A light was on in the bedroom, horizontal blinds slightly open. Just in case the freaks had come out at night, I grabbed the phone and sat on the floor.

I chuckled out a pleasant "Hello."

"Yes." The woman paused. "May I speak with Calvary?"

"I'm sorry. You have the wrong—"

"I meant Vincent Calvary Browne," she said, then caught herself. "Is this the correct phone number? This is the number that was on the check I received."

She had a sterile way of talking that I couldn't place. Add that to the mention of the word check, and my mind went into bill collector mode, especially since she'd said Vince's entire name like she was reading it from something.

She went on, "I'm sorry to disturb you. Your accent threw me."

"No problem. May I ask who's calling?"

"This is Malaika Quinones."

My heart dropped to the center of the earth.

In my mind I saw her. Saw her body wrapped all around Vince's body. Her cream complexion waiting to get stirred by his coffee. Heard his voice telling her how much he loved her. Heard her phony-ass moans.

In the background, wherever she was, I heard children playing. A television sounded like it was on a kiddie channel, could've been a video.

I said, "Sorry, you have the wrong number."

Softly and ever so sweetly, I hung up the damn phone.

Correct me if I'm wrong. We'd talked about him not sending any more checks until everything was straightened out. I guess my words went unheard. Either that or I wasn't as important as I thought.

My eyes went to the closet. I stared at the wooden

sliding door like I could see through it, like I could see the black tape on the top shelf.

Malaika naked, touching her own breasts, waiting for Vince.

In front of me were the pictures from Vince's old life, standing in front of mine like a solid family tree, my own photo in the shadow. My hand was led by my heart, eased my picture in front.

The argument next door rose in volume. Somebody got their emotional shout on, somebody countered in a sharp pitch, then the ruckus died down.

The phone rang again. I picked the receiver up before the first ring finished, then hung up in the face of whoever was calling. Waited a few seconds. Picked the receiver back up. Got a dial tone. Dialed 72#, followed by my pager number—forwarded all calls to my service.

With that, I headed back to the bathroom, leaned against the counter, droplets of water still dripping from my body to the peach marble.

That was wrong. What I just did was wrong.

When Vince got out, he asked, "Was that Womack or Gerri?"

I kept my lips tight and shook my head.

The phone hummed once. Seconds later, my pager vibrated.

Every day I've passed by his closet and hoped that black tape on the top shelf would poof, be gone. Hoped that he'd realize that he'd forgot about it, see it right there and toss it. Or burn it. That hadn't happened.

Her fire waiting for Vince's hardness to spread her wide open. It wasn't a fistful of love like the black Kennedy tape that everybody and their momma had a copy of, wasn't as weird as that Pamela Lee tape, Vince wasn't steering a boat with his penis or nothing like that, but seeing your man booty naked on top of another woman, whether she was his wife or not, well, it was more than enough for my eyes to bear.

Yep, I was angry. Should've went off on Vince.

But the end of that tape, what happened after that twenty minutes of groaning and moaning was done, that's what I remembered the most.

For now, my size-eight foot was on the neck of that monster.

Vince stood behind me, patted my backside, asked, "You okay?"

I smiled. Kissed him.

Vince put on his black jeans, an acetate/Lycra muscle shirt under his leather jacket. I put on dark stretch jeans, black top, soft leather jacket, braids pulled back and tied down.

Malaika's voice was swimming laps inside my brain, bugging the hell out of me because her voice seemed so familiar. Maybe from hearing it on the tape, but then again, she wasn't regular talking like she was on the phone.

Lips got lined and war paint colored in, things I can do even with a distracted mind, eyes done to make me look mischievous and mysterious. Southern Exposure. Smells too good to be true. I dabbed the brew on my pulse points, loved the aroma because it was light as a feather.

Once again Vince read through my mood and asked, "You okay?"

Again I smiled.

As we were unlocking our door, the landlord's door flew open.

Naiomi backed out, snapping, "I can't believe you did that."

Her woman's voice pursued her: "Address me with respect, please."

"You were talking to her in my face. What kind of respect—"

Naiomi closed her door on those words. Then she saw us standing there looking stupid and awkward, our eyes wide open. Her face jumped. We shifted. Naiomi spoke like she was humiliated, then shuffled down the stairs so fast her golden braids and tight skirt became an orange blur.

By the time we made it to the courtyard, Naiomi's golden Jeep was zooming west up Stocker, bouncing over the deep dips.

We walked at a decent pace up the pine-tree-lined Degnan. It was Sunday night, cruise night on Crenshaw, and LAPD were out in full force, motorcycles and squad cars all over the joint. The boulevard was crazy and neighborhood traffic was bumper to bumper, a nation of hip-hoppers riding with their tops down and music up, creating atmospheric chaos. A mirror of the turmoil that was a pool of acid inside me.

I said, "A full moon."

"Means it's gonna be a romantic night."

"Drama. It means drama."

Womack and Rosa Lee had already shown up and had saved us seats outside of 5th Street Dick's, right next to the rows of tables filled with dominoes and chess players. Barbecue smoke was in the air, no doubt drifting from Phillip's BBQ around the corner.

Womack's Jheri-Kurl was pulled back into a ponytail; he wore white Fila tennis shoes that made his feet look like boats, black jeans tight enough to show the outline of his family jewels, and a burnt-orange rayon shirt underneath his Levi's jacket. Something about him, his color, that wavy do on his head, was more Belize than plain old African American. He was outdated but in a cool kinda way. Sorta like Billy Dee Williams.

Rosa Lee's reddish brown skin glowed with her yellow blouse; her black skirt showed off her cute little figure and those robust calves. Full bottom lip, thin top lip, kind of a big forehead, keen eyes. Her funky 'fro made her look stunning. Her keys were in front of her, a red leather thingee that had mace on the ring. Gerri had a gun. I had a stun gun under the front seat of my car. Rosa Lee had mace. This drive-by society has turned women into urban warriors.

Rosa Lee stood and hugged Vince. Hugged me just as

long. Her first words were flattering, "You look nice. And your perfume, that smells so good."

"Vince bought it for me. It's Terry Ellis's line."

"Who?"

"One of the girls from En Vogue."

"It smells sophisticated. Sensual. Gonna have to get me some of that."

Womack hugged me too. Threw a few compliments my way.

Rosa Lee jumped right back in. "Now, let me see that ring. Wow."

I smiled, stared at that promise of forever.

A minute later we had 7-Up cakes and Kenyan coffee at our table, friendly words waltzing in the winds.

I said, "If you don't mind a sister being honest, Rosa Lee—"

She waved her hand. "Go right ahead."

"—but you don't look like you have four kids."

She made a funny face. "Let me guess. You thought my uterus would be hanging out like a slip that's three sizes too big?"

Rosa Lee was so chatty tonight. That day we'd met at church, homegirl was weird, as distant as the Milky Way. I didn't understand her new spunky disposition, made me think she was a bit schizo in the membrane. Then, in the middle of my next breath it dawned on me why she was so free. Because Vince's lies were out in the open. Because they knew I knew.

I told Rosa Lee, "We're meeting my buddy Gerri and her boyfriend for dinner in Hollywood. Why don't you come and hang out with us?"

She answered, "Rain check. Have to get the kids from Harmonica. Always have to get back before it's too late. We haven't been in a club in eons."

Womack's fingers were tapping along with the Coltrane-style jazz, but his big brown eyes were on a fresh batch of chatty sisters who were passing by Melissa's Bridal and Formal. Young sisters in high and ugly Herman Munster–style tennis shoes, sporting acres of cleavage and butts.

My attention went to Rosa Lee. Her radar was on; she'd noticed. A subtle frown came over her face, then a curt smile.

She said, "Womack? We're over here, honey."

Womack's focus came back, first to his wife, then to the rest of us.

My pager hummed.

Oh, Malaika, what the fuck is going on?

I tried to keep myself in the here and now, told Rosa Lee something I already knew to start a conversation. "You're a schoolteacher."

"Yep. Middle school."

"How you like it?"

"Let me tell you about last week." She leaned in like she was about to tell a fantastic story. "I have this student, she's black, twelve years old, almost six feet tall, and her breasts look better than mine ever will."

Everybody laughed.

"The girl never does any work, and I was going to write a referral and send her to the office, you know, not participating, whatever, because I'd had it up to my eyes with her attitude. But when I got to her desk, she had her makeup case—"

I said, "A makeup case?"

"Yes, she did. I looked inside the makeup case—"

Vince added, "Uh-huh."

"She had a pack of condoms."

Womack asked, "What brand?"

"That's not the point." Rosa Lee waved him away. "She was twelve, and she had condoms. An open pack, not a new pack, and a couple were missing. That sent a nippy feeling up my back."

With wide eyes I asked, "What you do?"

"I scowled down at the condoms. Shot daggers at her. She looked at me. I said, 'You have condoms at school.' She nodded at me like I was the town idiot, perked up, picked one up, extended it toward me, and had the nerve to say, 'You need one, Mrs. Womack? Take it. You might get lucky.' "

I wailed, "No shit?"

By then everybody at our table was howling.

"All of you, stop laughing," Rosa Lee said, but she was cracking up too. "That was somebody's daughter. A twelve-year-old child. Womack, stop laughing and spitting; cover your mouth before I get cooties."

Vince said, "You said the little freak had body."

"That's irrelevant. She was twelve. Her mind was less than that. Yes, with her big boobs and long hair, she could pass for high school, maybe even college. All I could do was look at her and see her in the backseat of somebody's ride, trying to be a woman before she could spell the word. Acting like she's grown, getting knocked up, then spending the rest of her life living down a bad decision just like—"

Rosa Lee stopped laughing. So did Womack. Exasperation was in his eyes. Uneasiness came off Vince, I smelled it. He eased back. Rosa Lee shifted, like she was catapulting her mind away from a bad memory.

Boy, oh, boy. The mood had definitely changed.

"No more talk about school or children," Rosa Lee announced, and ran her fingers through her wild hair.

Vince nudged her playfully. "No problem, schoolteacher. We can talk about the time LAPD beat down people at a poetry reading right here in Leimert Park, causing yet another mini-riot."

Rosa Lee smiled a bit. "Don't start with that. Don't upset me."

Vince joked on, "Or about our favorite African American congressmen selling out and taking away the free parking. White people getting business permits in black neighborhoods easier than black people."

Rosa Lee said, "That's because, even with all this, we have no power. We have no power because we have no community. We put on Stepin Fetchit smiles and pretend to support each other, but we don't."

Vince said, "Some of us do."

Rosa retorted, "Not enough. Like I said, no community."

I leaned forward. "What do you mean, no community?"

"Look around. Little by little our culture has been amputated. You have a Chinese laundry on this corner. Another Asian business across the street selling black hair products. Non-black people own and operate every gas station in the neighborhood. And over half of the so-called soul food restaurants in the area have Mexicans doing all the cooking. And to further my argument, Compton, Watts, Lynwood, all of that is mostly Hispanic. We're a vanishing minority."

Vince said, "Well, the truth be told, all of this used to be owned by white folks."

"Right, and we always settle for leftovers from other people's plates. Our problem, in my opinion, is that we've been so busy trying to get integrated and be like white people that we forgot to keep on being black people. No, we don't have a community. No structure. No goals.

"Chinese have Chinatown. There's a Little Hanoi. Little Havana. In a true community, the people of that community have rules and run that community. There are boundaries. They support each other. They have their own rules; they have discipline in their community.

"They take our money right back to Chinatown. Oh, I could go on and talk about how we don't recycle black dollars, how most people will run up to Starbucks before they keep places like Fifth Street Dick's in business."

So much passion. And that sister could ramble. Everybody had to lean back and catch a breath after that.

Womack broke the silence. "See what happens when you get her started? You have to take the batteries out."

We laughed.

I added, "You are definitely a schoolteacher."

"No more politics, not tonight. Let's keep it simple." Rosa Lee took a breath. "Dana, tell me about New York. The subways. Where did you hang out? What's it like to have that much snow on your doorstep?"

Rosa Lee was longing. She wanted to be somewhere else. Or maybe she read through my smile and saw my disturbed mood. She saw mine and I saw hers. Her cute little foot was on the windpipe of her own beast.

I smiled, blinked away all those troubled feelings, and said, "Okeydoke, Rosa Lee. I'll tell you all about New York."

With soft laughs and a sentimental sensation, I went down memory lane.

Rosa Lee beamed. "Ice skating at Rockefeller Center?"

"Yep," I said. "Momma took me every year."

Womack chipped in, "We go snow skiing up in Big Bear."

Rosa Lee said, "God, we haven't been to the mountains in years."

"Why not?" I asked. "It's a couple of hours from here."

"When you have kids, you stop doing a lot of things. So, you two should take your time before you do. This is a twenty-four-seven, three-hundred-sixty-five j-o-b. And no time off for good behavior."

Vince and I shared an uneasy glance. Kids were something we hadn't brought up. Maybe, considering his true status, I should say more kids. And now I wasn't too sure I wanted to throw my hat in that arena.

I brightened up. "We should plan to go snow skiing."

Rosa Lee said, "All of us used to go all of the time. We'd hang out with Winter Foxes, rent a cabin, stay all week."

All of us. They'd all been friends for years, so there was no telling how many women Vince had taken on weekend sojourns with them, how many fingernails had raked across through the sweat on his back while he released his energy inside them.

My pager vibrated again.

Rosa Lee laughed hard and that jarred me big-time because I thought she was laughing at me, thought she heard my pager humming, thought she knew about Malaika's call. But her laughter was shot at her Jheri-Kurl–wearing hubby.

I asked, "What's funny?"

She said, "Womack, Vince, you bad boys ever tell Dana about when you two were trying to be big shots and run scams?"

I lit up and gazed at the pay phone. "What did they do?"

Rosa Lee added, "Outside of putting rocks in TV boxes and trying to scam people, these two did all kinds of mess back in high school and college. Oh, let me tell you about this one. Womack and I had a cute little red Celica that we'd bought at the auto auction. Spent our last money getting the stupid thing. After about two months it turned out to be a lemon, and we were sinking money in it every week."

Vince and Womack groaned.

She waved them off and went on, "So Vince drove it out to Downey, parked it behind a Goodyear, stole the seats and radio, poured gas all over the inside and engine, and introduced it to a match."

"Oh, crap. I'm engaged to a con man. When did they do that?"

Rosa Lee was perky, said, "That was when he was with Malaika and he'd gotten laid off for a while. Malaika was pregnant then, right?"

Vince shifted like he was uncomfortable. So did I.

Womack's eyes wandered over another girl—brown-skinned, long dark hair, oval face. Midriff top showing off her stomach.

Rosa Lee said, "See what I have to put up with, Dana?"

Womack snapped back, "What I do this time?"

Rosa Lee sighed.

"What I do?" he asked Rosa Lee again.

"That girl is young enough to be your daughter. But I guess that's how men like them. After we get all fat and have your babies—"

"Who? That girl? Rosa Lee, you gotta be joking. That girl so ugly that she could get handicap parking at a freak show."

She shook her head. "Get a clue from Vince and learn how to hold my hand every now and then. Not just when you want to crawl on top of me."

Womack reached for her hand.

She pulled it away. "Too late now."

Wow. Too late sounded too strong.

Rosa Lee got up. "I'm going to the ladies' room."

Womack sighed. I grabbed my purse and followed her.

Once we were inside the shotgun-style coffee house, standing in the mouth of the crowd enjoying the jazz, I touched Rosa Lee's shoulder and spoke up over the loud music. "You all right?"

Rosa Lee gave me a trying smile. I'd had that kind of smile so many days that I knew exactly what it meant.

I told her, "I'll tell Vince to talk to him."

"No, I'm fine. I've been all right for ten years."

There was a moment between us. Empathy and understanding.

Point-blank, I asked, "Would you do it over?"

Rosa Lee laughed. "You are unquestionably from New York."

"Nope, just nosy like my momma used to be."

"Out here, we're not so forward. We sugarcoat everything."

I smiled.

"Hope I didn't spoil the evening for you."

"Puh-lease. You're a better woman than me. If that was my man doing that crap, I would've had my foot all up in his ass."

Rosa Lee cracked up. "What's your fee?"

"Buy me a cappuccino and I'll break out some Tae Bo on his butt."

"Cut that curl out of his hair while you're at it."

"I ain't touching that greasy mess."

Again, laughter.

Rosa Lee said, "I've known Vince for years. And I'm not saying this because I like him, but you've found yourself a good man. Enjoy each other before the babies come along."

"I was hoping we could before anything or anybody got in the way."

Rosa Lee missed my hint and kept on. "You two have romance, freedom to get up and go wherever, whenever. I envy that. I went from my mother's house to getting pregnant to getting married and living with Womack. Never had my own place. Never had my own space. Never really dated."

"Dating ain't all that."

She shrugged. "Well, from where I'm sitting, dating looks good. Most of the time I feel like the woman in *Bridges of Madison County*."

When somebody opens up, sometimes they want you to open up just as much. I've been closed off for so long, so unable to trust in people that I'm not sure I know how to open up like that.

"Would I do it over?" Rosa Lee asked. "The truth?"

She answered her question by shaking her head.

Rosa Lee walked away, but stopped at a counter long enough to browse some handbills advertising poetry readings in NoHo—North Hollywood. She grabbed several leaflets. A decent-looking brother wearing awesome dreads and a schoolboy grin tried to be slick and ease into her space. Had a can-I-get-your-number smile. She stood there, blushed, and absorbed his flattery. Womack's wife didn't stay long, just long enough for me to think that if she were here alone, she would've been sitting at his table before the Billie Holiday record finished playing "Strange Fruit."

She saw me, looked exposed, then said an abrupt adios and left the brother longing. He watched her as she bumped through the crowd, moved by the long line of jazz and caffeine junkies. She fluffed her wild and stylish hair as she sexy walked her way toward the bathroom.

Four children. And looking like that. If only I could be so lucky.

The pay phone by the front door was vacant. I headed that way, did like ET and phoned home, checked the messages. All the back-to-back calls had been from Gerri. Her voice was fast, choppy, panicked. She'd been calling because whatever had happened after she made it home this evening was "jacked up" and she had to talk to me before she killed somebody.

I called her house. When the answering machine came on, I put a finger over my other ear and raised my voice so she could hear me over the jazz. She didn't pick up. I called three times in a row. No answer each time.

My eyes went outside, to that moon.

Back at the table, we all started saying our good-byes. They had parked on Leimert Boulevard, between the blues club and the Korean inconvenience store that had bulletproof glass spread the length of the counter. Just like New York, all the stores, banks, fast-food joints around here were bulletproof. The aroma from Phillip's BBQ joint was so strong it had made my stomach turn cartwheels. If we were going to eat, it would have to be soon. L.A. closed down early, so a sister could starve to death after midnight. And that's no joke. They should call this place the City That Loves to Sleep.

With my arms around Vince, I winked at Rosa Lee.

Rosa Lee was holding Womack's hand. She winked back.

We hopped in their Explorer, and they drove us back up Degnan so we could hop in our car and go get our grub on.

I asked, "Anybody want some gum?"

Everybody did.

I whipped out my pack, took out two sticks. I handed the pack to Rosa Lee. I opened one stick, licked the stick top to bottom, then teased the cinnamon stick in and out of Vince's mouth before I put it all the way in.

He asked, "Why do you lick my gum?"

"To make it sweeter."

Everybody talking. Windows down. Air cool enough to chill me.

I looked up at the full moon.

12 Dana

"Wow. Amber walls, and check out this serious
grillwork, classy art, vaulted ceilings. Know what?
This reminds me of the French Quarter. Much
nicer than the Shark Bar on Amsterdam."

Vincent playfully bumped me. "Why do you always
say exactly where something is when you talk about
New York?"

"What do you mean?"

"Sylvia's in Harlem. Or whatever in Manhattan, or
this place in Brooklyn between this and that avenue, or
that place in SoHo."

"That's what we do."

We had valet-parked and stepped from the traffic on
La Cienega Boulevard into the bustle and hum of the
noisy, shoulder-to-shoulder crowd.

This was a hot spot.

Brothers looked good. Sisters were lounging near the
piano, a couple dressed in tight and slinky Chiquita Gon-
zales dresses. Even the fat sisters were skinny. Made me
feel like a whale. Showing off aerobic bodies, looking more
dangerous than the svelte curves on Mulholland Drive.

My stomach grumbled hard. Hungry as hell. Salmon,
seafood gumbo, sautéed crab cakes, barbecued ribs, vegetables, all of those flavors were mixing with the soft
music in the air. The skinny hostess said that we'd have
to hang out at least two hours to get a table for dinner.

I said up over the bustle, "I'm going to the ladies'
room."

"Go talk to your bladder and I'll wait by the piano."

"Don't serenade anybody while I'm gone."

"Not even if she was in *Waiting to Exhale*?"

"Don't start nothing."

I squeezed through all the mingling and macking going on at the bar. Actors, football players, basketball players, singers, all in Cary Grant poses, holding hard-to-pronounce-the-name drinks in their hands.

A heavy hand touched my right shoulder, practically shot out and grabbed me, rudely pulled me. And you know I was about to snap my arm free and read the brother the riot act, tell him that booty gawking was free, but please don't squeeze the Charmin. Then his oh-so familiar voice stole its way inside my ear. "Dee Dee, I know that ain't you up in here."

My eyes widened. A gasp slipped out with my startled breath. I turned and made eye contact with the bald-headed brother and almost fainted. Nut brown complexion, gray eyes, broad shoulders.

Before I could move, he'd hopped off his bar stool, pulled me to the side, and smothered my body with his. Held my breast to his chest like he'd found his dream woman. The caresses felt good, compromised the hate and anger I thought I'd feel if I ever saw him again.

In a rattled tone all I could do was say his name, "Claudio?"

His thick-lipped smile was so close I could taste his wine.

Claudio said, "Damn, you're looking good, Dee Dee."

My mind told my legs to move, but my foot had landed in the snare of a memory that would not let me go.

Claudio adjusted his green suit jacket, his high-fashion, multicolored tie, and said, "Didn't think I'd run into you."

"Surprised to see you too, Claudio."

"Chris Rock asked about you."

"Tell him and his wife I said hello."

"Saw him at the VH-1 Music Awards. Hard to get his ass now that he's blown up. No time for the little people who gave him his first work."

For a moment we were frozen, memories swimming in both of our eyes.

Yep, once upon a time I had left him hanging, waiting for my call.

His pretty eyes fell down on my ring hand, and that happy-to-see-me grin vanished. "Guess you wasn't joking. You got engaged to a West Coast nig."

I raised my ring, moved it side to side. "No joke."

"You didn't waste no time."

"Well, my eggs weren't getting any younger."

I'd never seen a big man look so hurt.

The crowd wormed by and bumped me into Claudio, pretty much made us into a sandwich. My soft breasts rubbed all over his hard arm. I backed away.

"You never did tell me how Tia was doing."

"C'mon. That was over before that night. I told you she was trying to get back with me, mad because I wouldn't return her calls."

"I should've kicked her ass again when I got out of jail."

Emotions rolled those words off my tongue.

Claudio sulked. "Look, what about Timothy, Charles, or what was that other dude I found out you were seeing?"

"Anybody I was seeing was when you were MIA. Nobody walked in on you in the middle of the night and went psycho. You didn't go to jail. I'll never forget how they sprayed me between my legs like I was an animal."

I stopped, killed that memory, raised a palm in a way that said I wasn't going to create a scene, that I was cool and back in control.

He said, "That's over and done with. Let go. Look, let's move on. I'm doing a show at the civic center in Carson next week. Edwonda White, Emil Johnson, D'Militant, a few other West Coast comics on the show."

"Good for you."

"I'm gonna be in L.A. awhile."

"What's awhile?"

"Few weeks. I'm kicking it at the Wyndham in Fox Hills."

He said the name of the hotel like he wanted me to get in contact with him in the wee hours of the night.

I responded, "That's a pretty expensive hotel. What's up with that?"

He licked his lips. "Let me buy you a drink. We'll talk."

I wiggled my engagement ring in his face.

Claudio said, "Where's your man?"

"He's that fine brother over by the piano."

Claudio saw Vince. Saw my thick-armed man dressed in all black. Claudio's bushy eyebrows knitted; he made an *unh* sound, amplified his voice, "Dee Dee, can he take you farther than the A train and higher than the top of the World Trade Center?"

My trite grin turned upside down. "Did you have to go there?"

We stared at each other, knowing what that meant.

Years ago we had made love on top of the World Trade. An exhibitionist sort of thing, brought on by a dare from Claudio. Back when he was my teacher in the department of freaky deaky. On the A train, late one night when we were coming home from an event we'd put on with WBLS down at Le Bar Bat on West Fifty-seventh, I'd dared him and he'd given me oral love on the subway.

Those old feelings of yesterdays and yesteryears stirred in my chest, tightened my throat, created a sudden swelling in my breasts.

My tongue spat out words that were nothing but business: "Let's cut to the chase. Do you intend to pay me back for all of those charge cards?"

"Whoa, now a lot of those charges were yours too."

"Most were because of you."

"I told you to be patient, but you were the one who jumped up, ran out here, and filed bankruptcy. Nobody told you to do that."

"Well, you weren't the one getting stressed every time the phone rang. I had to disguise my voice when I answered my own damn phone, then lie and tell people I had moved. Creditors didn't garnish your wages, call your job all day, or ring your phone at the crack of dawn."

"Let's hook up and talk about this, one on one, not in a crowded joint like this where we have to yell back and forth." He slid a stylish Mont Blanc pen and paper toward me. Always smooth, so damn hypnotic and convincing. But now, I have to admit, success was written all over him. I'm not surprised. He could sell a fish a glass of water. In a gentle voice he went on, "Give me your digits. We'll talk."

I shook my head. "I'm living with my fiancé."

He looked like he'd been slapped with a skillet, but he recovered. A lot of urgency in his tone as he told me, "No problem. Drop me a number where I can reach you. My money is tied up—"

"Don't bullshit me. Untie enough to reimburse me."

"You need it that bad?"

"Well, yeah. My money is kinda funny."

"Your man not taking care of you?"

"That's not the point. I'm planning a *wedding*. That costs a grip."

Another pause while he stared at me. Pain was his middle name. Finally he said, "I'll kick you down something after Carson."

"You joking?"

"I don't joke about money. I'll need a way to contact you."

"Leave the cash with Western Union, then leave me a message. I can pick that up anywhere in the world."

"Dee Dee, c'mon. All I want to do is talk to you, nothing more."

I'd been here too long. I hurried and gave him my business card.

He grinned. "Real estate? You went out and got a real job?"

I nodded and felt good. "A career. I have a career."

He said, "I'll send you two tickets to the show. Cool?"

"Keep your tickets. Send my money."

With that I turned around, headed through the crowd toward Vince. Felt Claudio's eyes and thoughts crawling all over me.

Small fucking world. Getting smaller every friggin' day.

Vince said, "I thought you had fallen in the toilet."

"Long line at the ladies' room. You know how it is."

"Want to get a drink at the bar?"

I held his arm and stopped him from moving that way. "Vince, it's too crowded. Let's go to the Cheesecake Factory."

"You all right?"

"Yeah."

"You're shaking."

"I'm cold."

"You're sweating."

"I must've sipped too much Kenyan coffee at Dick's."

Vince stalled, eyes searching to see what had upset me. Wanting to protect me from all the evils that lurked behind my back.

I glanced toward Claudio. Wish I hadn't done that and just left the building.

He was bumping his way through the crowd, eyes on Vince, coming toward me. He stopped right outside of our personal space, stood there like a black gangster from a Donald Goines novel. And if he was a black gangster, I definitely felt like a black girl lost.

Claudio's lips crept up into a shrewd and determined smile. He winked at me, then walked right by us.

Vince asked me, "Who was that?"

I shrugged and made sure I didn't look behind me.

Again I tugged Vince's arm. "Just some fool trying to flirt. Let's go. I'm hungry."

We waited out on the curb, a few feet away from Claudio. Vince gazed at Claudio a time or two. His hand tensed each time, squeezed my hand. I was discombobulated. These light brown eyes stayed on the ground, smiling and counting cracks, pretending I was so interested in everybody's shoes. My hand was inside Vince's, so he knew my palm was sweating.

A dark Lincoln Town Car with tinted windows pulled up, the driver hopped out. Claudio stepped off the curb. The driver opened the back door, and Claudio crawled into the backseat of a Dav-el limousine. Fine as wine, that I couldn't deny. Doing well, from what I could tell, just like Renee had said.

No regrets, I told myself. No regrets whatsoever.

He rode away the way Prince Charming does at the end of the fairy tale.

13 Dana

The next sunset, my troubled mind was at Gerri's condo. Her crib is in Carlton Square, a secluded tract next to the Great Western Forum in Inglewood, where the L.A. Fakers used to pretend they were a basketball team. Her place was laid. Quiet. An African American borough of about four hundred homes that was damn near under the incoming flight path for the planes floating into LAX; the hum and roar of a plane echoing every thirty seconds or so. Her private life hidden behind castle-high iron gates, pine and evergreen trees, acres of manicured grass. The kind of place that when the L.A. riots broke out, armed guards kept the greedy misguided bastards from jumping the walls and stealing peeps out of house and home.

Jefferson's voice rang out: "That's the truth."

Gerri retorted, "Don't touch me."

My road dawg was in the bedroom with Jefferson. Sounded like they needed a couple of guards; they'd been going at it nonstop. Accusations and denials rang louder than a church bell.

I fidgeted from corner to corner, sat down on the light green leather Italian sofa for a moment, moved to the love seat, adjusted my black suit and stared at the vaulted ceilings for a while, played with my braids, then went and looked at her reproductions of Van Der Zee photos.

I was a wreck. Nobody could tell—well, outside of watching me chew the pink and purple nail polish on my baby finger, nobody could tell.

Jefferson's voice boomed, "You're wrong."

And of course, Gerri's did the same. "We'll see, but I'd advise you to start packing your Hush Puppies in the meantime."

"I don't wear Hush Puppies."

"Then pack up your ugly ass overpriced FUBU shoes."

Gerri had a framed poster that was time-worn around the edges. Big-lipped, bubble-eyed caricatures of charcoal-colored Africans depicted over an announcement that read:

July 24, 1769—TO BE SOLD On Thursday the third Day of August next—A CARGO of NINETY-FOUR prime healthy NEGROES consisting of Thirty-Nine Men, Fifteen Boys, Twenty-four Women, and Sixteen Girls—Just Arrived—In the Brigantine *Dembia,* Francis Bare, Mafter, from Sierra Leon, by Claudio & John Deas.

All around the room were Gerri's daughter's gymnastic trophies, her son's basketball trophies, pictures of Gerri and her kids in suits and dresses. The perfect Christian family.

Last night, the weirdest thing happened. I stared in Vince's face and went blank, forgot his name. Now, that was some scary shit. I prayed. Asked for understanding, needed to know what was going on inside me. At daybreak, that ball of confusion was still rolling around inside my belly.

I went to Gerri's kitchen table, picked up the newspaper. Read, word for word, a full-page article that the Langston Law Center had in the *Sentinel* about child support, a page that Gerri had highlighted. Her day planner was open. Two dates were circled in red. One said TRAFFIC FUCKING SCHOOL AGAIN. The other MELVIN/COURT 8 A.M.

Her bills were in her day planner too. Gas. Electric.

Cable. Air Touch Cellular. Car note. MasterCard. The one that stood out was in a white envelope with a thick red trimming. Red trimming always meant bad news. It was from AIS/MERCURY, I think that was her car insurance.

The kitchen phone rang. My butt jumped away from dipping all in Geraldine Yvette Green's financial business.

Gerri rushed out of the bedroom, legs moving like she was riding a bike. My road dawg was dressed in a beige skirt suit with the double-breasted jacket open, low brown heels, matching camisole, reddish brown hair pulled back and slicked into a conservative bun.

I asked, "You okay?"

"I'm sorry you had to witness this, Dana, but—"

"You need to calm down. You're getting a bit too loud."

"Sorry. This is just so unbelievable." She pressed her palm on her forehead like she was holding a bale of thoughts inside, took a deep, cleansing breath before she answered the phone in a calm, corporate voice: "Gerri Greene, how may I help you? Uh-huh. Give her directions."

All six foot five of Jefferson hurried into the living room, stumbled over a magazine rack, his roan complexion looking flushed. He had on a colorful FUBU sweatshirt, matching jeans, and Timberland hiking boots.

"Who that on the phone?"

"It's Mister None-a-ya-damn-biddness."

"You can't speak to a sister?" I interrupted, did that so that maybe, with me in their presence, both of them would take the insanity down a notch or two. "What's up, Jefferson? How's the rap group you managing?"

He responded, "We, uh, they're having problems."

Gerri snapped, "Probably because you were screwing two or three of those non-singing video-ho bitches. I've been struggling so I can help him save enough to do a good demo, and his dick runs amok and fucks it up."

I asked Gerri, "Where are your kids?"

We made eye contact. Gerri's posture changed, became motherly. "I sent them to View Park. I don't want them to see me like this."

Jefferson said, "You running my business all into the cordless. That's an open frequency, and you know how we keep picking up other people's conversations. Ain't no telling who can hear you."

"You want me to chill? I don't think so."

"Aw, Gerri, calm down. Don't believe the lies."

"If she lied, how did she get pregnant?"

"How would I know? If she is, it ain't mine."

"You're supposed to be producing records, not producing babies."

Gerri marched away; Jefferson rubbed his neck, mumbled, and followed. Even with those big feet and long legs, his pace was half of hers.

I moved the stray braids from my face, pulled my hair behind each ear, went back to the balcony, and watched a world of lesser chaos.

Giving Claudio my biz card was a bad move. He's sent flowers to my job—roses, tulips, carnations—three days in a row. Every delivery came with I'LL ALWAYS LOVE YOU messages. Can't count the messages he's left on my service. Or count the e-mail. WE COULD STILL MAKE A GREAT TEAM.

And he'd FedExed me two tickets to the comedy show tonight.

Tickets that were wiggling in my purse right now.

Gerri's voice calmed down a bit. So did Jefferson's.

Gerri, Gerri, Gerri. Girl, what kinda mess have you gone and gotten yourself into? Her life looks so together. Very nice condo. Kids in private school. Doing it without getting her C.S. Hardworking, determined woman. I wondered how much spare change she was pulling down at Blondies.

I jumped when the doorbell ding-donged three quick times.

Jefferson rushed out of the back room, bumped into a wall, and almost stumbled over nothing. Gerri was right on his heels, closer than his cute little mustache. He looked through the peephole and exhaled, "Shit."

"Open the door," Gerri declared firmly. "Since she insisted on paging me every other minute, I called her and told her to bring her lies on over here so we could straighten this out. That was the guard down at the gate on Manchester who just called and told me she was here."

Jefferson gave up a distraught breath and opened the door.

A thick, mustard-colored girl was outside. I remembered her from the night I'd seen them perform at the Townhouse. Butter Pecan. She had on tan capri pants, three-inch black sandals, a sleeveless cotton blouse that showed off her boulders. The only thing that was tacky was the fluorescent pager clipped to her front pocket, and I wasn't too fond of hooped nose rings. I don't think people should draw attention to the place where stalactites originate.

Jefferson sighed, "Butter? How you know where my woman live?"

Butter's swollen eyes were almost the color of ketchup. Her tone feather soft when she spoke, "You tell me, Jefferson."

Gerri maneuvered around Jefferson's huge body, opened the black screen door, and let Butter in. The girl's posture and movements didn't have any real femininity. She had that manufactured hardness that was attractive to certain type of peeps.

Butter said, "I write the songs. Everything was fine before you hooked up with Gerri. Now you want to control everything—"

Gerri snapped, "I'm not trying to control. You need to learn to lis—"

"Butter," Jefferson said, "don't do this. After all I've done for the group, don't playa hate because I switched lead singers on a few cuts. Okay, you know this here my woman, and I don't know why you tripping."

"I write all the songs, put the group together, and now you trying to make me sit in the back of the bus."

Butter had a deranged scowl that didn't quite go with her pretty face. I had a feeling that something wasn't right about this girl. Her eyes told me that.

Jefferson stood as close to Gerri as he could.

I asked, "How old are you, Butter?"

She hesitated. "Nineteen."

Startled, I asked, "Then, you're in school?"

"Uh-huh," she said. Her tone was a lot nicer when she talked to me, maybe because my tone was a lot nicer when I talked to her. She added, "I go to LACC."

"Well, good for you," Gerri said with undisguised sarcasm. Then she cut to the chase and moved the meeting forward. "You sticking to the same story and telling me Jefferson screwed you on a regular basis?"

"Yeah." Butter paused. "We got busy a lot."

"Whoa, whoa, hold up here," Jefferson was shouting. "Why you up in my crib sweatin' me? Stop lying, Butter."

Gerri asked Butter, "Without a condom?"

"He didn't like the way they felt. Said one of them, I think the one with the suicide stuff—"

I corrected her, "Spermicide. I think you mean spermicide."

"Yeah, that stuff. He said it made his thing itch or something."

Jefferson laughed and threw his hands up. "She's lying."

"We can settle this real quick." Gerri opened a Ralph's grocery sack on the kitchen table. "EPT time, sweetheart. If you're pregnant, you won't mind taking this pop quiz."

My heart was a rock. Butter's shaky hands took the box from Gerri. Jefferson's mouth opened, eyes bugged out like the slaves on the two-hundred-year-old poster.

Butter fumbled with the box, turned it side to side. Her forehead wrinkled in a way that let me know she was confused about the directions.

I asked, "You ever had to do one of those before?"

She shook her head. "Have you?"

"Too many times," I mumbled. I went over and gently put my arm on her shoulder. "You pull the strip out, pee on it."

Butter looked at me and asked, "Then what?"

"You pray you don't get two dots."

"What does two dots mean?"

Gerri jumped in with venom: "That means you're knocked up and somebody's about to be homeless. One dot means you're not pregnant and somebody's lying. Either way, somebody's lying to me in my house. You'd just better hope it ain't you, Jefferson."

With his face hung low, Jefferson massaged his neck, looked flushed. He hopped up and grumbled, "Enough of this madness. I'm going down—"

"If you walk out that door, *don't look back*."

He sat back down, rubbed his face. He looked so young. Gerri, so old. Butter was aging in front of my face, frozen by indecision.

I found some tissue in my handbag right next to my never-used stun gun, then blew my nose. Cleared my sinuses and wondered how this day would change the rest of Butter's days. How it would change Gerri's.

Butter's chest heaved. She shifted to and fro, made me think that she was going to make a mad dash for the front door.

"You see, she lying." Jefferson chuckled like the girl was insane. "Butter, fess up. Nobody gonna be mad because you jealous and told a lie."

Butter said, "My major is criminal justice. I want to be an entertainment lawyer—well, I used to want to be—so that's why I know what Jefferson and Gerri, that contract ain't right. You trying to pull the same shit they pulled on TLC. That's why they went bankrupt, because they wasn't handling their business. I ain't stupid. Just because I'm trying to be a rapper doesn't mean I'm stupid. I don't like the way you let Gerri talk down to me, Jefferson. You've mistreated me ever since you met her."

She sounded smarter, had dropped that hip-hop persona she had whenever she was with her friends. A tear rolled down the girl's face, but was wiped away before it got beyond her pudgy nose. Butter looked at Gerri in a way that made me think she'd changed her mind about the pop quiz.

Gerri told the kid, "Want me to show you the way to the bathroom?"

"I already know where the bathroom's at." Butter looked down on Jefferson, cringing like she was smelling the depths of his anus, but kept talking to Gerri. "Down the hall on the left. That one's small and the shower backs up if you turn the water up too high. The bathroom in the bedroom is bigger and always much cleaner. And you got some boss perfume on your dresser by your glass jewelry box. And your peach and green comforter is all that. Your sheets don't really match because you gotta different shade of green in 'em, but it's all good."

Gerri's face contorted a thousand different ways.

Jefferson gulped, dropped his oily face into his hands.

Butter wiped her eyes, lowered her voice. "Yep, I know where to go."

Gerri moaned, wiped her damp eyes.

When Butter returned from the bathroom, she moved with labored steps down the carpeted hallway, like she was on death row. She shot a watery-eyed scowl at Jefferson.

Butter mumbled, "Two dots."

14 Vince

I took my partner with the Rick James–looking hair-style up to the 24-Hour Fitness inside the Hilton on Century Boulevard, the one all the brothas and sistas flocked to. We ran into our old crew, Stomach Man and John Marshall, hit the free weights, worked chest, some back, threw in some abs. Then we did Evelyn Orange's advanced-step class. Showered. By eight o'clock we were at the pool hall on Crenshaw and Jefferson, not too far from the unused train tracks and the overused probation department.

"Why you shooting so hard?" I asked as I fanned a cloud of the clove odor from my face. "What are you trying to do, make the balls explode?"

"Play your game how you wanna play," Womack said. He took a draw on his Djarum. "I'll play mine my way."

"What was the point of us going to the gym if you're gonna fire up a cancer stick as soon as you get out of the sauna?"

"This is my first smoke in two days, so lighten up."

"You've got four kids and a wife."

"That'll drive any man to smoke."

Womack had been snappy all evening. In the locker room at the gym he'd been talking about Rosa Lee, his marriage, the kids. He felt he was doing all he was supposed to do, but Rosa Lee was always complaining, had been in the habit of making snide remarks. And since meeting Dana, Rosa Lee wanted to go to New York and visit Times Square—without him or the kids.

When we were in the step class, he was in a world of his own. Good music and a funky class brought out the rhythm in a brother. He was footloose, fancy free. Womack has always been a good dancer, could do all of that pop lock'n, break dancin', moonwalkin' crap, so he put an ethnic twist to the moves like the hurricane, snake, double dutch, merry-go-round, and got his clown on in class. Had everybody watching him, was the center of attention, like he used to be when we were in high school, hanging out in the same halls that Lisa Leslie and Byron Scott walked every day.

But that aerobics class was over and the music had ended.

I asked, "You all right?"

He nodded. Sighed.

The CD machine near the double white doors was thumping out the tune "Harry Hippie." Those melodies masked the sounds of arguments, laughter, and pool balls colliding at the nine or ten tables around the room. A den filled with restless, energetic people who exchanged gambling monies in the guise of a handshake.

I asked, "Sure you all right?"

Womack sank the eight ball and said, "Rack 'em up."

A couple of African sisters walked up, laughing and smiling, talking in their native language, and put their pool balls down at the table next to us.

Womack said, loud enough for the light-brown-skinned women to hear, "Two Somalian women are really pretty."

They didn't speak back.

Womack responded with a big smile and a lot of humor, "Damn, y'all can't speak to your African American brothers?"

First they made incredulous faces at each other, then said something in their native tongue. Their brows rose and their light brown faces didn't have pleasant expressions. They shot us scowls like we were peasants who had spoken to the queen.

Me and Womack looked at each other.

He said, "I think we've been dissed."

I shrugged and muttered, "Inter-fuckin'-nationally."

"They act like somebody trying to get in their draws. It's called being cordial." Womack spoke again, a little clearer, a little louder. Asked them, "How are you lovely ladies doing this evening?"

Both of the women were early twenties, that age when a sister didn't have too much mental luggage. At least that's what a brother would assume, because a man never knows what a woman has been through. One had on a dark, fall-flavored miniskirt, the other a spring-time sarong. Long, wavy-haired daughters of Africa living in two different seasons.

As for Womack's last question, no response from the motherland.

Womack blew out his Djarum's smoke. "You Somalians treat all yo' African American brothers like that?"

"Arrgh." The shorter one frowned and gave us stiff words. "We are not Somalians. How dare you. We are Ethiopian. Learn the difference before you speak with ignorance."

Womack shifted his lean to his other leg, shrugged, chuckled out, "Lighten up. We all from Africa, one way or another."

"Arrgh!" Once again the shorter one frowned like she was having a root canal with no anesthesia. "What part of Africa are you from?"

Womack leaned back on one of his legs, tilted his head sideways. "What you mean, 'What part of Africa'?"

"You *black* Americans are always talking about Africa, waving our flag and screaming about the struggle and the cause, and know absolutely nothing about the land. Your *black* American women dress head to toe in my country's Kente cloth and can't find my home on a map without a tutor."

Sounded like it was the wrong time of the month for

that nation. I knew when to hold 'em, knew when to fold 'em.

But Womack said, "Woman, I know all about Africa."

The tall one in the sarong walked and stood in Womack's face. A straight-up dare. She said, "Okay, Mister African American, name ten nations in Africa. South Africa not included."

That nose-to-nose challenge was enough to make me and a few more brothers put their lives on pause and turn around. Womack hemmed and hawed, but nothing came out. The girls chuckled. He'd opened himself up for this, but I had some empathy for the man. For my friend. What he was doing was harmless. Every now and then a brother just tried to flirt to see if he still had it.

I spoke up. "Womack, ignore 'em. It's your shot."

The women said something rugged in her native tongue, walked away shaking their heads, their hair and backsides bouncing in an aggravated rhythm.

"We in America," Womack shouted at their table, "I don't need to know no geography about no damn Africa no way, right, Vince?"

I nodded.

"That's why I can't stand them Africans. Hell, we were slaves for four hundred years, and how many of them left their cozy little colonies and tried to help a brother or a sister catch a rowboat back home?"

"None that I know of."

"Well, that makes two of us."

"Tell it like it 'tis, Brother Womack."

"Name ten countries." He mocked her better-than-thou tone, then frowned. "I bet she can't name ten damn states east of the Miss'ssippi River, Miss'ssippi not included."

"That's right."

"Better yet, name ten freeways between here and the 710. I bet they don't know about the Red Summer of 1919, when there were twenty-six race riots here in America, or the Tulsa race riot back in 1921 or . . ."

"Preach it out, Womack, preach it out."

He sucked his teeth. "Nobody wanted to talk to her big flapjack-looking forehead noway. And ain't neither one of 'em got no kinda ass. How the hell you gonna come all the way from Africa and forget to pack up the booty? They probably from Compton."

I joked, "Or Santa Ana."

"Yeah, they probably from Orange fucking County. They needs to hop on John Wayne's horse and ride back down the 405 with all them Republicans."

Womack preached through two games. He lost both of 'em. That put twenty extra dollars in my pockets.

We hopped in Womack's car and headed back to Stocker and Degnan. The air was cool, the area pretty calm, so we sat out on the three concrete steps in front of my building for a while.

That was when I told him what Dana had told me about Rosa Lee being unhappy. Told him about how he had embarrassed his woman down at 5th Street Dick's, the night when he let his eyes wander all around. Womack could be as sensitive as a woman with tender nipples, so I had wanted to creep in that direction, but sometimes the best approach was the direct approach. That struck a nerve that made his curl straighten out.

"Look, Vince, I've been with Rosa Lee for twelve years."

"I know."

He emphasized, "Twelve."

I said, "Yep, you have."

"And for the last seven, she's the only woman that I've slept with. And it's not like I can't pull no women, you hear me?"

"Right, right."

"When she got pregnant the first time—which was my fault for not pulling out in time—I wasn't ready to be nobody's daddy, but I told her I'd be there for her and make sure she got her degree."

"I remember."

"And you also remember that I told her one of us had to finish college because I wanted my children to be able to see that in one of us."

"Right. Remember that too."

"Then the pill didn't work. Either that or she wasn't taking 'em every day like she was supposed to. Either way, she got pregnant again. The foam didn't work and, bam, another baby come popping out crying. She got her tubes tied and, bam, the knot must've jiggled loose."

I playfully pushed him. "You must've been rocking too hard."

Womack almost laughed. "Must've been."

I asked, "Right. Now what's the problem?"

"We've had four kids. And I've done what I promised."

"Ain't no doubt about that."

"A man does what a man's supposed to do and they still complain."

"Definitely ain't no doubt about that."

"Now, in the course of a relationship," he said, sounding like he was talking to an amateur, "one that lasts for umpteen years, beaucoup PMS cycles, umpty-ump mood swings—"

"And twelve Super Bowls and twelve NBA championships—"

"And eleven World Series. People fall—"

I stopped him. "Wait, how you get eleven World Series?"

"It was canceled back in '94 because of that stupid strike."

"Oh, yeah," I said. "Right, right."

"And we only had half a NBA season in '99."

"That was whacked."

"Anyway, when you're with somebody that long, you fall in and out of love more times than you'd ever imagine. Love ain't constant. You have highs and lows."

I just nodded that time.

He was quiet for a minute.

I asked, "So where are you now?"

"What do you mean?"

"In or out of love?"

Without hesitation he replied, "Oh, I'm in love. Ain't nobody better than Rosa Lee. The question is, where is Rosa Lee? Every night she comes to bed in some funky T-shirt, never puts on any sexy stuff like she used to. First thing she does is run to the kids. And when she gets done breast-feeding Ramona, don't let her have a Patti LaBelle book, or a Gladys Knight book glued to her hand. That's why I just go get on the computer."

"Turn the PC off, snatch that book out of her hand, and play Tarzan on her ass. Women like that shit."

"Black Man Negro, that's how we ended up with four kids." Womack lit up another Djarum. "If you want to hear what I think the real problem is, I think she thinks that she's outgrown me."

I made a strange humming sound. The kind that a man makes when he finds out something he'd never thought about. Still waters run deep.

He mumbled, "Hell, maybe she has. She's the one with the degree. I only got half of one. I got a family, a duplex that my daddy won't pay rent on. I can't relocate, can't afford to change jobs. So it ain't like I'm gonna have a lot of career opportunities knocking at my door."

We were quiet for a moment. I was pondering my own future.

Womack smirked and asked, "Ginger or Mary Ann?"

I shook my head. "You know I ain't into white women."

More silence.

I said, "Mary Ann. Ginger would've freaked Mr. Howell for a fur coat."

We laughed.

Then the laughter faded. I glanced over my shoulder, up to my landlord's bay window. I heard it shut, like we were making too much happy noise. Maybe being too ethnic at night. I didn't think the silhouette I saw in the window was Naiomi's because her Jeep CJ-7 wasn't out front.

Womack asked, "After all you did for her, after the way you busted your balls getting her anything she wanted, you ever wonder why Malaika was screwing that dude?"

"All the time. She slept with me that afternoon, and I caught her fucking him before my semen had dried. Used to wonder what I did, or didn't do . . ." My words faded, like every black radio station does when you're heading east out toward Palm Springs.

"And?"

I shrugged. "You know what? I came to the conclusion that it wasn't about me. It was some need she had, I suppose."

Womack said, "Don't you sound psychological."

"I guess. Probably from those self-help books I read after they vanished. Maybe that's what kept me from snapping any more than I did."

"Shit, Black Man Negro." Womack laughed those words out. "If you'd been any worse, your ass would've been locked up for premeditated. And me and Rosa Lee would've been accessories for hiding your ass out."

Again, I knew when to let silence talk for me.

He paused. "Now I'm gonna ask you like Poppa would've asked me. What did you learn from all of that?"

I said, "Never trust a big butt and a smile."

We laughed awhile, then Womack's face got a strange look. Our minds were in sync.

I said, "You still think Rosa Lee's messing around?"

"I wasn't gonna say anything, didn't know if I should've told you at first, 'cause now I'm feeling all suspicious and shit, but yeah, she did it again. Came home from the gym. Didn't have any wet clothes."

My face became haggard with worry.

"Yep. I'd be the last to know." He chewed his lips. "What do you think I should do?"

"Start dating your wife. Take her to a club one night."

"Vince, she complains about going to a club, but the last time we went out, she just sat in a corner. I'm not paying fifteen dollars to get in a club to watch her hold up the wall. You know how many packs of diapers I could buy with the thirty dollars we'd have to spend to get in?"

"At CostCo—one."

"A big one that would last ten years."

"Womack, that's not the point. Just take her."

It showed in his eyes. I asked him what he was afraid of.

His voice lowered. "What if it's already beyond the point of no return?"

Rigor ran over my chest.

Womack looked at me.

It might've been a bad time for me to bring it up, but I said, "Something might be going on on this side of town."

I told him what happened at the Shark Bar.

"Dana vanished, then rushed back like she'd seen a ghost, turned us around like a pack of wolves was about to chew her ass off."

"That would be a lot of chewing."

"Shut up, fool. And this brother was staring her down."

He asked, "What was up with that?"

"Then the motherfucker followed her, walked right up to her face."

"Damn. Probably a brother from the Eastside. You know how bold those niggas are."

"Same way we used to be."

"Wish I could count the fights we had with those fools."

I went on, "It wasn't him that got to me. That's the crap that happens when you with somebody that's half decent. What got me was her reaction to the situation. Looked like she was about to shit on herself."

"She knew him."

"Yep."

He asked, "An ex or what?"

"Hell if I know. I'm pretty sure I'm the only man she's dated since she came out here."

"Man, you better wake up. You know the game. A woman will never tell a man about all the dicks she's had the pleasure of meeting. She can be forty with five kids and she'll still be crying virgin."

"Lower your voice, Womack. Respect my side of Crenshaw."

"Sorry. Just trying to fit in."

"Anyway, where was I—yeah, Dana said the wait for a table was too long, and she grabbed me, damn near dragged me out of the joint, said she'd rather go to the Cheesecake Factory."

Womack understood what I was saying. My partner in crime said, "Dana made you drive across town to get to the Shark Bar, then as soon as you get to the place, made you leave the Shark Bar and drive all the way to Marina Del Rey to the Cheesecake Factory, a forty-minute drive from Hollywood."

"Plus . . ."

"What?"

"It's simple, but it was something. Maybe that's what got me to thinking there was more to it that what she said."

"What was that?"

"All that time she was gone, she said she went to go pee. When we got back in the car, she still had to pee. Made me stop at a gas station."

Womack stiffened his tone. "Why didn't you rattle her cage right then?"

I shrugged. "Thought I might've been overreacting."

"Damn." Womack puffed out some air. He got up and headed toward his car, said, "Keep your ear to the ground."

"You know it."

"Gotta go tuck my crew in bed, if they ain't already 'sleep."

He took half a step before he turned around and asked me, "You got books about Africa in your crib?"

"A couple."

I knew what that was all about. The Ethiopians had hit a sore spot. It's always bothered him that he didn't get that four-year degree. There have been times when he wanted a promotion, stepped up to the office, told the man, and the man told him that even though he had the experience and the know-how, that even though he was always on time, hardly took a sick day, he didn't have that little piece of paper that separated folks like us from folks like them. Between wife, four kids, work, Harmonica having up and down health, Womack has given a lot of years to others, but the years haven't given Womack the time to do anything for himself.

He said, "Next time you're over my way, if you remember, drop them off. I wanna read up on them places. Kids had me so wrapped up in *Barney* and *Bananas in Pajamas* that it's been a while since I had a chance to sit down and read. I'm starting to forget a lot of stuff."

"I'll bring 'em by tomorrow."

"Thanks."

Womack walked away, a load pulling his face down. All of a sudden, he looked as ancient as a pyramid. Older than Harmonica would ever live to be. With the little that he's had, my friend has done a lot. Has taken care of everybody in his reach. Left his dreams behind and became a man. Not the man he had planned on being, not that civil rights attorney he'd dreamed of being, but in some ways, a better kind of man.

I yelled, "Womack, you never answered my question the other day."

He yawned out his words, "What question?"

"Tracy Chapman or Whoopie Goldberg?"

He laughed so hard he started wheezing. I did the same.

When I calmed down, I caught my breath and said, "Okay, okay. I withdraw that one. Nia Long or Vivica Fox?"

"Now you talking." He perked up, fell into a mack-daddy stance, held his crotch. "Nia Long on my love jones bone. I'd have her in the bathroom, leg skraight—and I did say *skraight*—skraight up in the air, just like she was in *Soul Food*."

"Hey, why don't you try that with Rosa Lee?"

A wicked smile crept across his lips. "How you thank we ended up with four kids, fool?"

It was nine-thirty when Womack headed home. I went to my one-bedroom apartment and lay across my bed. Stared at the picture of Dana.

Then I picked up the ones of my child.

And my mind went back to when I was sitting with Kwanzaa in the ICU at Daniel Freeman. She showed up two months early, weighing two pounds, fifteen ounces, looking like a little yellow gal. She was in that room filled with preemies, on her belly, eyes covered, under some sort of light thing. Watched her stretch, yawn, make waking-up faces. Skin so soft and warm. I changed her diaper before her mother did. A tube was up her nose, going down into her belly, so I could feed her breast milk, sat there every evening and watched it go down. Dreamed about her last night. Dreamt she was big and strong. Woke up scared. Scared and hoping she was okay.

All I have of her are those pictures, images stuck in time.

I showered to ease my mind, picked up a book on financial planning. I read through a few pages before something crossed my mind. Most of my books, outside of a James Patterson or a Walter Mosley, were nonfiction. Those didn't include my technical books. I checked out Dana's selection in books. Some were non-fiction, a lot were self-help and recovery, but most of them were those fiction, borderline Cinderella stories.

Stories so far from reality that I couldn't understand the hype.

I put in the videotape me and Dana made. Fast-forwarded past the parts we taped in this apartment, nights of strawberries and honey.

We were in Kenneth Hahn Park, in the brightness of a weekday when hardly a soul was around. I'd skipped work that day, met Dana for lunch at Subway; then we went to the park to eat and talk. One kiss led to another and we ended up taking a chance on getting caught, her face against a tree while I loved her from behind, her beige dress hiked up just enough, colors that looked wonderful against her dark skin. We moaned soft at first, then louder, the birds fled the trees, squirrels ran around in a frenzy. In my mind, I inhaled the scent of our passion, experienced the gentle breeze on our skin.

I come before she does, but the bliss in her eyes, the imperfect smile on her face tells me that she doesn't mind.

So much love in her eyes. Can't wait for her to get home.

15 Vince

Whoop WHOOP Whoop

I'd turned the tape off, fell asleep reading, then was jarred awake. Grunted, knocked the financial-planning book off the bed. A helicopter was flying overhead. LAPD was showing how much they loved us at 2:15 A.M. Back-to-back cars sped over the dips outside my window, music blasting. The streets were alive with the fools of the night.

I called out, "Dana."

No answer.

It was that drive-by time of night. The time of night when thirteen-year-olds kidnapped and raped young women, then tried to burn their bodies to make a slow night have some meaning.

I paged Dana.

Whoop WHOOP Whoop

The noise from the ghetto bird faded. Somebody came up the concrete walkway, heels click-clacking toward our stairwell. The click-clacking slowed, the way a person pauses in thought, then the pace stopped about halfway up. Keys jingled. Then nothing, no more sounds.

I went to the window. Didn't see Dana's car.

I pulled on my favorite worn-out Levi's, opened my door, slow and easy so it wouldn't creak, took a peep out. A feminine figure lingered on the stairs, stalled in the darkness of the hall, halfway up the fifteen-stair climb. Her head was down, braids dangling and covering her face while she massaged her temples. Her skirt hugged her hips, made her look like a sexy sister standing in silhouette.

I spoke softly, "What'cha doing, sexy?"

Her bracelets rattled as she moved a stray braid that was tangled in her earring. She whispered, "I'm not Miss Smith, Mr. Browne."

"Naiomi?"

"You always step into the hall with your chocolate pendulum hanging?"

"Yikes." I jumped, looked down at my pants; my jeans were buttoned up, nothing hanging.

Naiomi slapped her hands over her mouth to smother her belly laugh.

"Psyche, Mr. Browne. You should've seen your face."

We laughed, lightly, like we didn't want to wake anybody up.

Her eyes touched the hair on my chest, then my abs, then my eyes.

I said, "Fix the light so people can see who the hell is out here."

"In the morning I'll do it," she told me. She came up two more steps. As lovely as the sun was warm. She gave up a sweet smile as she repeated herself, "As soon as Home Depot opens up, I'll take care of it."

"Get me the bulbs and I'll save you some work."

"Okeydoke. Don't let me come between you and your testosterone."

She yawned, stretched a little, twisted side to side and made her back pop. When she moved, her blouse loosened, broadcasted the swell of her breasts. Dignified C cups living inside a purple satin bra. Wine mixed with perfume floated from her pores. Intoxicated and beautiful.

She put her back to the wall. It didn't look like she was in a hurry to take those last four steps and get to her home plate.

We chitchatted, low and easy. Her chuckles made her breasts bounce. My insides were filled with Mexican jumping beans.

But black was the color of my true love's hair.

Our about-nothing conversation was cut off when Naiomi's door swung open. Juanita stepped out. Damn near leaped out. Dressed in mauve satin pj's and a red robe. I hate to admit it, but next to my ex-wife, Juanita was the most gorgeous lemon-colored sister I'd ever met. Her green eyes darted to Naiomi, back to me, glued themselves on my bare chest.

Juanita's words flared: "What's going on with you two? You're pretty ... not exactly appropriately dressed, are we, Vincent?"

I said, "Thought I heard Dana, but it was Naiomi. We were just speaking to each other."

"That was a lot of speaking," Juanita said. Her eyes went back to Naiomi. With a soft voice she politely asked, "Where've you been, baby?"

Naiomi said, simply, "Out."

Juanita paused, like she was looking for the right words. She was so composed it was frightening. "How many times are you going to disappear and come sneaking back in the middle of the night?"

Naiomi snapped, "Don't you think it was disrespectful to talk to her on the phone in front of me for over thirty dang minutes like I didn't exist?"

"She's an old friend."

"Then why couldn't you speak to her in English, so I could under—"

"Naiomi, come inside and let's discuss . . ."

Naiomi came up two stairs, slow, methodical steps. "She know we live together?"

Juanita glanced at me like I was standing in their comfort zone. I closed my door, but didn't move my ear away. Both of them had some inaudible words. A moment later their door closed hard and locked.

Their voices rose for a short moment, then fell silent, the way people do when they stop talking and start kissing. Heat was in my chest.

I've always wanted to know how women made love

to each other, how they did what they did when they did the do, especially since they weren't equipped with a pole for the hole—unless they'd bought something made by Ronco. I couldn't imagine two vaginas rubbing coarse hairs against each other like kindling trying to get a spark to start their fire of love.

A car alarm went off. I peeped out. Dana was struggling to get her Q45 into a spot right under the window. She bumped a Montero truck; its alarm came on. She bumped the black Chevy van behind her; its alarm came on. She'd pissed off half of Leimert Park.

I slid under the covers, closed my eyes until she sat on the bed and changed the radio station from R&B to soft contemporary jazz. She leaned over, kissed my face. Rum spiced her breath. Her hair held pounds of fresh smoke, perfume fresher now than when she left this evening. A nasty combination.

I asked, "Where you been all night?"

"With Gerri."

Dana saw my eyes go toward the digital clock: 2:59. She shifted.

She yawned. "I'll be drinking coffee and taking No-Doz tomorrow."

She told me that a girl from Jefferson's rap group came by and told Gerri that she was sleeping with Jefferson.

She said, "Hell broke loose."

Dana stepped into the shower; I stood on the other side of the clear plastic curtain and eye-savored Nubian excellence in motion. Wondered what our children would look like, sound like, act like. I watched her scrub her skin like she was trying to make herself two shades lighter. She gargled with Plax, gently washed her face with Noxzema. She wiped the cream off her skin, saw me staring, blushed, and the tipsiness made her glow. Dana was definitely tipsy. Too tipsy for me to let it slide.

"Dana, you shouldn't be driving around like that."

"Like what?"

"After you've been drinking."

Her response was, "There are a few things you shouldn't be doing too."

"Like what?"

Dana turned around, let the water run over her back, looked me in the eyes, and said, "Have you heard from Malaika?"

"That came out of nowhere."

"Well, Malaika, Kwanzaa, all of that came out of nowhere."

"Why did you ask me that?"

"Why are you so evasive when I ask you about your daughter?"

"I'm not evasive."

"I could ask you a thing or two, but it's late, dealing with Gerri drained me, so I'll tell you what I know just to save some time." She hesitated. "You've still been sending checks to Malaika."

I tried not to blink, tried to hold that same blunt stare that Dana had, but she'd softly pushed me into a corner.

I asked, "You've been going through my checkbook?"

She chuckled. "Maybe Malaika called and told me. Am I wrong?"

"Dana, don't play games."

"Well"—she put soap on her scrungie, soaped her body down—"if it's a game, you're the one who made it that way."

"Is this your liquor talking?"

"I'm buzzed, yeah. Not as much as you think. Enough to let you know shit's on my mind. And it hurts me to pretend that everything is okay."

"Like what? What's on your mind?"

"We talked about that situation you have with your ex-wife, and as a team we made a decision how we would handle that issue financially, and you've gone behind my back and done your own thing. Is that behavior what I should expect from you after we get married?"

I didn't say anything. Not a dime of the money I was sending had come out of her bankrupt pocketbook.

She rinsed the soap off her body. Turned the water off. Motioned for me to hand her a towel.

I confessed, "I sent a check. So what? It was only a few dollars."

She asked, "Okay, then what did you mean by a few more dollars?"

I didn't know what she knew, so I played it down. "It's no big deal."

"It is a big deal. You said that you might be looking at another layoff. A couple of houses fell out of escrow, my desk fees are behind, so I'm not pulling down as much money as I thought I would."

"What if my child grew up hating me because I didn't send money?"

"You've been watching too much Ricki Lake."

"Well, the last thing I need is to end up on the *Ricki Lake Show* trying to explain my side while I'm getting booed by her audience."

Dana turned the shower off, then looked at me and rat-tat-tat-ed her words: "Hell, how important can you be to them if two years go by and they can't take the time to at least send a ten-cent postcard?"

Silence.

Dana softened her quick-tempered tone, tried to sound more rational than emotional. "See it from my point of view. You've been sending them money, living in a second-class apartment, driving a second-class car, and Malaika and her second husband have been getting all the benefits of watching her grow up. I hate to be the one to burst your bubble, but if you asked me, they don't need you, don't want you, don't care about you."

I didn't like what she'd said, not one bit, but maybe there was some hard truth in Dana's argument. They'd been gone a couple of years, and they would be away four more. Not a postcard. To them I was probably as

significant as a single grain of sand blowing across the
Mojave Desert.

"Vince, let's call this an amnesty moment."

"Okay."

"Have you lied to me about anything else?"

"Nope."

"Think real hard."

"Nothing to think about."

"Sure about that?"

"What, you know something that I don't?"

"Last chance to get the skeletons out of your closet."

"Dana, if you have something to say, then say it."

"I'll give you the utmost respect if reciprocated."

"Meaning?"

"Do unto others as you want done to you."

"Is this how you get after you've had a bit too much
to drink?"

"If it is, then I need to drink more often. Maybe you
need to have a drink with me. Well, Vince, I've done
some hellified thinking, and you know what? From now
on this relationship is like skydiving."

"Once again. And that means?"

"You're up to strike two. You've got one mistake left."

"What was strike one?"

"Play stupid."

Dana threw her towel across the room, then went and
got on the phone. She called Gerri. Talked loud enough
for me to hear that something was really brewing on her
buddy's side of town. Only talked a hot second. I had a
feeling that she did that for my sake, to ease my mind
about her being gone until the middle of the night. After
that she pulled on a big NYU T-shirt, went into the bedroom, and sat on the bed. I followed.

She went to the dresser, fidgeted with her jewelry box,
and glared at our bills, most of them hers, glanced at
Kwanzaa's pictures.

Dana said, "Why haven't you ever put our picture in
a nice silver frame to match your daughter's?"

"They're just pictures. Don't start tripping."

"I'm not tripping, I'm just asking. Geesh, can't I make any suggestions without you biting my damn head off?"

"They're just pictures."

She picked up the wooden frame that housed our studio photo, then eased it down in front of Kwanzaa's photo.

I asked, "Why did you do that?"

"They're just pictures, right?"

"Dana, don't come in here at three in the morning trying to make something out of nothing, all right? It's time for us to hit the bed."

"And that's just a bed too, right? Your old honeymoon bed."

Dana strolled toward the kitchen. I let my toes open and close, made fists with my feet, did the same with my hands, massaged my temples, closed my eyes as tight as I could. Wished she'd've stayed her black ass out in the streets.

A second later she came back over and eased into my lap. She had please-forgive-me eyes. Her mood had changed. When she touched me, my mood changed too. I hated she could soften me up like that.

She kissed my forehead in some sort of an awkward apology. "Are we going to be okay?"

"I hope so."

"Head hurts. I'm hungry." Dana shook her head like she was rattling secrets around, then kissed my lips. "Be my hors d'oeuvres and kiss me for a few minutes."

The mood was broken, but I tried to get it back with a bucket of smiles, and a few soft kisses on the spots that usually made her wiggle, rubs on the tender areas that usually make her purr. Things got warm, but they never heated up. No wiggles. No coos. Her tongue had no passion or flavor. Rain had fallen on our flames. She broke away, went into the kitchen, and made herself a plate. When she came back, a blank expression was on her face.

I asked, "What's wrong?"

She took a bite of her spicy baked chicken wings. "We need to get out of this box and get a house before we get married."

"Where did that come from?"

"Guess since I was at Gerri's condo. Hell, if she can do it and she's by herself with two kids, I don't see why we can't do the same."

After she ate, I took her plate into the kitchen, washed the few dishes we had. I dried my hands, put the dishes away, and headed toward the secondhand bed. Knew nothing first-class would be happening between our sheets but sleep.

The top of the chest of drawers had been rearranged. My child's picture had been put into the plain wooden frame. The picture of me and Dana had been put in the silver frame and stuck up front.

At five a.m., while Dana slept, my second sight woke me up. I slipped from between our sheets, eased her purse from the foot of the bed, and took it into the bathroom. She had tickets to a comedy jam in Carson.

I moved her stun gun to the side, searched top to bottom, and didn't find anything else. No phone numbers.

Nothing at first.

Underneath her letter from the IRS was her pager. It was turned off; the messages might've been rolling over to her answering service.

I scrolled through the numbers. My after-hours pages weren't the last ones she'd received. Two had come in within the last thirty minutes. From the same number. And it wasn't Gerri's 310-671-whatever number over in Inglewood's Carlton Square. I didn't think that a client would be calling way after midnight to ask about an open house, maybe just searching for some legs to open, so I wrote the number down.

A jackhammer was living inside of my chest. I put the pager back, left her purse where I found it, and crawled back into the bed. But ten seconds didn't pass before I pulled the covers back again, tipped into the kitchen, and dialed that number. Had to know what was up.

"Thank you for calling the Wyndham Bel Age Hotel."

That caught me off guard. I asked the sister to repeat the name of the hotel. Asked where they were located. They were on Green Valley Circle in Culver City. Five minutes away.

I hung up. Wanted to know who'd call my woman from a hotel in the middle of the night. There was no extension on the pager, that meant she knew.

New feelings crawled over my skin like an army of African ants. My first mind told me that I should've done like Womack said, grabbed her shoulders and rattled her cage right then, but Womack had suggested that I do something that he wouldn't do his damn self.

Something I knew I could never do again.

Dana woke up long enough to murmur, "You all right, sweetie?"

I nodded in the dark. She hadn't called me sweetie in a while.

"What's the matter, baby? Why you keep getting up?"

I replied, low and uneasy, "Nothing. Go back to sleep."

Dana softly said, "Vince?"

I waited a couple of seconds. "Yeah."

"Sweetie, I love you so much it scares me."

"Same here."

Dana spoke in a sensitive tone, "I'm just going through some changes, I guess. Things are on my mind, and I'm scared, so fucking scared because this is new territory for me, and I don't know how to address the issues."

"Wanna talk about it?"

"Ignore me. I'm just looking for reasons to argue, I think."

"Why?"

"Frustrated?"

"Why?"

"Shhh. We have to work in a few hours. Close your eyes."

I kissed her head. "Don't let that worm dig too deep."

"I won't."

She wrapped around me like she never wanted to let me go, like she owned me. Her affectionate touch made that jackhammer feeling go away.

Just that quick she was asleep, almost as if she'd never woke up.

My fingers drifted back and forth across her satin scarf. Rubbed her pea-size head like she was mine all mine. I moaned out a gust of worry, stared at the ceiling until sleep robbed me of consciousness.

16 Vince

I made it home around six. Put on my purple nylon shorts and running shoes. Purple was a neutral color, didn't belong to any gang. I conquered Stocker, tackled two-mile-high hills in Baldwin Vista—Cloverdale and Veronica—then jetted back down Hillcrest and found my blue-collar world, made it home around eight.

I cranked the shower up and hopped in with eight miles of aches, and the pain felt good. The music was bumping, so I got my bathtub boogie on.

The shower curtain swayed when the front door opened quick and closed hard. Bags rustled. Soft singing. Heels clicked across the tile on the kitchen floor. Then Dana came down the hallway into the bathroom. Smiled.

She had on a long woven skirt and top, maize and burgundy colors flowing in a horizontal pattern. The outfit was new. Hair pulled up like a queen. Silver geometric jewelry I'd never seen before.

New clothes. New jewelry. Subtle changes.

I asked, "Where've you been?"

"Food shopping. Want to make my world-famous turkey nachos."

"Close the shower curtain."

She eased the curtain back some more. She lowered her voice. "Maybe the nachos can wait. Room for two?"

"Yeah."

She undressed where she stood. Folded her clothes

and took them into the bedroom. First there was a new darkness from the curtains being drawn, the sound of matches being struck, then the smell of incense romanticizing the air. The radio was changed from the hip-hop on KKBT. I heard the cassette door open, then close. Instrumental jazz kicked in a new kind of mood. A second later her craving came to me with a smile, nipples hard with anticipation.

The shower rained over us. I cleansed my fiancée's back, ran my soapy hands over the molds and curves I knew so well. She murmured. All lights were off; all bets were on. The aroma of the Black Love incense mixed with the sounds of the Boney James *Seduction* tape rippling from the boom box in the bedroom, his sax blowing out smooth rhythms with a gentle bass line.

Dana turned to me and we shared a wealth of insatiable kisses. Water bounced off the wall and drizzled our faces like a spray from a river gone wild. She kissed my face, moaned, loaned me soft sucks and lagged her tongue over my neck, back to my mouth, over my chest, enjoyed my nipples. I loved the shit out of that. The shower steamed like soft clouds from heaven.

She said, "I know what you like."

"Do you?"

"Yes, I do."

Her kisses flowed south, below my equator, my hot spot. Heat and moisture from the inside of her mouth. I gripped the shower wall and tried to keep my knees sturdy, fought to keep the sensation from overwhelming me. I gazed down on her motions, watched her fill herself with me, watched her work it.

I moaned, closed my eyes. Imagined myself being a man who controlled everything around him. I opened my eyes. Let the light from reality shine through. Dana rubbed that rigid part of me on the side of her face.

She brought her mouth to mine, her damp breasts to my chest, let her hand massage the part of me she'd seasoned.

"I want you inside me."

"Let me get a condom."

"Without one. I need to feel you."

"We've never gone bareback."

"First time for everything. Please me. Come inside me."

"We can't. Not without a condom."

"You been with somebody else?"

"No."

"What's the problem?"

"You've never wanted to do me without one—why now?"

"I'm gonna be your wife. Can't I feel you for a minute?"

"What if, you know."

"What if what? What if I get pregnant?"

"Yeah."

"Why you have to say it like that?"

"You know we're not ready for that."

"Chill out, sweetie. I'm not ovulating."

"We shouldn't take that chance."

"I just came off my period. It's safe. Don't you trust me?"

"This ain't about that."

"Well, if you want to, you could pull out before—"

"Dana, let's not play that game. Let me get a condom."

"Never mind. Never mind. Never mind. Forget it."

Dana slid an inch in a new direction. Pulled her braids back, held her face toward the shower, rinsed the soap off her neck, stepped out, water dripping from her body, dried off in two seconds, wrapped a green towel from her breasts to her hips, put one over her hair, grabbed the Listerine from underneath the cabinet, and gargled deep, hard, and long. Over and over she spat, rinsed, gargled again.

"You can stick your dick in my mouth, but you want to put a condom on to go inside me. Makes me feel less than I am."

I was still in the shower, alone with the warm water turning cold, my penis harder than an ancient Chinese writing block, throbbing for relief. My handle took on a life of its own, screamed and aimed at Dana the way the provoked creatures in *Invasion of the Body Snatchers* pointed at the humans who needed to be changed.

I switched the water to cold and calmed myself the best I could. But some days my best ain't good enough.

By the time I got out, Dana was in the kitchen pouring herself a glass of juice. I stood naked with liquid almond soap creeping across my flesh and stared at her. She swallowed her juice, then returned my glare.

I went to the bedroom and picked up the frame with my child's picture in it, the wooden frame she'd crammed the photo into. I took the picture of me and Dana out of the silver frame and put my child's back inside. Dana's was put back into the wooden frame.

Dana went back into the kitchen, nodding all the way.

I went into the bathroom, grabbed a towel, dried off what water hadn't been burned away by the heated anger brewing deep inside my soul. Sat on the edge of the tub, head down. My hands doubled up into fists. I was about to come apart, but I found my cooltivity, pushed the troubled man in me aside, let the feeling of control take control. Slowly opened my hands.

I'm a peaceful man by nature. Can't afford to get riled.

When I raised my head, Dana was standing over me. One foot on top of the other, leaning against the door frame, her eyes burrowing in mine.

"Would it be so bad if I did get pregnant?"

"Dana, please, babe."

"Maybe that's something we should talk about, if we want kids. How many, if any at all. We've never talked about it, and I assumed you do. Assumed you did. But that was before I knew you already had a child."

"Well, right now we don't have any real savings, no room in a one-bedroom apartment. We're living on top of each other as it is."

"I can't get pregnant. Not today. I know my body."

"That's not the point."

"Would you want me to kill it because you already got one?"

"Let's not play hypothetical right now, okay?"

"This isn't play, this is for real. This is the kind of shit people should talk about before they go this far."

"Not now."

"Then I know your answer. You know, I'm telling you that you can trust me with anything, but your message is loud and clear. That's another reason why I never wanted to get with a man who had a child. It's always that sorry-eyed, selfish 'I already got a baby, I can't afford another one, here's half the money, why don't you run down to the corner and get an abortion' crap a brother sobs and spits out when he fucks you pregnant."

"You saying you're pregnant?"

"No." A moment passed. She said, "I'm saying I love you, Vincent Browne. Loved you damn near from the moment I saw you."

An intermission in the conversation lasted ten seconds. Dana said, "It wasn't about the damn condom. I needed a new level, a deeper connection with you. I really needed to feel you. Really wanted you to feel me without that barrier taking away some of the feeling."

Her sweet, sensitive personality had resurfaced. The vulnerable side she had shown me out on the beach, the woman I'd met and fallen in love with.

"Vince?"

"Yeah?"

"I apologize. You okay?"

"I'm cool."

"Forgive me?"

"Yeah."

"Can I have a kiss?"

"Yeah."

We did.

Dana said, "Cheer up."

"Nothing to cheer up about."

Dana opened her hand. Two golden condoms were inside.

I gazed at my limp manhood. Pillow-soft ebony flesh with no definition. My mood had become a casualty. It wasn't impotence. Not a Viagra moment. It was missing desire. I had less appetite for Dana than a corpse has plans for tomorrow.

Dana kneeled, came closer, reached for my penis. Her head lowered, eyes focused, mouth eased open. The warmth of her breath was on my wrinkled skin. I intercepted her face with my hand.

I said, "Later."

"I need you now."

"Too much on my mind."

"Try, okay?"

"Later. I need to get out and get some fresh air."

Her lips curved up into a mutilated smile. "Sure."

She stood, held my hand. I stood, let myself dangle. Disappointment was in her eyes. I followed her into the bedroom. We both found our own space, dressed without looking at each other. Her reflection was in the rectangular mirror on the wall. Like a merry-go-round, her eyes kept floating about the room. To the bed. To the dresser. Toward the pictures. To me. To the closet. To her reflection.

She clicked the tape off, then lay down on the mattress.

Five minutes later, I told her I was about to drive over to Womack's for a while. Don't know if she heard me. She was breathing hard and deep, holding herself, like she was asleep.

I put my hand on the doorknob. The phone rang. Dana picked up before the first ring was done.

Her soft voice, a short pause, pure silence, then she yelled, "Vince! Phone."

I crept into the doorway. Dana had dropped the phone next to her hipbone. She sighed with a weary smile, fidgeted, picked at her toenails. I'd have to be up under her when I answered.

I cleared my throat, put the phone to my ear: "What's up?"

"Vincent. This is Malaika."

17 Vince

My world stopped revolving.

I took a slow breath and said her name: "Malaika?"

"Yeah, it's me." Her voice, unsteady. "How's it going, Vince?"

Hearing Malaika's voice jarred me down to the bone. It was like getting that middle-of-the-night call from a relative who never called, and you know they're going to tell you something horrific had happened.

I asked Malaika, "How's Kwanzaa? I mean, every-thing okay?"

"We're blessed." Malaika's tone was hesitant. "I called to thank you for the little package you sent. That was unexpected."

"Your mother forwarded it to Germany that quick?"

"Momma ...." Malaika started, then: "We're in San Bernardino."

"You're in San Bernardino?"

That blue-collar strip of desert was less than two hours away.

Dana ran her finger through her braids and mumbled, "Are they back to stay or visiting?"

Malaika's end was filled with static, fading in and out. She must've been on a cordless phone, walking around the house.

"Yes, we're in country."

"How long have you been back in the States?"

"Six months."

"Six months? Why are you just now calling?"

"I called last week."

"Last week? Well, why didn't you leave a message?"

"I spoke with the same female who just answered. She said that you didn't live there, that I had the wrong number."

My eyes went to Dana. Her eyes went to the carpet.

"Vincent, this is long-distance, so I'll be brief. I just wanted to call and thank you on behalf of Kwanzaa—"

"Where's Kwanzaa? Put her on the phone."

"She's not with me."

"Where is she?"

Malaika wavered. "I just wanted to acknowledge your gift."

"Can I talk to her?"

A lengthy pause. "That wouldn't be a good idea."

"What do you mean, not a good idea?"

"She's adjusting to our positive lifestyle—"

"What, you think my lifestyle's not positive?"

"I'm not saying that."

"What are you saying?"

"This is a difficult situation. Stressful to all parties. I don't think it would be fair to her to get her confused at this point."

"Confused? I'm her daddy, nothing to get confused about."

"I don't think that would be a good idea."

Dana's breathing roughened. Her knuckles popped when she opened and closed her hands. She said, "Vince, sweetie, don't beg her."

I shushed Dana, then asked Malaika, "Where can I reach you?"

"I'll contact you if the need arises."

"If the need arises? C'mon."

Dana said, "Vince, sweetie—"

My heart thumped. I shushed Dana so I could hear Malaika.

"Don't disrespect me in front of her." She hopped off the bed. "Sweetie, Vincent, don't shut me out."

I rubbed the bridge of my nose to fight the new stress. "Malaika, let me talk to Kwanzaa."

"I can't do that, Vincent."

"Malaika, c'mon—"

Dana snapped, "That's enough, Vince. Don't beg. Don't stand in my face and beg—"

"Dana, stop."

"Vincent." That was Malaika. "Is everything okay over there?"

"Enough is enough," Dana cried. She came across the room, stood in front of me, nose to nose. "Baby, listen, understand what I'm saying. I just don't think you should have to beg to see—"

"Malaika, lighten up." I put my hand over the phone, muffled my irritation, and said, "Dana, c'mon now, baby, chill."

Her response was a harsh whisper, pure frustration. "No, I'm not gonna chill. I'm watching you suffer. And that hurts me."

"Look, Vince," Malaika sighed. I imagined her massaging her round chin, just like she used to do when we were married. "I'll have to see how you're living before I even think about risking my daughter's well-being."

"She's my daughter too."

"If we do let you see her—"

I repeated, "We?"

"—at first it'll be from a distance."

My tone turned extreme: "Why from a distance?"

Malaika said, "I don't want you confusing her."

I paused long enough to realize what she was telling me. My tone was squashed by apprehension. "She thinks your husband is her daddy?"

Me and Dana were eye to eye when I said that.

Malaika's voice was fractured: "He is the only father she knows."

"That's your doing."

"Those are my terms if I let you see her. No compromise."

Dana said, "Hang up the damn phone, Vince."

"Stop pulling the cord!" I snapped at Dana, then, since I had no real power, I spoke cordially to my ex: "Whatever you think is best for her."

Malaika hung up on me. At least that was the way it seemed.

Dana was in the corner, breathing hard, the telephone cord dangling in her hand like she'd jerked away my life support.

By then my head was pounding. I snapped, "What is your problem?"

"I'm the one over here scrubbing the skid marks out of your funky-ass drawers, and the moment she calls, you're ignoring me, disrespecting me."

Dana stood toe to toe, dared me in her own way. When I walked away, she followed, practically walked on my heels. I pushed her off me.

"Don't push me. That's your first and last time pushing me."

"Don't get up on me like that, Dana."

"Help me understand this, Vince. If she loved you so much, why did she walk out on you and marry somebody else just like that, huh? That might not even be your baby."

"How can you say something like that?"

"Because I know women."

"You don't know Malaika."

"Well, from what you told me, that makes two of us."

I gritted my teeth, wished I hadn't told her so much.

"You should get a blood test," she said in an unrelenting, logical tone. "Ten years from now you might be in court crying because you just found out that child that you've been supporting wasn't yours. Let me correct that. If we were married, we might be in court crying because that child that we'd been supporting with our income wasn't yours."

She was in my face. I eased her off me. "What's wrong with you?"

She shoved me away from her, said, "I never should've gotten involved with you. Never should've let you put your damn dick inside of me. You got me sucking on your damn dick to please you, and when that bitch calls I ain't about shit. It's always some other bitch . . ."

The back of my neck feeling dirty and gritty, I headed for the door. Had to get away from the madness, had to escape this space that was closing in a foot with every breath.

"Vince, don't walk out on me."

I waved her away. Stopped with my hand on the doorknob.

"You going out there?"

"Just might."

"Well, can I go?"

"Get away from me."

"I'm sorry. But you should see yourself."

"Get the f—" I started. "Look, get away."

"So, I don't mean shit to you?"

I shuffled down the stairs, had to catch my breath.

In my mind I was cursing the world out, damning everybody from here to eternity. I strolled toward the bungalows on Edgehill, kept meandering until I made it two short blocks over to Audubon Middle School.

My baby was back in the States. Had been here since God knows when. Nobody contacted me. Made me less important than a single blade of grass in a field of dreams. They've always had my phone number, always had my address. Somebody could've at least bought a stamp and sent me a *fuck-you-nigger* postcard.

Malaika had my flesh-and-blood calling a stranger daddy.

Damn.

I sat on the concrete, whispered, *"Focus. C'mon, focus."*

After my head cleared a bit, when my heart cooled and its beat was close to normal, I dusted the grit off my butt, and admitted that I didn't handle that too well. That call blindsided me, woke up a lot of hidden feelings, denials that had been plastered all over our four walls.

I didn't want to lose Dana too. Didn't want to relive the pain. I hurried back up Stocker, damn near sprinting, went upstairs so fast that my feet touched every other step. I needed Dana to understand where I was coming from.

A thin river of smoke clogged the air. A glow prettier than a golden-orange sunset was dancing on the walls.

A fire was in the kitchen.

The blaze was dancing on top of the white gas stove. Fumes from the burning had blackened the wall, were reaching up for the ceiling. The last-chance smoke detector kicked on just as I got inside.

"Dana! Fire!"

The flames lit up the room enough for me to see Dana was biting her nails, gazing out the front window, ignoring my yelping and fanning and throwing tap water on top of a pile of papers that had a riot-sized blaze going. She didn't turn around or flinch. When I got the crackling fire out, I stepped across what felt like a broken window. My silver frame was on the floor, smashed. I coughed and gagged and spat into the sink, waved away the smoke and saw what was burning were my child's pictures.

My voice became shrill. "What's wrong with you!"

She stepped up to me and snapped, "They don't give a shit about you."

I pushed her off me. She stumbled three, maybe four steps, then came back at me. Her right hand came up in a blur, with the fury of a tigress. That was a slap heard around the world, a blow that made my world turn bright red. My face stung, pain from her wide swings.

In that moment I hated her. Hated Malaika, hated Dana.

The next thing I knew, Dana was across the room, upside down, sprawled in front of the sofa, holding her mouth. The tips of my fingers were stinging. My reaction scared me. But I was too far gone. I was in a zone called the fuck-its. That was when a brother stopped giving a fuck. And I had the mother-of-all-fuck-its.

She touched her lip, glared up at me with I'm-gonna-hav'ta-kill-your-ass eyes. She sprang to her feet, about to charge at me with her fists doubled, but something she saw in my face scared her.

I rushed to meet her halfway. She screamed for her life, stumbled backward toward the sofa. The smoke detector kept chanting its maddening song. Dana screeched at a bone-crushing volume, "Let me go, Vince!"

We tussled over the love seat, fell hard to the carpet, rolled on the floor. She raced on hands and knees. I chased on knees and hands. She was fumbling for her purse. I caught her, grabbed her waist, flipped her over. Everything in her purse fell out. Including her stun gun. That had to be what she was trying to get.

I grunted.

Dana kicked. Fought. Wriggled. Twisted. Tried to knee me off her. Pushed my chin back with the palm of her hand. Dug her nails into my back.

I pinned her down, held her until she wore down.

I struggled to unzip my pants.

Salty moisture dripped into my eyes. Burning pictures, all I could see were the burning pictures. Heard Malaika's cold-hearted voice telling me I couldn't see my baby.

Pushed. Shoved. Abused. Cheated on. Ridiculed.

Somebody had to pay.

I held Dana down with one hand on her neck, my pants down at my knees. Wiggled myself around, tried to force my way inside her. She slapped me, shifted side to side to buck me off.

Then I stopped.

Wondered if I was losing my motherfucking mind.

Tried to find myself in my frenzy.

Stunned eyes. We grimaced. Panted. Faces dank head to chin.

Dana's features slipped into innocence, like glitter on a child's drawing. Then I had a vision of my own baby. The baby who came from me. Created by my sperm. I thought of someone trying to do this to Kwanzaa, someone trying to control and violate her when I wasn't around to protect her, to save her from somebody like the man I'd become right now. Somebody with the fuck-its.

I let Dana go. Let go of all the anger. Said I was sorry.

She took short, ragged breaths. Nostrils flared. Her mouth almost opened. Her hostile eyes widened. First she pulled her knees deep into her chest, then she snarled, leaned over and slapped me. Again, again. I backed up. Her braids fell and swayed when she came after me.

I tried to get away. She reached up and grabbed the back of my neck and tried to yank me back. I fought to escape the madness. Sweat had left me slippery; she lost her grip, then struggled to grab part of my shirt, and when I stumbled backward, it ripped. Buttons popped off and spun.

Then I was going for the stun gun, but she cut me off.

We struggled, bumped into the furniture until she cornered me in front of the beat-down sofa. She was stronger, determined; she pinned me down. I wanted to fight, wanted to tell her to get the hell off me, but I was too weak from my spiraling emotions to do anything.

She jumped on me. I tried to shove her off without throwing her into the stereo and hurting her head. Her hand lunged between my legs and gripped my dick, squeezed it, twisted it. I thought she was going to yank Mr. Happy off my body, but she was trying to force me inside her. I squirmed, fought to keep her from sitting on me. I didn't want to go there, not in the middle of lunacy and madness.

Then I was tired of fighting.

Tired.

She put her hand on my cheek.

Made me look at her, absorb her passion until I relaxed.

She whispered, "I know how you fucked her."

"What are you talking about?"

"I know it all." The words floated from her face. "Vince, I know."

She put soft kisses on my eyes. Ran her fingers through the sweat on my face. So much passion was inside our anger. I touched her skin, kissed her hand. Dana relaxed and licked around my lips. She flirted her fingers between my legs and took control with a loose grip, kept kissing me, brought me to her, led me inside a warm, wet place.

She went into the rocky bump and grind. Her body did a slow hum, like she was keeping tempo with a gritty song inside her mind. We fought each other some more, me with my grunts and groans, her with her stroking and dancing without a single word. I didn't want to come. Didn't want to give her my seed. Fought it. Then it felt so good I didn't want her to ever stop. I tried to hold back. It was there. Heat rising to the top, weakening my muscles, the beginning of a flood seeping out the gates, numbing my body with a bittersweet recipe of agony and pleasure. I tried to push her off me before it was too late, but she wouldn't move.

My breathing changed from pants to harsh breathing. I became light-headed and jerked around inside her. She shrieked out pleasure that sounded like anguish, pumped fast and hard like she was trying to get all of the pain and fury out of her system. Trembled and repeated what I had just done.

Body hotter than a match, she moved her hips in intense circles. Dana finally slowed down, caught her wind, swallowed a mouth of her own saliva, wheezed a hundred times while she stared deep in my face.

That was how we remained. Our eyes on each other. Anger was still floating here, but it was different, diluted, mixed with shame and uncertainty. Her hands drifted across her sweaty breasts. Then she wiped my face, put her fingers in my mouth, let me taste the end of her wrath, rolled over next to me. Collapsed like she was drunk with power and put her head on my chest.

We lay there like we were bolted into the ground.

I tried to understand what had just happened to us.

No damn condom. I wondered if I had done something that couldn't be forgiven. Wondered if I'd forgive her for what she had done. The smell from the fire, the ashes I saw, even with my eyes closed, was my answer.

The smoke detector stopped yelling.

Footsteps charged up the stairs. Our narrow hallway rumbled like we were having an earthquake.

Juanita was outside my door screaming. Radios squawked. Outside my window red and blue lights started flashing like crazy—rainbows chasing rainbows. Hard knocks rocked my door.

"LAPD. Open up."

"Dana," Juanita yelled. "Oh, my God, she's not answering. Dana! *Dana!*"

"Ma'am, stand back, please."

"But she was screaming that he was trying to kill—"

"Ma'am, stand back. Go back inside and close your door."

There were a bunch of 'em. I could tell. There had to be more blue suits than had shown up for the Rodney King party.

My pants tangled at my ankles. Dana must've been in shock because she held me tighter, pinned me down. My shirt was ripped, buttons everywhere, half on, half off. Some furniture was knocked over, pillows were off the sofa, CDs scattered, a few things zigzag. The place was tossed like a jail cell. Dana's panties were on the carpet by the front door. Ceiling to carpet, the room held the lovely aroma from what we'd done.

"LAPD. Open up."

"I'm the landlord. I've got a key."

The door swung open before we could get our bearings.

Police swarmed into my apartment like cockroaches drawn to spilled Kool-Aid. We were half-naked in a sea of blue suits and dark guns.

I wrenched my pants up, trembled head to toe, ached in between.

Dana took a sharp breath, quivered, struggled to get up. I helped her to her feet. Strange eyes were all over us. Juanita was in the background, yelling. Dana made a terrified sound and hid her naked body behind mine. Hid behind me and held my hand like I was her daddy.

18 Vince

Ten minutes passed.

Minutes that felt like years of nonstop sweating.

LAPD left the door wide open while they raged inside my life and pushed me to the side. They had even been kind enough to send a ghetto bird to fly over our building and let it shine its lights down brighter than Parliament's flashlight. All of our lights were turned on. Outside, eight patrol car lights whirled and lit up the night like a fucking West Coast Mardi Gras celebration was going on in the center of my courtyard.

Seventeen policemen stood sentry in the middle of my life.

Dana had thrown on wrinkled jeans, a worn Harlem Book Fair T-Shirt. She was escorted to the other side of the room by two female officers in Kevlar vests who looked at me with disgust.

I was led out into the hall. Handcuffed. They said that embarrassment was for my own safety. My pride almost resisted that first step of dehumanization, but I remembered videos when brothers did contest the police, remembered how they were beat crippled and crazy.

What happened in the kitchen?

You left some papers on top of the gas stove and it ignited?

Would you like to come down to the station with us, ma'am?

Are those your panties by the door?

Did he force himself on you?

You can file a restraining order to give yourself time.
We can lock him up for at least forty-eight.
So you were making love and got carried away,
ma'am.
The neighbors heard you scream.
Please don't cover for him.
Brother, if that was my sister, you wouldn't be standing
here.

Voices surrounded me on the landing, right outside
Naiomi and Juanita's open door. Then they paraded me
down to the courtyard, handcuffed, hands behind my
back, made to stand in front of my whole neighborhood.

An officer of the goddamn law asked, "Why are you
tense, Mr. Browne?"

I used my shoulder to wipe the sweat off my nose.
"I'm black. You're police. We have a history of conflict
and misunderstanding."

Juanita and Naiomi were in their bay window, their
backs to me. An officer was with them. Juanita was as
animated as a Disney movie, gesturing, pointing.
Naiomi was calm, arms folded.

The police said that Juanita had dialed 911 and told
them that Dana was screaming for her life. Described a
murder in progress.

Seemed like an hour passed before they raised me
from sitting on the curb and took the shackles off. I massaged my wrists, held my head high. The officer stared at
me with disdain until I marched away from all the eyes.
LAPD's convoy left with disappointed faces.

I stood in the dark of my apartment, in the window.

Dana was on the floor, hands in her hair, her back to
the wall.

"Unbelievable. Malaika calls here, first you let her
talk down to you, then you stand in my face begging her,
then you jump on me."

"I jumped on you? We need to push rewind and see
who popped who."

She sat there with haunted eyes. She looked incurably sad.

I said, "Wake up and stop tripping."

She chuckled. "Well, let me show you who is really tripping."

Dana left, went into the closet, rifled through my personal stuff, came back with a videotape. Put it in the VCR. Grabbed the remote. Turned the television on. Pushed play. Me and Malaika came up on the screen.

Dana said, "Why do you have a tape of you and her fucking?"

I didn't say a word. I was numb.

The tape played. Tortured me. Tortured Dana.

Me and Malaika were naked. Her short brown hair. My body was thinner, not much, but enough. And I wore a Bobby Brown–looking flat top fade. We were squirming on the bed that's in my bedroom right now.

I cleared my throat.

She said, "It disgusts me."

I went to the VCR.

She said, "Don't stop it. Look at the end of the tape. Watch what happens. That tells all. You go get her a towel. See the blank look on her face? She forgot the tape was on. She loses that smile, sighs, shakes her head, and frowns up at the ceiling. She bites her bottom lip and stares off into space. With you was the last place she wanted to be."

My body ached when I stooped. Pain from running. Pain from fighting. Pain from living. I pushed eject. Tore the tape to shreds.

She said, "How would you feel if I had a damn tape of me and somebody else having sex right up under your damn nose? How would you feel?"

The future walked in, very slowly. Thick lines were in her forehead, but she was a lot calmer. Like a burden had been lifted.

This had been turned around. Now I was the bad guy.

"You know that Malaika's called. I know about your

funky little tape. I feel so much better. So much better. I don't know what else to say."

"Dana, Malaika has nothing to do with what's between me and you."

"That's bullshit," she snapped back at me. "The money that you'll have to dish out to Malaika's household could make the difference between our children going to public and private school. A difference in the type of loan we could qualify for. Kind of car we can afford. The difference between us having nice family vacations, getting to visit other countries, places like Africa or France or Australia, or have to pack up government cheese sandwiches and catch a bus to Disneyland. Life's expensive, and I want to be able to give my kids a decent life too.

"If she's half the scrub you said she is, the more you make, the more they'll take. And every time you make another dollar, she'll be downtown at the courthouse asking for two. And if we have children, that'll be just like taking the food and opportunity right out of my children's mouth."

Dana used the wall to help herself to her feet, followed me to the door. Her voice was strained: "If I was willing to accept your lie, to give up a chunk of my income for the next umpty-ump years, do you know how I must feel about you? How many women do you know would be willing to do that?"

"You've got a problem."

"If telling the truth is a problem, then I wish you had the same problem. Now is when we need to sit down and talk."

Her words made my soul ache. She was telling the truth. So many truths at one time. I just didn't know if her truth was my truth.

She said, simply, "You don't understand, do you?"

"Understand what?"

"My passion for you."

"Can you have the same enthusiasm for my child?"

"After watching how you lost your mind the moment

you heard Malaika's voice, I should be asking if you'd have any left over for me."

It was time for me to find my own corner in the sky. I walked away. She ran to the top of the stairs and called out my name.

I turned, faced her.

She asked, "You still love your ex-wife?"

"I love you more than I loved Malaika."

"How do you know?"

"Because I didn't kill you ten minutes ago."

She chuckled. "I wish you had. It would've made my life easier."

"Wouldn't've done much for mine."

A moment passed.

"What I know is that I love you, Vince."

"Do you?"

"If I didn't, I would've stabbed you in your heart when you hit me."

The landlord's door jerked open. Juanita's cute little voice snapped, "Did I just hear you say that he hit you?"

Dana said, "Mind your own business."

Juanita's door slammed like a gunshot. Then our door closed, easy.

Inside a coffin-size hallway, I leaned against the wall, wiped away the dampness the burning smoke and loss had brought to my eyes.

Voices were still on the street.

I was ashamed to step out into the streetlights because my neighbors might still be out, in lawn chairs, eating ham sandwiches and waiting for the second act of the Negro Follies. I'd been handcuffed. Slave-marched in front of the whole damn neighborhood.

A faint voice said, "Mr. Browne? You all right?"

It was Naiomi. She'd opened their door. The light in the hall had been replaced with a sixty-watt bulb, so her concerned expression was clear.

Naiomi was talking, but I wasn't in the mood to listen.

I was bewildered. Didn't know how I got where I was, didn't know where I fit in life. Wanted to know how I could set an example of righteousness for Kwanzaa if I couldn't set an example for my damn self.

Naiomi suggested, "Stay somewhere else tonight."

I nodded.

She spoke like she was reading my corrupted mind. "We're rowing in the same boat, Mr. Browne."

My eyes rose and met hers. Feelings were shared. Her empathy was strong. I wanted to tell her not to gaze down on me like that at a time like this, not while everything in my life was jumbled.

Juanita called Naiomi's name. She followed her commanding officer's voice back inside.

The people outside had gone on about their business. That was the attention span of the big city. They'd moved on. Cars screeched over the dip at Degnan. Across the street a sister was having a church gathering in her one-bedroom apartment, playing her gospel so loud that angels needed earplugs to keep from going deaf.

I coughed. Fumes mixed with the sweat drying on my skin. Flesh smoldering. Ashes clung to the sweat on the back of my hands.

From the courtyard, I saw Dana standing in our window, arms folded underneath her breasts, rocking side to side. She closed the blinds.

19 Vince

Womack said, "Damn. She got you pretty bad."

Velvety music was gliding in the background, drifting on the wings of KUSC, USC's classical music station.

Rosa Lee said, "Womack has some more sweats that you can wear."

I shook my head. "I'm cool."

My agony had been taken to Womack's duplex, in his bathroom.

Rosa Lee was dabbing peroxide on my back, mothering me while she chastised me with sisterly words.

She shook her head in disbelief. "Vince, there's no way you're going to make me believe that Dana did this."

"I told you what happened."

Womack had Ramona, the girl of his dreams, on his shoulders. She was crying when I came in, but had fallen asleep with him bouncing her. Womack headed down the hallway, took Ramona to her crib.

Rosa Lee asked, "How soon before they go back to Germany?"

I answered, "Don't know. Didn't get a chance to ask."

Womack was back in the doorway, wearing checkered boxers and a T-shirt, a Djarum hanging off the tip of his lips. If he had a smoke on the tip of his lips, something had him rattled. He had an oversize Tommy Hilfiger shirt slung over his shoulders. He tossed that to me.

I'd calmed down enough for me to realize that the kitchen smelled like flowers. Roses that came from their front yard. A six-dollar bean pie was on the counter next to the Black & Decker toaster. Their fridge had a fresh harvest of kiddie drawings taped to the front. Love Mommy. Love Daddy. Love Grandpa. Two *Goosebumps* books were on the kitchen table next to little toys that might've come in boxes of malnutrition disguised as Happy Meals.

I said, "You guys play Beethoven all night?"

"That ain't Beethoven, idiot," Womack said, then turned to Rosa Lee. "That one's Peter Tchaikovsky, right?"

Rosa Lee added, "Symphony Number Five, The Destiny in E minor."

She microwaved us orange spice tea seasoned with honey, then glanced at the time on the microwave.

"Keep an eye on Vince." She shook her head. "I'm going to sleep for a while. Ramona's going to wake up wet and hungry in a little while."

Then she was gone.

My back stung like an insect was gnawing me to the bone. I rubbed my wrists; the handcuffs were still there, invisible but there, cutting deep into my flesh.

Womack said, "Damn-di-damn-damn. Dana burned Kwanzaa's pictures up?"

I didn't answer; it wasn't a question.

He said, "You can crash upstairs at Poppa's."

"You sure about that? I can get a room somewhere."

"No problem. I don't want your butt driving into a light pole or running off a pier somewhere. You know he's got a hideaway sofa in the front room. Louie and Mark are up there sleeping in the bunk beds."

His two older boys stayed upstairs most nights. A two-bedroom duplex with two parents and four kids can start to feel cramped, so everybody spread out. I'd seen his youngest son asleep on their bed. Which was good. I'd hate for the little ones to see me looking torn up like this. That's why I had called from a pay phone before I came over.

Moments like this, when Womack, Rosa Lee, and Harmonica all worked together, made me realize that Womack lived in a village. A true community. Everybody under his roof took responsibility, helped raise the children. Raise each other. Tonight I was younger than his youngest son.

Harmonica woke and went into the bathroom. Stale water mixed with hard water as he emptied his bladder. When he came into the front room, Womack told him that Malaika was back and I'd gotten into it with Dana.

His jowls dropped some. I'd disappointed him. That hurt.

He said, "Even a worm will turn when she gets riled."

I nodded. "Yes, sir. I know."

He stood in the doorway, scratched his belly. "Both of you are young pups on a long chain. Live and learn. Can't sang the blues with no bad times living on yo' breath. It just so happens that a fastidious woman brings out the funereal of a man's soul, takes away his right to felicity."

I said, "Guess you've mastered the F's."

Womack looked at me. "See what you created?"

Harmonica said, "I done got emancipated in the head."

We laughed and yawned. Womack smiled at his old man. Only Harmonica could make a man feel like a juvenile delinquent and have him cracking up when not a damn thing was funny.

Harmonica told me, "Stay long as you need, son. This your port in a storm. Sleep on it. We can talk on it tomorrow if you like." He went back to the bedroom.

When I got settled, I noticed Womack was uneasy.

I whispered, "What's the problem?"

"Rosa Lee did it again tonight. Her gym clothes were bone dry."

I waited.

He said, "I might be getting some outside help I don't need."

Womack went into the bedroom and checked on his two boys. When I headed to the bathroom to drain my anaconda, I caught a profile of him standing in the doorway, smiling down on the little rascals. Never saw a man look so happy. I was a little jealous. Actually a lot jealous.

My best friend left. I went and stood in the bay window and gazed out on South Fairfax Avenue. So quiet over here. I thought about Womack and Rosa Lee. About what Womack had asked me to do.

Rosa Lee was my friend, but I'd known Womack longer. We'd been together as boys, were still tight as men. And I owed him. If I hadn't rented a car from Hertz and had Womack follow Malaika from my home to her lover's den, I never would've known where she'd been creeping. Womack was my backup the night I went rampaging through Moreno Valley and knock-knock-knocking on that door in the middle of the night. I wasn't a fool. He didn't want to do it back then, because, just like I'm Rosa Lee's friend, he was Malaika's friend.

All he was doing was calling his favor in.

I lay down in the dark, stared at the ceiling for an hour. I sat up, scratched my head, pulled my pants back on, grabbed my keys, and headed out the door.

As soon as it opened, Harmonica's voice came: "Son?"

"Yes, sir."

"Thank before you do anythang foolish."

"Yes, sir."

I eased the door shut.

I drove La Brea, took the 10 freeway toward San Bernardino. I was going to ride deep into those drought-ridden boondocks and find Malaika.

I chug-a-lugged as far as the 710 freeway, twenty-five minutes from home, fifteen minutes east of downtown, before my senses came back to life and I realized that the inside of my car smelled like a gallon of gasoline. Damn car was twitching like the fuel injectors were on their last legs. My rearview mirror showed me that I was hell warmed over. And, to be honest, with my mood, it wasn't the best time for a family reunion.

I turned around, headed home.

When I went up my stairs, my landlords' door yanked open. Juanita rushed into the hall, her teardrop-shaped earrings and golden bracelets rattling an anxious waltz. She was barefoot. Pink toenails. Short jean skirt. Sleeveless red shirt tied loosely at the waist. Belly exposed.

Her dark red lips were pursed, but came unglued when she saw me.

I said, "You're up late."

"As are you." Her voice was severe. "Have you seen Naiomi?"

"Afraid not."

She paused like she was waiting for me to change my answer.

I put my keys in my door.

"Vince, I need to have a word with you."

I left my keys hanging in my door, faced her.

She said, "This has been a truly heinous evening."

"Pretty much."

"This situation makes me feel uneasy, and I don't want you to think I'm overreacting. I thought about it all evening. It's best I voice my problem with what seems to be happening. If I don't say what's on my mind, I get too resentful. Nothing personal. I'm being real."

I stood firm.

"How could you hit a woman?" Her finger was aimed at me as she went on, "You're just like them. Billy Dee, Warren Moon, Rodney King, Darryl Strawberry. You're just like them."

My chest was swollen, branded and inflated by misunderstanding. I took a gentle breath and chilled. Told myself not to disrespect Juanita. She had the right to say whatever she wanted tonight. Tomorrow would be different.

"You're uncivilized and unruly. Certain types of behavior have zero tolerance in this building. And a code of ethics, what is necessary for expulsion from the property, is outlined in your rental agreement. I'd suggest that you review that document."

We stared. Her face and body were positioned like she was waiting for a rebuttal. In my Rolodex of insults, outside a bunch of "your momma" snaps, all I could find to say was, "I see."

"I don't want Naiomi associating with you."

"You're saying, don't speak to her anymore."

"After this conversation, to us anymore."

"I see."

"I've made myself clear." The less I said, the bolder her tone became. "I don't want anything to be misunderstood by you, Dana, or myself. Naiomi and I have our own problems that we're trying to work through, and I don't want her getting distracted."

I leaned forward. "Distracted?"

Juanita's expression told me what she meant.

"You think I'm after your woman?"

"I see the crude way you look at Naiomi. I don't appreciate that."

"The way I look at her?"

"Naiomi is very naive. She grew up in Oklahoma, hasn't been exposed to her own culture, and needs to be around positive African American people so she can build herself some solid character. So I don't want her around anyone like you."

I nodded, not in agreement, but anger.

She stayed firm. "Everything understood?"

Seconds passed before I opened my mouth.

"I'll put it to you like this. Your girlfriend has a mind and a mouth. If Naiomi tells me that to my face, then, yeah, understood. Other than that, roll up all that bull you yacked off and use it for a tampon."

"You abusive, misogynistic, lowlife jerk—"

I went inside my own cave, closed the door on her insults.

My place was spotless. Dana had put a new umbilical cord on the phone. The air smelled like Pine Sol, Carpet Fresh, incense. The ashes had been scrubbed away, but the scent from the fire was still in the air.

Dana was gone. Two or three outfits were on the bed, like she couldn't make up her mind what to wear. None of her other clothes was missing, her briefcase was in the corner, so that meant she was coming back. Eventually.

No messages on the machine from Malaika.

They were back. Had been back half a fucking year.

Heels click-clocked up the concrete stairs. Relief cruised through my blood. She'd made it back home okay. There was a pregnant pause. Like she was waiting for me to open my door and stick my head out. Either that or I was witnessing the birth of contemplation. Keys jingled.

The door across the hall opened. Closed. Juanita's voice came, went. Naiomi set free a few leave-me-alone sounds. Then silence.

This had been a pretty fucked-up day. I didn't know if I should laugh, cry, or ask God where the reset button was so I could do this one over.

20 Dana

Gerri was onstage wearing fishnet stockings. Captivating and stimulating, bebopping and hip-hopping. She came out like she was Janet Madonna Jackson—adjusting her glittery bra, slinging off her brown tam, then tugging off the elbow-length leather gloves she had on.

Ten minutes after that Gerri had thrown a white shirt on over her bare skin and headed toward my table.

Gerri said, "Come on in the back."

"You sure about that?"

"C'mon. I have to change. No time to waste."

When I went into the den of mostly naked vixens, nausea set in. My nose scrunched, eyes burned a little. I could've OD'd on the thick smell of nail polishes alone, not to mention all of the different perfumes.

Somebody asked, "Is she a new girl?"

"She's cute."

Gerri shook her head. "Friend of mine. Knock it off."

Eyes rose from the mirrors and vanity tables. A couple of the girls smiled. Others gave me gangster stares. A couple had catty glares sharp enough to cut diamonds.

Gerri changed her outfit, slipped on a black leather G-string that was the size of an eye patch on her kitty cat.

The dancers forgot about me, started back rumbling, helping each other with their wigs and lipstick. Like actors getting ready to go onstage.

Mesmerizing and obscene. I took a glimpse of each woman: black, brown, and pale faces. Wanted to ask what their relationships with their parents were like. Most of them sounded like silly girls who thought they were grown.

Gerri finished in less than a minute—not much to change—then we stood to the side. I told my road dawg about the phone call, about the pictures I burned, the fight, about the police coming and humiliating me.

She shook her head and said, "Jealousy arouses a man's fury and—"

"And he will have no mercy when he takes revenge. Yada, uh-huh, whatever. The same goes for a woman."

She shook her head. "I would've kicked your ass from here to Iraq."

"I didn't do what he—"

"Not the point. Mind games'll get you hurt."

"He came in, foaming at the mouth, making all kinds of accusations—"

She slapped one hand with the other and raised her voice enough to scare me. "The bottom line: what you did was fucked up."

"Shit, thought you were my friend."

"No, you thought I'd say what you wanted to hear."

"Mustang Sally" was bumping wall to wall. The Asian girl was center stage, swinging from that golden bar, showing the world how flexible she could be for a few buckeroos.

Gerri put her hand on my shoulder and said, "Look, youngster, I'm sorry. With all of my shit hanging over my head, I haven't been in the best of moods lately."

"I know. How're you feeling?"

She shrugged. "Worn out."

"You talked to Jefferson?"

"Yeah. This situation is jacked up."

Another pause.

I asked, "How long are you gonna do this?"

"Two more sets, then I'm home to the rug rats."

"No, I mean, how long?"

"Don't, Dana. Not tonight."

Her eyes turned to the women who were getting ready to hit the stage. I don't know what Gerri thought about all this, but I thought of that poster on her wall at home, the one with the slaves.

"Gerri?"

"Yeah, babe."

"Can I ask you something?"

"Make it quick. Gotta go and wrap up this paper route."

I asked, "Is it possible to be in love with two men at the same time?"

My question stopped her in her tracks, made her blink a few times. "Yes, in different ways, yes. You can love somebody, they can stimulate you in some ways, and love somebody else in a different way. It's selfish and frustrating as hell, a hell of a dilemma, but hey, youngster, that's why God gave you two breasts."

She adjusted her blonde wig, and we headed back down the hallway, left the overwhelming odor of perfumes and nail polishes behind.

She went to work. I clutched my stun gun and crossed the room, strutted through the smoke like a 767 cutting through the evening clouds.

So much anxiety. I needed to talk to someone, had to calm down.

Out in the middle of the decadence and carbon monoxide that was funking up Sunset Boulevard, I thought I saw Butter standing across the street. Lingering near a homeless man who was sleeping in a furniture store's small doorway. Dressed in all black. Right underneath a rainbow-colored neon sign flashing in Asian writing. I could have sworn it was Butter, but so many girls in L.A. have that same wanna-be-a-ghetto-superstar look that I couldn't tell.

I forgot about Butter before I made it to my car.

Claudio smiled at me. "I didn't think that you'd call a brother."

"I didn't either."

"So this is the famous Melrose Boulevard," he said.

"That's what the street sign says."

"Sounds like you're in a mood."

"Sounds like."

We got out at a corner. Claudio told the limo driver that we'd meet him back here in an hour. A limo. Claudio had a driver at his disposal. Living larger that I would've ever imagined. A few people stared at us as we put our feet on the pavement, tried to figure out who we were. Stupid people probably thought we were Jada Pinkett and Will Smith.

I was impressed with his apparent success, but I played it down.

He straightened his nylon sweatsuit and peeped around at the secondhand clothing stores. Then we walked by tattoo shops, drug paraphernalia businesses, and sidewalk eateries.

He said, "Looks better on *90210*."

"Everything looks better on the idiot box."

"Here or back home?"

I shrugged. "Babylon is Babylon, no matter where."

"I doubt if you could look any better."

I didn't respond, just absorbed and observed.

He said, "You've lost weight."

That perked me up some. Positivity in the form of vanity. I said, "Few pounds. Gym memberships are cheaper out here, so I joined."

Competition is the life of a woman. Always competing. You look at a sister, even a woman as thin as a toothpick, and no matter how happy you are with yourself, if she gives you a look that says she thinks she's better, it makes you want to lose weight, to be like them, just so you can give someone else that same better-than-you look. Makeup, hair, toes, nails, wardrobe, you go broke so you can look like you're not broke, have to be part of the game and get your share of the attention.

Vince said I had been tripping. Not tripping, just plain old competing.

Claudio asked me something.

I cleared my throat, did the same with my mind, asked, "What?"

"The gym, is that where you met your husband-to-be?"

"Nope. Met him at a club in Ladera. The Townhouse."

"Did he save your life?"

I didn't answer.

Claudio held on to his crooked smile. That pretty smile. Those warm, gray eyes. "I like you better the other way. You know, real brothers like some meat on a woman's bones. Real brothers. Not fake West Coast nigs."

This walk brought back memories. The first time I strolled down Melrose, I was on my fourth or fifth date with Vince. I'd browsed the trendy shops, ate at Georgia's. This was the closest thing to the Village. A place where the car-dependent people of Lazy Angels actually walked more than a block without cramping up.

Claudio said, "Tell me about your future husband."

I slid my tongue back and forth over my lip. The edge had a sting.

I responded, "Let's get something to grub on."

A lot of overpriced eateries were open, but we stayed low-budget and ended up at a small booth in the 1950s-style hamburger stand Johnny Rockets. The place was crowded both inside and on the patio for ground beef on a bun.

Claudio started acting silly, putting change in the jukebox and playing Chuck Berry and Elvis Presley songs.

He asked, "What's it gonna take to get you to come back home with me?"

"A miracle on Thirty-fourth Street."

"Dana, cut that brother loose. I'll get you a much better ring, and we can get married at Canaan Second Baptist."

In a wistful tone I said, "Canaan Second Baptist. God, I miss my church. Miss getting off the A train at 110th, coming out of the subway at Central Park, getting a doughnut at Make My Cakes, then seeing me and my momma's church sitting right across the street. Right there in my face."

Across the street a white couple crossed the street against a red light. Out of nowhere, a policeman pulled up on a motorcycle, light flashing, and motioned for the couple to stop.

Claudio asked, "What's that all about? Shoplifters?"

"Worse. Jaywalkers. Might be a hundred-dollar ticket."

"Shit, they'd have to catch my ass."

"You and me both. That's so damn stupid."

We watched the policeman write the couple up. The white man was livid, his arms flailing. The officer was so nonchalant, just writing away.

Claudio changed the tone of the ludicrous moment: "I went to your mother's grave last Mother's Day."

That made me look at him. "You did what?"

"Yep. I took her a dozen yellow roses."

My words became warm. "You did?"

"You know how much she loved yellow roses."

A huge smile came over me. "Yeah. My girl sure did."

"I talked to her, asked her to forgive me for the way things turned out between me and you. You know she wanted us to be together."

My eyes locked on his gray eyes a long time. My insides warmed.

The waitress came over. Brown skinned. Meaty. Beautiful sister. Young, with a motherly demeanor. Hair pulled back so tight her eyes looked more Asian than mine. Five earrings in each ear. One in her eyebrow.

"Are you and your daughter ready to order, sir?"

Claudio made a hard face and said, "My daughter?"

I laughed so loud half the room turned around.

The waitress blushed. "Oops. It's not that you look old, she just looks so young. I thought you were a teenager at first."

Claudio let out a half-baked chuckle. He took it pretty well, even sounded happy when he said, "Get me a cheeseburger and fries. Well done."

I told her, "I'll have the same."

Claudio added, "But make hers super well done."

"Right," I said. "Make sure I don't get salmonella poisoning."

The girl smiled. "You guys are from New York, right?"

Claudio nodded. "Yep."

That was when I heard it myself. My New York accent had thickened just that quick, in the few minutes since I'd been around Claudio.

"I'm an actress. I study dialects, so I notice that kind of thing. Might learn a thing or two listening to you guys talk." She laughed like she was the genius of the year. "Would you care for anything to drink?"

"No," I said. "Water is fine for now. For both of us."

I was surprised that I'd said that, *For both of us*.

Five years of familiarity with an older man. My father figure, that's what I used to call him. I guess a father figure is what a woman gravitates toward when her daddy ain't been nowhere around.

The waitress took her sweet voice and smile to another table.

Claudio cracked up. "That sister sounded whiter than Wonder Bread. If my back was turned, I never would've known she was black."

"I know that's right."

"So damn polite. Did you check that out?"

We fell into a very old groove. Talked about everybody in the place. Until I saw Claudio was staring at me.

I said, "What're you looking at like that?"

Claudio forced a grin, leaned forward, and lowered his voice. "Damn, you always smell so damn good."

"I still bathe regularly."

"That's a new perfume you got on."

"Yeah, it's Terri El—yeah, it's a new flavor."

He hummed. "Can I kiss you?"

"For what?"

"I want to find out what heaven tastes like."

I didn't move. My eyes stayed firm. Claudio reached to hold my hand, to touch my flesh with his flesh. I moved away, put my right hand in my lap, away from his reach. Wiped the anxiety and sweat and desire from my hands onto my thighs.

"What's on your mind, Dee Dee?"

"Just thinking about Momma. When you said you went to talk to her, now you got me thinking about my favorite Harlem girl."

"Ain't nothing wrong with that. I think about her a lot."

The waitress came back and left our steaming burgers on the table.

Claudio said, "Let's get our grub on and enjoy each other's company."

"What about my money? You said you had some of it, right?"

"I'm gonna hook you up."

"Hook me up? All you have to do is hand it to me."

"You haven't changed a bit when it comes to money."

"A hungry woman always thinks about food."

"Good. Let's eat. Bless the food."

I told him, "The man should always bless the food."

He reached his hands out to me. I hesitated, then gave him mine. Let him touch me again. A touch that was so familiar. That had so much history. Years had gone by, but when we pressed flesh, seemed like only seconds had passed since we were together.

Claudio did his usual childish blessing. The one I'd listened to him do for five years. "God is grace. God is good. And we thank . . ."

In the middle of his prayer, I opened my eyes and looked around. Condom shops on the street next to drug shops next to teenagers who were trying to sell their bodies to get their next meal. Wide is the gate and broad is the way that leads to temptation.

Claudio said, "The food doesn't taste as good out here."

"It's the water. They need to import New York water to add some flavor. And bagels. Somebody out here needs to learn how to make bagels. Or pizza. Out here they actually think Domino's is good pizza."

"Tell me about it."

"Claudio, the water out here is so bad I wouldn't even wash my car with it if I could help it. That's probably why they don't have mosquitoes."

"Or rats the size of dogs."

"God, that is so true."

We ate some more. I enjoyed kicking back and talking about nothing.

He asked, "So what's the problem between you and your man?"

"What makes you think that there's a problem?"

"You're with me."

I blinked twice. A good old tear came from nowhere, was rolling before I could find the strength to wipe it away.

"Shit, Dee Dee." Claudio sat up straight. "What's wrong?"

I told him. Told him about Vince, how he didn't tell me that he used to be married and had a kid until six months after we'd been together. About the arguments, about how he'd moved my picture to the side, about how he'd dissed me in my own space when Malaika called, how he made me feel like I meant absolutely nothing, told him about the fight we'd just had.

"Did he touch you?"

"Let it go."

Claudio looked like he wanted to protect me. He was saying the right things. Not pushing the issue. Listening. Seeing my side of the whole thing. Not like Vince. Or like Gerri.

We ate. Talked about old friends that I'd left behind. People were getting together. Others getting divorced.

Having babies. Some had succeeded, found their dreams and moved away for good. Some had failed at whatever and had gone back to Sugar Hill on midnight trains from Georgia.

So much drama that my West Coast life seemed sane.

Claudio offered me an Altoid. "Remember how we met?"

"Why do you have to go there?"

"I've thought about that every day."

I laughed about it now, but back then it wasn't funny. Not at all. I was so much younger, on my way to another temp job. On the musty subway platform, waiting on the E train in the winter's frigid air with my Walkman on my head. The moment I relaxed and stopped watching my back, my purse was yanked away so hard and fast that I twirled and almost fell facedown into the pits of the tracks. I would've fallen if a man in an Italian business suit hadn't caught my arm. That was Claudio. Miles of people watched the brother run away with my good purse. Not one chased except Claudio. He did his best to run the thief down, but he was caught in the crowd.

Claudio had loaned me thirty dollars, right there on the spot.

My Statue of Liberty had been replaced with the Hollywood sign, Sylvia's in Harlem with Roscoe's in Hollywood, Puerto Ricans with Mexicans, but the intimacy that Claudio had brought me in the last few hours, the emotional closeness in the air made it feel almost as if we had never broken up. Me and New York. Me and Claudio.

The black limo pulled in front of the hotel, its headlights brightening up the palm trees and pavement. The driver came around, held my hand like I was a queen, and let me out. Let Claudio out, treated him like he was a king. Then Claudio told him what time to pick him up tomorrow, dismissed the limo, and came and stood in front of me, smiling.

He asked, "Coming up?"

"Going home."

He came close. Too close. And I let him kiss me. Something that I swore would never happen again. He tasted my tongue. And I tasted his. So familiar. Under the half moon and a starlit sky, there was something I had to know. About my past. About these unresolved feelings. The kiss felt good. Then he tried to massage that growing part of him against a part of me that was becoming damp.

I pushed him away. "Good night, Claudio."

He groaned. "C'mon, Dee Dee."

"Don't let the bedbugs bite."

"It ain't like we just met."

He caught my arm and pulled me back to him.

We kissed again.

He rubbed his hardness on me the whole time.

I moaned and pushed him away. "You probably have a hundred freaks back in Harlem waiting for you to come home."

"Nope. I ain't like that."

"You're lying."

"I'm serious. Come up for a while."

Again I said, "Don't let the bedbugs bite."

"Dee Dee, you shouldn't go back home to him."

"Give me one reason to stay. Shoot your best shot."

"How can you stay with a man that treats you like that?"

I laughed. "The same way I stayed with you."

His voice was fractured, wounded. "Low blow, Dee Dee."

"All's fair in love and war."

"We don't have to do nothing. I just want you to be safe."

"Good night, Claudio. Thanks for the burger."

He asked, "Is it okay to call you at work tomorrow?"

"For what?"

"You said things were tight, right?"

"My cash is shorter than Webster."

"Let me see what I can do."

"Well, if you have a limo at your door, you can do something."

"Anything for you."

I smiled. Felt a rush from the energy and dominance. I took a slow, smooth breath. Relished the feeling. Let it creep into my body, felt its majesty as it filled these lungs.

Then from behind me, in the darkness, I heard my name: "Dana."

Every ounce of air was sucked out of my body.

It was Vince.

21 Dana

Vince was a few feet away, under a streetlight. His body was tight, standing close to where my car was parked. He had appeared out of thin air like the Ghost of Christmas Yet to Come.

"Shit," was the one word that slipped from my mouth.

I blinked, tried to make that shadow vanish, but he was there.

Claudio said, "Look like homeboy followed you."

I wanted to know how Vince knew where I was, wondered if he had trailed me down on Melrose, or even by Gerri's midnight paper route, wondered what he had heard, wondered all of that in the blink of an eye.

Claudio put his hand on my shoulder, said, "Want me to—"

I moved his hand away and said a curt "Stop, Claudio."

Just like that, I was coming apart at the seams. I'm used to busting them, used to being the bust-er, not the bust-ee. No idea what to do.

A stare-down was going on between the men.

Claudio tried to step by me, but I jumped in front of him, politely pushed him back. Vince was watching.

I reminded myself to breathe.

I told Claudio, "Let me go take care of this."

"Unh-huh, no can do. I'll go with—"

"No, Claudio. I can handle this."

Vince lowered his head, turned around, and took unhurried steps to his car. He drove away. Didn't screech, didn't peep back, never called my name again, just drove away.

Again, the word of the night was, "Shit."

"C'mon inside. Dee Dee, c'mon inside. Let that punk ass nig go."

I pretty much jogged to my car, did the same thing that Vince had done. I drove away, sped up until I saw Vince's taillights. My heart pounding, hands sweating. I slowed down when I made it to Centenilia, let him go on, let myself get caught at a light or two. He vanished around the curve. And I sat there, aching, thinking.

"Shit."

Hands wouldn't stop trembling. Ain't no telling what he might do when I got back to the apartment.

I clicked my heels three times. Nothing happened.

The moment I opened the door, I saw Vince was lying on the living room floor, on the carpet, face up, like he had collapsed when he came in the room. The phone was cradled in his arms. Vince moved enough for the hall light that was behind me to lighten up his frown.

I swallowed. "Were you stalking me?"

No answer. His eyes held so much hatred. His breathing filled the entire apartment.

I said, "You walked out on me. I needed you to stay and talk to me tonight. But you walked out. I'd been humiliated. The damn police saw me without my clothes on. Juanita and Naiomi saw, so you know they blabbered it to everybody in the building. I lied to LAPD to keep you out of trouble. And after all of that, you walked out on me like I wasn't shit."

"And you ran to somebody else."

Nothing came from my mouth.

"That was the brother we saw at the Shark Bar."

"Yeah."

"Who is he?"

"My ex."

"How long has he been out here?"

"Not long."

"How long have you been in contact with him?"

"Not long. This was the first time I saw him. I needed to talk, that's all. You wouldn't talk to me, I had to talk to somebody."

Palms wouldn't stop sweating, fingers tingling like I was on the road to a stroke. Heart attack. My heart, so weak just like my mother's.

He asked, "So, you fucking him?"

"Nope. We haven't made any tapes."

"Blow job?"

"I don't believe you said that."

"The night you were out until three, is that who you were with?"

"I was with Gerri."

"What about the tickets to the comedy thing?"

"What, you've been going through my purse too?"

"No more than you've been going through my closet."

We let it rest for a moment.

Finally he said, "All the way back here, my insides were mixed up with thoughts of forgiveness and revenge. That sound familiar?"

I shifted, said, "Yes. I said that to you."

"Must be nice, riding around on a moonlit night in a limo."

"It wasn't planned, if that's what you think."

"I saw you kissing him. Over and over, you kissed him."

I swallowed. "Like I said, we didn't make any tapes."

Vince laughed. Nothing was funny, I was terrified, trying to act cool and confident, wanted him to be to blame, and he laughed.

"I was wishing I had a .22 on my hip. That was scary, wishing that. I've been there before. I know how this story ends."

Remorse was so heavy I could hardly stand.

His voice was ragged. "It's time for you to move."

My throat tightened.

Vince continued, "The woman I marry has to be in my

corner, support me, and accept my daughter. I'm gonna do everything in my power to make sure Kwanzaa knows who her real father is. Those are my parents' only grandchild, the last branch on this tree. If I have to keep living right here on Stocker and Degnan and work two jobs and sacrifice so she can expand her mind and have a life better than this shit I've got, that's what I'll do."

By then my breathing was choppy; I was suffocating.

Vince's voice lowered. "That's my child. You're just a woman I met in a bar. If I had done what I was thinking about doing, it would have been hell for you, jail for me. You owe my child. She saved you tonight."

My chest heaved with regret.

"You burned up my child's pictures. What kinda woman are you?"

He stomped toward the bedroom. My legs were so weak. On the other side of the wall that stood between us, the springs creaked when he finally lay down.

I wiped my eyes; my hands came back dry. I gazed at the old cracks and new cobwebs in the spackled ceiling until everything became blurry, until my eyes watered more than I could stand, until focus was lost.

Then my pager went off. Startled me. I knew who it was.

I muttered, "Fuck."

Vince released a tormented *"Now."*

I responded, "What?"

"Move now. Start packing. Don't be here when the sun comes up."

A chuckle of disbelief came from me. "You serious?"

"Do I sound serious?"

"It's the middle of the night."

"Pack or I'll start throwing your shit out a window."

"I can't take all of my—"

"Take what you can take in one trip. Start packing."

This was some shit. I shook my head and made my way into the kitchen. Clicked the light on. Looked on the counter. They were still there. Vince hadn't been in the kitchen since he came back. Never looked down when the police came knocking.

I picked the photos up, went in the bedroom, and dumped them in his lap. It was hard to talk; one by one, my words crawled out, "These are yours."

He saw that I'd given him the pictures of Kwanzaa. All four were intact. Not a single dent, not a scratch.

His eyes came to mine for what might've been the last time.

"Vince, I burned up pictures of you and me. Pictures I paid for with my own money, that was what I burned. I was upset with you. With me. Mad at us. All I was going to do was change the pictures back in the frames, but I got frustrated. What's funny was you were so stuck on those pictures that you never noticed that the ones we took were gone too."

He stared at the photos in disbelief.

"They were on the counter. Have been there all evening. You ran right by them, came in screaming and accusing, assumed I'd burned them up. I burned up the picture of you, the one I paid for."

His heart-shaped lips parted enough for me to see the tip of his pearly whites, but whatever he wanted to say was trapped in his throat.

My words marched on: "Yes, I have feelings, and if need be, I can be vindictive," I admitted and used the back of my hand to wipe away tears. "I'm not evil like you think I am. I'd never hurt somebody I care about. I'd never burn up a baby's picture."

I wiped my eyes, grabbed a suitcase, started packing.

22 Dana

I woke up underneath a comforter, my head on a pillow as soft as a cloud. As homeless as I wannabe.

Turkey bacon, oatmeal, and toast were in the air. My eyes focused on a huge framed picture of Little Rock Central High School over my head. Took me a second to remember who I was, where I was, that I was in Gerri's bedroom. My overnight luggage and three boxes with a handful of my junk were in the corner, next to her six-drawer dresser.

Somebody tapped on the door. "You awake?"

"I'm always up after three hours of sleep. Come on in."

Gerri came in wearing a red hooded housecoat, slippers, hair in a ponytail, smelling shower fresh. She said, "Good morning."

I took the yellow satin scarf off my head. "Good morning."

"You were tossing and turning."

"Don't you sleep?"

"A mother never sleeps."

I yawned. "A tsunami is doing a number on my insides."

"Right now, I know how you feel."

Again I yawned. "Misery loves company."

"Then I'm your Woman Friday."

I straighted out my cotton NY Giants pj's, something I hadn't worn in a while. I'd grown used to sleeping skin to skin with Vince most nights, with the window up for the fresh, cool night breeze. I ran my tongue over my teeth, licked the sour taste.

A beep-beep-beep came from the microwave. Then the voices of her two rug rats arguing. Everybody in this world was wide awake and talking.

Gerri's daughter squealed, "That was my toast. Put it down."

"Move, fathead." That was her son. "Make yourself another piece."

"Momma, he's eating my toast."

Gerri spoke firmly and softly, "Don't start acting like idiots with me this morning. Give your sister her toast."

"Momma, yesterday she ate my—"

"Give her the doggone toast."

Her son stuck his head in the door. "She ate my toast yesterday."

Gerri snapped, "It's a new day. For the last time, give up the toast."

"Why y'all females always siding up with each other?"

Gerri answered, "Duh, hello, O ye creature of useless testosterone in a queendom of estrogen and eggs."

"What?"

"Because we're females, dodo brain," her daughter said as she pushed Trench aside, stuck her head in the door too. "You're a boy. We rule."

He made a face. "You wish."

"Who got the toast? Useless creature of test-off-you're-wrong."

Everybody laughed.

Trench smiled and straightened his teenage posture. Gerri's daughter, Stacy, was five six with a small waist, caramel skin, shoulder-length auburn hair, round Bambi-like eyes. Dressed in a plaid skirt and white blouse, her school uniform. Her son had the same dimples and happy-go-lucky smile, only he was six feet plus and growing, shaved bald to the bone, with big silver hooped earrings in each earlobe.

"Yo, Dana." Trench slid his leather backpack off his

arm, straightened out his Shawn Kemp jersey. When he smiled, he showed a mouth filled with braces and rubber bands. "What you been up to?"

"What's up, player? How're the grades looking?"

"Dag, why you always on my back?" He frowned, then laughed. "I got a C in English, a B in social studies, the rest are strong A's."

Stacy boasted, "I made straight A's."

Trench playfully pushed her. "Nobody talking to you."

Stacy asked me, "Did you and your boyfriend have a fight?"

"What I tell you about that? Stay out of grown folks' business," Gerri said, then told her son, "Make sure you talk to your English teacher you claim gave you a C and ask what you can do to bring that grade up to a B. Talk to your teacher today, as soon as you can. Show him you're serious. Page me and let me know what he says."

He grumbled. "All he gonna do is make me do extra work."

Gerri shot him a momma look and said, "What was that?"

"Yes, ma'am."

"That's more like it. Don't show off because Dana is here."

Stacy jumped in, "PTA meeting next week. You're on the committee."

Gerri sighed out, "Okay. Did you ask your daddy?"

"He's on the committee too. I want you to sit together so people won't be asking me all kind of stupid questions."

"Be asking?"

"Ask."

"Okay. As long as his breath don't stink."

Trench said, "Momma, I need some new tennis shoes."

Gerri rolled her eyes. "If I have some extra cash, we'll go up Manchester to the Footlocker outlet this weekend."

"The outlet? Aw, c'mon," he griped. "I can't be walking around in no whacked last-millennium shoes from the outlet."

"Then get a job."

"Mom, c'mon. People will diss me like I'm crazy. Shoes up there are played out like the eight-track."

Gerri sighed. "I'll see what I can do. You're gonna have to get a job, and I'm talking soon, so you can get your hands out of my pocket."

She sounded so much like a mother. Gerri wore so many hats in her twenty-four-hour day. And her voice owned a different tone every time. Had to become so many different types of women.

The kids left the room, got ready so Gerri could drop them off. She came in and threw on black spandex tights, two sports bras to hold her load down, cross-trainers, a large T-shirt that made her look like a modest mom, pulled her hair back, slapped a cap on top, shades on her eyes.

Gerri massaged her cheeks. "I'm so stressed my skin is breaking out. See those pimples on my forehead? The makeup I wear at night's not helping either. I've got to go to the dermatologist to get some cream."

I asked, "That bad?"

"When a sister's epidermis starts to feel as rough as Godzilla's backside, it ain't good."

The stress level in her voice went off the scale. Her words thickened and her eyes turned darker than the bra she was wearing.

I asked Gerri, "What's on your agenda today?"

"Well, I was going to ride out to Upland and get my do did at Cuts and Such. I can't be riding around L.A. looking like a Groovy Ghoulie."

"A groovy which-a-what?"

"The Groovy Ghoulies, Horrible Hall. Guess that was before your time."

"Anything before Pac-Man is before my time."

"Damn, I'm getting old."

I laughed. "Getting?"

The smile left her eyes when I teased her, made me feel bad that I did. She went on, "I have a quick meeting down in Manhattan Beach—"

"With a client?"

"One's business, the other personal. Insurance company is tripping, so I have to go see them later. So, I might call Jackie Lynch and tell her to reschedule me for tomorrow or the next day. I think you and I need a break from the madness. We need to get off this merry-go-round for a few hours."

"I know I do. Tired of going in circles."

"Since we are two self-employed divas—"

"That we are."

"—let's cancel our appointments. Play hooky."

"Sounds good to me."

"Two things we can't talk about for the next eight hours."

"What?"

"The first is men."

"The second?"

"Men."

Our workout took us to Manhattan Beach, to a secluded strip right off Rosecrans Boulevard called Sand Dune Park. A hellified hill of sand that climbs toward the sky. We've walked the stairs in Santa Monica a time or two, and those are no joke, but this is the ultimate workout. Gravity and sand make you work your booty muscles and thighs and calves like you wouldn't believe. Every time I put my bare foot in the sand, my foot sinks. People were all over the hill, huffing, puffing, giving out, cramping up, sweating buckets so they could reach the top and catch a view that led straight out into the ocean.

Halfway up, my legs were burning like somebody had cut me and poured Tabasco sauce on the wound. Last night, yesterday, so many days before were on my mind. I know that Jefferson, the singing group, her kids, and her ex-hubby were on her mind, but we talked about other things.

I huffed and told Gerri, "Come on, slowpoke."

"I'm coming. Man, this hurts like hell."

A sister who looked like Lisa Bonet, slender and curvacious, pretty much all legs, went by us like we were standing at a bus stop.

Gerri muttered, "Heifer. Why she gotta make it look so easy?"

We stopped talking and fought the hill, our feet sinking in the sand with each step, butt trying to cramp up, grunted our way to the top. We were in so much pain that we made ugly orgasmic faces over and over. Caught our breath, then ran back down, kicking sand everywhere.

I asked, "How you feel?"

"This is excruciating. But I love it. Back in the day, me and Melvin used to do this hill every Saturday morning."

After a few moments of panting, we hobbled around in the sand with our hands on our hips, down where all the stay-home moms had congregated with their babies. We stretched and stared at that monster hill.

Gerri said, "Back to the top."

"Shit. You must be on ginseng and caffeine."

We tortured ourselves five times, each time getting a helluva lot slower, then twice we sped-walked the stairs that were next to the dune.

We grabbed our bottled water, squirted our faces to wash away the sand and sweat, then sat down on the concrete table in front of the little kiddie playground, talking about what we had promised we wouldn't talk about for the next eight hours.

She said, "So, after last night, the wedding is off."

"Roll the credits and tell somebody to say, 'Sit, Ubu, sit.' "

"Then why are you still wearing the engagement ring?"

No answer from me. Just a surge of heat in my heart. I sipped my water, put more on my face, tried to cool off.

We struggled through two sets of twenty push-ups.

Gerri told me, "At least be the man's friend."

"You care about Vince, don't you, Gerri?"

"You want the politically correct answer or the honest-to-God truth?"

"Let's try the truth."

"Yep. Hell, right now I wish I had seen him before you did."

"He's single. Go for it."

Then she looked sad. "I don't like feeling old. Don't like feeling used up. Don't like this dating thing. I'm feeling old, feeling tired."

I asked her if she was still seeing Jefferson.

"For now," she added. "We have too much business."

"You sleeping with him?"

"Sex is in limbo. It's not about sex anyway. Hell, I've gone two years without sex. I can do it again if I have to."

"Well, good for you. Coochie lockdown ain't my style."

She spoke in a distant whisper, "This was supposed to be my cash cow."

I asked, "So, what's up with the Butter Pecan situation?"

Gerri picked at her nails. "We had to have a business meeting."

"We being who?"

"All parties involved in this stupid three-way. Look, I've invested; I have to protect my kids' money. This record deal could be our cash cow."

"How much you spend so far?"

"Too much to throw my hands up. Studio time ain't cheap."

"And what happened at the meeting?"

"Well, Jefferson told her he loved me. Typical stuff a

man does when he's up against the wall. Did all of that drama in front of Butter Pecan."

"So, he dissed her."

"She played herself. He just told her where his heart is, that's all."

I sucked my jaw inside. "How did Butter react to that noise?"

"Pissed off. Rejection ain't easy."

"Been there, done that, wrote a postcard."

"After our group discussion, I made her an appointment for tomorrow."

"You made her one?"

"Her money is nonexistent, so I'm paying."

"Whose idea was this?"

Gerri swallowed. "The girl has no money, no job, can't take care of herself, no maternal skills. Raising a kid is more than a notion, Dana."

"If you're making her do that, I don't know. That's a crime."

Gerri sounded full of remorse, bothered down to her bones when she said, "Butter is young. She'll recover. Time is on her side."

I didn't know what to say. At the moment I really wasn't too sure if I wanted to be near Gerri.

Her pager hummed; she had it attached in the X of her sports bra, under her sweaty T-shirt. She read the display. "Some idiot's been paging me all week, and all they put in is three digits."

"Probably some pervert who got your pager number off one of your bus benches."

"Wouldn't be the first one. I don't recognize the prefix, unless it's a cell phone. Information said it's a West Virginia area code."

I rocked a second. A light blue truck pulled up behind us, stopped where the street ended and the park began. Two young brothers were inside. One was on a cellular phone. I'd seen them checking us out while we went up and down the hill. Watching butts at sunrise.

They saw me looking back, played it off, and stared at the ground.

I asked Gerri, "Why don't you let Butter and Jefferson handle their own business, then you go on and meet somebody else?"

"With my luck, I'd meet a preacher, he'd embezzle church funds and buy me a big house, then his wife would come and burn it down."

"Not funny."

"Not laughing."

"You are too cynical this morning."

"Dana, my situation ain't like yours. You can date whoever, whenever. I get leery every time I have to start over. I can't bring anybody into my home. For all I know, he could be a woman beater, have bad credit. Hell, I have a daughter who is ten minutes out of her training bra. And I can't have my kids see me with a lot of men. Outside of their daddy, they know I've been on a date or two, but Jefferson is the only one they've met."

Seconds ago, a pin pricked my heart when she said bad credit.

She rambled on, "My outlook has changed, I'll admit that much. Anybody who stays in this wretched dating game long enough will change. A fool buys you a snack at KFC, he thinks he's gonna get a coochie coupon."

"At least you get offered a snack. Men I meet just want a coupon."

Light-hearted chuckles came from our sweaty faces.

She said, "They talk about us, but the brothers have twice as much baggage. And the ones hitting forty, damn, when they take those fly suits off, their guts look like a tub of Jell-O. You can see how they've let themselves go to the dogs. Not the kinda man I want in my bed."

A cool breeze came up and raked our skin.

I said, "Jefferson is fine."

"That the man is. Too fine. He's gonna be a hard act to follow."

She shook her head and chuckled.

I asked, "Wanna share that joke?"

"You know why it's hard being a woman?"

"Nope," I said with mucho sarcasm. "I have no idea. School me."

"You watch TV and all they talk about is being an independent woman, how we don't need men, uh-huh what-the-fuck-ever, and the moment you step into a supermarket, every magazine from *Essence* to *Cosmo* to *Body and Soul* has articles on how to get a man, how to lose five pounds so you can keep a man, how to get rid of a man, how to find your soul mate—we get so many mixed signals, what we're supposed to do?"

When her words faded, I asked, "You believe in soul mates?"

"Whoever invented that crap needs to be shot. If I have a soul mate, and he has a soul, with my luck he's a short man living in China."

"I take that as a long-winded no."

"A big *fat* no. You find somebody and you work at it, good or bad."

"Then why aren't you still with Melvin?"

"Why aren't you with Vince? Why did you leave Claudio?"

No answer, just a lot of thoughts.

I asked her what I'd asked her before, "You love Jefferson?"

"Falling in love is easy. Being in love sucks."

"I take that as an evasive yes."

"Some days it feels like life is passing me by. I want a chance at happiness before this cow goes dry. Don't want to be sad and lonely." She whispered that, then gave me a painful smirk. "Jefferson makes me feel like I'm still young. Melvin, every time I see him, the wrinkles in his face make me feel old."

"Wow."

"Dana, that older-woman, younger-man thang looked easy in the movie."

Another breeze came to visit us.

I told her, "Close your eyes. Think beautiful. What do you see?"

She did. My road dawg started smiling wide, looked almost like a child, and talking so crisp and clear: "My folks' house on Sterling Street and Giles Road. St. Mark Baptist Church on West Twelfth. Little Rock Central High School. Daddy coming home from his job at Kroger. Momma making Sunday dinner on Saturday night. Us on the road to Hope, Arkansas, to see my momma's people, car smelling like fried chicken and sweet potato pie."

She opened her eyes and that smile slowly went away.

"I never should've left Little Rock. Should be with my momma, teaching social studies at Central High or something."

I whispered, "You can always go back. That's why it's called home."

"Nah. Too late. Too much water under this bridge. Cost of living is cheaper back there, I could get a huge spread for what I pay now, but it would be too much of a culture shock. My kids wouldn't be too thrilled to be hanging out at a watermelon festival with a bunch of mosquitoes."

We laughed.

"And you think the picking is slim out here," she said. "How do you tell the single men in Arkansas?"

"How?"

"They have both teeth cleaned."

Gerri laughed. I didn't get the joke. It was too South for me.

"Pager is blowing up." Gerri shifted and took her pager out. "Same number again. I have over twenty messages from the same idiot."

We headed into downtown Manhattan Beach and grabbed some grub on Highland and Thirteenth. The Good Stuff was another spot with an ocean view, where the world was European and shorts and sandals were the dress code.

Earlier, Gerri said she had a meeting with someone. Ten minutes after we made it to the restaurant I saw who it was. It was Melvin.

They stayed to the side, away from me so I couldn't hear, talked for a while, ended up laughing about a few things. He reached out and held her hand. Gerri smiled and blushed, the way a woman does when a man tells her how good she looks. She walked him back outside. I saw them cross Thirteenth Street to the meter parking. She tiptoed and they kissed, lip to lip, and hugged again before she came back inside and sat at the table with me.

I asked, "What was that all about?"

"Nothing. He's picking the kids up when he gets off today."

"Is he working?"

"Yeah. He found a gig at a small company not too far from here."

That was all she said. We ordered. She was still quiet.

Me and Gerri made eye contact. A weak smile came over her face.

Her words were so human. "Yes, Dana. It is possible to be in love with two men at the same time."

23 Vince

"Lisa Leslie or Tina Thompson?"

"Lisa Leslie."

"Man, you a natural-born fool."

"Takes one to know one."

AAA showed up and got ready to drag my ride over to the Nissan dealer, the one in downtown L.A. If the leak in my injectors became any worse, a spark would start a flame and the fire department would be hosing down belts and wires that had been burned like toast. Like what had happened between me and Dana. I'd been in a defective relationship, living in a powder keg, and that phone call from Malaika was the spark that caused the explosion.

LAPD came by. Seeing them made me tense, but they stopped and held off the impatient traffic so the tow truck driver could do his thing.

I said, "That's the thing about police, one minute you hate 'em for what they do, the next you love 'em for what they do."

Womack put out his cigarette. "Just like women."

"Tell me about it."

I'd called Womack so I could use his AAA card, and he'd driven over before the dial tone was gone. A friend in need, a friend indeed. And indeed I was in need. Harmonica was watching Ramona. Womack had a little while before he had to pick his boys up from school.

Womack said, "Don't forget, Nissan has a recall on the fuel injectors for all those Z cars. Any dealer has to fix 'em for free."

My ride was strung up like it had been caught by a lynch mob.

"Mr. Browne?"

Naiomi was coming out of the building, heading for her golden Jeep. Her silver jewelry sparkled in the sunlight. She stopped close enough for me to see she had an open jean shirt over dark blue spandex.

She tilted her blue-lensed shades from her eyes. "What happened?"

I told her that my car would be in the shop for at least a week, maybe two. Nissan had a backlog of defects to deal with.

She said, "Need a ride anywhere, let me know."

"I'm taking vacation from work this week."

"Still, you might need to go somewhere. I'm here for you."

"Juanita will kick both of our butts if I do."

"Let me worry about that."

She smiled and waved at Womack.

She asked me, "How're things between you and Miss Smith?"

"That's a done deal."

"Aw, that's so sad. I was hoping for the best."

"You and Juanita?"

"I'm not sure. One day chicken, next day feathers."

Our eyes, expressions lingered a moment.

Naiomi hopped in her Jeep and zoomed up Stocker, bounced over the dips.

Womack came and stood by me. "Jamaica got hot eyes for you."

"Not her type."

"And Michael Jackson marries black women."

Womack signed the AAA papers, followed us downtown, waited for me to TCB with the dealer. Then we went over on Slauson and grabbed Chinese food at Yee's. Across the street, Gerri Greene's cinnamon skin and freckled face was on a bus bench, light brown hair flowing down over her shoulders,

Kool-Aid smile like she owned this corner of the world.

We sat at a booth. I broke down and told him what was burning to get out of me. Let him know I'd seen Dana getting out of a limo at the Wyndam Belage, kissing her ex-boyfriend, her arms up around his neck, his hand on the round of her ass, slow-grinding their way to the edge of heaven.

"You saw her kissing?"

"Busting slob like it was prom night at Morningside."

"Damn-di-damn-damn. How did you manage to bust her?"

I told Womack that I'd stolen the hotel number off Dana's pager one night, had been checking her pager off and on, saw that number popped up around four times a day. When I got back from his place, the night after LAPD put me on display, and I saw all of her clothes spread out, her dress clothes, that left me feeling uneasy. My male intuition pulled me back to my car. I drove to that hotel, saw her car parked in the lot, its hood turning cool. No parties were going on in the hotel, I'd gone to the lobby and asked. Then I waited. Would've waited for three mornings if I had to. Then that limo pulled up, she got out like she was Queen Sheeba.

After that, I saw what I didn't want to see.

He asked, "What did you do when you saw 'em locking lips?"

"Called her name. Let her see me. Walked away."

"Why didn't you bust his chops like you did, you know . . . ?"

"Dana's not my wife," was my honest answer. "If a man who had done her wrong could show up and get her back in fifteen minutes, she never was mine for the having."

Womack mumbled, "Like Poppa said, a man would be the last one to know."

We ate, let the world pass us by. After the food was

gone, he drove me by the Chinese dry cleaners next to the Dance Collective, then he brought me back home. Small boxes that belonged to Dana were in the bedroom. Those were things she had packed when I asked her to leave, things she didn't take, so I wanted them moved to make some walking space. My buddy helped me lug them down to the garage.

I opened the double locks, and we raised the door on the garage I hardly ever used. The space I shared with my landlords. More of Dana's books, a few boxes filled with other things, waiting for pickup.

Womack motioned at the furniture. "Whose sofa and love seat?"

I said, "Naiomi's. The furniture, the stack of boxes with U-Haul on the side, all of that stuff is what she had when she was married."

A voice called out from the other side of the gate. "Hello. Excuse me. Hello. Who's back there in my garage?"

I stepped to the side so I could be seen. It was Juanita.

She was in jean shorts and a T-shirt, a red silk scarf around her head, pieces of her golden hair sticking out. She was coming out of the laundry room, a bright yellow basket of white clothes on her hips. Womack spoke to her. She returned a brief hello, nothing for me, but her gaze told me that conflict and misunderstanding lived between us.

She left. Her stride, soft and easy. As indifferent as the wind.

Womack groaned out a sorrowful feeling.

I said, "What's wrong?"

"You see those legs. That's a waste of natural resources."

We headed through the back gate, passed by the row of plastic garbage cans, moved toward the wooden stairs that led to my back door. Womack wanted to talk. Mostly about Rosa Lee. About his fears that were clogging his heart. My ill feelings were sheltered.

He asked, "When you want me to get that rental car?"

I asked, "You sure you want to do that?"

"What you mean?"

"Look where it got me."

"I really need you on this one. Like you needed me."

I told him that I'd been through West Hell over the last few hours. Couldn't take anymore, not right away. Told him to think about it a day or so. He made an unsure sound when I didn't give a solid answer.

Womack left, massaging his neck, head held low.

I checked my messages.

Malaika had called.

Around eleven the next morning, Juanita and Naiomi

24 Vince

Around eleven the next morning, Juanita and Naiomi were out front hugging like schoolgirls at recess. Juanita ran her fingers through Naiomi's braids, a glow in her eyes. Minutes later, Juanita headed toward her car; Naiomi was out front in her gray sweats, playing with the brim on her Mighty Ducks baseball cap, leaning against a dirty Chevrolet.

Juanita's little red Toyota backed away from the curb and putt-putted toward MLK Boulevard. They waved, blew soft kisses.

Naiomi ran upstairs, and soon she banged on my door.

"Hurry." She had changed into a peach skirt and an upscale multicolored blouse. No bra. "Thought she'd never leave."

"Why were you two brawling at the crack of dawn?"

"Oh, she had her panties in a bunch because I played one of her funky CDs and didn't put the darn thing back on the rack in alphabetical order. I put Sade after Sting, and that heifer had a cow."

"Kind of meticulous."

"More or less. But the real reason she's mad is because she don't know where I was most of last night. She thinks I was out cat'n."

"Where were you?"

"Out cat'n." She laughed. "Now hurry, walk up and meet me up at the mall. Be on the bus stop outside of Founder's in about twenty minutes."

* * *

Naiomi's temperamental Jeep rattled down La Brea toward Pico Boulevard and the Mid Town Shopping Center. While the winds tossed a Snickers candy wrapper around the cab, Naiomi told me to stop checking my face in the mirror and quit wringing my hands. There was an oil leak, and the grease stink drifted in through the vents. Extra cans of 10W40 were in the back bouncing around along with extra water in an antifreeze bottle.

Naiomi leaned forward, struggled, pulled a pack of cigarettes from underneath her worn seat cover. "Closet smoker."

I wasn't paying attention. My mind was sorting through my past, getting ready for the future. A rap tune came on. Naiomi frowned, changed the radio to soft rock. An old Madonna love song was playing. Naiomi's cocoa face turned ecstatic, like she'd found the goddess of blue-eyed soul. Naiomi puffed and yodeled along, sounded like a whale in heat.

She laughed a little, confessed, "Closet rocker."

"Anything else you plan on bringing out the closet?"

She laughed a lot. "Never knew you had a sense of humor."

"I don't. Naiomi, why you going out your way and risking yourself by bringing me out here?"

"I want you to see your child." Then her voice went soft, deepened and sounded serious. "I understand what it's like to miss your baby."

"What do I owe you for the favor?"

"Put your money away. I might get you to do me a favor."

I asked, "What kind of favor?"

"Get your mind out the gutter."

"That's your mind slumming."

"I can't get my modem to work on my computer."

"What happens?"

"Juanita lost her mind because I was on the Internet,

chatting with somebody I'd met in blackvoices, and she did something to it. Now when I try to log on, the stupid computer says that it can't find the modem. I was hoping you could look at it for me."

"That's an easy fix. Sounds like Juanita has unplugged it."

"Unplugged?"

"Yeah. The same way somebody unplugs a telephone. Look at the back of the computer and see if the phone line is running to the modem."

"That cow."

I asked, "Anything else?"

"Since we're on the subject, pillow behind the headboard."

"What?"

"Pillow behind the headboard. Next time you have a woman over and you're getting busy, put a pillow behind the headboard."

"You heard us?"

"A time or two. Y'all be moaning on that squeaky bed. You need to work on your rhythm. Sounds like you need to work on your endurance, too, 'cause the moaning don't last till morning."

I said, "If you do it right, don't take all night."

World on Wheels was the urban skate haven where I used to take Malaika. Back in the day, it was our Friday night hideaway. Womack, Rosa Lee, all of us used to come here. Thought those days would never end. Friday night was the night that the riffraff and gang-bangers didn't show up to get their boogie on because it was gospel night. Upbeat, spiritual funk.

Malaika was outside at the door, waiting in a crowd of hip-hop'n teens who were lined up with roller blades dangling over their shoulders. First my heart stopped, then it did an anxious dance. I nodded at my ex-wife; she barely responded.

Naiomi mumbled, "Oh, boy."

I hopped out. Naiomi went to park on the side nearest the Bank of America. Malaika's shoulder-length hair had been cut, colored golden brown, slicked back in a wavy style. Her loose jeans, black military-style boots, and FUBU top showed how well she'd been taken care of. She stood there, brown leather purse over shoulder, restlessly jingling her car keys.

Yesterday had become today.

We looked at each other for a second. I smelled her perfume, soothing and sweet. Her attitude had a stench like pork gone bad. That sent a chill up my back.

Malaika said, "I was just about to give up on you."

"You're pretty good at giving up."

"Don't start."

A rough second passed. "How've you been?"

"Blessed. And you?"

I shrugged away her righteousness. "Surviving."

I took short steps, moved the unsure way an intelligent man approached a wild horse. My bygone took her fist off her narrow hips, the hand with the glittering wedding ring, slid the other into her back pocket and held on to her butt. Her right hand came up to her neck, massaged like she was reliving the pain from when I'd touched her in anger. I saw that memory in her eyes. She saw the memory of me finding her fucking somebody else in mine.

She was my first love. The one I would've died for. No matter how many times a man fell in love, he never tumbled like that again. Never as far. Never as deep. Never as hard.

Malaika cut to the chase, said, "Remember our arrangement?"

"Yeah." My mouth smiled under my frowning eyes. "Sure."

She wanted to go in first, said she had a seat inside with some friends, to the right by the video games. She told me not to skate, just to stray to the left and stand near the rail.

She said, "Don't go near my child."

"My child."

"My child. Don't go near her."

"I won't."

"Don't let me down, Vince."

Another nerve was struck. "Malaika, if she doesn't re-member me, what difference would it make if I went in with you?"

She fingered her wedding ring. "Don't cause a prob-lem."

To tell the truth, I was afraid. Afraid to see my own child, because I was afraid of what she would see when she saw me. If she was indifferent, that would hurt just as much as it would if she despised me.

At least three hundred people were inside, ages eight months to eighty years. Mostly black people. I moved toward the benches, stood next to the rail, and watched Kwanzaa. My insides were on a roller coaster. She struggled to skate lap after lap, but she fought and did it. She'd slimmed out, more than doubled in height. Overprotective Malaika had her decked out in a hel-met, knee, and elbow pads. Other than the battle gear, she had on jeans and a top the same color as her mother's. It was easy to tell that my child was her daughter. That they fit into each other's lives. And I was the man on the sidelines, out of the game. Kwanzaa's mane was pulled back into a shiny dark brown goddess braid. Seeing her so big kept me wondering what parts of her life I had missed. Made my heart bleed.

Malaika put on her in-line skates, danced backward for a few laps, mixed with the serious skaters, then slowed down and took Kwanzaa's hand. The last time I was with Malaika, she couldn't skate backward. Back then Kwanzaa couldn't talk or walk without falling on her rear.

I scanned the room and tried to find the thief who had put on my shoes. When I looked to my left, Naiomi was smiling.

"She looks like you, Mr. Browne."

I blushed. "Think so?"

"Thick eyebrows. Thick fingers. Ashy elbows."

Naiomi had put on skates. She grooved with the beat, rolled over the lime carpet, passed video games, and whizzed out onto the floor. After a couple of laps of bouncing, rocking, and rolling, she slowed next to Malaika and Kwanzaa. Naiomi said something. For a brief second Malaika turned toward me, then smiled and shook Naiomi's hand. Naiomi pointed at Kwanzaa's shoe. They stopped. Malaika held Kwanzaa steady while Naiomi bent over and tied the loose string. Kwanzaa laughed. A joyful sound I longed to hear. Malaika smiled. Kwanzaa went right back to skating. Naiomi sped off in the bopping crowd. I stayed put. I wanted to run out and grab my child, but I did just like I had promised. Stayed put.

Naiomi tried to get fancy by crisscrossing her legs and doing a 360-degree turn. She fell flat on her booty, tripped two little boys. She held her skirt so her draws wouldn't show. Damn near every booty-watching brotha on the floor tried to skate over and help her. They left the little boys stretched out like dead men in a coffin.

Malaika left Kwanzaa with some adults, her friends I guess, searched for me with her eyes, head-signaled to meet her near the exit. When she passed me, I let a few people get in between us, stayed a few feet behind and followed her into the lobby.

She led me outside, up the asphalt walkway, took me around the corner on the side of the building.

I asked, "Where's your second husband?"

"Why?"

"Thought I might get introduced. Formally. It'd be nice to see him under more reasonable circumstances."

"You came to see my daughter."

"Our daughter."

Malaika put her hands in her back pockets, exhaled, and said, "Kwanzaa's smart. Too smart for her age."

"She got that from my side of the family."

She coughed, ignored me, said, "She's asking questions."

"About what?"

"I was teaching her to write her name and my name—you know, just in case something happened—and she realized her last name was different from mine. She wanted to know why her last name is Browne and mine is Quinones. People say things that make her ask about things."

"What kind of things?"

"Things that make her ask questions I'm not sure how to approach. The other day she asked me if she was adopted."

For a moment Malaika's voice softened to the point of pain.

I waited for her to tell the rest.

She went on, "She saw something on TV, then came to me almost ready to cry. She's sensitive and gets upset very easily. And one of her friends has a different last name, because her mother has remarried too, so Kwanzaa wants to know if she has two daddies like her friend does."

"Why don't you tell her the truth?"

We caught a view of Kwanzaa when she and the other children ran across the parking lot. My ex touched my arm, moved us behind an SUV.

She said, "I'm going to have a talk with her about you."

"What about Drake?"

"Thanks for the money you've been sending."

"Don't thank me for doing what I'm supposed to do."

"Thank you, anyway." She nodded. "I'll be in touch."

Malaika stalled and stared. She intimidated and irritated me. That uncaring face housing her insensitive words.

Malaika said, "She might be singing in L.A."

I grinned. "She sings?"

Malaika smiled. "She got that from my side of the family."

We shared a laugh, a positive moment.

Malaika shifted back into her all-business persona. "I might invite you. Just to watch your daughter."

The sun rose over my soul. I asked, "When?"

"If it happens," she said, didn't smile, but her words were friendly, "same conditions as today. Agreed?"

"Okay, sure, no problem. When?"

"I'm just going to think about it, that's all. Vince, it's just that she doesn't know you."

"Not my fault. Not my fault at all."

"Stop placing blame. Listen, I know she's going to hate me for what I've done. That worries me. I don't like the fact that I've lied to my child."

Sounded like Malaika had told Kwanzaa the same lie that I'd told Dana. So many lies had been told, and I wondered which ones were forgivable.

She moved restlessly. "Are Rosa Lee and Womack still together?"

"Yeah." I smiled. "They just had another baby."

"Rosa Lee's popping them out, huh?"

"Yeah. But she's done. She's quit at four."

"Thought she was going to quit at three."

I chuckled nervously. "So did Womack."

"You haven't had any more, have you?"

"Nope. Not yet."

There was a pause. A very uncomfortable pause.

"The Lord willing and the creek don't rise—" Malaika stopped. She bobbed her head, finger combed her hair. " 'Lord willing and the creek don't rise.' Remember, Harmonica used to say that?"

I said, "He's still living. Strong as an ox."

"Good. I think about him from time to time."

Seeing Malaika now, seeing her doing so well, got me to thinking about what I'd been doing for myself. I'd been treading in place since she left. She'd moved on.

Then she jarred me, "My momma died."

"Miss Joanne died? When?"

"Six months ago. That's why I came back. I had to put everything in order. Then you sent another check. So I called."

"I know."

Malaika said, "Until I collected Momma's mail, I didn't know that you were sending Kwanzaa any money or keeping in contact."

"She didn't tell you?"

Malaika shook her head. "She sent money, but she never said that any of it was from you. Guess she took that secret to her grave with her."

"She hated me."

Malaika didn't deny my accusations.

She continued, "What I was saying was, if the Lord's willing, I'll be having my second baby in about six months."

I kept the twinge of jealousy subdued. I smiled some, said my warmest "Congratulations."

"Vince, I'm sorry things turned out like this. It's just that, well after . . ." Again she paused. "Things were pretty bad between everybody. Not only Momma, but Drake thought it was best for me to cut all ties with you. Especially after we left the country."

Regret was the mask that covered her face. Mine too. I let her know what I felt: "This ain't right, Malaika."

"I'm trying to keep my marriage together."

"He doesn't know you talked to me since you've been back?"

"No. But I'm going to tell him."

"Why do you need his permission?"

"Vince, this is hard enough as it is."

I stood and listened to how she'd let another man take control of her life. She didn't say control, but when you gave up your right to do what was right, that was what you gave up. Control.

"Well, I'd better go. Kwanzaa's looking for me."

Her face blossomed into a wide smile as she jogged off and called my only child's name. I mumbled the same name and remained hidden in the shadows. Played by the rules. They held hands and hurried to their Paseo. Kwanzaa jumped into the front seat. The Mexican child got into the back.

I stood on the side, wondering what Kwanzaa's voice sounded like. What girlish texture it had. I wanted to hear her laughter. The pitch of her cries when she woke from a bad dream. Wondered what kind of food she liked. What she didn't like. Her favorite color. Her favorite song. What she smelled like if I held her close and tickled her belly.

There were a lot of things I didn't know.

And if all that was true, that meant I didn't know her. And if I didn't know her, I couldn't expect her to call me daddy.

Naiomi came to where I was, under the shade of the awning.

She touched my hand and said, "Mr. Browne?"

I pushed my lips up into a polite smile. "Yeah?"

"It'll be all right, Mr. Browne." Naiomi slid her fingers between mine and held my hand. Her voice softened. "Stop crying before you make me start boo-hooing like a fool. You gonna be okay?"

I wiped my face. "Everything's cool."

We went to her Jeep but didn't get in. Stood in the shade. Words running low. Emotions running on high.

She sniffled, shifted, did nervous things with her hands.

I asked her, "You okay?"

Naiomi said, "I was thinking about my little boy. Your ex seems like a good mother. I could tell by the way your child reacted to her with smiles and hugs. Made me miss being with my son all the time, that's all."

"When was the last time you saw him?"

She smiled, wide and strong. "That's where I'm coming from when I creep in late at night. A lot of times, I miss my boy and I cruise down the 605 to Cerritos and stay until my baby boy goes to sleep."

"Oh, I see. Creeping with your ex husband?"

"Heck, no. He's remarried. To somebody his own age."

"How old is he?"

"Sixty-five. I married to get citizenship."

"You married to get his discount at Denny's."

She thought that was knee-slapping funny. "We had a kid, tried to stick it out, but it didn't last three good months."

I asked, "Not seeing anybody else?"

"Nah. I'm a one-woman kinda woman, or a one-man kinda woman." She laughed like she'd told the world's best joke. "Depends on the season."

Her laughter was contagious, made me chuckle a while as well.

At first we were strangers, then neighbors. Today I needed a ride, and we were friends.

I wondered if what Dana felt was normal, so I asked Naiomi, "So, how does Juanita feel about you having been married and having a kid?"

"She could care less. She wants me to bring my son to live with us. And I'm not comfortable with that thought."

"I see. Your problem is one hundred eighty degrees from mine. But your situation puts a little more on your table."

"Not because I'm living with Juanita. I'm comfortable with who I am." She bobbed her head. "It takes harmony to raise a family. And my ex would drag me through court. It's not worth it. The pain, I mean."

A beat later, she laughed lightly. "Mr. Browne, let's run away."

I winked. "Changing horses doesn't mean the ride'll get any better."

"You get Kwanzaa, I'll get my Otis, and we'll go to Mexico. I'll be your *señorita*, you can be my *papi*. Enjoy sunsets. We can do this."

I said, "And live off of beans and corn?"

"And whatever fattening food they eat down there."

Now we were parents joking about our troubles, expressing a longing. In between the jokes, Naiomi put her hand on my shoulder, got my attention. Gave me soft, womanly eyes. Stared deep, sent a dangerous message, one that couldn't be misconstrued. When I turned away, she moved her hand.

"You know what, Mr. Browne?"

"What?"

With warm eyes she said, "You're decent."

What I saw in her eyes was what I wished I got from Dana.

We went to the Beverly Center, ate downstairs at California Pizza Kitchen. I paid. We weren't ready to go home to play out our individual dramas, so we rode the Pacific Coast Highway, drifted close to Malibu, ended up parked near Gladstone's restaurant. We sat on the rocks, right over waves that were wetting the debris in the dirty brown sand. Just like I'd done on my first date with Dana, I closed my eyes and inhaled the ocean's salty breath. Ocean air, a fading sun, a rising moon. Night was on the way. Naiomi sat close to me, her back to my shoulder, using my body to block the light breeze and keep warm. I needed her heat.

She told me, "No more talk about your ex-wife. Or Miss Smith. No talk about Juanita. Or our children. Let's let it all go for now."

"Okay."

We talked about nothing. Communicated about everything. Had pleasant moments. Which was dangerous for two people with rumpled feelings.

The heat from her breast was resting on my arm. I closed my eyes and ached with that good feeling. My hand eased around her waist. The ocean was spanking the shore when she leaned into me. Seagulls sang when I kissed the silver ring in Naiomi's eyebrow.

Her lips glowed. She made a pouty face, spoke like her insides were on fire. "A romantic, moonlit night on the beach, and that's it?"

Her lips parted. I went inside her warmth. Her tongue was stiff at first, reluctant. Her eyes were open. I did a slow move and groove, did the taste test, relished the flavor I savored, was amazed by her rhythm, and hoped my breath wasn't too funky while I harmonized. Her body relaxed, eyes slowly closed, tongue softened up. Breathing became heavy, her hand on my face, rubbing my beard. She made an orgasmic sound and pulled away.

"Okay, all right, okay." She fanned herself. "That's enough."

"What's wrong?"

"You kiss like . . . hmmmm . . . you know."

"What?"

She shook her head, said, "Like you're having oral sex."

That line had been crossed.

I leaned away, but she pulled me back. Kissed me. Kissed my neck, danced her tongue up to my ear, moaned her way inside my mouth. She trapped my tongue, sucked it in and out, like she was giving me some serious fellatio.

She said, "Do you want to go to the Hilton?"

I chuckled.

She didn't.

We tongue-danced again for a while, until it felt right. She put her head on my shoulder. That excited sensation that came from doing wrong—I wondered if that was the thrill that Malaika felt when she was creeping. Wondered if that was what Dana felt when she tipped out with Claudio.

I asked, "How did you hook up with Juanita?"

"We were both going out for the LAPD. I'd run into her when we took the written test out in Hollywood. I was just leaving my husband then, trying to understand, reinvent myself, struggling to be independent again. We were up by Dodger Stadium, at Elysian Park taking the physical agilities test at the same time."

Naiomi laughed.

I asked her what was funny.

She said, "Neither one of us could get over that damn six-foot concrete wall. Both of us were miserable because we have allergies, and it was springtime, so everything was in bloom. By the end of the day my eyes were swollen like golf balls."

"And you've been together ever since."

"Yep. We dated awhile. Movies. Dinner. Dancing at this gay club down in Long Beach. Think I fell for her in Starbucks in Marina Del Rey, over a cup of flavored coffee while we sat and talked. We made love that night. It was awesome. She was awesome."

"So she's good in bed."

"She's good. Very enthusiastic and creative. But I'm better."

Just like she'd heard me through our wall, I'd heard her. I gave ear to the waves. Seagulls added their melody to the music of the night.

Naiomi said, "Communication."

"What about it?"

"Strange things happen when people talk and get to know each other. When they get comfortable with each other."

I agreed by not disagreeing.

"Naiomi? Can I ask you a personal question?"

"Sure."

"What do you see in another woman?"

"Same thing you do, Mr. Browne. Same thing you do."

A moment passed. The waves crashed a few times, water splashed high and spread up on the rocks near us. The moon was tugging and the tide was getting higher. Behind us, up over the short hill, sixty-mile-per-hour traffic sped down PCH. Boats were drifting out in the Pacific.

And Naiomi was drifting closer to me.

I never wanted to leave this place.

I asked Naiomi, "How're you going to get over the wall that's in front of you now?"

"What wall?"

"Your relationship."

She said, "Nice metaphor."

"Thanks."

She smiled. "The same way you are, Mr. Browne."

"How's that?"

"I'll either get strong enough to pull myself over, walk around it, or turn around and go back from where I came."

"Back to Oklahoma?"

"Nah. I've outgrown Guthrie. I don't think the Jehovah's Witnesses would take me back, anyway. I'm a gypsy at heart. I try to stay in one place, but my feet start itching before long. I want to see the world."

I asked, "How does Juanita feel about that?"

"What she doesn't know won't hurt her until I'm gone."

Naiomi shrieked, jumped, grabbed my arm so tight it hurt.

I jumped with the pain. "What's wrong?"

Her words came out fast: "I saw a rat."

"A mouse?"

"No, a rat about the size of Mickey Mouse."

It was time to go.

On Highway 1, when we were near her Jeep, Naiomi said, "You never answered my question."

"Which one?"

"Would you like to go to the Hilton?"

It was almost nine o'clock when Naiomi dropped me off a few blocks from my place. She didn't want Juanita or anybody in our building to see us together.

She ditched her Jeep in front of the homes on Edgehill, waited a few minutes, then tiptoed up the seedy alley behind our building. She stayed close to the garages, moved like a cat. There was enough music and chatter coming from the house behind our building to cover her footsteps.

I prowled into the darkness from Degnan, gravel and debris crunching under my shoes. Me. Naiomi. Sneaking toward each other, slow and easy.

Nobody strolled the alley behind our building at night. At least nobody sane. We gave each other warm eyes, glanced toward our building. The light was on in the laundry room. Neighbors' windows were pitch black. Naiomi stared at her apartment. Her kitchen light was on. A dish clanked. Juanita was moving around, laughing. Powder blue satin robe on her light skin, on the phone, making sweet faces as she yakked and poured herself a glass of wine.

I said, "She's waiting for you."

"Let her wait."

There were six double garages for our twelve units. Two locks on the opposite side of each door. Naiomi undid the padlocks to the garage we shared. I pulled the wooden door up, slowly, to minimize the creaking.

We stepped inside.

Silence.

No dry wall between the attached garages. Could see from one end of the building to the other, echo to echo. Cars and trucks were in the other stalls. I eased the door back down, kept it from banging and rattling.

Me. Naiomi. In the dark. An awkward moment.

I said, "It's dusty in here."

"Mr. Browne, we didn't come in here to talk about dust, did we?"

"No, we didn't."

She danced her warm tongue around my mouth as soon as my words faded, ran her fingertips across the small of my back.

She whispered, "Welcome to the Hilton."

No wine. No candles. No room service.

Naiomi led me around dusty boxes, across oil-stained concrete, beyond cobwebs. We moved back until we bumped into the cream-colored leather sofa and love seat.

I threw the dusty cover over her washer and dryer.

She dug a condom out of her purse, waved it at me. I had a virginal chill. Once again I was sixteen, cutting class at Morningside High, sneaking inside a girl's house while her momma was slaving at work.

She sat me down on her throne. The soft leather sighed. I pulled her silky blouse up, kissed her belly, lagged my tongue across her small brown breasts. She leaned and sucked my nipples *mmm* and put a zillion tingles in my belly. Then she bit me. Pain felt so good.

My thoughts strayed to Dana. Seeing her face in my mind made me impotent. But Naiomi soon made me hot enough to boil water. Steam rose in thick vapors, clouded the vision of Dana's face. Lifted that heavy troubled man who was holding me down. I turned her around, hiked up her skirt and nibbled her buttocks. A mixture of soft and hard bites.

I rolled the condom on. Naiomi slid her thong panties off.

Her jewelry clanged an anxious sound. She lifted her skirt, put a knee on each side of my thigh, smirked like she was living in the land of victory.

I was there. Inside Naiomi's hideout.

Naiomi was a little woman with a lot of space. I was about to feel inadequate, but she moaned, did a sweet measuring, like she was calibrating her love to what I had to offer, eased into a sweet rise and fall. I was praying that I didn't shame myself and come before she did. Her kisses were the sugar that made this coffee taste so sweet. I struggled to open her blouse. She was just as rushed and frantic as I was. She helped me with the buttons. Her breasts, I squeezed them softly, lagged my tongue over the tips, moved my hands up to her neck, across her braids, a tingle inside me turning into a blaze, fire growing in my gut, curling my toes.

If this was the sensation of sin, the world should go to hell.

One of her block heel shoes fell from her feet, clopped on the concrete floor. Our rhythm became severe, deep. Her other shoe slipped off.

Music blasted from nowhere. Right outside the garage door. Might've been another one of our neighbors getting ready to park back here. Naiomi stopped on a dime, shut her moans off like water in a faucet, then shifted her weight like she was preparing to hop up and hide behind the boxes.

The car kept going.

She panted out the breath that she'd been holding, whispered while she rolled her hips and chewed my lips, "Mr. Browne?"

"Yeah."

Her sweat dripped in my face. "Relax. Feel my rhythm."

She made me feel comfortable, no pressure to perform or impress. Just sit back and enjoy the ride. Work on my rhythm.

Oh God Oh shit Oh Juanita—I mean Mr. Browne.

Practice endurance. Be submissive.

Oh God Oh shit Oh Mr. Browne.

I was inside a dusty garage, but the gratification I was getting took me far away. My sweat and her sweetness made me feel like I was on the island of Waikiki, loving under green spectacular mountains, thundering surfs, and powdery white-sand beaches. And Naiomi was my Polynesian dancer, giving me a feeling so good that I could spend a million days lost in her loving, smiling while her braids danced a hungry tempo in my face, letting her drops of sweat rain on me and wash away all the bad times. Every last fucking one of 'em.

Naiomi trembled. Her forehead bumped into mine as she asked in a horrified whisper, "Where did it go?"

I shifted her to the side, put my hand up and down my

penis. Nothing there but moisture and softening skin. "Hold on."

Her body tensed, locked, and her voice, growing with panic, bonged out like a prayer. "Mr. Browne, please tell me the stupid thing is still on you. You got it, right?"

"I can't find it. It must've come off."

Naiomi sneezed twice, both times her vagina tightened around me.

She asked, "Inside of me?"

"Nowhere else for it to go."

"Oh God Oh shit Oh Mr. Browne. Damn, damn. When?"

"I don't know."

"Before or after?"

"I don't know."

She snapped, "You couldn't tell when the thing came off?"

I said, "No more than you could."

Somewhere between the *oohs* and the *ahhs* and the magic that wouldn't last forever, Mr. Latex had done a disappearing act.

Naiomi shivered and panted while I eased her off me.

She jumped up, squatted like she was trying to squeeze it out. Nothing came out of her body but a couple of farts.

Panic. Heavy breaths. Rustles in the darkness. Fear crackled.

Her voice was in tears. "I don't need any more drama right about now."

I pulled my pants all the way up.

She trembled. "Well, don't just sit there. Help me find it."

"How?"

"How do you think?"

Ten minutes of her lying on her back with me acting like the gynecologist of the year, and I couldn't find the damn thing. That sugary song of pleasure we'd been singing had become a melody of blue.

She snapped, "Are you sure you put the condom on?"

"What do you mean, am I sure?"

"I mean, are you sure?"

"Yeah, I'm sure."

Naiomi yanked her skirt down, ran her fingers through her braids over and over. She found her shoes, held one in each hand, stared into space.

Her voice had an arctic timbre, a side of her I'd never seen. "I know it's too late, but can I ask you a personal question, Mr. Browne?"

"What?"

"Have you had any questionable sex?"

I kept my tone level when I asked, "What do you mean?"

"You know," her voice softened more, "questionable sex."

My brows furrowed. "You mean, have I ever been with a man?"

"Yeah."

"*Hell, no.* Why you ask me something like that? You had the condom."

Her words were quick and snappy. "I work part-time at a center, that's why I have condoms, to pass out for prevention."

"I only go one way."

"I don't believe this. Don't believe this."

I said, "What about you? Any questionable sex?"

"I'm cleaner than the board of health." She put her purse over her shoulder, didn't glance back before she eased the garage door half open. Words labored from deep in her throat, "See you around, Mr. Browne."

She slipped out and eased the door closed on the Hilton.

The aroma of her rose from my lap, through the dust, into my nostrils. My head was low. Again, I'd become the kid on *Leave It to Beaver.* I'd learned my lesson, forgot my lesson, then was reminded of the lesson I'd lost.

Barefoot, low-spirited footsteps moved up the back

street toward Edgehill, tipped over crunched debris. A
Jeep's engine started. Tires rolled east to west through
the alleyway. Gears shifted. Zoomed toward the streets.
Sped away from Stocker and Degnan.

25 Dana

Vince didn't see me. When I saw him with Naiomi, my braids wanted to stand straight up. I was right there the whole time.

I had picked up the information off the answering machine, wrote down what Malaika had said about meeting her at the skating rink, used my little old Thomas Guide to find my way over to Mid Town. Ya know, sometimes this other side gets a grip on me and I have to go with that flow. That's why I was down at World on Wheels before Vince and Naiomi showed up. Took my booty down there early and hoped that Malaika would be there before he arrived and not get here up CP-time.

That sister-girlfriend-ex-wife was there before I made it to the skating rink. I walked right by her three or four times, smiling every time, stood right next to her while she bought Kwanzaa a soda.

I told her, "You child is so pretty."

Malaika thanked me and smiled.

"You and her daddy brought her out for some fun?"

She chuckled. "It's just the girls today."

No hubby on the scene. She looked right at me, smiled, heard my East Coast accent, had no idea who I was. Her eyebrows were plucked to perfection. Her jeans, a little tight. She'd carefully chosen what she was going to wear.

Kwanzaa ran over to the video games with the other kids.

Malaika told a lady with her, "He should be here any minute."

"You nervous?"

"Yes. Just hope I'm doing the right thing."

It's not the kid. Was never about Kwanzaa. It's the other woman that makes me uncomfortable. If I hadn't seen that tape from their marriage, hadn't heard him begging her, it wouldn't be so bad. I don't know any other woman who could stand to watch her man become weak the moment another woman's voice reached his ear. No woman wants to see her man crumble for another woman.

I went back outside and sat in my car. Then I saw Vince get out of Naiomi's Jeep. Watched his body language, so confident, back so much straighter since I wasn't with him, clothes perfect, like he'd made sure he'd worn the right thing too.

Him and his ex went inside.

Naiomi went inside a few seconds later.

I told myself to go rent skates, join the party, just happen to be there. But I left and drove to my office.

"Shelby Williams? It's Dana Smith from ReMax."

"Hey, Dana. What's up? Any word?"

"Hey, new homeowner!"

Shelby screamed with joy. "Everything went through?"

They were out of escrow, out of purgatory. That dream house was all theirs. "Sounds like you're having a party over there."

"Book club meeting," she told me. "About forty sisters are here."

"I'll talk to you tomorrow sometime."

"Okay."

"Tell Tyrel I said congrats."

"Hey, before he left for Australia, my hubby told me to tell you he was passing your fiancé's résumé around Dan L. Steel. Jordan Greene or Stephan Mitchell might end up calling him for an interview."

"Thanks."

"Maybe when you guys get married, we'll end up being neighbors."

I was glad that over the phone, people couldn't see your face. Couldn't see what the eyes couldn't hide.

I hung up and gazed out the window.

Late afternoon sunshine was strong. Up the street golfers were out, having fun in the sun. Beaches had to be packed. I decided that I might not work tomorrow. If I did, I wanted to leave work early, go to Santa Monica, buy a thong bikini at the mall, and hang out on the beach until the sun was swallowed by the ocean. Maybe have strangers with broken accents lust after me, maybe buy a disposable camera and have them take pictures of me half-naked sporting a West Coast tan, smiling in the Cali sun, photos to show my friends when I made it back to Harlem.

That was a maybe for tomorrow.

But for now I closed my eyes. An angel with my momma's voice whispered in my ear, invited me to escape everything west of the Mississippi. I followed the wisdom of that unseen heavenly spirit and imagined I was back in Harlem, in a season of cold with snow falling all over the city, on Malcolm X Boulevard between 126th and 127th Street. At Sylvia's, sitting underneath pictures of Courtney Vance, Dru Hill, and Hi-Five. That Mo' Better Blues poster on the paneled walls leading downstairs to the bathroom. Dishes rattling, silverware clanking against plates as people ate. NY1 playing all the bad news from the five boroughs on the small television over the bar. I was in my favorite spot facing the boulevard, in a straight-back chair, at a table that had green tablecloths under the glass tops. All around me were waitresses in black slacks, white shirts, and ties. Jamaican accents. Dominican accents. In front of me was a huge plate: sardines and grits, sautéed chicken livers, pork chops, salmon cakes, pattie sausage, cornmeal fried whiting, pinto beans, black-eyed peas, and a big-ass bottle of Sylvia's kicking hot sauce. I wanted every bit of it too. I inhaled and smelled every spice, felt the meal's heat.

When I opened my eyes, I was still in California.

* * *

Gerri used me as a cover, told her kids that we were going out together, eating at La Louisianne and then getting our party on. She did all of that in front of Melvin. He'd come by to snatch up the rug rats, was taking them to the movies, then dropping them off later after they were done doing that bonding-slash-nurturing thing. When they left, Gerri packed up her gear and headed for Blondies. And there was no way I was going to sit around her condo and stare at the walls, not with this much on my mind.

I'd dialed Vince's number four or five times—all evening he was MIA. My imagination filled in the blanks.

Had to find my own peace of mind.

Allowed myself to gravitate toward where I was wanted.

To where I was safe.

At nine-thirty I had on my favorite wool LBD—Little Black Dress—and beaded jewelry. Classy, sexy, and hipness rolled into one. All that and black strapped heels. The sweetest perfume I owned.

Claudio said, "So, this is restaurant row."

"Yep."

From my window at the Warehouse, I took a deep breath as I gazed toward the ocean and saw thousands of stars standing high in the sky. In front of me were just as many yachts. The area reeked of money, old and new.

Claudio said, "This area is nice."

"A lot of exotic food places are down here."

"Ain't a damn thing more exotic than you."

"Claudio, knock it off."

Above us, sweet-faced couples were at candlelit tables, chowing down seafood and steaks while a jazz band did their thing. On the other side of my reflection, outside on the wooden deck right below us, were tables of buppies, muppies, and yuppies pigging out underneath the table warmers. Couples were holding hands, eyes glinting with pleasure, laughing, sharing entrées and feeding each other in between smiles.

The salty smell in the air, the echo of the tide breaking on the rocks, even the overweight white lady in the green muumuu singing angelic Billie Holiday tunes made the place pretty extravagant.

This looked like just another first-class restaurant, but I knew better. This was a place of seduction, one big foreplay party for the sophisticated.

Claudio was holding a glass of chablis. "I wanna make a special toast. To seeing you again."

"Thanks."

He said, "Was smoked salmon and a salad all you wanted?"

"Yeah. I'm trying not to get fat."

He laughed. "There you go with that weight thang again."

He wolfed down the last of his fillet of sole meunière. I sipped my wine, then nodded. "The salmon was fine, Claudio."

"You can have as much of anything you want. If they don't have what you want, I'll tell the driver to ride around until we find it."

I glanced at my engagement ring. Yep, still had it on. Why, I do not know. I asked Claudio, "Where are you getting all of this money?"

"Comedy is hot. The King of Comedy tour made way into seven figures. If I can do a corner of that, hell, I'll be set. You know how black people love to laugh."

"How many more shows do you have out here?"

"One at the Comedy Emporium in Hollywood. Need to meet with Guy Torry, maybe Joe Torry too. I'll leave you a couple of tickets at the door. Bring your tall friend. One of my homies wanna meet her."

"I'll let you know. Then what you doing after L.A.?"

"Going to San Francisco and Oakland, doing a show at Geoffrey's in the Bay, then hitting Seattle and Tacoma. That'll take about a week."

"Then what?"

"Back to N.Y. and do the same in the Village."

"Sounds like you're coming up."

"That's why you need to be with me. We could do this together, you know. Travel. Make some pocket change while we see the country."

I said, "So, when are you going to pay me what you owe me?"

"You sound like a bill collector."

"Is that a hard question to answer?"

"Don't make tonight about that. Let's roll back to my hotel."

"And why would we do that?"

He smiled. "Kick it with me."

"And?"

"I miss you like crazy." His eyes pointed at my engagement ring. "We both know that should be my diamond on your finger."

"When we were together and I brought the subject up, all I remember you saying was that marriage was a three-ring circus. Engagement ring, wedding ring, then suffering."

"I said that?"

"Yes, you did."

"I was a straight-up fool. Dee Dee, baby, I wish like hell that I could have you forever, keep you at my side as a king—"

"Oh, since you're coming up, you're a king nowadays."

"That's right. Got tired of being a field hand working for the man. And I'm a king who should have a smooth and elegant queen, like yourself, at my side so I can cherish her beauty and grace forever and a day."

"Two snaps down. Where did you read that stupid mess?"

"I'm being serious over here."

"You sound silly."

"I'm serious. I'd love to get married. Start my own

family. Should've married you five years ago. We could have two kids by now."

"And I'd be as big as a horse."

"But you'd be my horse."

I didn't respond, but I savored his verbal warmth.

"I've missed you so much, Dee Dee."

"Stop, Claudio."

"Tell me you haven't missed me half as much as I've missed you."

I sighed. "Can't tell you that. You know that."

He stroked my hand with his finger. Over and over he did that. "Let's see if we can get back what we had."

In the back of my mind I knew that Claudio would come back. Knew he would find me. They always come back on bended knee.

Again I stared out into the endless miles of calm waters.

Claudio said, "I'm serious."

I blinked out of my trance and murmured, "What?"

"Your skin is the most beautiful thing on this planet. See, a real brother appreciates a sister that looks like a real black woman."

"Thanks."

"I've always had a thing for your skin, you know that, right? Dee Dee, your complexion is so smooth and perfect. You been using Ambi?"

"Cut the bull, all right?"

"I'm serious. I changed hotels, upgraded, got a boss suite at the Bonaventure, a high floor that looks over Los Angeles and'll put us so close to the heavens you can snatch a feather off an angel's wing."

That time I laughed. "Angel wing or a Kentucky Fried Chicken wing?"

Vince had stared at me with disdain. Had shut me out. Claudio was staring at me with a wanting, absolutely no shame in his game. A hunger that the wine and candlelight dinner had weakened me for.

Vince had gone to see his daughter. To see his ex. Not

that I had expected, but he hadn't invited me. That pretty much solidified where we stood. Or where we didn't stand. Would never stand again.

Right now I was as powerful as Atlas, the way Gerri looked when she was up on that pyramid-shaped stage, when men bowed like paupers at her feet and begged. Large and in charge. There was a victory in being face-to-face with Claudio, being able to see his regret for leaving me. His yearning told me that I was better than Tia. Another triumph.

Feelings I had for him were rising to the top. We were older, had grown. Maybe it could be different now. That second-time-around thing.

I let Claudio's hand go, stared out at the Pacific Ocean.

New York was my home, ran through my blood like Broadway through Manhattan. L.A. was pretty, a paradise with one season, but this was the type of place a woman like me was supposed to visit. Maybe this had been my vacation, and now it was over.

He asked, "You okay?"

I took my lipstick out of my purse, saw the receipt for the package I had at Culver City Trophies. Cost almost a hundred dollars. One of the most important projects I've ever done.

Again he asked, "You okay?"

"Let's have another glass of wine, then maybe we can go to heaven."

He raised a brow, pulled out a charge card, waved down the waitress.

Kissing started in the limo. Riding through the marina, the privacy glass up, my shoes off, champagne in the back.

I said, "You don't just want my stuff, do you?"

"I want you, Dee Dee."

"If that's the case, don't pump me up. I already want to share myself with you. And it amazes me whenever I think about us going there again."

He opened the champagne, dipped my toes in the glass. The chilled brew excited my warm skin. He sucked all the liquid off, had me in a corner, muscles twitching. He touched my hair, rubbed my back, kissed my neck.

"Claudio, there were times I thought about you, and it felt like a part of me was missing. Hard to explain what I'm feeling now."

"Don't try. I just want to know if everything can be okay between us."

"I want to know that too."

We talked the whole time, all of our words barely above a whisper, about what, I don't remember. From the look on Claudio's face, all the smiles and laughs, it must've been a pretty interesting conversation.

He asked, "You want me to stop and get some bubble bath stuff?"

"Not this time."

"Honey?"

"Ain't I sweet enough for you?"

"Let me see."

He raised my dress, did it slowly, waiting to see if I was going to stop him. His tongue snaked from my toes up into my subway; my temples shook. We had stopped at a red light, and three people were right outside the tinted windows. He wiggled that soft flesh over the edges of my goodness. As he went inside, my eyes were on the strangers, watching them laugh and talk. That tongue found my spot, my back curved, moan-gasmed so fast I know the driver heard my long and winding love cry.

I put my hand deep in Claudio's pants, stirred up his protein.

By the time we made it to the hotel, it was too late to turn back.

Claudio stripped me naked, used lotion to massage my legs, my feet, licked all of my toes over and over, my eyes on the stars, staring at the heaven hovering over Stocker and Degnan.

It was a cool night. I pulled the sheets back, nice and slow, checked to make sure they were clean. He took off his shirt. I slid out of my bra. Unzip. Unsnap. My heart was beating strong. I smelled him. I know he could smell me, the envy of every rose in town.

Then we were in the rented bed, covers pulled back, bare skin under moonlight.

Kissing my neck. My breast. Standing tall for me. My legs easing open. Thick fingers roaming in my condensation. Kissing my nipples. Biting my nipples. Licking me from my navel down. What I thought would never happen again was actually happening. His body on mine. In mine.

"Claudio," my words were slurred a little, "slow down, baby."

"Shhh, quiet . . . right there . . . yes . . . coming . . . yes . . ."

The first time was always fast. Hard, fast, and good enough to make my insides shiver, body convulsing. He grew. Not as long as Vince, a little wider. Became intense, but not as intense as Vince could get. Better in some ways. Everybody's love was so different. Vince's love was like jazz with slow-burning candles; Claudio's loving was hip-hop all the way. Harsh breathing on my face. His pre-come wail in my ear. I turned my head. He was there, losing control, feeding me his liquid energy, beyond the orgasmic point of no return, groaning out a burst of pleasure loud enough to shatter my eardrums.

He caught his breath. "You feel how much I love you?"

"Yeah, baby."

"Did you?"

I kissed him. Wanted to cry. "Get the condom before it comes off."

My head was on Claudio's chest, his hands running through my braids. My mind was down at Stocker and Degnan. That part of my life was officially over. It was always a matter of when. Inviting Claudio inside of me was the ultimate when.

Twenty minutes after that, Claudio's mouth was on my breast, hungry for some more of me. I leaned to the nightstand, grabbed a condom, handed it to him. This time would be longer, more for me than it was for him. If I could relax my mind and stay focused, I'd be able to have back-to-back multiple moan-gasms. He lay on his back, and I sat on his magical flute with my back to his face, my eyes closed, listening to the pornographic music he made, my breathing curt, heart pounding with the feeling of power. I leaned back as far as I could, one of my knees up, my hand holding me steady. A moan-gasm rippled through me like fierce electricity.

I leaned forward, watched him disappearing and reappearing.

"Oh, damn, Dee Dee, baby, oh baby, damn."

After he came, he lay on top of me, his body getting heavy, breathing slowing. I rubbed his bald head. My eyes stayed on the ceiling. Hardly a breath came from my face. My thoughts on the other side of town.

"Claudio?"

"Yeah?"

"I hope you're not falling asleep on me."

"Damn, I'm sorry. You wore me out. And this three-hour time change, ain't used to that yet."

He rolled over, pulled me close to his body. A body that was so relaxed. A second later I had to lean away from his asthmatic snores. I scooted to the other side of the bed and balled up in a fetal position, held myself, rocking and thinking. Wired like I'd had two cups of cappuccino. I lay back down, my left arm dangling off the bed, the white sheets draped over my lower back, covering part of my left leg and half of my cool butt, my foot bouncing.

I glanced at the digital clock. Thirty-five minutes. That was how long we'd been here. It was almost as if it hadn't happened. But it had. I was resting in the middle of the evidence. And the condom had left a chafed feeling, the one thing I hated about using protection.

I peeped at the clock for the umpteenth time. Was anxious, kind of scared, very nervous. Heavy snoring was still behind me. He stirred a little when I moved. I eased to the other side of the bed, peeped and made sure he was knocked out, then gingerly picked up the phone. Dialed. No answer before the machine clicked on.

I hung up. Butterflies in my stomach went wild.

"Who you calling?"

I jumped, the inside of my head tingled. "Thought you were 'sleep."

"Who you calling?"

"Stop acting jealous. I was checking my messages."

"Why you gotta check your messages this time of night?"

"I was supposed to hook up with Gerri at a club called Duets after I did dinner with you. Never called to cancel."

He patted the bed next to him. I moved to that spot.

I said, "Claudio, this changes everything in my life."

He asked, "For the good?"

"Depends."

"On what?"

"You really want me to come back home with you?"

"Yeah."

The red light on the phone started blinking. Claudio had a message. The phone never rang and he had a message. Unless they called while I was on the line.

I got up. Claudio's voice followed me: "You leaving?"

I smiled back at him. "Bathroom. You know how my bladder is."

"You staying?"

"I don't know. Have a lot of work to do in the morning."

"We could have breakfast at sunrise."

"Can't. Need to be dressed for an open house."

I went to potty. I thought Claudio would be pissed off when I came back into the room, but he had that look in his eyes.

He sat up. "Dee Dee?"

"Yeah?"

"If you can't stay, do me a favor."

"Okay."

"Let's do it again."

"We've never done it three times in the same night."

"See what you do to me?"

I said, "And?"

"I don't want but two people in this bed."

"What does that mean?"

"Unless you're the Green Lantern, take that ring off your left hand."

I did. It was hard to do, took a while to do, but I did.

This time felt different. I couldn't relax, maybe because he kept changing positions so much. Behind me, beside me, at one point his leg flew by my face and he turned me into a pretzel. Thought he was trying to damage my insides, with all the pushing. He was going so fast, hitting me so hard, asking if the dick was good. It was getting crazy. A headboard-banging, hair-pulling workout session that had me trying to keep up with his pace. The condoms had me so chafed I wanted to scream. I used my inner muscles to squeeze, tried to make him come as soon as I could, started making all kinds of noises like his dick was the best I'd ever had.

And when he was done and had fallen into a deep sleep, I showered, then put on my clothes. I stood in the window for a while.

Sore. I was so damn sore.

I kissed Claudio on his forehead. Kissed him and grabbed my keys. Part of me wanted to stay in this room and wait to see what that good old sunrise would bring, but this other part of me told me I had to go.

26 Vince

Light was losing its battle with darkness when Rosa Lee left home and headed up Sixty-third Street. I was parked a few duplexes back. I cranked up the six-cylinder rental I was in, made a quick U-turn, then followed her Ford Explorer through the residential area. She turned right at La Cienega, went the opposite direction of the gym.

This had to be how Womack felt the night he did this for me. A hole was being drilled in his heart. I'd have to be witness to his torment.

This morning at the rental car company, I'd made a deal with Womack. He wanted this favor. And for his favor I had made my price known. An extreme price, one that made him almost call the whole thing off, but in the end, he wanted this so badly that he bowed down to my demand, never mentioned that he made no demands of me way back when.

Twenty minutes passed as I trailed Rosa Lee into Hollywood. Passed by acting studios and dance clubs on Highland, cruised by stores specializing in religious supplies and beeper activations. She ended up on Santa Monica Boulevard, driving toward the theater district. This street has more drama houses than 7-Eleven has Twinkies. A good place to creep and meet somebody.

Rosa Lee changed lanes without signaling, sped up, and made it through a red light at Las Palmas. I didn't change lanes fast enough and I was left trapped at the red light, craning my neck. Her brake lights came on under the bright lights near a Honda dealership. Then she whipped a quick left and vanished into the residential area.

That light cost me a good minute.

I took off like a horse at Santa Anita racetrack, zoomed down to the Honda place, had to wait for traffic to thin so I could bust a left at Hudson. All the while I was staring that way, toward a stream of single-story houses. Rosa Lee could be anywhere. I didn't see any fading taillights.

Paranoia set in. I wasn't sure this was the side street where she had turned. She could've turned back at Seward. I was about to floor the accelerator and race to the end of the block, but then I spotted her coming out of the fenced pay-parking lot on the corner. Head down while she stuffed her wallet and keys in her black backpack-style purse.

A Ford Excursion was coming up the narrow street. Not enough room to get by. The SUV tooted its horn. Rosa Lee raised her head. We made eye contact.

Damn.

The SUV went by. I let my window down. My friend's wife sent me an empty wave. I nodded, checked out what she had on: Capri pants, black mules, a denim shirt with Bugs Bunny and Daffy Duck on the pocket. Her hair fresh, jutting out in that wavy Afro, bouncing with every step.

She held a yellow legal pad to her chest and said, "When you follow people, let a car or two get in between."

I slapped the steering wheel. "Shit."

She smiled. "Well, since you're here, you'll have to park in the lot and pay three-fifty because the streets look like they're full, unless you want to drive around the block a few times and see if you can get lucky. I'm going to Lucy Florence."

"Who's Lucy Florence?"

"Lucy is not a who, knucklehead. It's the coffee house on the corner that's connected to the Hudson Theater."

"What's going on here tonight?"

"Poetry. Find a table and I'll meet you."

"What's the rush?"

"My bladder's killing me. Gotta go do number one real bad."

She hurried across the street and vanished inside the opening between the theater and the coffee house.

The entire drive, I hadn't been hiding. I'd stayed behind her in plain sight because I wanted her to see me. I just didn't know what to do when she saw me.

It took me a minute to park and hurry through the side door. No sign of Rosa Lee.

The crowd was laid-back, almost everybody in up-to-date, oversize and baggy fashions. Incense mixed with the aroma of cakes and pies, did a ballet with the scent of caffeine. A saxophone player made his horn sing a tale of bewitchment. Congos added that ethnic twist. A dread-head sister was playing the hell out of a magical flute, making the soft music in the background sound funky.

A couple finished their cappuccino and left. I bumped around people and claimed their small round table, copped a squat next to a nice mellow crowd of brothers, sisters, and a couple of kissy-kissy white folks. Coffee-sipping Mexicans were in the house too.

Minutes went by. I ran my hand over my beard, then tapped my fingers on the table.

Rosa Lee came into the room, but she didn't come from the direction of the bathroom. She appeared in the doorway that faced Santa Monica Boulevard. She waved, went right by me, bumped around the people at the circular counter, got in line. She came back with two cups of tea.

Rosa Lee asked me, "Chamomile or Darjeeling?"

"Chamomile."

She set one cup in front of me, the other at her side of the table, then went back to the counter. She came back with two slices of cake.

Rosa Lee asked, "Lemon or Sock It to Me?"

"Lemon."

She slid the lemon across the table.

I said, "I was beginning to think that you'd fallen into the toilet or something."

She laughed. Her laugh was different from the throaty one she usually had, was the kind of shallow laugh that needed some accompaniment, so I threw in a chuckle or two to make a nice melody of uneasiness.

Eyes were heating up our space, and I looked around. A brother near the doorway had his eyes stuck on her. Sized him up. About five ten. Short dreads. An Eric Benet kinda look. In jeans and a jean shirt. Rosa Lee glanced at him, at me, then turned her head toward the musicians. My eyes went to the brother. His eyes were pointing this way. On Rosa. On me. He wasn't smiling. Not at all. I nodded to let him know I saw him. He turned away.

I asked, "Who's that?"

"Who's who?"

"The ni—the brother in the door who looks pissed off."

After my what-is-he-to-you question, she shrugged, sipped her tea, sorta whispered, "Don't know. Men look at me all the time."

"You got it like that."

"With every man except my husband."

"He looks at you."

"Like I'm the mother of his children, not like I'm a woman."

"I see." I sipped my tea, stirred up the honey, sipped again, added more honey. "Your husband's concerned about you. About your relationship."

"How so?"

I told her that he didn't think that she'd been going to the gym as often as she claimed. She was accumulating unaccounted-for hours away from home. "What about those nights you were AWOL?"

She shrugged. "I went to book signings at Zhara's or

Eso Won. Poetry at World Stage. Depends on what is happening, depends on my mood. It was my free time, so I did whatever I felt like doing. Problem?"

"Why didn't you tell Womack?"

"Because sometimes I like going places on my own. I'm married. I have four beautiful children, but I also have individual needs. My husband and kids can't be one hundred percent of my life. I have to have something just for me. I have to create my own corner, have to not lose the last piece of Rosa Lee I have left, or I'll lose my mind."

My eyes told her that I thought she was full of shit.

"Vince, I love you. If I hadn't married Womack, I'd've been scratching at your door from noon to midnight."

We laughed a bit.

She said, "Now, get out of my Kool-Aid."

The brother finally stopped gawking at Rosa Lee, then strolled deeper into the room and mixed with the crowd at the counter.

Rosa Lee's eyes went his way for a moment. Her face lost its distance and innocence. She saw me watching her watch him. She sipped her tea, gazed straight ahead at nothing.

Light sweat on her nose. Slight shake of her hand.

I asked her, "When did you start liking poetry?"

"Guess you forgot that I used to write poetry in high school. Some of it made it to the school newspaper."

"That's right, that's right."

We had to speak up so we could hear each other because the table next to us was loud, speaking in so much new and improved slang that it sounded like they were talking in Morse code. A couple at another table was holding hands and flirting in between talking about the post-riot rebuilding of the black community. Somebody else mentioned a slow-moving project to clean up Baldwin Village.

I asked, "So, what's really going on with you and Womack?"

"Don't get pushy."

"I care about you guys. You're all the family I have left."

"Don't get sentimental either."

She sighed. Peeped at her watch. Looked rattled.

I offered, "Wanna talk about it?"

"No. Hush. They're starting."

The band played while the M.C. threw down something that rang out like strong pro-black poetry. Very political, social. It voiced a lot of the same concerns that our forefathers had, so it let me know that even though we could now get haircuts in Westwood and enroll in UCLA, not much had changed. He finished to a strong applause, then humbly introduced a short sister who looked like a chubby Erykah Badu. Her words were satiny, soulful, like the lyrics to a song, but the message crossed the line of political correctness, was closer to antiwhite slogans that rhymed.

Another sister did a spoken word about the sins of the black man dating the white woman. She called them "blue-eyed cave bitches." The eight or so white people in the room shifted, but didn't get up and run out. They were in the thick of the crowd, no way to leave. An interracial couple near the door left without finishing their cake or coffee. Somebody claimed their table before they made it out the door.

I said, "She's kinda raw."

"Lighten up. Freedom of speech."

"So you say. When white people speak that freely—"

"Hush."

The sister finished her poem to a stupendous applause. I sipped my tea, tasted my cake, loved the way it melted in my mouth because that reminded me of the first time I kissed Dana. It would take a lot of kisses to dilute the flavor she'd left in my mouth.

I asked Rosa Lee, "How did you find out about this place?"

"The night all of us were at Fifth Street Dick's I

picked up a lot of fliers. A few of the handouts adver-
tised the local jazz bands. Some of them were for poetry.
One mentioned this place."

I shut up for a while. Checked out the lyrical flow.

One beautiful, bald, brown-skinned sister in a bright
sarong acted out a sexy piece praising her "good pussy."
It turned the room out. Women were high-fiving each
other, and before it was over, brothers were licking their
lips and drinking boiling coffee to cool off the lust she'd
built.

Rosa Lee leaned forward on her elbows, smiling just
enough to show her teeth, making sounds like "ummm"
and "yes, God, yes," mumbling "whew, tell it like it is." She
wrote a couple of things down on her yellow legal pad.

I asked, "What're you doing?"

"That inspired me."

From the counter, the brother was staring at Rosa
Lee.

She put her pen down. Smiled. I did the same.

I asked, "How are the kids at school treating you?"

"They're thieves, liars, promiscuous. They get caught
smoking on the way to school. They drink like alco-
holics, won't do their homework. If I give them the exact
questions in the same order that they will be on a test,
and give them the correct answers to study, ninety percent will still fail. So damn lazy." She blew out some air.
"What more can I say?"

"Just like we were."

She nodded. "Outside of MTV and the Internet,
nothing's changed."

For a moment I thought about our problems now. I
said, "Most of us are just kids with decent jobs and better clothes."

She became animated. "Let me tell you what happened
today. This kid was caught having sex in the classroom. My
student aide. In my classroom, of all places. During first
period. The same girl who had the condom. I called myself
giving her a chance and letting her be my aide."

"No shit?"

Rosa Lee looked sad for a moment. Heartbroken. That kind of look that a person gets when they've tried their best and made it nowhere fast.

She said, "I had a parent-teacher conference with her and her mother. Mom's under thirty, has four more kids—a single parent, works two jobs, and she's crying and telling me and the principal how her child has been smoking since she was five, was caught sexing after she turned eleven."

"That's scary."

"They drop those kids in our laps and expect us to work a miracle."

I thought about my own child. Wondered how she'd turn out. Rosa Lee's brows were tight. I bet she was thinking about her little girl, Ramona, having the same fears. Parents are always afraid that their children will do the same shit they did.

When it was all said and done, Rosa Lee checked her watch, said it was time for her to hit the road. We walked out together.

She asked, "So, you gonna tell Womack where I was?"

"Nope. I'll leave that up to you."

"Vince, you're paranoid. Both you and Womack are paranoid."

She said that like she meant it. I ached because it might be true.

Rosa Lee kissed me on my lips, hopped in her SUV, and pulled out of the lot first, turned right, headed toward Highland. Back toward Ladera. I followed her as far as the 7-Eleven, then slowed and pulled in the inconvenience store parking lot. I went in, bought a bottle of Sharps. I asked the man behind the counter, "This a twist-off cap?"

"Yeah."

I paid for it. Headed outside. Stopped at a pay phone. Dialed Womack's number.

Harmonica answered, then yelled for Womack to come get the phone. They were at home playing the parts of Two Men and Four Babies. Womack answered, sounding winded, like he'd raced to get the receiver.

I said, "The mother of your children went and checked out some poetry."

"Who she with?"

"Nobody."

Too quick. I'd answered too quick.

He waited a moment before he asked, "She see you?"

"Nope." I paused, waited for him to say something. He didn't. Listening to him breathe made me anxious. I added, "She sat at a table by herself the whole time, wrote stuff down, sipped tea."

He was a childhood friend who knew me too well. Some days he knew me better than I knew myself. He released a brief chortle, said, "If it was something else, you'd take care of it, right?"

"You know it." I shared some of the thin laughter. "She'll be home any minute. Tuck the rug rats in, then cuddle up."

"Okay, okay. Talk to you tomorrow or the next day."

"Womack?"

"Yeah? What's wrong?"

"Nothing. Kiss the wife for me."

"Sure you didn't already kiss her?"

"I did my best, but she's hooked on you."

We laughed, for real this time.

"Thanks," Womack said. "I mean it. Thanks a lot."

"No problem. Hey . . ."

"What?"

"Jennifer Lopez or Janet Jackson?"

"My wife. Just my wife."

The serious way he said that got to me. I hung up, rubbed my eyes. I was tired. From the inside out, I was tired.

I drove back toward the theater, parked a block back

on Seward, hoofed it down. Bounced the Sharps against my leg while I treaded in the shadows.

I stood on the corner, eyes trained on the coffee house. The brother who was hawking Rosa Lee was still there. I waited. Rosa Lee hadn't done like I thought she might and double back. People came and went. Ten minutes passed. The brother who'd been feenin' for Rosa Lee stepped outside. He'd never said a word to another soul. Never stared at another woman. He wasn't part of the poetic ensemble, not interested in iambic pentameter or the making of a haiku. He crossed the street, went up the avenue on the side of the Honda dealership.

I was right behind him, moving down a deserted side street, stepping when he stepped so I couldn't be heard over all the street sounds. I was here, but my mind was swirling in the sands of the Inland Empire, mixing past memories and present fears at the same time.

I had to put an end to this shit.

He slowed and pulled his cellular phone out of his pocket, punched digits, listened.

He started to turn around. I raised the bottle and brought it down across the bridge of his nose. He cursed with the pain. His c-phone twirled back toward me while he wobbled into the fence and bounced away grasping for anything, like a bird that had forgotten how to fly, but touching nothing but air.

His face was covered with blood.

I stood over him. "She's married."

"I don't know what you talking about—"

"Shut the fuck up."

"Okay, okay, all right already. Whatever you say."

"She's married. Remember that. Respect that."

The fool lay in the night's shadows, legs kicking like a rebellious toddler, scraping across the asphalt and its debris.

His phone rang. I picked it up. Clicked it on.

"Hello . . . you there?"

I said, "It's me."

"Who . . . Glenn?"

"My name is Vincent."

They hung up.

I envisioned Malaika on that rainy night. Heard her laughing while I was at work trusting the woman I'd married to be what she couldn't be. Not for me anyway.

I tossed the phone into the street and said, "You understand?"

His head nodded up and down. Sounded like he said, "Whatever you say, man, whatever you say."

Inside me, past and present were colliding, leaving me light-headed. The beer bottle slipped from between my fingers.

It broke; foamy liquid drained across the sidewalk down into the sewer.

Vincent.

My name lived on the night's breeze.

I turned around.

Malaika was behind me, hair loose, lipstick the color of my heart, her suntanned skin in a green satin robe. Rain dripping from her body, leaving puddles at her bare feet. I stepped toward her; she scurried a step back.

Malaika's hand came up, massaged her neck. Her lip trembled.

In the distance, a baby cried, my child calling for its mother's milk.

I was afraid. Sorry for all the wrong I had done in the name of right, and afraid. I backed off a step or two, stumbled into the fence, blinked.

Malaika's image vanished.

Nothing was there. Nobody at all. The ground was dry.

With the exception of a bleeding brother and a broken bottle of nonalcoholic beer, the pavement was barren.

I ran like the wind.

*   *   *

A voice called out, "Who's back there, please?"

I yelled, "It's me, Juanita."

"It's after one in the morning. What are you doing?"

I was in the T-shaped alley by the garages, leaning my mattress and box spring against the wall.

Dana might have been right about one thing. My holding on to that bed might've been my way of holding on to Malaika. And the videotape was my VHS trophy. That's not what she'd said, but I think that was what she meant. Given time, every trophy grew old.

Juanita came through the gate and asked, "What's all that noise?"

She saw my mattress leaning against the side of the garage.

Naiomi was behind her. She saw me, and her eyes dropped for the pavement.

Juanita asked, "Couldn't you do that at a more decent hour?"

"I could."

Both were dressed in jeans, sandals, and rainbow-colored T-shirts. And they were standing shoulder to shoulder with cutlery knives in their fists. Naiomi's weapon was in her right hand; Juanita's was in her left. In this land of Uzis and Mac-10s, I wondered what they thought a couple of three-inch blades would do back here.

Naiomi stared at me for a moment. In her eyes existed no trace of the woman who had sat in my lap, chanted out her lust while she asked me to run away to an exotic land with her and live on rice and beans.

She was somebody else now. So was I. Calmer. Clearer.

Juanita said, "Naiomi and I had a discussion. Let me be direct. Things I said to you were of the emotional nature, and I had no right to express my opinion in such a manner."

"Apology accepted. What I said to you was disrespectful. A man shouldn't address a woman like that. My momma wouldn't like what I said."

"Apology accepted."

That was the end of that. A warriors' truce.

Juanita asked, "Where are you putting that mattress?"

"I'm leaving it outside the gate for the trash man."

"Why didn't you donate it to one of the neighbors?"

"Don't want to see it. Don't want it in my geographical frame."

Juanita made a delicate sound, took a few steps, then turned away like she was leaving. She took a few steps, looked back and said, "Naiomi?"

Juanita paused, waiting for her woman to catch up. Naiomi went to Juanita and kissed her. Juanita smiled a little. Naiomi patted Juanita on the butt, then said, "Go ahead. I want to check the locks on the garages."

Juanita and Naiomi shared eyes for a moment, then Juanita glanced my way. That was interrupted when the sound of a car alarm pierced the lull in our conversation.

Naiomi said, "Baby, that sounds like your car."

Juanita let Naiomi's hand go. "Yes, it does, sweetheart."

Juanita stared at her woman, then at me, waited another moment before she trotted toward the front of the building. Her house shoes scraped and slapped against the narrow concrete walkway, made a hurry-hurry noise as she jogged around the corner.

Naiomi sighed.

I asked, "You find it?"

"I found it. Not that finding the thing makes it any better."

I sighed.

She said, "Mr. Browne, it shouldn't have happened."

I nodded.

She went on, "There was no future in what we did."

The car alarm shut off.

Naiomi continued, "I want to apologize for the way I reacted when, you know. When I couldn't find it."

"Are you ovulating?"

Naiomi's eyes widened with surprise.

"Are you?"

"Not that it's your business, but no." She cleared her throat, blew some air. "You didn't cover my furniture before you left . . ."

I said, "The Hilton."

No reply from her.

I shifted, put my hands in my back pocket, held on to my butt.

Naiomi said, "It didn't happen, Mr. Browne. As far as I'm concerned. For what it's worth, our curiosity has been satisfied. Let's move on."

The echo of house shoes flip-flopping stopped her flow. I made out Juanita's voice having a saucy conversation with somebody. Naiomi hurried out into the alleyway, put some distance between us, and started pulling on the garage door locks, making it look like that's what she'd been doing while her soft-legged lover was absent.

Juanita appeared. Dana was with her. Her braids were gone. Hair jet black, bone straight, parted down the center. Permed, hot-combed, I don't know. Dark lipstick. Dressed in black stretch jeans, gray stretch blouse, black mules, leather backpack purse hang-ing from one shoulder.

Dana was irritated. "Juanita, my car barely bumped your funky little car. That's why cars have bumpers. Just in case people bump into them."

Juanita said, "Dana, either invest in a driving class or find some other alternative place to park. I don't like you banging into my car, and neither do the neighbors."

Dana's spirit had changed as well. Strife was in her cat eyes.

Naiomi came back, stopped side by side with Dana. To me, there was no comparison. After dealing with Womack's problem, a load had been lifted, my head clearer than the moonless sky standing over my head.

Dana finally said in a heavy voice, "Hey, Vince."

"Hey yourself. What's up?"

"I got your message about my laundry. And I need to get my mail."

Dana didn't come close enough for a hug, but her perfume touched my nose. A different brand, not by Terry Ellis. No more En Vogue for my senses. She reeked with freshness, with newness.

Dana made a strange sound, said, "You threw the bed out."

"Yeah."

Her lips twisted; she sucked in one side of her jaw.

She asked, "Why?"

"It was time."

Juanita and Naiomi left, hand in hand.

Dana's pager went off. She turned it off without checking the digits.

She said, "I want to talk to you, if that's okay."

"It's okay."

Dana headed up my stairs. I finished up, then followed.

With the exception of the streetlights slipping through the venetian blinds, the apartment was dark.

I called out, "Dana?"

She answered, "In the bathroom. Leave the lights off."

"Why?"

"What I have to say will be easier this way."

My feet followed her voice. I knew my way around my cave and there was enough light to outline everything. The bathroom door wasn't closed all the way. The night-light was on, so I could see that she was sitting on the toilet, body forward, head between her knees.

I said, "Constipated?"

"Thinking."

Conflict was in the air. I leaned against the wall in the hallway, slid down until my butt rested on the brown carpet, rested my cheeks in the palms of my hands.

Soft sensual noises slipped from Juanita and Naiomi's

apartment through my walls. They were humming a chorus of sweet sexuality and eternal forgiveness. Either Dana didn't notice or she didn't care.

Dana started peeing. A long, hard squirt.

My stomach ached like I'd eaten some of that mad cow beef that Oprah had warned people about. Nerves gave me gas. I shifted, let that silent killer ride, closed my eyes, tried to make the darkness darker.

She told me, "I'm going back to New York."

"For how long?"

"Forever."

My phone rang and interrupted us.

A guy said, "Vince?"

I responded, "Yeah. Who this?"

He hung up. Malaika's husband came to mind. Made me want to know if he'd found my phone number laying around and dialed my digits.

I went back to the hall, picked up on our conversation.

For a few minutes we sat in a sea of apologies. We acknowledged the fight. Told her I was sorry, never meant to touch her the way I did, but those straws of discontent had worn me down. Her apologies were just as strong. We both tried to take all the blame instead of placing the blame. At some point we called a truce, let it be a no-fault.

She said, "Claudio wants me to go back to Harlem with him."

"He'd say anything to get you to sleep with 'im."

Matter-of-factly she responded, "Just like you did, right?"

I paused. "What if I want you to stay here?"

"I can't do L.A. anymore. This place just ain't me."

"Thought you liked the weather."

"Weather? L.A. has two seasons: wet and dry. And my season has been dry since I landed here. If I went back home, would you move there with me?"

"You know I couldn't."

"That's what I mean."

"What's what you mean?"

"My feet are in quicksand; yours are trapped in concrete."

Her clothes rustled when she leaned to pull off some tissue, rustled again when she leaned forward so she could clean herself.

I asked, "You love me?"

The toilet flushed. She washed her hands, then stepped into the hallway, sat on the floor across from me, her back to the wall.

Dana said, "That's always been part of the problem. Falling in love is easy. Being in love is so damn hard."

The *oohs* and *ahhs* that were traveling through my walls faded.

"What's the deal between you and your ex?"

"What do you mean?"

"You love the guy, is it a physical attraction?"

A moment went by.

She said, "This is weird."

"What?"

She ran her fingers through her straight hair. "Us talking like this."

"Want to stop?"

"Too bad we didn't do this in the beginning."

"Nobody talks like this in the beginning."

"Yeah, honesty is like seeing a crackhead up close: it ain't that fucking attractive."

Soft laughs.

I stared at Dana and I saw this little girl. An innocent child who played double Dutch like a demon before misery moved into her life. Sometimes I saw this twinkle in her eyes, and I swear to God that she was still six years old, skipping over cracks as she laughed all the way to public school. Soft eyes the color of a ripe potato. Full lips with no war paint, but ready to do battle at the drop of a hat. Hair a little nappy at the roots, pulled into four plaits.

Now she was a woman. The idealism has faded.

"Would you go to hell for me, Vince?"

"Considering where I've been, hell would be an upgrade."

It wasn't the child, but the innocence in her eyes, the sparkle behind her frustration, that was what I loved. In some ways the misery and suffering, I was attracted to that too. Maybe because of my own misery and suffering. Shit that made me more human.

Dana went in the living room and came back with her tote bag, the one she kept all of her ReMax papers in. She hesitated, then eased down the wall, sat down on the same exact spot where she'd rested before.

She told me, "This is my present to you."

It was the size of an eight-by-ten, wrapped in brown paper. I tore the wrapping paper off. She'd made copies of Kwanzaa's pictures, blown them up and had them perma-plaqued. Black, trimmed in old gold.

I said, "This is more beautiful than beautiful. Thanks."

"You're welcome."

"This is so—unexpected."

"Told you, I'm unpredictable and uncontrollable."

Dana gathered her mail. Her laundry was hanging in the doorway to the bedroom. She grabbed those clothes, read the receipt, then took out her checkbook. I had moved into the kitchen, put a teapot on the stove.

She put a check on the counter.

She said, "I get a commission check in a few days. I'll pay you my part of the rent, utilities, phone bill, what have you then."

"You don't have to."

"I have to pay my debts. I'm not that kinda girl."

She watched me. I watched her too.

Our gazes were broken when the yellow teapot whistled its song.

I asked, "Tea?"

She shrugged. "Sure."

I made two cups. We walked over to the love seat, took out two silver coasters, ones with Egyptian designs and soft felt bottoms, and put one close to her end of the coffee table. She sipped and cleared her throat.

"Vince, I wasn't ready."

"For what?"

"For you. For another relationship."

I listened. Sipped my tea and loaned her my ears.

She went on, "I have unresolved stuff."

"We all do."

"Honestly, you ever really got over Malaika?"

I shrugged, looked for the answer in my palms. "I guess not."

We pulled down our walls and we talked. I think I started it off. Told her things I should've told her from the get-go. Told her all about Malaika. How we met. How I went out of my way, did everything, spent every waking moment and every dime to woo her into my life. And about the comings up and goings down, told her how we broke up on that rainy night. Told her all about that night. It wasn't easy and I didn't sugarcoat it.

She said, "Damn, Vince. That was pretty fucked up. You were paying the house note, bought her a new car, and—damn. What did she do?"

"All she had to do was be my wife."

"Shit, wish I could've had that job back then. I'd've been one cooking, cleaning, soap opera watching—shit. I wish."

Some laughter.

She said, "Well, I guess we've been through a lot of the same crap."

We sat, sipped cup of tea after cup of tea and talked. We should've done that from the start. Then the end wouldn't be staring in our faces right now.

But that's not the way love goes. You show the good, disguise the bad.

I didn't tell her what I had done for Womack tonight. Didn't tell her that every time I heard a police siren my insides jumped, wondering if they were coming back for me. Womack had a wife. His kids lived under his wings, were being raised by his words. He had a parent, living to be witness to all he had done, to testify all that he stood for. While I had a breath in my body, nothing was going to take that away. Nobody was going to force him to wear shoes like mine, heavy boots too tight to the fit.

Dana motioned at the wall. "Sounds like they were going at it tonight."

I nodded. Naiomi never happened. All in my mind.

Somewhere down the line, we ran out of tea and conversation, but not necessarily in that order. Yawns came from both of our faces.

She said, "I'd better get going."

Dana put her cup in the sink, went to go potty again. The rest of her stuff, she said, she'd pick up when her plans had been solidified. I told her there was no rush. I'd be here.

I walked her downstairs. I stopped at the top of the three steps that led to my U-shaped stucco complex. Listened to the birds chirping in the trees. Hardly a whiff of smog in the air. Very few cars on the road. Two people jogging. One walking a Doberman. We stalled for a moment and watched this side of L.A. come to life.

I wished her well.

She handed me back the engagement ring. It was deep inside her purse. Finger was already empty when she came here. I wasn't going to ask for it, but if she gave it back, I wasn't going to be foolish and tell her to keep it. Maybe one day down the road, it'll fit on another finger.

I said, "Dana?"

"Yeah."

"The keys."

She took those off her plastic key ring.

"Make sure you call before you come over."

She pushed her beautiful lips up into a smile. "I will."

"And get your stuff in one trip. No need to drag this out."

"I plan to."

An awkward pause.

I told her, "Be safe."

"I will."

We waved good-bye.

Then she left. I walked away. As if we had never happened.

27 Dana

Hollyweird's Sunless Strip was crowded, loud, and rude. People hanging out in front of the clubs and bars. Miles of nonstop, impatient traffic zooming down the street. I parked in the paid lot at the Hyatt, across the street from the House of Blues. Me and my road dawg rushed down the steep hill on the back side of the Comedy Emporium. I had on black boots, jeans, fuchsia blouse, short leather jacket. Gerri hadn't changed from the dark pantsuit she'd worn when she was pushing real estate all day. She'd loosened her coat, put on a colorful, sassy scarf, undone a few buttons on her blouse, gave herself some after-five cleavage.

She checked her watch. "I hear people laughing all the way up here."

"It's almost nine. What time you need to be at Blondies?"

"By ten-thirty. We're ten minutes away, so as long as we're in the car by ten, we're cool. Dag, look at the line."

"All of black L.A. must be out tonight."

"Look around, look around," Gerri said with a smile. "There are more black men down here than they have locked up at the county day room."

An orange-haired, heavyset brother with earrings in his lip and eyebrow was at the glass door. His satin Comedy Emporium jacket rustled when he eased off his black wooden bar stool.

He said, "Seventeen-fifty to get in."

"I'm Dana Smith. I'm on Claudio Tillman's list."

"Got some ID?"

I whipped out my California driver's license. I wouldn't need that pretty soon. It would be walking, cabs, and A trains.

He clicked on a pen flashlight, read the license, then handed it back. "Hold up. Let me find the guest list."

Gerri said, "Hey, Chubby Checker, what's the point of looking at the license if you don't have the list?"

The bouncer shot Gerri a look as he waddled away.

I said, "Gerri, you're on a roll."

"I watch *Comic View*. Hell, I can be funny from time to time."

"So can *Comic View*."

More laughter in the background. The crowd was cracking up.

I asked, "I wonder who's onstage."

"Sounds like Emil Johnson."

I leaned so I could see what the inside of the place looked like, tried to peep past the black walls covered with pictures of every comedian from Buster Keaton to Robin Williams to Stepin Fetchit to Eddie Murphy. Black and white checkerboard floors and glass-topped tables. Typical club decor.

It happened in a flash. A sister in a lime-colored miniskirt passed by on the other side of the velvet rope. Big breasts that reminded me of Tyra Banks in that new Wonder bra by Victoria's Secret. She was laughing with a crowd of women, having a good time. Hair down her back, almost to her waist. She went by so quick that I didn't see her face, just her back and those too-big-to-be-real breasts.

I mumbled, "Couldn't have been."

Gerri asked, "Who you see?"

"Nobody."

Another bouncer, about double the girth of the first, stretching his black satin Comedy Emporium jacket to the limit, came to the door.

He was the bearer of bad news. My name wasn't on the list.

"Can you get Claudio Tillman for me? He's the promoter."

"Nope."

"Can you page him?"

"Nope."

"What can I do?"

"Your problem."

Gerri interjected, "This is his girlfriend."

He chuckled. "His problem."

I ran my tongue over my teeth and sang, "Okay."

Gerri said, "Minimum-wage-working idiots can be so rude."

He huffed, "You ought to know, Weaverella."

Gerri retorted, "This is my hair, Pork Chop. Guess you ain't heard of fat-free food, have you, Chunky But Funky?"

I politely asked, "May I see your list?"

He handed me the list. The name I didn't want to see ever again was at the top, scribbled in Claudio's block-style handwriting.

Gerri said, "What's up with the *Silence of the Lambs* face?"

"Nothing," I said. I cursed as I opened my purse and grabbed my wallet.

I handed the bouncer two twenties. He didn't take them.

He said, "Miss Thang, this is how you do it. You and your hair-club-for-women-looking friend need to jiggle those booties around the corner to the ticket booth right inside the front door, buy the tickets, then come back and get in line again."

I snapped, "What? We've got to get in line again?"

"Now step to the side so other people can get in."

I shuffled through the crowd with Gerri in tow.

Gerri said, "You're gonna buy the tickets?"

I lowered my eyes to the ground, headed for the asphalt hill that led to parking, but slowed down as I experienced a déjà vu: Claudio's body lying on top of mine, pleading for my affections, pang in his eyes as he apologized.

I broadcasted, "He ain't shit."

"Who you telling? His fat, arrogant ass needs to ask Richard Simmons to give him a ride to a Jenny Craig meeting."

"I'm not talking about the brother at the door."

"Dana, slow down before I break a heel."

I sneered. Heard the nonstop laughter behind my back. L.A. was laughing at me. Silly fool. I stormed back toward the club.

Gerri shouted, "Now where you going?"

I asked, "Your gun in your purse?"

"In my car."

"We should go get it."

"You think the jokes are going to be that bad?"

"Nothing's gonna be funny tonight."

Thirty-five dollars later, Gerri followed me around the perimeter of the club, through the chortles and shadows, until we came to a table of four brothers and two women sitting in the heart of the VIP section. Enough drinks and entrées for King Arthur, all of his knights, and their fair maidens.

A dark-skinned, broad-shouldered brother made a nervous motion for Claudio to look my way. I expected Claudio to look guiltier than Ted Kaczynski.

Claudio smiled and said, "Surprised to see you."

"Why is that?"

"You jetted on a brother in the middle of the night."

I reiterated what he already knew. "I didn't have clothes with me, had to work the next morning, told you that."

"Why didn't you call?"

"I left messages at your hotel."

"A day later. I rode you in the limousine, treated you better than you've ever been treated, wined you, poured my heart out to you, offered to let you stay with me in Harlem, offered you the best, then poof, didn't hear from you after you ran out on me. Paged you eight or nine times."

"My pager was off."

"Why was it off?"

I ran my hand over my hair. "Look, fine. You said your friend wanted to meet Gerri."

"Yeah, Raymond wanted to meet her. He's from Long Beach."

His friend waved at Gerri. My road dawg didn't respond.

I put my hand on the back of a chair, said, "Nobody's sitting here, so I guess it's okay for me and Gerri to sit behind the velvet rope with you, right?"

"Hold on, wait." Claudio's butt rose slowly from his seat. "What's up, Dee Dee?"

"What happened to your putting my name on the guest list?"

"Looks like you made it inside okay."

"I had to pay thirty-five dollars. Can you get my chips back?"

"Let me check in a minute. Go grab yourself a table up front."

"This chair is unoccupied, and you want me to go somewhere else?"

"Dee Dee . . ." Claudio's eyes searched the room for a second, then focused on me again. "Let's step to the hallway and talk."

I told him, "I saw her."

"Please. Can we step out in the hall and talk?"

"Talk right here."

Women of at least five nationalities lowered their watered-down drinks, put the laughter aside, and surveyed my scene with eyes of experience.

Gerri touched my arm. "Go into the hall and talk to him."

He headed toward the crowded hallway, and I followed him. A couple of sisters had stopped right behind him, ears wide open. Our body language let everybody know that there was a rumble in the jungle.

Claudio had the nerve to say, "Don't get loud on me out here."

"What about wanting me to come back to Harlem?"

"I did want you to come back."

"What do you mean, 'did'?"

He went off on me. "Don't come up in here tripping. When shit was low for me, you left me in New York, didn't even say good-bye. Then you got my hopes up, had me packing to come out here, and you changed your number on me as soon as you met that nig. Did all I could to find you. I came out here, stayed this long just to be with you. The nig showed up at my hotel, waiting for you in the parking lot, and what did you do? I begged you to stay, and you ran to him like what I offered you didn't mean shit. You're engaged, living with a nig, getting with me. Then as soon as you bust a nut, you're running back home to him the same night."

"What are you saying?"

"I've spent a lot of money on you. Dinner. Flowers. Limo. We made love. Don't trip on me. Fair exchange is no robbery."

"Fair exchange? Are you calling me a—"

"Tell me this: who did you call when you thought I was 'sleep?"

"What do you mean?"

He stressed, "When you were in my room, after we had made love, when you thought I was 'sleep, who did you sneak and call from my phone?"

I tilted my head sideways and looked at him like he was crazy.

He went on, "Cut the bull. You said that you called your homegirl."

"I said I was checking my messages."

"Dee Dee, I ain't stupid. When you snuck out, I

called down to the front desk and got the number. I called it up."

I sucked my jaw deep into my mouth, chewed my own flesh.

He rubbed his neck. "I'm the fool who saved your life. You were right. Maybe I should've let you fall. I'm the man who was there for you when your momma died. Hell, I helped you pick out the coffin."

"Leave Momma out of this."

"All I did for you. If I wasn't blowing up, you wouldn't be up in here now."

"Is that what you think?"

"That's what I know. Your actions're speaking loud."

"What about that girl? I see she's here."

"That chickenhead? I was gonna curb her ass, get my life right with you. Tia ain't nothing, you know that. Ain't never been nothing to me."

"So, you were gonna drop her for me?"

"This ain't about that chickenhead. Don't change the subject on me." He had the nerve to look pissed off. "What was I saying? Oh, yeah. That dude you engaged to answered the phone. The nig you live with. Vince, right?"

I ran my tongue over my teeth, my head barely moving up and down.

He got a little loud. "How's that supposed to make me see you? Plus you had your damn engagement ring on the whole damn time. You think that didn't hurt my feelings? Don't come up in here tripping at my show." Claudio stopped rubbing the bridge of his nose. "This is my gig. Could've been yours too. Don't trip. I got your pager number."

"You brushing me off?"

His words were firm, very final. "I'm working."

"So, that's how it is?"

"That's how it is."

My teeth clenched.

These words came from behind him: "So, I'm a *chickenhead*?"

It was Tia, the flight attendant with breasts the size of Mount Rushmore. She was with one of her girlfriends. They had been standing behind him the whole time, listening to all he said. Her mouth had been wide open. Sister was good, more patient that I would've been. Not a word had to come from my mouth. He had told it all.

My eyes moved up and down her frame, from the light brown hair flowing down her back to her tight lime miniskirt and beige blouse. Tia's eyes focused with recognition, flickers of the past.

Tia sighed. "This makes sense."

And just like that, her eyes watered. Her lip trembled.

Claudio walked away. I was right behind him, my hand down inside my purse.

Tia was right behind me, calling Claudio's name over and over, each time a few more tears weighing her voice down. So, we ended up at the VIP section. Drama, tension, evil eyes all over the place.

Claudio's homeboys' eyes bugged out when all of us came back together. Gerri was off to the side, but came back near me.

Tia went on, "You've been using my charge cards to rent your hotel rooms and fly your women out here?"

I said, "I live out here, Tia."

"No wonder he was breaking his neck to get out here and get the ball rolling. Now I know why you wanted me to wait before I came out here."

Then all of a sudden, I don't know why I didn't see it from the get-go, but the name of his company made sense. TNT. I had believed him when he said it meant TNT like dynamite, because he was blowing up. It meant Tia and Tillman. Or Tillman and Tia. What-the-fuck-ever, that's what it had to mean.

Tia stayed close to her girlfriend. I guess she remembered the pain from that middle of the night ass whooping I put on her in New York. Her girlfriend backed away; she wanted no part of this crap. I wasn't about to do anything, not to her. Sometimes it was nice to have a wicked reputation.

My stomach was knotting, face feeling hot, muscles twitching in my jaw. The room was shrinking, my vision blurring. I was Mother Nature: unpredictable and uncontrollable.

Claudio said, "Tia, sit down and shut up. Chill out."

Gerri jumped in, "Sister-girlfriend, I don't know who you are, and I know this ain't my cup of water to be drinking, but you're going to let this bald-headed fool disrespect you like that?"

He faced Gerri like an animal trapped. "Hey, bitch, nobody's talking to you."

My hand came out of my purse; the stun gun gripped in my fist. I was going to fire his butt up. Had it in my hand, finger on the trigger, and I froze. Took short breaths through my wide-open mouth and told myself that he wasn't worth it. I was worth more than this.

He was right about one thing. The night I tried to recapture old wants with Claudio, I'd been overwhelmed with desire for Vince. And I was lying in his rented bed thinking about Malaika, how she looked on that video, because that was exactly how I was feeling.

This was over. Was over before I ever made it to California. I'd mistaken the heat of a dead relationship for the warmth of real love.

Gerri's hand slid down my right arm, eased down my leather jacket until her fingers made it to the stun gun. At least, I thought that was Gerri touching me. But Gerri was in front of me, going off on Claudio.

The hand belonged to Tia.

She yanked the stun gun from my loose grip. Watery eyes, snot running from her nose, lips pursed so damn tight. I wanted to stop, drop, and roll before she sent all of that electricity through my body, but she rushed by me and thrust the fifteen-dollar weapon deep into Claudio's back. There was the loud static discharge. Claudio made a crowlike noise, cawed, and twisted. Agony was flowing through his body in ocean-size waves. He gagged, choked on his own saliva, all of that noise blending with the sounds of light applause from the comic's closing routine.

She shocked him again.

Tia's friend finally got enough wind to let out an animal-like scream. Claudio's friends were leaping over seats, tripping over the rail, the men leaving the women behind, sisters squealing, jumping out of the way.

Tia did it again, sent another electrical discharge up his spine. His face twitched, convulsed, eyes were rolling into the back of his head. He struggled to get away from her, staggered toward me like a zombie. I pushed him off me. He bumbled back toward Tia. And homegirl extended that stun gun and sent another shock up his spine. Opened the rest of his nerves.

That was when I screamed.

Claudio's bald head glistened—just that quick he had sprouted gallons of sweat. His mouth was wide open, but he was quiet, like he owned too much agony to create words. Looked like his muscles had locked up.

I tried, but I couldn't breathe.

A faint voice said, "Help him . . ."

Someone else yelled, "Stop blocking the stage."

"That what his ass gets."

Claudio fell, slammed across a round table, sent wine and beer and shot glasses flying every which-a-way. He ricocheted to the ground, bounced and twisted, twitched, head bounced off the black and white tile.

Tia was frowning at me. Holding that stun gun and grimacing at me like I was the grinch who stole her Christmas. She came toward me.

Sounds faded. The world was getting darker. I was about to pass out. Told my legs to move, told myself to concentrate. Get control of my body and get away from that psycho flight attendant before she got to me.

Coldness made my teeth clatter. Tia's thin lips moving

so fast while she raised the stun gun. Pointed at me in a you're-next kinda way. Couldn't hear the words rushing from her tight lips. Everything muffled. Air too thick. Knees about to fold. Stun gun coming toward my body.

Darkness surrounded me.

28 Dana

A zillion lights flashed in my face. Buildings and bill-
boards and homeless people went by me in a blur. My
body was thawing out at thirty miles an hour. I was in the
passenger seat of Gerri's car. She was concentrating on
traffic, whipping from lane to lane. I moved my tongue
around the inside of my mouth, tried to add moisture to
the dryness.

"What—what . . . Gerri, what happened?"

"Well, welcome back."

"What happened?"

"I dragged you out of there."

Yellow. I saw yellow lights behind us.

The stun gun was welded into my palm.

I asked, "How did I get this?"

"She gave it to you."

"Gave it to me?"

"After she messed up Claudio, she sashayed right up
to your face and put it back in your hands, bounced out
of there with her head high in the sky, like she was leaving church on a Sunday after service."

I dropped the damn thing to the floor.

"You think she killed him?"

"Can't kill something that doesn't have a heart."

"I'm serious."

"He was twitching like an epileptic when we ran out.
He'll recover."

"Oh, God."

I let my window down. Still couldn't breathe. Was getting claustrophobic. Wanted to stick my head out and pant like an overheated puppy.

Gerri drove the side avenues, took the smutty streets by the Pantages Theatre and the Capitol Records building. In my passenger mirror, I saw those lemon-colored lights again. Two cars back. We turned. The yellow light turned too. We turned again. Those lights turned.

I said, "Somebody's following us."

"Nobody's following us."

Then the yellow lights vanished.

I relaxed into the soft leather seat. We ended up getting trapped at a light over on Gower at Franklin, across from the Roosevelt Hotel and the entrance to the 101 freeway.

Claudio's words, every last insult was inside my head.

Gerri's engine stopped; she took her keys out of the ignition.

I jumped. "Why you cut the car off?"

"I want my Temprees CD out of the glove compartment."

"How can you be in the mood for music?"

"When I'm stressed, I need my old school music."

"Give me the keys. Make sure we're not being followed."

"Relax, if they're after anybody, they're after the other girl. They probably have an APB out on her breasts right now."

"Not funny. How do I open this thing?"

"Is funny. Turn it left. Okay, then turn it right. She could've breast-fed Egypt with those things."

"Your CD's not in here. All I see are NAS and Q-Tip."

"Jefferson must've stole my music. That pisses me off."

Gerri sat back for a second and massaged her temples. Massaged like that was the main memory she had been trying to avoid.

A few thoughts passed before I asked, "You love Jefferson?"

"Enough for this to make my skin break out, and that's too much." Gerri finger-combed her hair. "So much money. What was I thinking? I've sunk too much money into that dream. I at least want to break even."

"What happened with Butter?"

"Nothing yet. She started off talking crazy, but I put her in her place. Had to put my gun on the table."

"You what?"

"She threatened me."

"Damn."

"Nobody threatens me. I've got that ragamuffin too scared to pee. I told the gold digger to get rid of that problem."

That jarred me. "Told her or suggested it? Whose choice is it?"

"I already made her appointment for tomorrow."

"What Butter say about the whole thing?"

"Don't ask me about that anymore."

I shifted my body, moved away from Gerri.

I asked, "You love Melvin?"

"Sometimes I want him back. Sometimes I don't. I want to prove I can make it without him. But I want my kids to have a relationship with their daddy. They love him. He's great with them. That's attractive to me, in a different kind of way. A spiritual way, I guess. Surprised?"

I shook my head, used my hand to smooth out my hair. I understood her wanting and not wanting at the same time. I knew how dangerous and misguiding left-over love could be. I understood Gerri. Love ain't never been a rational beast. And I understood my momma.

I should've been crying, but I chuckled. "You see the look on Claudio's face when that wacko zapped his butt? Never seen anybody look that damn ugly."

Gerri bounced around and imitated him.

We laughed. Laughed so hard that I had stopped watching my back. Vibrations from another bass system made it to us before the music did. A car rolled up the hill toward us. Cheap sound system, too much volume.

It was a truck with the lemon-colored fog lights. It zoomed up on my side of the car. Before the truck stopped, a brother leaped out the back, landed flat-footed, and rushed toward my window. The truck jerked to a halt, and the driver hopped out and followed his friend into the broken light.

"Oh, shit."

"Go, Gerri, go!"

"Where my keys?"

"In your hand! Go!"

Gerri fumbled the keys, dropped them on the floor.

Two young brothers ran into the thin light. Mustaches that hadn't thickened with age. Sweaty faces filled with acne.

"Get out the car, bitches." One of 'em pulled his shirt back, showed a gun sticking out from his checkered boxers. "I said, out the damn hoopty!"

I fumbled for the door.

Gerri screamed, "What are you doing?"

I yelled, "We're getting jacked. Get out."

"Hell, no. I'm not giving up my ride."

I tried to duck down in my seat. "Then drive!"

One of the thugs grabbed my door handle. The door opened. Interior light popped on. Sensor dinged. The boy grabbed my shoulder.

I thought about Vince. Wished I could get him a message, tell him my last words. It was strange that that desire came when the Grim Reaper had pried open my car door.

Gerri raised her right arm, brought her gun up, pointed the pistol right between his pretty brown thighs. She spoke as calm as a summer breeze: "Make my day, and it'll be *hasta la adios.*"

"Damn." He cha-cha'd a step backward. "My bag, my bag."

Gerri snapped, "Idiot! It's bad, not bag. Bad, as in wrong, as in mistake, as in error, like the one you just made."

There were two pops and a scream. Quick pops from a small and cute black gun that rang as the bullets flew by my head, whizzed though my open window. The pops had come from Gerri's gun. The scream came from me as I grabbed and covered her ears. The truck's window exploded. The boys cursed, yelled, dove to the concrete. Gerri ran the red light, zoomed to the freeway entrance, passed two cars before the end of the on-ramp.

My heart was a mile in front of us, racing at its own pace, about to explode. As my ears cleared, I heard Gerri laughing. I was about to go off on her. Until I saw her tears.

"I'm having a messed-up week," she said, then wiped her eyes.

Gerri had an anger, a darkness that made me forget about all the drama I'd gone through in the last hour. Her words were molten lava. "Jefferson's stressing me. I'm hiding up under a ton of makeup at least twice a week, messing up my damn skin. I'm in love with an ex-husband I can't stand. Kids won't stop begging. And now fools on the streets too young to pop a nut are treating me like I ain't nothing."

"You didn't have to shoot at them."

"Should've shot their damn nuts off."

"You're crazy."

"They tried to jack me and I'm crazy? They had a gun. For all you know, they would've had us somewhere butt naked—"

"They didn't care about us."

"Duh, hello. That was obvious. What clued you in?"

"You know what I mean. They wanted the car."

"They didn't want *the* car, they wanted *my* car. I make my living driving this car. I drive my kids to school in this car."

"Your insurance would've paid you for another one."

"No damn insurance."

I said, "What?"

"You heard me."

"No insurance?"

"Too many speeding tickets. Nobody'll insure me without wanting to charge me an arm and a leg. And having a kid in my house old enough to drive ain't no help. Even the people who advertise that they'll insure anybody hung up on me." Gerri wiped her eyes and let loose a bitter smile. "Always something. Always, always, always."

"Stop sounding like a damn victim."

"Get a grip," she snapped, damn near exploded. "Dana, I've watched your self-defeating behavior for months. You can have anything you want, if you'd just stop getting in your own way. You're your own worst enemy. You're carrying luggage and trying to swim at the same time. That's what your problem is."

She'd insulted me without a thought. Her wide eyes said that she was terrified and trying to play it cool.

I said, "And your problem is that you're attached to material things."

"Don't playa hate."

"I was the closest to them, so they could've killed me. Hell, for all I know, you could've shot me in my head a minute ago."

Gerri said, "And if you want to know the truth, all that crap you say about Vince hurts me, 'cause I know men are probably saying the same thing about me. You probably feel the same way about me."

"What are you talking about?"

"Hell, if you ain't noticed, I'm a single parent. With two kids. I wish I could count the number of men who disqualify me because of that, and because I was married to Melvin. That pisses me off every time. You think that just because I have a failed marriage, because I've reproduced effectively, you think that means I don't deserve to be loved anymore?"

I had no answer to that.

Gerri said, "Niggas like you make me sick."

"I'm not a nigga."

"Then stop acting like one."

I went off on her ass. "Since we're talking about niggas, as you say, you're the worst one I know. Jefferson fucks you over, and now you're going to make Butter get an abortion. What kind of mess is that? Hell, you have a daughter. What if somebody like you did the same thing to her?"

"Shut up, Dana."

"I hope you rot in hell. You'll do anything just to keep a man. Niggas like you is why women like me feel the way we do."

A moment passed. All she said was, "Ouch."

I blew a ton of heated air out my nostrils. "Gerri, we need to reevaluate our friendship."

Gerri hissed, then mimicked me, "Reevaluate?"

"We can't be friends. Can't be friends if you could do Butter like that. Especially over some no-good that's dogged you out."

"I don't believe this shit. I let your no-credit, no-money, homeless ass sleep in my house, eat my food, shit in my toilet, ain't charged you a damn dime, and this is the thanks I get?"

"Whatever. If some bitch was doing that to your daughter, you'd have a different attitude. What goes around comes around."

I'd said it. No way for me to take it back. Didn't want to. Should've said that a long time ago.

"No wonder Vince slapped your silly ass."

That pretty much wrenched my heart out of my chest.

Both of us were crying, too choked up to talk. All this drama, everything that had happened tonight had both of us a little crazy. I know that it had me running too high on emotion, about to O.D. on adrenaline. It was dangerous, both of us being so high-strung in a speeding car that offered no space.

I put my hand on top of Gerri's. She held mine tight.

"Sorry, Dana."

"Guess I needed to hear that."

"Me too. Guess I needed to hear that too."

My sister. My friend. My road dawg.

If we weren't friends before this day, we were definitely friends now.

"I mean it, Gerri, don't encourage Butter."

"Maybe I'm pissed off and saying it wrong. I wasn't trying to encourage her. I was explaining to her her options, in a realistic kinda way. The same way I would talk to Stacy if she was in that predicament. Butter's young. If she popped out a baby right now, with no skills, no income, she'll be raising a county baby. That's what I told her."

"And her reaction?"

"She didn't want to hear it, just started shouting, 'Jefferson can afford it.' Told her what I've gone through with my kids, that she can't depend on Jefferson. She couldn't see through those resentful eyes, told me I was playa hatin'. That's where her head was at."

"That bad?"

"All I can say was, it got ugly. It's hard to act like Iyanla Vanzant when you're dealing with the Jerry Springer generation."

"Well, leave that drama between Butter and Jefferson."

"You're right," she said after a second went by. "Time for a reality check. I need to take my losses, stop before I get in way too deep, let Jefferson and Butter work it out. Ain't my pot to be pissing in."

I patted her hand. Squeezed it a few times.

"Dana, since we're telling each other off, you need to lose your childish vision of the world and grow the hell up. Stop thinking about what Dana wants and develop some sensitivity to other people's lives and learn to admit when you're wrong."

Simply, I said, "You're right."

A moment passed.

Gerri said, "Tonight."

"What about tonight?"

"This is my last night at Blondies."

"When did you decide that?"

"When I saw the gun in that boy's belt, I thought about my kids. Imagined myself in a coffin, being planted six feet under. Wasn't ready for that. That was a sign. I should be at home. I need to be at home. Need to be back in church, trying to get right from the inside out."

I stared out the window. Wiped my eyes with my ashy knuckles, licked the tears from the back of my hand, then found a tissue and blew my nose. I handed Gerri a tissue. She did the same.

29 Dana

I followed Gerri through a side door of Blondies. "Mustang Sally" thumped from every speaker. China Doll was onstage under the spotlight doing acrobatic moves, swinging from a pole, rolling into an upright split.

Gerri said, "Come on in the back."

"You sure about that?"

"C'mon."

When I stepped into the den of mostly naked vixens, my nose scrunched, eyes burned a little. Too many perfumes, so much nail polish in such a small space. Dancers' eyes rose from the vanity tables. Sharp looks at me. Gerri undressed, neatly hung her dress clothes up in a pink metal locker, pinned her hair, then slipped on a black leather G-string.

Gerri took over the conversation. "Some fools just tried to jack me."

She told the whole story, about what had happened at the comedy club, how Tia had shocked Claudio like he was at the end of his Green Mile, then gave blow by blow of what went down under the overpass. Women were applauding and pumping their arms in the air. Our whacked victories had become their victories. We'd changed from being Lucy and Ethel to Thelma and Louise.

One of the girls, who had an angry rattlesnake tattooed on her belly, jumped in, "Maybe one of the customers had you followed. When I was dancing at the Barbary I was followed; at Angels I was followed. Then when I was working over on La Cienega, these white boys tried to jack me in front of Trashy Lingerie. I came out of my heels and ran through six lanes of traffic all the way back up to Acapulco Mexican restaurant to get help."

Gerri's pager went off.

She cursed.

I asked, "Same three digits?"

"Why would somebody keep paging me and put in three digits?"

"What three digits?" one of the girls asked.

"Three-oh-four. It's a West Virginia area code."

Most of the girls paused, and half the room laughed.

"That ain't no damn West Virginia. Cinnamon Delight, somebody is calling you a hoe."

"What?"

"Any ten-year-old knows that if you turn your pager upside down, 3-0-4 looks like H-O-E. Just some fool playing games on your beep-beep. That's probably who was following you. Some customer after your kitty kat."

"Couldn't be. Those were boys. Too young to get in here."

"Never too young for kitty kat."

Everybody was ragging on Gerri, and even though a shallow grin was on my face, hiding the fear that had been in my heart all evening, once again I glanced from woman to woman, from sister to sister. Wondered how a room full of black women who came from a legacy of queens ended up like this, stripping for anybody with a dollar in his hand.

Then Gerri said, "Major announcement."

The girls listened up.

She said, "This is my last night. Y'all can have this crap."

"What're you gonna do?"

"Mind my own business and leave others alone."

They all laughed.

Gerri's eyes stayed on me while she made her short

speech. Still, the environment, I couldn't take it any-more.

I said, "Gerri, I'm going out front."

"I won't be long."

"When you shaking your rump?"

"Next. Slow crowd tonight. The girls say nobody's tip-ping, so I'll be retiring after one, no more than two sets. Going home, get a good night's sleep, then get up and have some oatmeal, wheat toast, and turkey sausages with my children."

I shifted back and forth.

She said, "You're staying at my place tonight, right?"

I shrugged. "Okay."

A dancer wiggled her breasts and said, "Cinnamon, I've been trying to go home with you for a long time. You trying to hurt my feelings?"

Gerri painted on her scarlet lipstick as she retorted, "It ain't that kinda party. I like mine dark, wide, and long."

"We can go by the Pleasure Chest and pick one up on the way."

Gerri gave her the finger. The other girls laughed.

Tonight, both of us were wound too tight. My mis-placed anger and frustration had been flying all over the place. Damn muscles were knotted up like monkey fists.

I put my hand back on Gerri's hand. A hardworking woman.

"Gerri, how does a person like me get to be as selfless as you, the way you are with your kids?"

"Time."

"How do you sacrifice when so much has been taken from you?"

"You just do."

"You make it look easy."

"I'm a mother. We make a lot of things look easy."

Then she shook her head; her red lips turned way down.

I asked, "You okay?"

"That three-oh-four thing. Wondering who that could be. None of the customers know I'm in real estate. Nobody in real estate knows about this. At least I hope not. That would be tragic. Couldn't be Melvin, he doesn't play games like that. I hope one of my kids' friends hasn't found out about my midnight paper route. That would be so embarrassing."

"After tonight you can deny it."

"Yeah."

I left the room. I bought a glass of wine, sipped half at the bar, and headed toward the back corner.

A crowd of women were a few tables over. My sensitive nose picked up their perfume long before I heard their girly-girly chatter rolling in the darkness. Barely noticed them because my mind was stressing over the scene with Claudio, but one of those women was checking me out in a major kind of way. Women did come in here to watch women too. And across the room a sister with golden hair was getting a lap dance. This was that kind of world.

I ignored them.

The night I'd lain with Claudio, another man was in my heart. I pulled out my c-phone and dialed what used to feel like home. The answering machine kicked on. I listened to the outgoing message, my own cheerful voice telling the world that nobody was around to take their call. A perky, cheerful message. I never realized how happy I'd sounded with Vince.

I pushed the end button. So symbolic. Turned power off.

My heart was still ringing.

Then it stopped.

Sand Dune Park. That truck was the same truck I'd seen at Sand Dune Park. That hit me all of a sudden. Had to be the same boys.

And somebody was staring me down.

The candlelight at that table was bright enough for me to see the sister had an earring in her nose, just like Naiomi has.

The sister leaned into the light and made strong eye contact with me.

I turned away. Didn't need any more shit, not tonight.

The instant I turned away, I realized who she was. I leaned and stared that way. She had turned her back. Their candle had been blown out.

That was scary. Very scary.

I spoke out loud, "No way. Can't be her up in here."

I headed that way, slowly walked through the darkness, moved through the old school beat of Ice Cube rapping "No Vaseline."

The D.J. did an upbeat intro, announced that crowd favorite Cinnamon Delight was about to take the show to another level.

When I was close to the table, the sister rose from her seat defiantly. Her face was made up to the teeth, and she was dressed in black Lycra pants, white cotton blouse, black jacket. Sister was pretty, looking grown, but still a child.

I said, "Butter?"

"Step off."

One of her friends, a dark girl with short hair, I believe that was Chocolate Starr, said, "Who that?"

Butter said, "One of that three-oh-four's friends."

Then I knew who had been paging Gerri.

I asked, "What the hell are you doing up in here?"

Butter and her friends shared expressions, then nervous laughs. Two of the girls were in Jefferson's group. My eyes went from face to face. And it made sense. This was the same crowd that I had seen out front the night I thought I'd seen Butter. I had seen Butter. She had been stalking.

"Butter, what're you—"

The sister they called Big Leggs jumped to her feet, pointed at the stage, and said, "This is the same stupid routine she always does. She's getting ready to turn her back and stick her old ass all up in the air."

Butter twisted her lips. "Y'all still down with this?"

Pooh Bear said, "We got your back."

"Starr, your brothers didn't do it right." Butter's eyes were locked on Gerri. "Never send a boy to do a woman's job."

I was almost shouting. "Butter, what are you—"

Then Butter growled and shoved me so hard that I stumbled and flopped over a plastic chair, hit the floor hard. Hurt my leg. Bumped my head. Aching and limping, I got right back up in pain.

I screamed Gerri's name, but the music smothered my warning. Ice Cube's song masked the sounds of the ruckus.

Those sisters had became wolves, howling and racing across the room. All of them bolted to the stage and jumped up on the platform before Gerri could stop vibrating her butt and turn around. All except Pooh Bear. She was mortified. That girl ran two steps behind her friends, then made an abrupt U-turn and raced for the front door. She wanted no part of this scenario.

They swarmed the stage and yanked Gerri off balance, snatched the blonde wig off, threw her from the six-foot-high stage, and were on the floor beating her down before the bouncers realized what was going on.

I screamed like there was no tomorrow. My throat hurt like it had first-degree burns, already raw from yelling half the night.

Curses and squeals came from Gerri.

Flying chairs.

Butter staggered like she'd been hit or kicked. Then she yelled, dove on top of Gerri, and the fight vanished from my sight.

I tried to get to her, but people were in the way.

Gerri was yelling for help. Her pleas frosted the room, an aching sound that filled the air like the howls of a wounded animal.

Waitresses dropped trays, ran topless out into the streets. Customers fled in the middle of lap dances and ran like hell.

Butter's friends were swinging at anybody who came close and tried to stop the fight. Ice Cube had stopped rapping. One of the bouncers shrilled that he had been cut. I knocked chairs out of my way, stumbled on other things, but before I could get to Gerri, a bouncer grabbed me, lifted me in the air with my feet kicking, tried to make me go the other way. I wrestled with him, clawed him, finally got free.

By then the girls were breaking for the emergency exit. Butter was hurt, her hair all mangled, blood on her face like she'd been slashed by a wolverine, stumbling into tables, clawing to get free from whoever tried to stop her, the white blouse she had on covered in blood.

The side door flew open and slammed the brick wall, allowed a streetlight to create a moment of visibility. Outside was the same truck. Yellow fog lights on the front. Its engine revving, lurching like it was ready to take flight. I heard the squeaky voices of the young boys panicking, screaming at the girls to come on and *hurry the fuck up*.

No more screams from Gerri. Not a single sound.

30 Vince

I woke at sunrise. No woman at my side. My mind ablaze. Dana had been my sunshine and happiness. The river that flowed through my life and quenched my every thirst. I'd have to thirst again. Would have to find a river that was truly mine.

This afternoon I had an interview over at Dan L. Steel. Was nervous about that. Job changes, just like the possibility of a layoff, raise a brother's stress level. At Boeing, unless a new contract dropped in their laps this week, I was the next one scheduled for involuntary unemployment.

Nikes were in the corner, so I put those on and ran the Crenshaw Loop. Eleven miles and some serious change. Ran the course in less time that it usually took me to run Inglewood Ten. Probably because while I ran, I blanked out, and with every step I became more nervous.

Dana was sitting at the top of the stairwell. I was about to go off on her for not calling before she came to get her stuff.

Until I was close enough to see her uncombed hair. Eyes bloodshot. Face oily. Trembling. Hands massaging each other.

She wiped her eyes. "I need a friend."

Dried blood covered her shirt.

31 Dana

It was right there in black and white. The metro section of the *Times* had an article about how Gerri Greene, real estate agent, divorced mother of two, former Cal State Long Beach honor student, was attacked at a strip club on the Sinset Strip. That summed up what was printed in the mainstream papers. Stories that had more empathy, that hit from that struggling single-mom angle, ran on the front page of the African American newspapers: *Wave, Crusader*, and *Sentinel*. *Gerri's face, the one grinning on every bench and bus stop on the west side of L.A., was on the front of every paper.*

Reporters called my job and asked me a question or two, but I hung up in their faces. The Asian girl who worked down at Blondies saw opportunity knocking like a Jehovah's Witness, opened her big mouth and told the whole world her version of what went down that night. Did that bull while she posed for the reporters, swinging upside down from the trapeze. She said that Butter and her friends had come down, said that they wanted to audition for the club, but wanted to sit in the back and watch first.

Played the owner big-time. All of that young T&A looked like a gold mine in the making. Let the whole crew in without checking ID. Even bought them a round of drinks. When the dust cleared, the owner of that gentlemen's bar had no comment. I pretty much expected that.

On that floor, I had held onto Gerri and screamed for

help. Hadn't ever seen anybody look the way Gerri did when I made it to her.

Fifty stitches to Gerri's pretty face, chest, arms, and back. A concussion. Ankle twisted, leg fractured from being pulled from a stage that was six feet high. Yanked from heaven to the hell below.

I was glad that she was going to be okay, in the physical sense.

The two teenage boys who had tried to jack us and two of the girls from Dangerous Lyrics had turned themselves in. They did that after their pictures were shown all over the news. Butter was still on the run. On the morning and evening news, reporters showed that girl's estranged mother in front of the camera, begging for her only daughter to come back home.

That wasn't the end of it. The midday news played a snippet from a Dangerous Lyrics tune, let it be known that the rough lyrics were written by Butter; they emphasized that a thousand times. By the end of the day, all of the local news stations had picked up the story. The struggling mom doing what she had because of her delinquent C.S. was a damn good angle. And to top it off, they rolled some video that had been taken with the security cameras, scenes from that night at Blondies.

It was all negative. But, like they say, any publicity is good publicity. And Dangerous Lyrics was getting pumped up like hell.

Within two days, Tower Records, the Wherehouse, Sam Goody—nobody could keep Dangerous Lyrics CDs on the shelves. That's what the paper said. I had to go by their word on that. But I did know, firsthand, that not one of the a.m. drive-time D.J.'s missed a beat either talking about it, taking a people poll, or doing wicked spoofs on the wretched situation. And I know how my people are; this time next week, every unfunny brother and sister would be using Dangerous Lyrics as a punch line.

Jefferson never called my road dawg. Never went to

the hospital. Didn't call a friend of a friend and ask them to check on her.

No note. No good-bye.

By the end of the week, I'd gone to UCLA Medical Center all but one day to see Gerri. The only day I didn't go was the day I used to finish most of my packing. I was so worried about my girl that I called a few times every day, but being there, seeing her laid up like that, puffed to the max, damn near unrecognizable, was too much for me.

Besides, her private room was a little bit on the crowded side twenty-four-seven. Flowers. Cards. Her family was there, standing over Gerri's tattered body and swollen face. Ex-in-laws. Parents had flown out from Little Rock. Her children. Her ex-hubby, Melvin, was boohooing the hardest. I didn't know if he was sobbing for Gerri, or his children, but he was dropping tears left and right.

Not one person from work had showed up. No one at all.

Gerri was on painkillers, using bedpans, slipping in and out of consciousness, but I watched her wake up and hold Melvin's hand like she wished she'd never let him go.

A tense moment came when Gerri told me, "Put a mirror up to my face."

"No. You don't want me to do that."

"Put a mirror up to my face."

I did. It took all my strength, but I did.

Gerri started to cry at the sight of herself. As a matter of fact, everybody started to cry.

In between, I tried to get some sleep, stay rested so I could handle driving all the way back to New York. Had mapped out my route, hotels I was going to stop at. Drive six to eight hours a day, depends on how much my booty starts to hurt, and sleep all night.

But sleeping was hard to do. Gerri's parents, other people from her family, her kids, everybody was at her condo, every spot being used as a bed. Too many people, not enough bathrooms. Melvin was over there every day, getting the kids to school, taking care of business for her. No space in her place for me.

At the crack of dawn I heard an argument on the Naiomi and Juanita side of the wall. Once again I was kicked away from dreamland. In my dream Gerri wasn't hooked to an IV, legs weren't in a splint, didn't have to buzz the nurse for a bedpan. She was herself. No scars. All smiles and laughs.

My pillow slipped to the carpet as I sat up on Vince's sofa. The furniture squeaked a little. I let the layers of covers fall from my bare chest to my lap. As I looked around for the peach-colored silk scarf that had come off my head sometime last night, Vince stirred on the other side of the wall. In the bedroom. On the floor. That's where he'd been sleeping ever since I came back to Stocker and Degnan. At night I closed the hall door and confined myself to the living room. He'd closed the door to the bedroom.

Sounded like something broke next door.

Vince came to the doorway.

I said, "Good morning."

"Morning."

That pretty much summed up our conversation.

His eyes fell on my packed suitcases, on the boxes that I'd have to cram inside my Q45 this evening. He hovered there, barely dressed in his green plaid boxers, nothing else on that brown skin.

I pulled the covers up, hid my breasts, and as I untangled my hair, I thought about how we used to be. So passionate. So much conversation. Heading for a hot shower, loving under hot water and steam. Kisses on my face so light and tender. How I'd jerk, then laugh, when he began to nibble on me. How flaming butterflies danced in my belly at that moment when we became one. In my mind, he whispered my name.

Vince was in the doorway, arms bare, chest out, staring at the wall between his apartment and the landlord's.

I asked, "Malaika called you yet?"

He nodded. "Kwanzaa's singing up at the mall today."

"You had a chance to meet her again?"

"Not yet."

"I don't think that's right, having you on hold like that."

"I know."

Then I encouraged him. "Take her to court."

No response.

Love for his child was in his eyes. Above all of the other madness that had invaded his life, our lives, that was what was important to him. That little girl would always be the most important.

If we'd had children, I'd want him to feel that way about what we'd created. I wish my daddy had felt that way about me. He loved me, I know that, but he didn't put me in front of other women in his life. He sacrificed his relationship with me to make his relationship with his new wife stronger.

I said, "Vince."

The argument next door sounded more like Juanita's voice.

Vince hesitated. "Yeah?"

"You know this is gonna be my last day here."

He went into the bathroom. I recognized the sound of water breaking water. The toilet flushed. Recognized the sound of him washing his hands.

The bathroom door opened. I called his name.

A while went by before he finally stood in the doorway. He was close, but his voice was faint, far away: "What's up?"

"I'm going by the office to close out my business. Make plans to pay them back for my delinquent desk fees. I have to call the IRS and do the same. Tonight, after traffic dies down, I'm driving back to New York."

"Why at night?"

"It's cooler. Less traffic."

Silence, for a long moment.

I said, "I just wanted to thank you for everything."

Finally he cleared his throat, said, "You want me to carry your stuff to the car after I get home from work?"

"If you're not too busy. Just the heavy things. I'll take my clothes down this afternoon after I finish running around."

"Okay."

"Maybe before I bounce out of here, we can ride up on Pico and get something to eat from Roscoe's, chitchat over some chicken and waffles before I go."

He said, "We can skip the chicken and waffles. You always said that place in Harlem has a better recipe."

I ran my tongue over my lips, slow and easy, let the covers drop and show the blackness around my nipples, saw Vince shift. I pulled the covers back up to my chin. His eyes made me ashamed of my nakedness.

I asked, "How do you want me to settle up what I owe you for rent, the phone bill, and what have you?"

"I'll leave that up to you."

"Will you take a postdated check for part of what I owe?"

"I'll leave that up to you."

I imagined us on a cool summer night, with the ocean breeze blowing through an open window, cooling off our sweat just when we needed it most.

Next door somebody shouted. Not like the other times. That one was a painful cry that made me jump. Vince did the same.

We looked at each other. Vince knew he should be the last one to get involved. And if they were fighting about what I thought they were fighting about, me sticking my head in their biz wouldn't be any better.

I said, "I'm about to eat a quick breakfast, maybe toast and a boiled egg. Want me to make you some before you go?"

"Nah. I'll grab something at Dan L. Steel in the cafeteria. Tyrel wants me to meet with some more people in metrology."

"No problem. How do you like your new job?"

"It's a much better gig than Boeing."

"Pays a lot more."

"Yeah." He smiled a true smile. "Benefits are better. Thanks for the hookup. I don't know if I thanked you."

"What are you going to do if Boeing calls you back?"

"Try and get on and work second shift."

"You're gonna work two full-time gigs?"

"If I can swing it. That'll keep me busy."

He'd said it like I was nothing more than a friend.

I said, "Guess since you'll be making all the cabbage, you'll be hanging out at the Townhouse on KJLH night."

He turned away. I stared at the back of his head, tried to read his mind.

He asked, "You're not going to tell Rosa Lee and them good-bye?"

"I hate good-byes. Tell them for me."

"At least go see Gerri before you raise up."

I shrugged. Didn't know if I could handle seeing her mangled body one more time. Didn't want to have an emotional good-bye. Just wanted to get on the road to freedom. Get to my future.

He asked, "Is that how you treat your friends?"

"I don't want to leave sad." Again I shrugged because I didn't know what else to do. "Give Harmonica and Womack a hug. Kiss Rosa Lee and her babies for me. Kiss Ramona twice. She's so beautiful. I want to have a baby like her one day."

The door across the hall opened.

"Naiomi," Juanita's voice carried, "I want you out of here. *Now.*"

Vince turned his head toward the demand.

I forgot about being naked and let the covers drop to the brown carpet. Reached down to the floor, grabbed my ripped 501s and pulled them on in a hurry. Hunted for my salmon-colored bra, but it was lost in the sheets.

He opened the door wide enough for us to see out into the hallway. I took baby steps until I was next to Vince. My shoulder touching his arm.

Juanita was there wearing jeans, a UCLA sweatshirt, hair pulled back into a ponytail, face fire red, arms folded tightly across her chest.

Naiomi was barefoot in gray cotton sweats, no makeup, her braids tied up at the top of her head, quivering a little. Right eye bruised.

Juanita stared at Vince like he was the worm inside her apple.

She snapped, "I'm going to do my best to get you out of here too, Vincent Calvary Browne."

Vince said, "Junior. My name is Vincent Calvary Browne Junior."

Juanita huffed her way down the stairs.

Vince asked Naiomi, "What happened to your eye?"

"Guess I fell, Mr. Browne."

Something was bound to happen. Maybe, considering all of the choices, this was actually pretty mild. Not many restful hours had been on that side of the wall, or this. I'd told Vince about Claudio, what had happened at the comedy club. Told him, yes, I'd been intimate with Claudio. Tried to ease my soul. Vince had told me about what went down between him and Naiomi in the garage. Hurt me to hear that. And when Vince wasn't looking, I went into the bathroom. And I cried like I did the moment the dirt was scattered on my momma's coffin. Solidified that me and Vince were a done deal. That's what sex does: it starts relationships and it verifies the end of relationships.

Juanita was at the bottom of the stairs. She yelled up at Naiomi, "Miss Smalls, how long will it take you to gather your belongings?"

Naiomi answered, "Not long. Fifteen minutes."

That was when I led Vince back inside. I went to the sofa, folded my covers, then sat down and watched Vince gaze out the window. Toward San Bernardino.

Then he went down the hallway and looked at my laminated pictures of his kid. He'd put my present up next to the photos of his parents.

I made herbal tea, toast. Offered some to Vince. He declined.

Twenty minutes later, there was a knock on the door. I answered. It was Naiomi. Shades hid the bruise on her eye. In the hallway was a stuffed green military backpack.

Naiomi said, "Miss Smith?"

"Yeah."

"May I come in?"

"Come on."

I stepped back. Naiomi came inside. Barely.

My scrutiny went to Vince. His eyes went to Naiomi, then to me. So much uptightness in this crammed space. I released a weary sigh to go with my understanding expression that might've looked something like a mother's smile. Over the last few days, since I'd dumped that luggage holding my leftover love, my spirt had aged, left me feeling much wiser. I wanted to cling to that new feeling inside of me.

Naiomi said, "It only happened once, Miss Smith. I don't want you to think that Mr. Browne was messing around with me the whole time I knew him. I hope that sounded right."

I sorta smiled. Not a happy smile, just an I'm cool smile.

"Just once. I was unhappy, for a long time. I went after him. If it makes you feel better knowing that, I went after him."

I shrugged and said, "We had broke up. He was a free agent. Still is. No biggie. You were human. Less than perfect."

"The truth be told, imperfection is one of my better qualities."

"Mine too."

Vince was living in silence, watching, listening.

I went to the kitchen, took out a bag of frozen peas.

My hips sang a simple song of empathy as I handed the peas to Naiomi.

I said just above a whisper, "It's for your eye."

Naiomi took the bag. "Thank you, Miss Smith."

"Where you going, Miss Smalls?"

She shrugged. "North, south, east, or west. All four in due time. It's a big world out there, and Stocker and Degnan is just an itty-bitty corner on a short block. A beautiful block, but it's just a block."

"Any chance that you might be heading toward Harlem?"

"East Coast isn't my style. Not today anyway. Right now I'm going down the 605 to South Street. Regroup in Cerritos after I square this away. Have to go see my little boy's brown eyes and lady-killer smile to relax my mind. I've been putting it off for a while, but I have to make some hard decisions about my life. You mind if I ask Mr. Browne something?"

"Go right ahead."

My eyes went to Vince; his went to Naiomi.

She asked him, "You ever hear from Kwanzaa, Mr. Browne?"

Vince told her that Kwanzaa was singing at the mall today.

Naiomi smiled. "Don't wait too long before you get to be her daddy again. They grow up so fast. Don't miss the best parts. Don't let her slip out of your life again."

Vince's face was solemn, trapped in thoughts.

Naiomi made it sound like it was just a sex thang, but she cared for him. A lot. It was in her eyes. In her words. In the curve of her lips whenever she looked at Vince. Any woman would be a fool not to care for a man like him. He wasn't rich, wasn't half the things that we put on our lists when we're fantasizing about our knights. He was better.

Naiomi grabbed her duffel bag and threw on a backpack. She told us to take care, grunted and headed down the stairs.

I called after her, "Naiomi?"

"Yeah, Miss Smith?"

"Take care of yourself, too, homegirl."

She adjusted her backpack, said, "Many blessings to you too. Peace and light on your darkest days."

Vince reached for the phone about the same time I was closing the door. I wanted to ask who he was calling this early. But instead I stepped to the window, peeped down on Juanita.

The window was open; I heard Juanita ask, "Naiomi, are you really leaving?"

"You told me to leave, so I'm leaving."

"Wait, sweetheart. Please, baby, please. Naiomi, come back. Wait. Listen to me for a moment. I was upset. Don't leave me—"

The revving of Naiomi's Jeep pierced the air. Tires screeched as she pulled away from the curb. Juanita's hysterical eyes were on Naiomi, lips moving like she was casting some sort of a mumbo-jumbo spell.

Juanita marched around in circles, arms folded. She strayed toward the street, peeped out like she was trying to see if Naiomi was really gone. She leaned against her car, bent over like she was hyperventilating. Crumpled down to the ground and sat on her backside, bowed her head and tugged at the grass.

I'd miss Naiomi too. I'd think about her off and on, do that for years. Yep, I'd miss her. Not the way a person missed friends, but the way a person missed someone they saw or heard every day.

When Naiomi drove her jeep over the dips at Stocker and Degnan and crossed Crenshaw, ten years would go by before I ran into her again. We'd hardly recognize each other. The years will have changed us both. Naiomi would be with her family, rushing to catch a flight to Puerto Villarta, the place she was calling home for that winter season. I'd be with my husband and some close friends, on my way to a ski trip. Seeing her again would be a moment to treasure. Would bring back so many memories.

Vince was on the phone. Soft, tender words going into

the receiver, spoke in a stimulating tone that let me know he was talking to a female.

He wasn't my man anymore. No right to the feelings I had.

But I was human. As imperfect as they came.

I asked, "Who are you talking to?"

"Rosa Lee," Vince said. He held the receiver out toward me. "Step to the phone and tell her why you're not going to tell them good-bye."

32 Vince

Malaika was outside the entrance to Robinson/May, arms folded over her cream-colored mohair outfit. Dark lipstick, lined. High fashion. Malaika shifted, frowned at her watch, made an impatient face.

She said, "You're late."

"Sorry. This is my lunch break. Was in a meeting."

"Remember our arrangement."

"Same as last time."

"Same as last time. Please, Vince, stay upstairs."

Malaika hurried off through the store. Sprouted wings, flew away and left her sweet smell behind. Something about the way she walked away from me like I wasn't shit bothered me down to my DNA. Like she had told me on the phone, I waited three, four minutes before I went after her.

I grabbed an ivory program, then caught a piece of the rail upstairs, right over the food court where Malaika told me to stand, and gazed down at the stage in the middle of the mall. The chairs were packed, shoulder-to-shoulder crowd leaning against the interior palm trees for the free show. The last black-owned and -operated R&B radio stations was broadcasting live over lunchtime, giving away T-shirts, CDs, the entire promotions thing.

In the middle of the masses, a few girls had on black Dangerous Lyrics T-shirts. I'd seen brothers hawking those shirts on the Shaw, in a variety of colors.

After a preteen hip-hop duo from a record company

did a rap and dance, the choir bounced out dressed in black robes with red, green, and gold Kente collars. Kwanzaa was up front with about six other children. Hair in curls, my mother's sweet features in her face, especially the cheeks. Same eyes. The skinny drummer kicked off a strong beat, the bass and guitar players followed. The lady on the electric keyboard didn't miss a note. Malaika threw out her million-dollar smile and floated up front, rocking and hand clapping, led the choir into a groove so funky the mall was swept into the spiritual vibe. People stopped moving; conversations under me at the food court died. Teenage girls by the cappuccino stand at the bottom of the escalator started doing some pretty hot moves.

Kwanzaa was passed a cordless microphone. Without hesitation she stepped out with her mother, both waving their hands side to side and singing so strong. I finally got to hear what she sounded like. Kwanzaa had a sweet little girl's demeanor and a devil of a voice. She held her little head back and raised a hand to the sky, the same thing her momma was doing. When the song was done and the crowd applauded, she left the stage with her mother. My child ran into the arms of Malaika's husband. He was down there in the crowd. All I saw was his back, his dark hair, but that was him. That was why Malaika wanted me to stay in the rafters, like I was the Hunchback of Notre Dame.

"Vince?"

This was a déjà vu. I had expected to see Naiomi standing near me, don't know why, could've been hope, but it was Dana, dressed in blacks and grays. I didn't ask her how she knew Kwanzaa was here, maybe I told her. Either way, I didn't question much of anything anymore. Just let it be.

She said, "I hope you don't mind."

My eyes went back to the people below.

Dana said, "Kwanzaa can sing her booty off. She's gonna be a Whitney Houston."

My child was being carried through the crowd toward

the Disney Store. Malaika stalled, broke away from her second husband, peeped up toward me, then dropped her eyes and followed her leader. Held his hand while he held my child. Looking like a family. All I offered was disruption.

I smiled at Dana. "I should've listened to you. You were right."

"About what?"

"They don't need me. Don't give a shit about me."

I left Dana standing near the rail.

When I passed through Sears, people were crowded in front of all the televisions, like they were watching a concert. A high-speed chase was being broadcast live. There was at least one a day.

Somebody said, "It's that rapper. They've been chasing her down the 5 for the last two hours. Looks like she's trying to get into Mexico."

Butter Pecan's face was down in the corner of the screen. I read the CLOSED CAPTION as the words floated by. Parents divorced.

Close to the border, the CHP put down spike strips. Blew out the tires. When the car limped to a halt, they surrounded her.

It took ten minutes for me to make it to Fairfax Avenue and Sixty-third Street. Yellow, red, and blue balloons were tied to the lemon trees in the backyard, a few on the wrought iron railing in the front and back. A sign that said the event of the decade was happening in the back was posted out front. Black, various brands of Caucasian, Armenian, Mexican—neighbors had come from as far as two streets in all directions.

Womack said, "Damn-di-damn-damn. Word sure travels fast."

"It's turning into a party," I said.

"That's what they told Joan of Arc."

I said, "Hurry up. I gotta get back to work. Running late as it is."

He was in his daddy's back door, gazing down at the crowd that was gathering, furrows in his forehead as he chewed his thumbnail down to the skin. A basketball bounced off the rim, ricocheted off the garage and rolled toward the crowd standing in a semicircle. Children were squealing, shouting. Harmonica had rented one of those tent things that kids bounce around in, so around twenty kids were over here for the moment.

I didn't tell them about Kwanzaa being at the mall. All of them would've come over, and I didn't want that kind of a scene. All for the best. I'd decided to let all of that go. To stop struggling.

Harmonica came up the stairs, his dark sweater wide open over his crisp white shirt. He told us, "Seventeen-ta-one."

I said, "Odds are that wide?"

"What?" Womack snapped, his nostrils open wider than his eyes. "They're out on my property taking bets?"

Harmonica repeated, " 'Bout seventeen-ta-one odds. I put five dollars on the one, hope I get the seventeen five times over."

"That would get you eighty-five dollars." I nodded. "About the same as it was on the Trinidad and De La Hoya fight."

Womack's lips were tense, pushed forward. He frowned at me and his chin dropped, tongue stuck out of his mouth.

He griped, "Ain't fair, Vince. This ain't fair. Not at all."

I told him, "Let's go. People're waiting. I have to get to work."

"Wait, wait, hold on. Let me go use the bathroom first."

"You just used the bathroom."

"I have to go again."

"Womack, son," Harmonica sang out in that rugged, bluesy voice. He smiled so broad, spoke in a teasing tone. "It's show time at the Apollo. They ready for you to sit center stage and release the grease."

"Oh, you so funny, Daddy."

"Release the grease, son. Let's go on down. Quit acting like you got xenophobia; get yeomanly like we expect you to be."

"Oh, now you're really cracking me up with those five-dollar words."

"Son—"

"Let me take a pee first, could ya?" His arms were flapping; his dejected stride took him through his daddy's part of the duplex, heard him fuming and grumbling as he passed by the African statues and masks. "This ain't fair, Vince. You know you ain't right. Didn't think you were serious. Invited the whole damn neighborhood to watch. Ain't that some crap. Never knew you could be so cold-blooded. Never knew, never knew."

Harmonica opened the door and waved his hand at the crowd. A signal. The ball stopped bouncing. A few people clapped, chanted Womack's name. One of Womack's boys anxiously pulled a metal chair out center. Another one of his sons ran out of the house, big smile on his face, a long extension cord in his hand. It was long enough to make it center stage. Another son hurried out with the hair clippers. He plugged them in. Clicked them on. Gave us the thumbs-up. We gave him the same signal. Same wide smile.

I said, "We got juice to kill the juice."

Harmonica nodded. "Seventeen-ta-one."

I put a hand on his shoulder. "I would've bet on the seventeen."

"Naw, I mean seventeen-ta-one that hair of his clogs up the clippers."

We laughed.

He went on, "When you get as old and have a zaftig belly like me, you appreciate all the zaniness you can get your hands on, even if you have to make your zealot son walk zigzag like a zombie."

"You finished the book."

"Done got a little mo' educated in my head."

More laughter.

He pulled out his C-band and he played. We walked down the stairs and he played all the way. The clippers were in my hand when Womack made it to the back door and headed down to take his seat. Harmonica was rocking this world. People were clapping their hands, even a few joined in and did a two-step to the beat that Harmonica had created.

Just what I needed. Harmonica always gave me what I needed, when I needed it. Yes, men like him should live forever.

33 Dana

I left the mall and went to ReMax. A visit that I wanted to last fifteen minutes, but it took two hours because everybody wanted to know what happened to Gerri. A story I'd refuse to tell a million times.

Since Gerri wasn't going to be around for a while, I referred clients to other co-strugglers. Went over Multiple List Services. Contracts. Files in escrow. Office manuals. Information on my primary farm area. Names. Addresses. Asked who wanted to buy my Thomas Guide, the book that diagramed all the streets and addresses in Los Angeles. Areas I'd grown to know like the back of my hand.

My Thomas Guide. A miracle book. From here to Palm Springs to San Francisco to San Diego, I could find any address I needed to find.

That was when I realized how much I knew about Los Angeles, how much I had learned about real estate and its hustle, how proficient I had become.

I went to ask a superior how I would set up a payment plan for what I still owed ReMax in desk fees.

She pushed a button on her computer, said, "Let's see. Your balance is . . . well, your desk fees balance is zero."

I repeated, "Zero?"

"Now leave before I change my mind."

I went into my office, pulled my bill from the IRS out of my purse, and closed the door.

I opened the letter from the IRS. A sigh later I picked up the phone and called the Uncle Sambo office in

Fresno to have a chit-chat about my delinquent taxes. After dealing with recording after recording, a real person picked up. I went through my hard-luck story, wanted to know if I could reduce my payment plan on my delinquent taxes.

The rep said that wouldn't be necessary.

My balance was zero.

I hung up before Sambo changed his mind.

A couple of hours later, I hooked up with Rosa Lee at the Vegetarian Affair. I'd promised her when she had me trapped on the phone, no way I could flake out. The schoolteacher looked like fine and sophistication in her copper-colored slacks, reddish brown blouse, open toe pumps, and big, curly hair that was always stylish on her little bitty head. There was a brief smile as I came in the door, but then the expression on Rosa Lee's face became all business.

I told her, "No way you have four kids."

"I tucked my uterus back in. Damn thing started hanging."

We laughed.

I copped a squat on a bar stool that faced Santa Rosalia Avenue. Ten-foot wrought iron bars went around the mall's perimeter. Five minutes later, I was wolfing down a barbecue sandwich made from soybeans. Waiting to see what type of conversation I was going to be having. In my mind, I was on the 10 heading east, leaving all the palm trees and dry air behind.

I said, "I'm surprised."

"At what?"

"You're the first person who hasn't asked me what happened."

"You want to talk it, you'll talk about it."

"I'd rather not."

"Me either. That's not the conversation I want to have with you." She chewed her bite of tofu sandwich at least twenty times before she swallowed. "We haven't had that much time to get together, which I really hate, so I wanted to steal a moment. After you head back to the Big Apple, never know if we'll ever see each other again."

"True. But the world ain't as big as it seems. People always run into each other again."

"That's the truth."

"How are things with you and Womack?"

"What do you mean?"

"Vince said that, well, that things were rough and, other things."

"I guess that means you're talking about when Womack told Vince that he thought I was having an affair?"

"Yeah."

Rosa Lee laughed.

I didn't. "Rosa Lee, what's funny?"

"We've had our ups and downs, like everybody else. Yes, some days are better than others. An affair? Get real."

She told me about the night she went to Lucy Florence.

"I saw him behind me. Can't hide a head shaped like his."

Some more chuckles.

"Dana, this brother, this actor on one of those silly WB shows was all over me before I could get in the building. 'Damn, my sister, lookin' good. I can get you in to see a taping of my show.' The whole spiel."

"What you do?"

"Told him his show was filled with trite buffoonery, programs like his were a disgrace to all people, hoped he had a day job, something better than the Amos and Andy role he played, and kept moving. Dana, that fool stared me down the rest of the night. If Vince wasn't there, I would've been scared."

I chewed and swallowed. Listened.

She told me that Vince had sold his Z. One of the mechanics at the Nissan dealer wanted to buy the car, and he sold it to him on the spot. Vince needed the money to do something for a friend. At first I thought he had loaned the cash to Rosa Lee and Womack, then I paused, a light came on. "He paid my bills?"

She smiled a little.

I asked, "Why?"

She shrugged. "He wants you to have a better start wherever you go."

My throat was getting tight, but I swallowed water, washed down the the emotional feeling.

She said, "I shouldn't've been the one to tell you."

"Now I want to cry."

"You should. If you left without saying good-bye, that would've hurt my heart. Never part like that. People remember you by your first impression, but they also remember how you leave."

"Makes me wonder what you think of me."

Rosa Lee said, "You've done things I can't condone."

"No doubt."

"You've got this up-frontness, this attitude, this daring that I've never had. At least not the way you do."

"My blessing is my curse. I talk a good talk, but I'm not as bad as I sound."

Rosa Lee ran her hand through her hair as she shook her head.

I asked, "What's going through that little head of yours?"

"The idea that after having four babies for him, Womack would still get jealous and think that I would even consider having an affair. I'd never do that to him, or to my children."

We ate a while.

"Dana, I know what happened between you and that friend of yours from New York. Vince told Womack and my hubby told me."

"News travels fast. That was a mistake. Major mistake."

"I'm not judging you, because it's your body, and your

choice. Only you can know the thoughts, the things in life that caused you to make that decision. But let me tell you something. Something that I believe when it comes to men."

"Okay."

"Every man that lays with you leaves his essence inside of you. All of that mixes up and becomes part of your unborn children."

"Is that scientific?"

"I failed science. Just my opinion."

She leaned forward. I got ready for one of her lectures.

She said, "I think that's why some kids are so messed up today. At work, as soon as I get a problem child, the first thing I do is look at his or her home profile. Ninety percent of them have the same thing in common: they live with single parents and the mother has to work two jobs to make ends meet, if she works at all. Then, if their mother is married, she has several kids by multiple men. Not saying that she did it intentionally, because nobody wants it like that, but that's how it worked out."

I smiled bitterly at my friend. "I hear you."

"It takes as long as three generations of hard work, three generations of sacrifice to correct the wrongs."

"What do you mean?"

"If you come from broken homes, single parents, you can't deny it, can't erase it, that's your legacy. But you don't have to continue it. You can relinquish what you want to make it right for your children, set the example. Then they have to do the same for their children, and so on. I don't come from a line of doctors or lawyers, but my family has two generations of lasting marriages. To me, that's more important than a Ph.D. This is Womack's first. He's given up a lot for his children, has struggled for me, just to make sure that his kids have a little bit better than what he had. There's no man better."

"I understand."

A moment passed.

She said, "That night when Vince followed me, all of that came to me. I made it back home, looked at my home, my family. And I cried. I think I had forgotten all Womack has done for me. Women take men for granted too."

I nodded patiently, but I experienced some discomfort. I wondered how deep Rosa Lee was going to get.

She continued, "That's why I hate Malaika. And I don't use the word *hate* too often. Hate isn't healthy. It damages the hater more than the one who's hated."

"That much I know."

"I've always seen right through her. So self-centered that she doesn't understand what she's doing to her own daughter."

She sipped her soda; I sipped mine.

Rosa Lee caught herself. "Listen to me ramble."

"No, it's okay. I understand what you are saying. Vince deserves the best."

"We all do. You deserve the best. Here or wherever, you deserve nothing less."

"I agree."

"Vince deserved a better hand than the one he was dealt."

I couldn't respond to that.

Then Rosa Lee said, "I was hoping you'd be the one to give it back. But that was just me hoping. Me loving my friend. He's not a weak man, but he needs a strong woman."

Just then Rosa Lee looked across the parking lot, and her red lips eased up into a smile. A brother was coming across the blacktop.

I said, "Look at you. You talk all that righteous smack, then flirt with the first brother that walks up."

"He looks so good, I wish I had a mattress tied to my back."

I stared at the man in jeans and a Negro League T-shirt, then shrieked, "Oh, my God."

Rosa Lee chuckled. "Yep."

"Womack cut all of that curl out of his head!"

"Got his ear pierced too."

Later on I'd find out that Vince had made a deal with Womack. The price he had to pay for spying was cutting that curl out of his head. Womack and Rosa Lee's beautiful self-made day-care center were all heading our way. Ramona was in a blue stroller. The skinny little boys were laughing and bouncing and helping their daddy push the carriage.

We high-fived, laughed like positive women. The kind of laugh that made the world feel better. I started to get up.

Rosa Lee touched my arm. "Wait."

"What?"

She reached into her purse, handed me an envelope.

"What's this?"

"Womack, Harmonica, and I are giving you four hundred dollars. It's not much, but maybe this will help you keep food in your tummy until you get situated in New York."

"No, I don't want to leave owing everybody."

"It's a love gift. We've been blessed a thousand times over, and we're sharing it. From me, my husband, his father, and my little rug rats."

Again, I held back the emotions. I whispered, "Thanks."

"One last thing. Friend to friend."

"I'm listening."

"You came to Los Angeles because you were running from something. I'm not asking you to stay, because you know what's in your heart, but make sure you know why you're really going wherever you're going."

"Harlem is my home."

"Don't misunderstand. If you don't know why you're leaving, whether you go to Harlem or Australia, it'll happen over and over. Don't pass that on to your children. Don't be alone on an island filled with people."

"I won't."

I knew that when I left California, I'd never hear from them again. They'd fall back into their lives, and I'd go on with mine. Remember each other from time to time, reach for the phone, but never get around to making that call. Become just another face in a photo album. A name that starts to escape.

"Now come on," Rosa Lee said. "Give my family some of those hugs and kisses before you drive toward the sunrise."

34 Vince

I left work a little early because I had to stop by a piece of rental property in the 3800 block of Edgehill. A nice two-bedroom house, large living room, lots of closet space, garage, huge palm trees in the backyard. This phase of my life was almost over, so I was planning my next two moves. I was going to go home, change, then run ten miles, but when I saw Dana's car loaded up, I parked and sat there for a moment.

Suitcases were in her backseat. Boxes in the window.

The streets were crowded with cars. Kids were getting out of Audubon Middle School, coming by in droves up Stocker, others were running through the alley, cursing each other like sailors.

Across the street a slim Hispanic woman was sitting in a red convertible Cavalier. She got out and stood next to her car. Jean shorts missing enough material to show her golden butt cheeks. Lime green sports bra. Hiking boots, thick socks hanging over the rim. Hair fire engine red with blond streaks.

She tilted her dark shades, looked at me.

I got out of Womack's car, loosened my tie, and went up the steps leading to my stucco castle. She was behind me, struggling with her luggage trudging up the steps that led to my cave.

I turned around and said, "You looking for somebody?"

Her head raised. Brown eyes penetrated her dark shades and met mine.

Juanita's door opened. She stepped in the hallway in a short red dress, make-up was done like she was an *Ebony* Fashion Fair model. I'd never seen her look so good. I nodded at Juanita. She ignored me.

She smiled and spoke to the woman who was behind me. "Hey, Soledad."

The girl came to life. "You look good."

"You're looking good too."

"Where are the rest of your things?"

"I'll get my television and stuff later."

After that, all of their words were in Spanish.

Their animated conversation kept on going. Me and Juanita passed by each other. Her eyes cut my way for a moment. A real quick, very sharp moment. I started to tell her then that I was moving out in the next thirty days, was going to let her know that I'd found a better place to live, a peaceful home that had a lease-to-buy option, but I kept my words to myself and walked through their walls of chuckles and hugs and laughs.

The shower was running when I stepped inside. Smelled Dana's strawberry and champagne shower gel mixing with the pasta aroma coming from the kitchen. I looked at the darkened barrier over the stove; smoke would always live in these walls. My eyes fell on the suitcases and garment bags at the foot of the sofa. Dana had separated the compact discs, made three stacks. Her books were in the living room.

"Vince, that you?"

I sat down on the sofa; it creaked under my weight.

"Vince?"

I finally said, "Yeah."

"Come here for a minute."

"What you need?"

"Can you come here for a quick minute?"

The bathroom door was open, but I stopped just short of the door frame.

"Yeah? What's up, Dana?"

"Step inside. I ain't gonna bite you."

I did. Saw her midnight skin. Light brown eyes.

Water ran over Dana's face; she gurgled.

"Vince?"

"Yeah?"

"This is hard for me to say. I mean to ask."

"Ask."

"Will you let me make love to you?"

"That was pretty direct."

"Pretty much to the point."

I paused. "When?"

"Right now." She coughed. "I have some unfinished business, and after I take care of it, it'll be too late for me to drive."

"I see. What kind of business?"

"If I stayed until the morning, would that be a problem?"

I answered, "Not really."

"Good. Well, can I make love to you or not?"

I didn't answer. But my insides were burning for her. I closed my eyes for a while. Shut out this world and thought back to those childhood days when I had a mystical playhouse. The illusion of a life where I made all the rules. If something wasn't the way I wanted it, I simply wished it away. It was that easy. In my play world, everything always turned out the best for me.

But this wasn't a play world.

This was the heart of Los Angeles.

Dana asked, "You gonna leave a sister hanging?"

"Sure. I'll make love to you."

Nothing was said, like neither one of us knew how to start this old-times-sake party.

I started having second thoughts.

Dana whispered, "Take your clothes off."

My voice softened. "Sure."

"What do you have to do tonight?"

"Nothing but load up your car. Why?"

"Later on, I need you to ride with me somewhere."

"Where?"

"Take your clothes off before the water gets cold. We'll worry about that later. If we have enough time."

We entered a language without words. After we showered, I grabbed the jojoba massage oil. Dana pulled my red comforter from the hall closet. Pulled curtains. Lit candles. Burned incense. She lay me on my stomach and poured warm oil in her hands, spread it up my body from my feet. Rubbed me down. My back. Neck. Shoulders. Circles with her thumbs.

She said, "You're so tense."

She kneaded the back of my legs. My arms. Palms of my hands. Each finger. Turned me over and saw how erect I was, but she ignored that part of me as it reached for the sky. Her touch had a syncopation, healed the aching that running had left in my feet. I fell asleep for seconds at a time. She anointed my genitals with warm oil. Held on to that part of me with her left hand, massaged with her right. Stroking in slow motions, then faster, her energy flowing into my body. The room became tropical. Gentle breeze creeping through my open window.

With the heated oil, I did the same thing to her. Massaged her head to toe, rubbed her temples, eyelids, lips, ears, breasts, worked the kinks out of her muscles. Touched her like it was the first time. Like it was the last time. With my mind trying to remember all of her. Her body had more tension, muscles harder than marbles, but I worked them until the rocks became pebbles, and the pebbles disappeared. So many sexy sounds came from her mouth, sensual expressions all over her face. I spread her legs and anointed her with oil. Massaged that womanly part of her, my fingers easing inside that passage to pleasure. Her breathing a sultry song. Her hand was on me, holding firm, massaging me high and low, close to orgasm.

"Let me get a condom."

She said, "I've got one in here with me."

*   *   *

I asked, "What's wrong?"

"Jesus, I feel like crying."

It was dark when Dana woke up and got up off the floor, the place we had made our last pallet. Both of us had made love, long and strong, but afterward neither one of us said much. Went right back to being polite.

She said, "Thanks for what you did."

"You're thanking me for sex?"

"No. My taxes. My desk fees."

"I don't know what you're talking about."

"Thanks anyway."

"You're welcome."

We hadn't held each other while we napped. No pretense. She eased into her ripped 501s, put her hands over her breasts, rummaged through the tumbled white sheets, found her pink bra, stuffed it into her back pocket.

"Thanks, Vince."

"You don't have to keep thanking me for your taxes."

"No, for the sex. I needed to release some stress."

"So you used me."

"You're stressed too."

"What makes you think that?"

" 'Cause you tried to kill me with your penis."

"You tried to smother me."

"I slipped. We had too much oil on us."

Soft chuckles, then awkwardness.

I said, "Stuffy in here. Want me to open the window?"

She shrugged. "A helicopter's out there."

"Didn't notice."

She said, "Wait till it goes by."

"You gonna shower?"

"No. I wanna smell like you for a while."

I grabbed my jeans.

She asked, "You heading for the shower?"

"I'll hang on to this fragrance."

She pulled on her NYU sweatshirt. "Get dressed.

Traffic should be better. It's time for me to make my run."

"It's almost nine. Where you gotta go?"

"Just get dressed."

"We going to see Gerri?"

"Just get dressed."

She wiped her hands on her backside, touched her face, tugged at the belt loops on her jeans, pulled her hair from her silver earrings. Did everything but look at me.

I said, "I hope you remember more than just us sleeping together."

"Me too. There's more to me than just that."

By the time I was dressed, she was at the door, jingling her keys in her hand, purse over her shoulder.

"Hurry, Vince. I need to pick this up before it gets too late."

Dana drove the 10 eastbound beyond downtown L.A. and the Arco Towers, sped by the 710 interchange. For a while traffic was meaner than Mike Tyson. Forty minutes and thirty miles went by. We zipped by Cal Poly Pomona, headed up Kellogg Hill.

I said, "You driving me to New York?"

"Gum?"

"Sure."

She opened a pack of Big Red, licked the stick top to bottom, then eased it into my mouth. It was so much sweeter.

Dana's troubled eyes matched her solemn face.

I stared out the window at the cars on the freeway. Eighteen-wheelers were clogging the two right lanes like cholesterol in a fat man's arteries.

I spoke in an even tone. "All the times that we've walked as friends and slept as lovers are over."

"No more cohopulating."

"Right," I agreed. "No more cohopulating."

Time for us to become strangers. Tomorrow she'd be taking this same freeway without me. The essence of her would diminish from my corner at Stocker and Degnan. Her taste would be overwritten by another woman's flavor, and the physical pleasures of what we had would only be a memory. That's the way love goes away. Details of nothing conversations become muddled. Words become vague. Images fade like a picture left out in the sun. But what's felt inside lingers for eternity.

Almost an hour passed.

Dana told me about her lunch with Rosa Lee, about the things she had said, the philosophy she had spouted over their vegetarian meal. The part about the guy who was hawking her, that actor she had insulted, should've made me feel bad. What Dana told me let me know that my paranoia made me overreact. It was easily explained away.

Dana chuckled. "She said you were tripping."

"I've been known to trip from time to time."

"I've noticed."

But what about the brother's cellular phone? When I stood on that barren side street and clicked it on, it was static-filled, not one hundred percent clear, yet it sounded like Rosa Lee's voice on the other end. After she got home, she had cried and talked to Womack half the night. About what, he never said. I let that be between him and his wife. But I do know this much: all the things Rosa Lee had said to Dana about being multi-generational, those were the things Womack had told her when she got in from Lucy Florence that night. Things that made her break down and cry in her husband's arms.

With the sunrise things were better over on Fairfax. Womack told me that he was a great father, but somewhere down the line he had forgotten how to be a great husband. Had to steal moments to nurture his relationship with Rosa Lee, treat her like she was more than the mother of his children, like she was a woman with the needs of a woman. He was working on getting that back.

I came out of those thoughts when I caught a whiff of cow manure coming through the vents. Saw stretches of freeway with no houses on the side, geography I hadn't seen in ages.

She'd driven past the 57 a while ago. We were at least eighty miles from home. She transferred to the 215 north.

I asked, "Smell that fertilizer. Where're you taking me?"

"I'm almost there."

She exited the 215 and drove past the Carousel Mall, Phoenix Information Center, cruised down E Street. A few minutes later, she parked in front of a one-story beige house made of stucco, double driveway, windows with dark brown awnings. Lights were on in the living room, also in the back.

We were in front of Malaika's mother's house.

She said, "A while ago I saw a letter you had mailed to Malaika's mother. This is the address. This is the house. I went on-line and used the Internet to print out a map of how to get here."

We stared at each other.

She said, "Everything that is faced can be changed. Nothing can be changed until you face it. On the Santa Monica boardwalk, you told me that."

I took her hand.

She said, "Something in there belongs to you."

Dana released my hand, patted my flesh with sincerity.

She sighed. She always did that when she didn't know what to say. I nodded. I always nodded when I was out of words.

She said, "I'll be right here. I'm your moral support."

I didn't make a lot of pomp and circumstance. I walked across the grass up to the door and rang the doorbell. Only rang it once. The porch light came on.

"Who is it?" I didn't recognize that voice.

I said, "Vincent Calvary Browne Junior."

Malaika's older sister Regina opened the door. Fear was in her eyes. It seemed like everybody was scared of me.

"Where Malaika at?"

Regina barely said, "In the kitchen. Washing her hair."

"Go get her."

Regina's older, petite body like her mom's. Her hair was cut boy short. She moved awkwardly, like she didn't know how to handle the surprise visit, then motioned like she was going to open the door.

I shook my head and said, "I'll wait out here on the porch."

Kwanzaa came into the living room. She had on Anastasia pj's. Hair in those goddess ponytails. Her eyes met mine. The eyes that I helped create met mine for the first time in years. She saw me. I wasn't invisible anymore. My hand came up slowly, and I waved at her. She did the same motion, slowly, without a smile. In her world, I existed.

I spoke gingerly. "Hi, Kwanzaa."

She sang, "Hello. Good evening, Mister Man."

"It's after eleven at night. You're up kinda late."

Regina cut in, "It's past your bedtime. What did I tell you about getting out of bed?"

Kwanzaa's eyes were still on me.

She sounded like an angel. Better than when I had heard her sing, because those words were for me. She looked even taller than she did at the skating rink, because we weren't so far apart. I could've pulled the door open and grabbed my child. But I didn't. Regina closed the door.

I went and stood next to the car.

Dana asked, "What happened?"

"Malaika's coming to the door."

"Go back over there. Don't come this far and back down."

The door opened. A tall figure with a short haircut stepped to the porch and looked out. Jeans. White V-neck T-shirt.

It was Drake. The last time I saw him, I was trying to

use my foot to examine his colon. He went back inside. He was keeping his distance. I was on their turf, keeping mine.

The door closed.

Then the front door opened again.

I heard them talking. Rushed words. Panic.

Malaika came out. Black jeans. Orange cotton blouse that was loose enough for me to see some of the swell of a new life in her belly. Her arms were folded across her chest as she came down the steps, marched across the grass. I strolled in her direction, away from Dana's car. Malaika stopped a few feet away from me, not too close, then glanced back at the living room window before she snapped, "What are you doing here, Vince?"

"You knew I'd come."

Her golden brown hair was wet, traces of soap on her ears and neck. She sounded irritated. "This isn't appropriate."

"But you knew I'd come."

"Yep." She sighed. "I did."

"I want to see my daughter."

"I'm not ready for you to meet Kwanzaa yet."

"You're not ready. What does that have to do with her being ready?"

"I haven't prepared her."

Once again my throat dried up and I was out of words. I nodded, all I could do. Behind me was the warmth of Dana's anxiety, her emotions giving me energy, making me strong in the right kind of way.

"Can I ask you something?"

Malaika glanced back at the house before she answered, "Sure."

"This is between me and you. It ain't got nothing to do with Kwanzaa. It ain't Drake's business."

"Everything in my life is my husband's business."

"If it was so much his business, he would be out here right now. Standing next to you, like you stood next to him that night . . ."

I let the pause sink in.

I said, "I'll be right here. Go get 'im."

"Ask your question."

Again, she sighed as she glanced back toward the house. The curtains in the living room moved, then stayed parted just enough for whoever was inside to spy out. The front door was open too. Maybe just in case I lost my mind and the calvary had to come charging to the rescue.

I asked, "I just wanna know what happened to us."

Malaika shifted, and her hand came up and scratched her head.

She asked, "What do you mean?"

"I mean what I said. Don't bullshit me. I just want the truth." I tried to keep my voice even. "That's all. I never understood. It's always bothered me."

Her eyes lowered. Hand made circles on her unborn child.

"Please, Vince. Don't do this now."

I said, "I loved you. Did you love me?"

"God, Lord have mercy, Jesus." Her eyes went to the sky, then to her feet. "I knew this moment would come."

"Be honest. Just be honest."

Her tongue was under her top lip, moving slowly back and forth. Her shoulders lowered a touch. She rubbed her belly and I waited.

Then we were eye to eye. No room for misunderstanding.

She said, "I never loved you, Vince."

Silence. And peace.

I said, "Thanks. That's all I wanted to hear."

Curtains moved again. Drake was in the door. Her sister in the window. Everybody was probably holding knives, waiting to dial nine-eleven.

"Vince?" That was Dana's voice in the darkness. "Everything okay?"

I waved at her. She stayed where she was.

Sweat was on my wrinkled brow, but I was as cool as I'd ever been.

I faced my ex-wife and said, "One more question."

"Sure."

Again I swallowed and closed my eyes. "Is she mine?"

Malaika whispered, "God, how can you ask me something like that?"

"With the way things have turned out, how can I not?"

"She's yours, Vince."

I said, "You sure?"

"I'm sure."

"She's mine. That settles that. When can I see my child?"

Malaika played with her wedding ring, turned it over and over, like she was twisting the thoughts inside her head. Finally she said, "He's going to be upset. Look, I'll talk to Drake, then I'll call you."

"When?"

"At the right time."

I said, "When it's appropriate."

"Yes." She drummed her fingers on her arms. "When it's appropriate. In the meantime, I don't want you driving out here and being disruptive."

"Who'll determine when it's appropriate?"

"I will."

"All under your terms."

"Vince, don't do this."

"Everything always has to be under your fucking terms. When you got tired of being married you leave, under your terms. You call when you feel like it, under your terms. Now, if I'm gonna see my child, you decide that you get to decide when and where. So everything has to be under your fucking terms."

"Don't curse me."

"You've already damned me."

Silence.

"Vince, I care for Kwanzaa."

"If you did, shit wouldn't be like this."

"I don't want her to be traumatized."

I shook my head. "It don't matter. I'm not dressed for the occasion. I want to look nice when she sees me."

Malaika nodded.

"Vincent?"

"Yeah?"

"Don't pop up over again, please?"

I told her good night. She told me the same, headed back toward their house in the same breath, rushed like she was on a timer. Her husband held the door open. Mumbles sprinkled the air. The door closed. Their porch light turned off.

"Well?" That was Dana. She was getting out of the car, pulling her hair from her face.

I got in the car. Got ready for my long ride home.

Dana got in for a moment. She said, "Vince?"

My voice was low. "Yeah."

"I was sitting up eating breakfast with my momma. We were laughing, planning on going to see a play over the weekend. She was looking good, healthy, happy. The next morning she didn't wake up. Talked to my daddy one week, the next I was getting a phone call. He was dead too."

My eyes stayed on my palms. A little kid. That's who I was. A kid with grown-up problems. Dana put a finger on my chin, raised my head until my eyes belonged to hers.

She whispered, "Nothing's promised."

"I know."

"Not the rest of tonight, not all of tomorrow."

In that moment I remembered that I thought my folks would be here a lot longer than they were. Thought about how this drive back to Los Angeles could be my last. And if something bad happened to me before now and whenever Malaika came to her senses, I didn't want to have to wait for my daughter to get to heaven before I kissed her face. I still didn't know her favorite colors. Her favorite foods. If she liked Big Bird or that purple dinosaur Barney, or if she played with whatever kids' stuff they're pushing at Toys "R" Us.

Dana said, "Let's bum-rush that house."

"Slow down. Be civilized."

"Stop being so passive. Damn, I never realized how much you need me."

"Dana—"

"Don't go back home not knowing."

In her eyes I saw some stubborn tears, saw she cared for me, and I saw she was right.

She was my second love. The one I'd live for. The one I'd always wish was there from the get-go. A diamond with a heart of gold. Her eyes told me she saw the same, felt the same undeniable magic when she gazed at me.

I opened the door. "C'mon."

Side by side we walked up to Malaika's porch. Didn't muffle our steps. Dana gave me some strong eye contact. Her cat eyes were ferocious.

I said, "You're going back to New York tomorrow."

She ran her hands through her hair. "Only if you don't ask me to stay."

"It wouldn't be a walk in the park."

"Might be like Central Park after midnight."

My voice wasn't easygoing when I said, "I'd make you suffer."

"I know. I'd suffer you back."

Softly I said, "Stay."

Her voice was just as tender. "Okay."

"If it don't work, there's always an open door."

"I know."

Everything would turn around in time. That thing with Gerri would do like most news—change from news to gossip to rumor, then, except for by a few, all would be forgotten. And forgiven. Dana would sell more houses than she ever imagined. We'd share years of smiles. Arguments. Tears. Three children and years of mostly smiles. And I know we were together in a carnal way countless times, numerous ways before we stood on the beach in Malibu with twenty of our friends and faced God, but for the record, let me say that there is no better feeling than when a man makes love to his wife. Nothing compares to that union.

She'd never mention Claudio.

She'd never ask about Naiomi.

But that five minutes of pleasure, that one-time experience in a musty and dusty garage, my crime of weakness that was done in an alley behind Stocker and Degnan would come back to haunt me.

The next time I saw Naiomi Smalls would be long after Harmonica had played his last song on his magical C-band and was summoned to the Upper Room to be with Edna and my parents. He'd live a few more good years, take care of those grandchildren, take care of all of us the best he could. But his time was short, as time will be short for us all.

Anyway, when my eyes fell on Naiomi Smalls again, Dana would be at my side. Ten years down the road. Today when Naiomi packed up her Jeep and headed over the dips at Stocker and Degnan, she wouldn't look back. She'd become a nomad and live where she stopped. Canada. Jamaica. London. South Beach. France. Living the life of a millionaire. I'd run into her again at LAX. Her hair would be longer, straight. Her skin tanned. She'd still be slim but not as tight.

Me and Dana, we'd be married, would be with Womack and Rosa Lee, Gerri and her second husband, all of us trying to catch a flight to Vale so we could tackle the slopes at the black ski summit. Naiomi would be rushing to catch a flight to Puerto Villarta, the place that she was calling home for that winter season. Dana would notice Naiomi first, because I'd be too busy struggling with our luggage to recognize her. She would be out of my memory. And I don't think that she'd recognize me.

We'd make eye contact and both of us would remember what had happened inside a dusty garage on Stocker and Degnan. Naiomi would have her son, Otis, with her.

He'd be tall like his father was, about sixteen, Kwanzaa's age. Naiomi would have a little girl with her too. A nine-year-old child with thick hair. A child with a British accent who looked like a female version of me.

Ten years down the road.

I have to deal with tonight.

Right now.

This moment.

I rang the doorbell one time.

The peephole went black. Excited mumbles on the other side.

Dana made it sing a sweet ding-dong twice.

No answer. More mumbles.

I ding-donged it two more times.

Malaika finally answered.

Before I spoke up, Dana cut in, using her real estate voice, "Vince came to see Kwanzaa. Will you go get her, please?"

Malaika's eyes went to Dana, then to me. "What?"

I spoke above a whisper, "Get my daughter for me, please."

My ex-wife didn't move. Neither did my future wife.

Dana added calmly, "Malaika, whether you like it or not, that's his child. You're just some sister he met at Mervyn's."

Malaika gazed at Dana. "Who do you think you are?"

Dana's lips curved up into a wicked smile. "A woman he met in a bar."

I said, "Dana, don't raise your voice. It's Kwanzaa's bedtime."

"Sorry."

I turned to Malaika. So much nervousness in her eyes.

Drake was standing in her shadow. Dana was in mine.

I said, "What's up, Drake?"

He said, "Vince."

He resembled a buffed Ricky Ricardo. Regina was there, her arms folded, eyes wide, cordless phone in her hand, body rigid.

I showed them open palms, the way African warriors did to show they could be trusted, and said, "I just want to see my daughter."

Drake held that eye contact. There was no fire in his eyes. No fire in mine. On a rainy night, I'd won that battle and lost the war. I didn't want what was his. I just wanted what was mine. I nodded. Drake did the same, backed away from the door, but didn't move too far from his wife's side. Regina moved too. Malaika pulled Kwanzaa up to the front.

I stayed next to Dana. I was in a lion's den, but with her I felt no fear. If she was born back in time, she could've ruled Cleopatra.

I said, "Hi, Kwanzaa."

She smiled the way little girls do. "Hello."

"You're a beautiful little girl."

The expression on Malaika's face was the same as the one I had owned the night I stood on a Santa Monica Pier, baring my soul to Dana.

Malaika stooped down to my child and said, "Kwanzaa, remember what we were talking about?"

"What, Mommy?"

"About why we have different last names?"

"Yes."

"Remember you asked me if you had two daddies, just like your friend?"

"Like Keisha?"

Malaika's eyes were getting misty. With a lot of tenderness, a tone that asked forgiveness, she said, "Like Keisha."

"Yes."

Malaika's voice splintered. "And I told you no."

"I remember."

"Well, Mommy did a bad thing. Mommy wasn't honest with you, baby."

Kwanzaa nodded and held onto my ex-wife, kept her face close to her mother's breast, but her eyes were on mine. Yes. In her world, I existed.

Acknowledgments

Well, Virginia Jerry's grandson is back at it again.

This book went through quite a few name changes, from the title *Imperfect People* I scribbled across the top of a sheet of typing paper to at last coming to a halt with *Liar's Game*. My fantastic editor, Audrey LaFehr, came up with the final title. And I dig it.

I love coming up with new characters, new situations. While I was in a writing class at UCLA I had started working on *Liar's Game* as a mystery with Vince as the lead in the story. Womack was in that story as well, but a very different kinda character. And Harmonica was a crusty old shotgun-carrying bluesman who ran a pool hall. And Dana, that New Yawk woman, was there as well. For me, her subplot with Vince was too strong, pretty much overshadowed the rest of the work. So I moved that part of the story up front and put the rest on the shelf. Like most of the stuff I save, bits and pieces, everything from dialogue to characters, will more than likely pop up in another story somewhere down the line. Yep, the original characters were pretty different. I still like their original story. And hopefully the winds will blow me back in that direction one day. All that is to say, characters evolve, plots change, and some stories take a while to get to their final form. My objective with each book is to write about new characters. Hopefully you'll find these peeps different from the ones in the other four books *(SS, F&L, MIMC, Cheaters)* I've completed so far.

Okay, back to the acks.

I have to thank the peeps at BrownHouse Productions. Steve Lapuk and Debra Chase are the bomb. And Leah Hunter is sooo crazy—not in a *One Flew Over the Cuckoo's Nest* way, in a cool way.

I have to thank Yvette Hayward back in New York. I owe her big-time. She took me around the city and helped me with all the New York stuff.

And a big shout out to my ace Tracy L. McKinley in Little Rock, AK. Thanks for that southern-fried tour when I was hanging at Garbo's bookstore. You be cool like that.

Tiffany Pace, your corrections (you know where!) are invaluable. Now, O ye queen of the LGB, the one who finds all of my mistakes and never lets me live them down, go finish your book!

Genny Ostertag, thanks for the info on "The Biz."

And no matter how many times she calls me a BONEHEAD, I have to thank Glenda Green for the real estate connection. Without her valuable input, Dana Ann Smith wouldn't have had a j-o-b. Thanks for letting me call you up damn near every morning and ask all of those questions. You're the best! I.O.U. lunch at Baja Grill.

Book clubs. All of the groups have been so supportive. I promised the sisters in Phenomenal Woman big PHAT shout out. (Insert SHOUT!) And this go 'round I need to hook up with Pages. And Reading with a Passion. And Jan's book club. Man, If I don't mention Tabahani, Denise will talk about me from now until ... and speaking of *Until* ... I have to thank Timmothy McCann for having my back. Nice to be working in the biz with a positive brother.

Much success to you! Your reviews are motivating for us all!

You know what. This is too much work. Almost like . . . writing a book.

I know what to do!

This book would not be possible without _____'s help. (Fill in your name if I forgot to mention you.) S/He was my inspiration, brought me Kool-Aid when I was thirsty, Colgate when my breath was humming, washed my dirty clothes, yada, yada, uh-huh, whatever.

LOL. Okay, all of that was fun. Now let's get serious. Thanks to the Creator. Much love to my friends, and thanks to the peeps who enjoy what I write. Thanks for supporting all of the writers who are both established and up-and-coming. Thanks for keeping me out of the unemployment line. I WANNA THANK EVERYBODY IN MY CREW! My wonderful agent (Sara Camilli), my fantastic editor (Audrey LaFehr), everybody in publicity (Lisa Johnson and Sara Golier), and Genny Ostertag.

Peace and hugs

Virginia Jerry's grandson signing off. . . .

—Eric Jerome Dickey
02/08/00

Eric Jerome Dickey delivers a superb
new novel that puts a startling
twist in the love triangle . . .

BETWEEN LOVERS
Available at bookstores everywhere from Signet

Fog walks the streets. Dark skies give Oaktown that
Seattle appeal.

I have on black running tights, white T-shirt, gray St.
Patrick's Day 10K sweatshirt. Nicole wears blue tights
and a black hooded sweat top, a red scarf over her
golden hair.

We take a slow jog out of the Waterfront, by all the
gift shops, head through the light fog. Rows of ware-
houses that are being converted into lofts line the
streets. All in the name of profit and gentrification, the
reversal of the White Flight is in progress. The homeless
are out peddling *Street Spirit* papers for a buck a pop.
The dirt poor, the filthy rich—all live a paper cup away
from each other in the land of perpetual oxymorons.

I say, "You want me to meet this chick—"

"Don't say *chick*. That's a misogynistic word."

"Nicer than what I usually call her."

"Which is disrespectful. Yeah, I think meeting will
benefit us all."

"So this thing with her is pretty serious?"

She smiles because I've given up the silent treatment.
"It's serious. There's more to it."

Acid swirls in my belly.

Nicole goes on. "I think we can resolve this situation."

"More like what?" I ask. "What more is there?"

"We . . . just more." She has a look that tells me this is deeper than it seems, but can't tell me all, not right now. She says, "Let's talk while we run."

We take the incline up Broadway, my mind trying to react to what she just asked me about meeting her soft-legged lover, whirring and clicking and whirring as we jog by the probation department. We come up on a red light and stretch some more while we wait for it to change. The signal makes a *coo-coo, coo-coo, coo-coo* sound when it changes to green—that good old audio signal for the blind folks heading north and south.

Before we make a step, a Soul Train of impatient drivers almost mows us down.

We jump back. Both of us almost get hit.

Nicole says, "Be careful here, sweetie. This is where all the assholes rush to get on the Tube."

Someone slows and allows us to cross.

I run behind Nicole. Check out the fluid movement of her thighs. Seven years ago they weren't so firm. Back then she had a whacked Atlantic Star hairdo that hung over one eye and she looked like Janet Jackson, not the *Velvet Rope* version, but the chubby-faced Penny on *Good Times* version. Now her belly is flat and the muscles in calves rise and fall, lines in her hamstrings appear, her butt tightens; all of that shows how much she's been running, doing aerobics, hiking up every hill she can find.

It fucks with me. I try not to, don't want to, but it fucks with me and I can't help thinking about her being naked with another woman. Keep thinking about all the videos I've seen with women serving women satisfaction, but refuse to see Nicole in that light, in that life.

Those silver bracelets jingle as she gets a little ahead of me, not much.

The light at 13th catches Nicole. I catch up and ask, "Why does she want to meet me?"

"Because. Curious, I guess. I love you; she knows that. Sometimes she sounds intimidated."

"Because I'm a man."

"Maybe. After seven years, we have a solid history, don't you think?"

The simple, five-letter word *solid* makes me feel good. The signal *coo-coo*s three times. We run north.

We race the incline toward Telegraph, a liquor store–lined street that leads into good old Berkeley.

I maintain a steady pace and ask, "This hooking up, is this for her, or for you?"

"For me. Because I'm in fucking purgatory."

"Where do you think I am? I'm standing next to you."

"Feels like I'm dancing naked on the sun."

"That sounds painful."

"Wanna see my blisters?" She clears her throat, spits. "It's important for her because she needs to get comfortable with my needs, and wants, with my love for you, to be secure. And it's for you."

"How in the hell is this hooking up for me?"

"Because I see how much it hurts you. You're an open book."

"Don't go cliché on me."

She goes on. "Be honest. Would you be this . . . well, for lack of a better word, understanding if I were—"

"I'm not understanding; I don't understand this whole lesbian shit."

"I'm not a lesbian," she says with force. Then she backs off. "Sweetie, I'm not a lesbian."

I tell her, "Look, I'm being patient. Waiting for you to get through this . . . this . . . this phase."

"Okay, patient. Would you be acting like a stunt double for Job if I were having a relationship, okay, even living with another man?"

"Hell, no. I'd break his neck. Go Left Eye and burn down the house. Not in that order."

She says, "Going Left Eye. Now that turns me on. That evil side you try to hide."

"Try me."

"I'm serious. I want you two to meet. We have to. I want

both of your spirits to be at ease. I want my spirit at ease. I want all of us to be able to have conversations, run races together. That way I don't have to be stressed and trying to figure out who I'm going to be with. It's a lose-lose for me, and I'm trying to make it a win-win for us all."

"So she's scared of me."

"You don't see her as a threat, not the way she sees you as a threat."

"Nothing that menstruates is a threat to me. Ain't *scared* of nothing that bleeds."

"Okay, Mister Macho."

Nicole has immeasurable passion when she talks about her soft-legged lover. I wonder if, when she's talking to her friend about me, she speaks with the same heated tongue, one that drips adjectives made of sweet mangos, verbs made of ripe kiwis, says my name as if it were a fresh strawberry.

I say, "So this is for me, you, and her."

"At this stage in my life, I do know what I want. And I'm going after it. I'm being honest with myself and I have the courage to follow it."

"How long did you practice that *Fantasy Island*–sounding speech?"

She extends both her middle fingers my way.

I ask, "You want it to be like that?"

"Ideally, yeah. If I could wake up every day knowing I was going to share my life with two people I adore, do that without any stress, yeah, my world would be perfect."

I say, "World ain't perfect."

"Our world can be perfect enough for us. We can create new boundaries, new love."

We. I notice she uses the word *we* a lot. The ultimate team player. A company woman.

"Dunno, Nicole. Dunno. Me, you, and your friend. That puts a chill in the pit of my stomach."

"That chill is your sense of adventure tapping you on your shoulder."

"You're quoting me."

"The unknown is always an added attraction."

"I told you that, too."

"Yes, you did. Got me to drop my drawers when that honey-rich baritone voice of yours whispered those words in my ear. Had me doing all kinds of shit for your ass. In and out of bed. Helped you out when your money was low, was your shoulder when your daddy gave you grief. I gave all of me to you. Your turn to give a little. Live up to your own standards."

Our pace gets closer to eight-minute miles. She's a great runner. Five inches shorter than I am, and a minute faster on a hilly mile. Arms low, nice smooth kick. I'm a slow starter and I use her to motivate my stride.

We keep heading toward a rolling hill that reaches up to the sky.

"Where you taking me?"

"C'mon."

Eighteen minutes later, we reach Highland, which is almost at the top of the hill, then head toward the row of mansions leading to Piedmont High School. She's sweating, face glowing with pain, back of her oversize sweatshirt damp, but not too damp because her T-shirt steals most of the moisture.

No nice way to put it: right now I'm hurting like hell and making fuck faces.

She slows a bit, says, "Think . . . about moving . . . up this way. Get some . . . investment property."

I wipe my face with the sleeve of my sweatshirt. "Sell crazy . . . somewhere else. A blacksmith in one village . . . becomes a blacksmith's apprentice in another."

"Smart ass . . . what does that . . . mean?"

"What kind of fool do I look like? Can't be your number two. Not going out like that."

"Dammit." Her breathing evens out. "There you go again. It's about love, not competition."

"Everything in this world is about competition."

"Not if we let it be about love," she says with enough force to show her inner struggle and frustration. Then she softens her attitude. "Not if we let it be about love."

In a tone that doesn't hide my jealousy and frustration, I ask, "Hypothetically, if I moved here, where the hell would you stay? Who gets you at sundown? Do I have to flip a coin every night, pull straws, what? Or do we go to court and get an order so I can get you every other weekend and every other holiday?"

She's offended. I want to offend her.

She takes off running, speeds up when I get too close, challenging me like I challenge her. We both move like we want to make up for lost time. But lost time is never recovered.

Nicole is in full stride by the time we come up on 6th, her tailwind stirring all the debris on the uneven, oil-stained boulevard, her bracelets jingling as she pumps her slim arms and races for the Tube.

Can't let her win. Ego chases ego.

She makes it out of the 980 overpass a good five seconds before me, flies across the entrance to the Tube, crosses 7th before traffic can take off. I break out of the darkness underneath the block-wide overpass and approach that good old Tube.

Death is waiting for me.

The light is green, the illuminated white man is on, those three sweet *coo-coo*s telling me I have the right-of-way. With me coming out of darkness from behind a huge column that supports the 980, and everybody and their momma rushing to get on the Alameda on-ramp before they lose the light, that is a deadly moment in the making. I'm sweating, legs aching, but feeling invincible, trying to catch the Roadrunner, in a zone. When I sprint off the curb, traffic doesn't give a fuck about me.

I'm facing a fast-moving death disguised as one of those ugly-ass PT Cruisers, that atrocious car that is built like a hearse for a midget.

The driver of the uglymobile is on the phone. Zooming right at me. I can't move. Can't break left because it looks like that bastard wants to do the same. Can't break right because that would throw me in front of the traffic that is zipping up Broadway.

The sparkling grill on that Chrysler widens; death is smiling. The engine rumbles out a soft chuckle.

The driver drops his cell phone, cringes, makes a wide-eyed, oh-shit face as he cuts left, his tires screeching a bit, then his side-view mirror slaps my arm so hard I think I'm shot.

Brotherman sends back his curses and speeds on, his radio blaring *"Shake Ya' Azz, Watchya Self."*

Nicole is still running, has no idea that I just cheated death.

I come alive, race through the other cars before they mow me down.

Nicole zips by the row of sushi joints and a plant store offering Psychic Reality, her heels smacking her ass with every stride. I don't give up. I lengthen my stride, arms pumping, knees high like Olympic great John Carlos. I dig as deep as I can. She's doing the same.

She never looks back.

Fifteen seconds later, which is a runner's lifetime, I catch up and stop next to her, my chest heaving, muscles burning, sweat coming from every pore, my face cringing with pain stacked on top of pain. There is a glimmer in her eyes, the shine she gets whenever she wins. She's pimp-strutting like she just left Maurice Green and Michael Johnson in the dust and won a gold medal.

I check my watch. We've covered ten miles in an hour and twenty. Not bad, considering we lost a good five to ten minutes talking. She spits like a pro athlete, wipes her mouth on the sleeve of her damp sweatshirt, and then walks in circles.

I take deep breaths, in through my nose, out my mouth, and tell her, "You run like a cheetah."

Her shoulders are tense, face cringes, fights to control her breathing. "You call me a cheater? It's not cheating.

If both of you know, it's not cheating. I have never lied to you. Never lied to her."

There is a pause. "I said *cheetah*. C-h-e-e-t-a-h. Not *cheater*."

"Oh."

"At least I know where your mind is."

A flash of embarrassment skates across her face.

I ask, "Are you comfortable?"

She gets animated, talks with her hands, like a teacher before a class breaking down a problem to its simplest terms. "A lot of women are attracted to women, but are scared to admit it."

I pause and we stare. "I meant, are you okay? I thought you were limping."

Her mouth becomes a huge letter O.

I say, "Let's try this again. How do you feel?"

"Like screaming."

"Because of me?"

"Because of my cellulite?"

I laugh. That's just like her, to jump to the trivial concerns stirring inside her head. "What cellulite?"

She groans. "Years of running and I still have big legs."

Her legs aren't big. And she hardly has enough ass to mention. There is no cellulite, not enough to worry about. She magnifies the flaws that Superman's telescopic vision can't see.

I remind her that she's the most beautiful woman in the world, that the anorexic airbrushed images on the covers of *Cosmo* and *Body and Soul* can't touch her.

She smiles. "Another reason I'm hooked on you."

"Let's go in before we get sick."

"Wait. Air feels good." She blows; her breath comes out like steam. She's hyped. "Miss being with you all the time. Move up here. It'll be so cool if you moved up here. Wanna take you to this salsa club in Emeryville. On the Black Panther Legacy Tour."

"Slow your stroll." I spit; wipe my mouth, too. "You're trying to wear me out."

Nicole scrubs her face with a corner of her sweatshirt. "Maybe I can kick in on the down payment if that'll help convince you."

"You're talking about a grip. Maybe thirty thousand."

"If all goes well, my sloptions are going to break through the roof in the next year or two."

Sloptions is San Francisco–Silicon Valley slang for stock options. Her soon-to-be-large techno Internet company offered her a chance to leave her old life and her program management position at Boeing in Anaheim to come here and be a contract renewal specialist.

I ask, "What you looking at, moneywise?"

"At least a million. I wanna be a baller like you."

"Nobody balling but you. Sounds like you got all the cheddar."

"With the cost of living and property, that's chump change up here. Hate thinking what the capital-gains taxes are gonna be, but either way it'll be a nice piece of change."

"Need any help before then, let me know."

"I'm cool. Thanks for offering. That's sweet of you."

I'd give her my all, but she relies on me for nothing but love.

A beautiful sister walks by. Both of us stare at her, then at each other.

Nicole puts her arms around my shoulders, kisses the side of my face, tastes my drying sweat before she tongues me with a true passion, each kiss asking me to accept her as she is, pimples on her butt, dry scalp, PMS, soft-legged lover and all.

She says, "Okay, now I'm getting cold."

As we stroll, she does a couple of gymnastic walkovers, first forward, then backward, then laughs, puts her face to mine and sucks my lips again. Even her moist skin is as sweet as a mango. With people rushing by, we close our eyes and kiss. Her bracelets sing and jangle as she hugs me. I pretend we're still engaged and that sound is the sound of wedding bells.